CONFESSION

Martin O'Brien was educated at the Oratory School and Hertford College, Oxford. He was travel editor at British *Vogue* in the 1970s and has written for a number of international publications. After twenty-five years on the road Marseilles remains one of his favourite destinations. He is the author of four previous crime novels – *Jacquot and the Waterman*, *Jacquot and the Angel*, *Jacquot and the Master* and *Jacquot and the Fifteen*.

CONFESSION

MARTIN
O'BRIEN
CONFESSION

arrow books

This paperback edition published by Arrow Books 2010

10 9 8 7 6 5 4 3 2

First published in Great Britain in 2009 by Preface Publishing

Arrow Books
20 Vauxhall Bridge Road
London SW1V 2SA

An imprint of The Random House Group Limited

www.rbooks.co.uk

Addresses for companies within The Random House Group Limited
can be found at www.randomhouse.co.uk

The Random House Group Limited Reg. No. 954009

A CIP catalogue record for this book is available from the British Library

ISBN 978 1 84809 056 9

The Random House Group Limited supports The Forest Stewardship Council (FSC), the leading international forest certification organisation. All our titles that are printed on Greenpeace-approved FSC-certified paper carry the FSC logo. Our paper procurement policy can be found at www.rbooks.co.uk/environment

Typeset in Times by Palimpsest Book Production Limited,
Falkirk, Stirlingshire

Printed and bound in Great Britain by
CPI Bookmarque Ltd, Croydon CR0 4TD

For Dottie and Joe and Rita,
and long-ago milky coffees
at 279 NKR

Saturday

7 November, 1998

1

Paris

THE GIRL DIDN'T LOOK BACK. Not once.

She came out of her building with a leopard-print plastic ruck-sack over her shoulder and a spring in her step. She wore pink Converse sneakers, grey drainpipe jeans and a blue woollen jacket belted at the waist, its shawl collar caught in a winding cashmere scarf just a shade darker than her sneakers. There was a warm bloom on her cheeks and her breath plumed in the chill winter air. She turned to the right, the concierge at La Résidence Camille later reported, as though she knew exactly where she was going, and from his desk in the foyer he watched her cross rue Camille, head down the slope towards place Saint Sulpice and pass out of sight.

Elodie Lafour was four days away from her sixteenth birthday, tall for her age with shoulder-length blonde hair parted in the middle and held back by blue enamelled clips in the coiling shape of serpents. Her eyes were the same deep blue – round and large for her face, as though her other features hadn't quite caught up – her nose thin and straight and freckled, her cheekbones high, sharp and haughty. She had a big wide smile that dimpled her cheeks, and a determined set to her chin. She could have been a model, hurrying for a go-see, all loose, long-limbed exuberance, not a care in the world, almost dancing down the street.

At the corner of rue Camille, Elodie looked left and right and crossed place Saint Sulpice at a happy skip, scarf lifting off her shoulder, rucksack bouncing against her back. When she reached the other side she glanced at her watch – as though she was late for something, the flower-seller on rue du Toit remembered later – then she turned down passage Guillaume. A few minutes later, she emerged from the narrow shadows of Guillaume into a splash of wintry sunshine on Carrefour des Quatres Carrosses, and here she came to a stop. She looked around as though searching someone out, checked her watch again then sat at a café table. When a waiter approached she ordered a *menthe frappée*.

Five minutes later, when the waiter returned with her drink, Elodie had gone, but had left a few francs on the table. The waiter remembered that when the police came by with her photo.

While she waited for her drink, Elodie played with the straps of her rucksack, winding them round her fingers, then looked up and saw the battered white Renault van draw into the kerb, thin blue smoke rattling from its exhaust. Leaving some coins on the table, she slung the rucksack across her shoulder and hurried over. The passenger door opened and Elodie climbed in.

'You didn't take anything?' the man asked as he pulled out into the traffic. He was dark and handsome, with a fall of curling black hair that spilled across his brow and over soft, promising eyes.

'Just like you told me,' Elodie replied. 'Toothbrush, some money . . .'

'Clothes?' He glanced at the rucksack on her lap.

She shook her head. Smiled. 'Just what I'm wearing. Like you said.'

Up ahead on rue Raspail a set of lights glowed red. While he waited for green the young man slid his hand on to Elodie's leg, leaned across and kissed her.

She kissed him back, still trembling at his touch.

So easy, he thought to himself.

Just so easy.

Wednesday
11 November

2

Marseilles

THE DREAM CAME AND WENT throughout the night. A girl running along a darkened street, rain lashing down, strands of sodden blonde hair licking across her cheeks. That was the dream, over and over again. Play, rewind. Play, rewind. But when Marie-Ange Buhl finally opened her eyes, woken by a coiling menstrual cramp, she could still see the girl, not so much running now as stumbling, desperate, head lunging forward, thin arms windmilling. How she didn't fall . . .

For a moment Marie-Ange lay still, eyes wide, a cool, sticky sweat in the hollow of her neck, the pillow damp and oddly cold, watching the images play out on the ceiling above her bed. Then she pushed herself up on her elbows and tried to blink it all away.

But the girl ran on, at the foot of the bed now, silently, the breath panting out of her, running towards Marie-Ange but never quite reaching her. For the closer she came, the more Marie-Ange seemed to draw away, until now there was a road between them, and traffic swishing past, headlights and streetlights lanced with a drilling, steely rain.

Yet still the girl ran on, out of the side-street and into that wider, busier road.

Marie-Ange tensed, drew in her breath, felt her guts coil.

She knew what was going to happen.

The girl had taken no more than three stumbling steps off the pavement, as though unbalanced by the drop from kerb to road, when she was swept off her feet by a pale-blue BMW. The driver braked too late, swerved on impact, his car mounting the central reservation, tearing through a wire fence and crashing into one of the concrete pillars that supported the flyover above. Over the gusting lash of the rain came a squealing of brakes and shrieking of tyres, a blare of horns from cars coming up behind, and under the cover of the flyover the tinkling of broken glass, the wincing creak of bent metal and a hiss of steam from a crumpled radiator.

The images finally faded with that hissing sound. But it didn't come from the ruptured radiator this time. It came from Marie-Ange, a long low breath forced out between her teeth.

It had been a long time. More than four months since the last episode. Up in the Luberon, that sweet little flower shop, Fontaine des Fleurs, on the *place* in St Bédard. Long enough for Marie-Ange to forget the deepening silences that always preceded her special 'moments', the dry dusty taste in her mouth, and that chill shiver of anticipation. Once, back when she was a girl, it had just been sounds and voices she'd experienced, but now there were images too. Dark, grainy images, jerky as a sequence on a hand-held camera, the action never quite matching the soundtrack, either slightly ahead or just slightly behind . . .

It had been raining in her dream and it was raining still, tapping and pattering against her window, flung around indiscriminately by a gusting offshore wind that had started up a few days earlier. Marie-Ange pulled aside the quilt, reached for her gown and pulled it round her. Barefoot, the tiled floor chill, she went to the glass door leading to her tilting one-chair balcony and raised the blind with a rattle of slats. Rubbing away a wet frost of condensation she looked across the stepped rooftops around Curiol towards the sea. On a clear day, she could see a small splinter of blue out beyond Fort Saint Jean and Marseilles' Vieux Port, but darkness and rain reduced her view to a few lighted windows across the street. Even when the sun came up over the Marseilleveyre beyond

Montredon, she knew it would never break through the low scud of black cloud that had settled over the city like a cold wet blanket, stubbornly resisting the wind's efforts to shift it, move it on.

Letting the blinds rattle back down, Marie-Ange accepted that she wouldn't sleep now and set about preparing breakfast. The scratch of a match, the pop and rush of a flame as the gas on her stove caught. Three spoonfuls of *café bleu* into the percolator, top half screwed to bottom half. A slice of *pain rustique* squeezed into a squeaky-springed toaster. Hard butter and sweet *confiture* from the fridge.

By the time Marie-Ange had cleaned her teeth, brushed her hair, and found her bed socks, the small apartment was filled with the scent of brewing coffee and warm bread. Taking her cup and plate to the kitchen table, she settled herself and reached for the previous day's newspaper. She was looking for a story, a news item, something to point the way.

Whoever that girl was, the girl in her dream, Marie-Ange had not the slightest doubt that she had died in Marseilles.

And recently.

The last day or two.

9

3

Cavaillon

JACQUOT STEADIED THE LOG and reached for the axe. Raising it above his head, smooth haft sliding through his hands, he brought the blade down with a satisfying precision. The log split with a splintery wrench, and the two halves sprang away from the steel. Six more logs and he'd be done, he thought. Enough for a week. Just six more and he'd call it a day.

He had come out to the yard an hour earlier, to find only the stack of thin kindling wood he'd been meaning to replenish, but hadn't got round to. Despite the rain they'd had, it was good and dry and plentiful under its lean-to cover, and tempting, but he knew that in the mill's mighty hearth it would burn too fast and be gone before the old stones began to warm. There was nothing else for it: he'd have to start chopping.

It was the slow, steady rhythm of the work that had kept him out there so long, adding to the woodpile – just one more swing, another splitting. The ring of the axe, the toppling woody sound of another log tossed on the pile. It hadn't taken long for his shoulders to ache, his lower back to burn, and his breath to cloud on the air. But now the daylight was sliding away and the rain had started up again, spitting through the trees. Time to stop. Far off, across the valley, thunder rolled and growled along the ridgeline of the Grand Luberon. Another storm was on its way, and over the red scent of freshly chopped wood he could smell it now. Cold, metallic, electric. In the hour, he thought to himself; another hour and rain would be hammering down again.

It had been a slow day at police headquarters in Cavaillon, and Jacquot had been pleased to get away from it – just tying up loose ends from his last case, noting down dates in his desk diary for forthcoming courtroom appearances, and checking forensic reports and number tags against evidence bags for those same appearances. Drudge work. Desk work. Everything he hated. Normally his assistant, Jean Brunet, would have done all this, but Brunet had called in sick. It had been building up, Brunet's sharply pointed nose reddening over the last couple of days from constant swipes of a sleeve or tissue or the knuckles of his hand, even seeming to swell a little. He'd sounded rough on the phone, and Jacquot wondered whether he'd been alone. He doubted it. Even in the depths of misery, Brunet would have found himself some company, someone to soothe his fevered brow. A real tomcat, Brunet. *Un vrai matou.* In the four years he had been working in Cavaillon, the man had cut a swathe through the town's womenfolk; it was astonishing there were any left for him to snag.

It was thinking about Brunet and his conquests that had brought Claudine to mind, just a few short kilometres out of town on the Apt road. After a late lunch at Chez Gaillard, a stunning *boeuf miroton* made up with the remains of Monday's *pot au feu* – Jacquot had been lucky to get it; there was never much in the way of leftovers at Gaillard's – he'd strolled back to headquarters to see if anything had come in. Since nothing had, he cleared his desk and headed for the car park. Twenty minutes later, he was back at the millhouse and steering a weakly protesting Claudine up the stairs. Afternoons in bed with your lover, thought Jacquot. After a good lunch. It really didn't get better than that.

Except lover wasn't quite the word, he decided as he reached for another log. Technically correct, but somehow lacking in substance. In degree. It's how they might have started out, as lovers, but two years after that first scrambling, breathless rush of passion

11

in his apartment on Cours Bournissac, kicking the door shut behind them, knocking pictures off the hallway wall, he and Claudine Eddé had become so much more. The axe came down again and Jacquot stooped to pick up the split halves, toss them on the pile. In just two years. So much more.

'Light me a fire,' Claudine had told him, after they'd made love, pushing her feet against his backside, shoving him from their bed. 'It'll be cold downstairs.'

When he'd tried to persuade her that staying in bed was as good a way as any to keep warm, she'd told him she needed to check the *blanquette de veau* she'd prepared for their supper.

'You didn't have any lunch, did you?' she'd asked, and he'd shaken his head.

'*Presque rien*,' he'd replied, picking up his clothes. Almost nothing.

So here he was, out chopping wood, not just to keep a fire fed and Claudine warm but to work up an appetite. And now it was done, enough logs to last a week. After the final swing and split, he laid down the axe, straightened slowly and tipped backwards, easing the ache out of his lower back. Too little exercise, too little action, he thought to himself, and too many lunches at Brasserie Chez Gaillard, or Scaramouche, or in the upstairs room at Cénacle. Back home in Marseilles, he took a meal when he could, en route to a robbery, or a murder, or a rape, or in his small apartment in the heights of Le Panier. In Marseilles he kept trim, worked off the excess. But here in the country . . . *oufff*, it was a different matter. Close on three years was starting to show where it shouldn't. Or maybe he was just getting older, he thought to himself, stacking logs into the basket. Closing on fifty. Where had it all gone?

Bracing himself, Jacquot lifted the basket and staggered to the kitchen door just as Claudine opened it in a warm, billowing cloud of *blanquette*. She was back in her jeans and *Aix Festival d'Art '96* sweatshirt underneath the apron she painted in, a brown care-taker's smock smeared with swipes and blotches of colour. She'd tied her thick raven hair into a knot held in place by a paintbrush, and she smiled as he started up the steps. Gypsy, he thought, glancing up at her. That's what she was. Pure gypsy. The dark hair, the tan, those laughing blue-grey eyes that knew every secret just by looking at you. Put up a tent and tell your fortune, you'd believe every word she told you. Forty. Twice married. A twenty-year-old daughter. But still a gypsy. A gypsy he loved.

'It'll be ready in an hour,' she told him, stepping aside as he negotiated the basket through the kitchen door. She did it with a feline grace, elegant and supple, like a matador stepping aside for a bull. 'You want to chop another forest of logs, or do you want to have a glass of wine with me?' She closed the door behind him and went back to the stove and a steaming Le Creuset dish. 'Make the wrong decision and you'll be having your *blanquette* in the yard,' she said, picking up a wooden spoon and waving it at him.

'Glass . . . of . . . wine . . . *s'il te plaît* . . .' he managed to pant.

'Correct decision. There's a bottle by the hearth.'

'I'll open it too, shall I?' he called over his shoulder, as he staggered down the passage. 'After chopping logs . . . and hauling this basket through the house . . . and lighting the fire?'

Claudine shook her head and grinned. 'That'll be just fine. There's a corkscrew on the mantel,' she called after him. You big oaf, she thought fondly to herself.

Struggling now across the salon, Jacquot dropped the basket by the hearth and, catching his breath, set to work on the fire. In no time at all, with just a handful of the kindling, he had the fresh-cut logs aflame and spitting.

Voilà, he thought, and getting to his feet he reached for the wine. He was pulling the cork when he heard the phone in the kitchen ring.

He stopped winding and listened.

'*Oui? Allo*?' he heard Claudine answer.

He held his breath.

'*Attendez. Ne quittez pas.*'

Jacquot looked across the salon and saw her lean out from the kitchen, hand over the mouthpiece. 'Daniel? Are you here?'

'Who is it?' he asked, going over to her, starting on the corkscrew again as though that single act would somehow dictate that the call wasn't important, had nothing to do with work, wouldn't spoil their evening.

'*Une femme*,' Claudine replied with a cock of the head and the teasing tilt of an eyebrow. 'Never give them your home number. Haven't I told you enough times?' She held out the phone to him. 'It sounded . . . important.'

Jacquot took it. '*Oui? C'est moi . . .*'

The voice on the other end of the line was instantly familiar.

'Daniel, it's Solange Bonnefoy . . . in Marseilles. I need to see you. Tonight, if possible. It's urgent.'

4

Marseilles

IT WAS DARK BY THE time Marie-Ange reached the Littoral
flyover, after a long day in the shop on rue Francis, in a tail-end
stream of rush-hour traffic threading its way west out of the city.
Keeping to Boulevard Cambrai, with the darkened belly of the
autoroute snaking above her, she followed the old coast road with
the docks on her left and the shadowy suburbs of Madrague coming
up on her right. It didn't take long to find the ragged tear in the
wire fence bordering the central reservation, the site plainly marked
by criss-crossing ribbons of chevroned police tape. This was where
the BMW had hit the girl and ploughed through the fence, and there
the flyover's supporting column which the car had smashed into.

But even without the tape, and the story in the newspaper, Marie-
Ange would likely have sensed that something had happened here.

As she passed the spot a rush of goose-pimples prickled on her
arms and spread across her shoulder blades. For a moment she
wondered whether she shouldn't just drive on, forget the dream,
ignore the summons. But she didn't. A hundred metres past the
tape, she turned her Citroën 2CV to the right and parked in a side-
street. For a moment she sat in the car, listening to the rain slap
and smack on the stretched fabric roof, watching it smear across
the windscreen. Then she pulled up the hood on her coat, opened
the car door and stepped out into the rain.

The newspaper report she'd read over breakfast – a single paragraph on page five of *La Marseillaise* – had told her where to come. Boulevard Cambrai. *Drunk Driver Deaths*, the headline ran. Henri Proche, 47, according to the report. From Carpène near Aix. Multiple injuries. Dead on the scene. And it was true. He had been drunk. Marie-Ange could almost taste the alcohol as she read the article. Sweet and strong. Cheap Cognac and beer. Not a man to kiss.

And the girl he'd hit, the one in the photo that the newspaper had run with the story, was the girl in her dream. Marie-Ange had recognised her immediately, even though the hair was dry and shorter, and the eyes wrinkled with laughter rather than wide with panic, glazed with terror. A pretty girl. Lucienne Viviers, 16. From Paris, a pupil at the Lycée Gordonne there.

And that was it. Nothing more.

Somewhere along Boulevard Cambrai, Lucienne Viviers had died. Just after midnight on Sunday. And Marie-Ange had found the place in an instant.

Locking her car, she turned to the left and hurried along the block. When she drew level with the police tape on the other side of the road, tied to the torn wire fence, she paused and peered through the rain, loud enough as it smacked off her hood and clouded around her boots to drown out the sound of unseen traffic from the flyover above, leaving only the intermittent whoosh-whoosh of cars passing by at street level.

There was no need to cross the road, to push past that tape, to rest her hands against the concrete span. Despite the rain, she could hear the shattering of glass again, that final crumpling crunch of metal on concrete, and the violent hissing of a split radiator. Now all she had to do was walk to the end of the block where Lucienne Viviers had run out into the road from a shadowy turning, to be hit by a bleary-eyed tiling salesman from Carpène.

Marie-Ange was nearly there, maybe ten metres from the turning, hunched against the rain, when from somewhere behind her a lorry let out two long klaxon blasts, horribly, shockingly, amplified under the arched flyover. She turned in time to see an old Peugeot come off a set of intersection lights, jerk itself into the right gear, spurt forward and speed away ahead of the lorry as though the klaxon burst had nothing to do with it. Heart beating wildly, Marie-Ange hurried on, pulling her jacket tight, and as she did so she sensed a silence settle around her and a dry dusty taste fill her mouth.

5

AS HE CAME OUT OF L'Estaque's road tunnel, two long sloping concrete pipes drilled through the hills above Marseilles, Jacquot wound down the window and breathed it in. The sea. The ocean. He'd been waiting for it, knew that this was where he'd smell it first. An iodine reek carried on the rain spattering through his window. Sharp, salty and strident, it reached up to him from the coastline below, gusting in from that wide black shadow on his right, a shadow dotted with a random sprinkling of ships' lights, its border defined by the sinuous golden glow of Marseilles' water-front and the warm twinkling reach of the city. A million souls unseen amongst the lights, in the dark geometry of squares and triangles and oblongs between them, going about their business, good and bad. Marseilles. Jacquot's city. Where he was born, brought up. Where he learned to pick a pocket in a crowd, steal fruit from a market stall, kiss a girl, ride a scooter, shoot a man. He might have left the city for a while, before the wrong track became the only track, but Marseilles was in his blood, as surely as the scent of the sea in his nostrils.

It was the ocean that had made him take the Martigues road, always his approach of choice, dropping down behind L'Estaque on to the Littoral flyover and sliding past the wharves and *quais* of Marseilles where that sharp salty tang acquired an oily sheen.

Commerce. Trade. The great port of the Mediterranean. What the city was all about. On his right ocean and docks, on his left a floodlit sprawl of container yards and railway sidings and ware-houses, and the suppliers and traders and workshops that serviced them. And there, up ahead, rising above the cranes and rooftops, the slopes of Le Panier where he'd grown up, the layered marbled bulk of Cathédrale de la Major, the squat stone buttresses of Fort Saint Jean and the quays of the Vieux Port.

Marseilles.

Home.

Except, for some inexplicable reason, Jacquot suddenly found himself in the wrong lane, spinning down the Chamant sliproad rather than keeping to the Littoral. He couldn't imagine what had possessed him to make such a stupid mistake. He'd been out of town too long, he decided, as he pulled up at a red light directly beneath the flyover and tried to work out how best to get back on it. As far as he could recall, he'd have to follow Boulevard Cambrai as far as the Pinède or Joliette sliproads before he could rejoin it and, in the process, add another ten minutes to his journey.

Not that Jacquot was running late. Half-an-hour after receiving the call from Solange Bonnefoy, he'd kissed Claudine goodnight – quiet and tight-faced when he'd told her he had to go – and was driving down the *impasse* which led from their millhouse to the Apt road. Twenty minutes after that he was through Cavaillon, across the Durance and heading south on the autoroute.

The call from Madame Bonnefoy had come as a surprise. It was two, maybe three years since they'd last spoken – also on the phone, Jacquot remembered, three months after his transfer to Cavaillon, at the end of the Waterman investigation. Marseilles' leading exam-ining magistrate had called for a debrief and then, in an unlikely exposure, had asked when he was coming back. They missed him, she'd said. He'd been touched by her concern, and by her annoy-ance at the dead-end posting he'd been given, taken off the fast track to serve out his time in the provinces.

For a policeman Jacquot had always had an unlikely fondness

19

for Madame Bonnefoy. He'd enjoyed their sparring, the mutual respect. They'd worked enough cases together for Jacquot to know that she was never less than thorough and resourceful, and it was a rare case when they didn't get their man. Hers was an intimidating presence, in court robes or casual clothes, easily a metre eighty in stockinged feet, with a long disapproving face set beneath a cap of wavy grey hair, blue eyes sharp and chill when she chose to pin them on you over the top of her bifocals. Madame Bonnefoy was no pushover; try it and she'd be down on you like a ton of bricks. It didn't matter who.

But the voice he'd heard on the phone this evening held none of the grit and growl he was used to. Instead there was a softness to her tone, an anxiousness and vulnerability that had surprised him. She wouldn't say anything specific and Jacquot hadn't pressed her. That she had called him, asked him to come to Marseilles, was all that was needed. He would find out soon enough what it was all about.

Jacquot came to another set of lights, changing green to red seconds before he could have chanced a crossing. Instead, he braked hard and waited while a convoy of lorries pulled out in front of him, backing away from a set of chained dock gates. There was no way through. The strike he'd been reading about had clearly started, with braziers already lit, hooded figures huddled around them. Dock transport this time, the newspaper had reported. Anything with a motor closed down until demands were met. Beside him the smaller set of traffic lights at window height ran through red and green three times before the lorries successfully negotiated their reversing and set off under the autoroute. Just his luck to get held up behind them, with another truck looming in his rear-view mirror.

It was then, waiting there at the lights, that Jacquot's eye was caught by a fluttering ribbon of blue police tape stitched across a rent in a stretch of wire fencing. Car crash, he decided. Some drunk piling into a support column of the flyover that he was now trying to get back on to. When they'd taken a few too many *pastis*, Jacquot

20

knew, drivers preferred to stay off the flyover, and keep a lower, slower profile on this older section of road. There was less chance of being picked up down here by the gendarmerie, or getting into trouble, though there was always the risk, late at night, stopped at the lights, of a tap on the window from the muzzle of a 9-millimetre – an invitation to leave your keys in the ignition and step out of the vehicle, *s'il vous plaît, monsieur*. In Marseilles it happened all the time, some random car-jacking that left you in the middle of the road, heart beating fast, relieved to be alive, watching your tail-lights race away.

From behind Jacquot came two massive klaxon blasts that shuddered through his old Peugeot. The light was green and the road now clear. Jesus, he thought, as he slammed the car into gear and jerked away from the lights, I'm getting slow in my old age.

Five minutes later, he reached the sliproad at Joliette, slid past the convoy of lorries and joined the autoroute for the last stretch down into the Vieux Port. All he had to do now was find the restaurant where he and Madame Bonnefoy were meeting.

At the top of rue Breteuil, she'd said.

A place called Kuchnia.

He'd never heard of it.

Which surprised him.

6

THE STREET MARIE-ANGE TURNED into was dark and cobbled, the stones rounded and irregular, glistening like raised boils in the rain, scabbed with patches of worn tarmac. The girl had been barefoot, that was Marie-Ange's first thought. The girl in her dream had been running down this street without shoes. Over these cobbles. As the silence settled on her like a warm, insulating blanket, Marie-Ange could actually feel a bruising hardness against the balls of her own feet, a sensation that made her boots feel suddenly tight and every step a hobbling discomfort.

There was more. A reeling breathlessness. A sweating, desperate panic. And the smell of vomit, the acid taste of it sliding across her tongue and puckering her cheeks and filling her throat. For a moment Marie-Ange stood still, looking into the street, the street from her dream. Just as she remembered it. The darkness, the rain-slicked shadows. No houses here, no cheerily lit windows. Just ancient brick warehouses, high double doors in the centre of each, barred darkened windows, and loading gantries jutting out like gallow rigs from the pitched upper storeys. On one of the brick façades, just below one of the gantries, Marie-Ange could make out the faded legend 'Savon Maréchal', in a blue wash thin enough to show the pattern of the bricks beneath. A soapworks from another time, as old as the flaking paint, but not yet as old as the narrow cart-ruts worn down the centre of the road.

Not a nice place to be, at night, all alone, thought Marie-Ange, shivering in the sharp November cold, still undecided. Ahead, burrowing into a distant darkness, were just a few dim street-lights fixed high on the warehouse walls, a silvery rain slanting through their gold haloes of light. Behind her, out on Boulevard Cambrai, traffic swept silently past, headlights flashing.

And there, suddenly, was the running, stumbling girl, or rather the sense of her, an invisible presence, rushing towards Marie-Ange.

Catching her breath, she tried to swallow the dryness out of her throat but all it did was make her cough, a rough retching cough that went nowhere.

Standing there on the corner, huddled under the rain, she knew what was coming next as that presence drew closer, passed her, a waft of air pressing against her. Instinctively, Marie-Ange tensed, as though expecting a blow, and a stinging bile rose in her throat, burning a sandpaper path into the soft tissue with every panting breath.

And then that breath was snatched from her.

The girl was out on to the Cambrai pavement, and from there into the road.

And, once again, it was over.

Just that sudden sensation of impact, brutal contact. Hit by a drunken Monsieur Proche, from Carpène, and flung high into the air, falling like a bag of dry, broken sticks on to the hard rain-slicked surface of the road.

Marie-Ange waited a moment, heard the distant blare of horns, the squeal of brakes, and then set off down the side-street the young girl had come from. Digging her hands into her pockets, feeling the rain kiss her cheeks, she retraced the girl's last desperate steps, the cobbles hard against the soles of her boots.

She couldn't see the girl, but as she walked Marie-Ange could hear her, the sound of her rasping breaths on her right-hand side, coming from the middle of the road. Half-way down the street,

Marie-Ange stopped and listened again, squeezed her eyes shut. The girl had crossed the road here, from left to right, and then come back into the centre, between the cart-ruts, where she'd stayed until Cambrai, as though she felt safer out in the open. But she hadn't come the whole length of the street, from what was clearly a dead-end thirty metres ahead. She'd come into it another way.

Marie-Ange took a few more steps and saw the opening, a shoulder-width passage between two of the warehouses. That's where the girl had come from. Without being able to stop herself, Marie-Ange turned into it and followed it, hands raised to shoulder-level, fingertips tracing the stone walls on either side of her, feeling a chill air spill past her, fan across her cheeks. Lucienne. It was Lucienne Viviers racing past her down that narrow alley.

Three times the passage Marie-Ange followed turned abruptly through ninety-degree dog-legs that finally opened out on to a patch of rough ground behind the warehouses. Some kind of over-grown track, a bank of weeds and a steel mesh fence laced with creeper that, in the darkness, looked like a black blanket draped over it. On the other side of the fence, through the rain, she saw the headlights of a lorry sweep into view, a few hundred metres away, and a good six metres below the slope that Marie-Ange stood on.

This was where the girl had come from: an overnight lorry park, wide and long enough to accommodate forty or maybe fifty trucks, a disused lot awaiting redevelopment, somewhere for drivers to rest for the night before catching a ferry, or delivering or picking up loads. Somewhere close by, Lucienne Viviers had climbed up the bank on the other side of the fence.

But where had she got through?

Looking to the right Marie-Ange could see no obvious opening, so she set off to the left and found the tear in the wire mesh not thirty steps further on. Holding the edges apart, she stepped through carefully but still felt her coat sleeve snag. She worked it free and wondered whether Lucienne had had time to be so careful, or whether she'd just pushed through regardless. Had the torn mesh scratched her? Snatched at her face? Her arms? Tugged at her hair? But Marie-Ange knew that there would have been no time for such considerations. Lucienne Viviers was on the run, needing to escape. That was all. She wouldn't have cared about a couple of scratches.

Once through the fence, Marie-Ange side-stepped and slithered her way down the muddy bank. Finally she reached the bottom of the slope and looked around. The lorry that had just arrived was now forty metres away, one of half-a-dozen trucks parked in a line. While Marie-Ange watched, the driver doused his headlights and engaged his hydraulic brakes with a slow and final wheeze. Moments later the cabin was bathed in a blue light. A television. He was settling down for the night.

With nothing to light her path save a scatter of twinkling lights from tenements on the slopes around the lorry park, Marie-Ange made her way across the rough, stony ground. The first lorries loomed out of the rain and darkness, their cabins high off the ground, lit and unlit, their towering sides billboarded with haulage company logos – Spanish, Portuguese, German, French – all of them parked up for the night.

Picking her way past them, she circled the lorry park, waiting for something to lead her on, point the way. But there was nothing. The trail she'd been following stopped here, and, without even realising it at first, she began to note the sounds of the city gradually gaining in volume – a distant beeping of horns, a police siren, a distant susurrus of traffic heading into and out of the city. And high in one of the lorries' cabins she heard the taped applause of a TV game show.

It was as if she had taken out ear plugs. She could no longer hear the pulsing of blood in her ears, no longer feel Lucienne's presence. And the rain seemed to grow if not stronger then certainly louder.

Marie-Ange looked around for a moment, moved her head from side to side like an animal tracking a scent, then acknowledged that there was no scent to follow, nowhere left for her to go. The trail had gone cold.

All she could say for certain was that this was where Lucienne Viviers had begun her dash for freedom.

And death.

7

AFTER REGAINING THE LITTORAL FLYOVER it took Jacquot another twenty minutes to drive around Marseilles' Vieux Port, negotiate the lanes and lights on Quai des Belges and head up rue Breteuil, leaning forward into the steering wheel as the road steepened. And the higher he went the harder the rain fell, gushing along the gutters in furious torrents, bubbling over the drains and streaming in glistening neon-ripples across the road, as though the golden spikes of La Bonne Mère's crown on Notre-Dame de la Garde had slashed open the swollen belly of a rain cloud.

But even in the rain, at night, it was good to be back in the city and Jacquot felt a stirring of fondness for the place. It had been six months, maybe more, since his last visit, yet it felt like a century. Such a long absence surprised him, now that he thought about it, and shocked him too. That he could stay away so long. How could he be so close – what, maybe seventy kilometres? – yet not visit more often?

Finding somewhere to park – a back wheel on the pavement, the Peugeot's front wing jutting a dangerous few centimetres into the one-way street – Jacquot spent a further ten minutes dodging through drenching rain trying to locate the restaurant Solange Bonnefoy had chosen for their meeting. After seeking directions from a bar on the corner of rue du Dragon, he finally found Kuchnia in a dead-end alley, just an old shopfront with a low sash window to each side of a glass door, the name 'kuchnia' painted in gold-shadowed green paint, the lower-case letters faded and peeling. It looked as if it had stood there for ever – the woodwork worn and buckling, any trace of an awning long gone – and Jacquot wondered again that he'd never heard of it. In Marseilles, he knew his restaurants. Hurrying towards it through the rain, he could just about make out a shadowy sense of movement beyond its lit but misted windows, confirmed when he pushed open the door and stepped into a wall of steam and heat and clatter and muffled conversation.

Squeezing into a narrow entrance hallway, made even smaller by overloaded coat-racks, Jacquot closed the door behind him, wrestled off his leather jacket and felt suddenly bulky and awkward. There seemed to be no room to move or turn, to go forward or backwards, so crowded was the hallway and the room it opened on to – a dozen Formica-topped tables with paper squares laid in diamonds crowded with diners, the whole place resounding to the kettledrum roll of cutlery on china and the muffled hum of guarded conversation. There was something canteen-like about the place, a workers' soup-kitchen free from any embellishment beyond the scruffy pleating of red gingham half-curtains, dulled brass curtain rails and wrought iron sconces on the wall, no more than forty watts shivering from their candle-shaped bulbs. The only other thing that Jacquot could make out on the walls was the same thin glistening sheen of condensation that covered Kuchnia's windows, reaching as far as he could see, into two more rooms at the back, each packed as tight with diners as a jar of Collioure anchovies. There didn't look to be a spare seat in the house.

Either the food was cheap, he thought, or it was very, very good. Judging by the smell, it was certainly going to be good, and by the look of the clientele it was more than likely going to be cheap. There was something creased and crumpled and well-used about their clothing, shiny and tight about the shoulders, the way they spooned and forked the food into their mouths, as though they were in a hurry to be out of there, or hadn't eaten a decent meal in

28

weeks. Once more Jacquot ran the word through his head – Kuchnia, Kuchnia, Kuchnia. Was it someone's name? A place? It sounded eastern European, maybe Czech, Polish, Hungarian; one or the other. What he knew for certain was that he had never heard of the place before. And living and working in Marseilles for as long as he had, that was saying something. The fact that Solange Bonnefoy, Marseilles' leading examining magistrate, knew of it – and ate here – made it all the more intriguing.

Piling his coat on top of a dozen others, Jacquot glanced around the first room, his eye settling on a glass display counter filled with salads and pickles and cuts of cold meat in plastic containers that ran the length of the side wall. Behind its sweating panels, wedged between counter and wall, stood a large, white-aproned woman in her late fifties, working away with concentrated energy and a prac-tised efficiency. Her hair was caught up and bound in a scarf, her chubby round face red with effort, and her bare arms squeezed sausage-like out of tightly rolled sleeves. For someone her size she managed uncannily well in the limited space available. With what looked like an octave span of fingers she hefted a pile of dirty plates off the glass counter, deposited them with a clatter on the top shelf of a dumb-waiter, removed a tray of fresh orders from the bottom shelf, shouted new ones into a small intercom, tugged on the rope then turned back to supervise the distribution of the steaming food to a line of hovering waiters – old, thin men in black jackets worn over stained white aprons who snatched up the plates with unlikely speed, balanced them skilfully on scrawny arms and scurried away with them. It was one of these old men who now approached Jacquot with an enquiring expression on his face.

'Bonnefoy. There is a table reserved,' said Jacquot.

'*Ach, Dobrawiara*,' the man replied, as though in greeting, and after a short bow led Jacquot past the glass display counter and into the second room where a single free table was crammed into a far corner. Pulling out the table an inch or two for Jacquot to squeeze in against the wall, the waiter smiled. 'I come back,' he said. 'Just to wait, please, and I return.'

The man's French was gruff and heavily accented, almost Germanic, and as Jacquot settled himself, freeing a corner of the white paper table-cloth that had caught on his belt buckle, he tried to place it. Eastern European, certainly. Possibly Yiddish? He remembered the two Hassidim sipping orange juice in the bar where he'd asked for directions, *payot* side-locks dangling beneath their fedoras, dark suspicious eyes, thick red lips and pale bearded cheeks, and he recalled there was a synagogue near by, just a block or two beyond rue Breteuil.

It was that rasping accent, his own language but spoken differently, that made him wonder suddenly about Solange Bonnefoy. Was she eastern European? Slavic? Jewish even? He'd never have guessed. There was, Jacquot had always thought, something classic, haughty, and old French about her. Pure Gallic stock – descended from one of those *familles anciennes* who'd survived the attentions of Madame Guillotine. With her height and her bearing and that searingly disdainful way she glanced at anyone who stepped on the wrong side of her, there was something almost regal about her, something undeniably magisterial.

But she didn't look anything like that now. Glancing up, he saw Madame Bonnefoy bearing down on him, as tall and elegant as he remembered but looking somehow diminished, her eyes red and cheeks hollow.

'Daniel,' she said, taking his hand and leaning over the table to press rain-damp cheeks against his. An uncertain smile flickered across her lips as she drew back. 'It's good to see you again,' she continued, in a low voice as wavering as her smile. 'And, *vraiment*, so good of you to come.'

8

Cavaillon

CLAUDINE THREW A LOG ON the fire and dumped herself on a sofa. She'd eaten her *blanquette* in the kitchen, alone, washed up her single plate, slotted it into the rack and come through to the salon. She reached for the TV remote and flicked through some channels – the nine o'clock news on TF1, a Schwarzenegger film on M6, a travel documentary on Canal+, a repeat on Arte. And the ads, of course. She couldn't be bothered to wait for them to finish, or to check TV listings. She just switched the TV off. Got up from the sofa to pour herself more wine, flicked on the CD without looking to see what was in it. A Pachelbel fugue. Appropriate, she thought, going back to the sofa. One of Daniel's. For a *flic*, he had an eclectic taste in music. Anything good seemed to be the rule, whether it was rock 'n' roll or the classics. Mozart and Howlin' Wolf; Handel and Dylan.

A *flic*. A cop, she thought to herself, punching a cushion into shape. So this was what it was all about. Always on call. Never off duty. Claudine didn't know if she liked it. Correction. She knew she didn't like it. He'd left the millhouse an hour earlier and she was still cross about it. Put out. That *blanquette de veau* had been as good as any she'd cooked. And it had taken time. Hours. The slow braising of that plump shoulder, getting the roux just right . . . and then being interrupted by Daniel coming home early, infuriatingly – and delightfully – seducing her away from her pots, making love to her, pretending to her he hadn't had anything to eat when she could smell the garlic in his sweat. It was their lovemaking then that made his absence now all the worse, the more pointed. Everything had been so perfect: the warmth of the kitchen, the ripening scent of the food, the sound of logs being chopped in the yard – just exactly how many logs did he think they needed? And then, fire lit, wine opened, the damn' phone. A woman. An old colleague, he'd told her when the call was ended. He was sorry. He had to go. Something had come up.

Just like that. No discussion. A done deal.

Well, *merci beaucoup, monsieur*. Thanks a lot.

Claudine took a deep breath and blew it out. Men, she thought. And a cop to boot. She must be mad, mad, mad.

Except . . .

Except she'd grown to love him. No matter what he did. Even if, sometimes, he let her down, like tonight, or did or said something without thinking, making her lips thin and tighten with annoyance.

She looked at the log she'd thrown on the fire, now starting to catch, curling yellow flames licking around it, and wondered where he was. In Marseilles, for sure, by now. She wondered if it was raining there too. If it was, that leather jacket wasn't going to do him much good.

And this Madame Bonnefoy . . . the one he was meeting, probably having dinner with. He hadn't said they were, she just assumed they would. And the word 'Kuchnia' she'd heard him repeating. Maybe that was the name of the restaurant. Sounded like kitchen in a foreign language. She wondered how old this Bonnefoy woman was. Married? Single? On the phone she'd sounded, well, it was hard to tell. She'd sounded . . . afraid? Or looking for a shoulder to cry on? Claudine knew the feeling. She just hoped that that was as far it got.

Over on the hi-fi Pachelbel gave way to Cesaria Evora.

The seventeenth century to the twentieth.
Nuremberg to Cape Verde.
Organ to soul.
Daniel Jacquot, she thought, I could wring your neck.

9

Marseilles

'THE LAST TIME ANYONE SAW Elodie was late Saturday morning, just before lunch. The concierge at her parents' apartment block, a street-corner *fleuriste*, and a waiter. That was it. She simply . . . vanished.'

Solange Bonnefoy sat back in her chair as though the effort of describing the disappearance in Paris of her niece, Elodie Lafour, had quite exhausted her. She looked spent, just a shadow of herself, thought Jacquot, as she reached for her bag, took out a tissue and blew her nose. As she did so their waiter, the same old man who had greeted Jacquot, bustled between them to clear their table.

Not that there had been a great deal eaten, neither of them with much of an appetite. But what Jacquot had managed was memorable.

'*Zupa grzybowa*,' Madame Bonnefoy had told him as the first course was served, a thick mushroom soup ladled into their bowls and a plastic basket filled with toasted crusts of nutty brown bread placed between them. 'Good, wholesome, peasant food. Real home cooking. So we don't forget.'

'"We"?' asked Jacquot.

'I'm Polish. Didn't you know?' Madame Bonnefoy seemed amused.

Jacquot shook his head. 'I had no idea. Your French is . . .'

'. . . good, but my Polish, believe me, is better.'

'But your name . . . Bonnefoy? And your father, wasn't he a minister under Pompidou?'

'That's as may be. But it doesn't alter the fact that my great-great-grandfather came from a town called Lomza in Masovia, eastern Poland, and was called Piotr Dobrawiara.'

When he heard the name, Jacquot chuckled. 'So that's what the old man meant,' nodding towards their waiter as he served out soup at another table. 'I thought it was a greeting. *Bonjour* . . . *ça va* . . . you know?'

'Translated from Polish, it means honesty, or sincerity, or good faith. Old Piotr changed the name as soon as he arrived. Paris first, then here in Marseilles. He was a cobbler by trade. And the family name wasn't going to do him any harm so long as his customers knew what it meant. Hence Bonnefoy.'

The small talk lasted as long as the soup. It was over the *gulasz* – ladled into the same bowls – that Madame Bonnefoy had told Jacquot about her niece, what had happened in Paris the week before. The reason she'd phoned him, called him down to Marseilles.

'She's sixteen today. Just sixteen,' she said, wiping her nose as the waiter bore away their plates.

'A runaway? It happens, at that age. Maybe a boyfriend?'

Madame Bonnefoy shook her head. 'No boyfriend I know of. Elodie's not like that – not yet. Not that kind of girl. Very sensible. Very . . . *composée*.'

'A problem at home? Some small thing. What about her parents? Your sister . . . her husband? Are they happy? Getting a divorce?'

'Nothing like that. And I would know.'

'And you say there's been no ransom demand?' asked Jacqout. 'You're absolutely certain?'

'I swear. My sister would have told me.'

Jacquot stayed silent for a moment. He'd have far preferred a ransom demand. If the girl had not gone of her own accord, no demand from a kidnapper usually meant no intent to return. Which meant one of two things. Either rape, followed by death within hours of being snatched and a shallow grave somewhere, or transportation. The prettier ones to whorehouses in Africa and South America. The less attractive sold to clinics for their livers, hearts, kidneys . . . Kept alive for as long as it took, to keep the organs warm and fresh.

Solange Bonnefoy tucked the tissue in her sleeve and held up her hands. 'I know what you're thinking, Daniel. I know, I know. A ransom demand would be better . . . But there you are. There hasn't been one. And after four days, the chances of getting one are growing slimmer by the hour. Which is why I want you on the case, Daniel. I want you to find her. If anyone can, it's you.'

'Here? In Marseilles? If you'll excuse my directness, Madame, if she's not already dead, your niece could be in any of a dozen ports – Cherbourg, Rotterdam, Hamburg, Genoa . . . Why Marseilles?'

Madame Bonnefoy leant forward, and Jacquot saw a thin gleam of hope in her eyes. 'Early Monday morning,' she replied, 'just after midnight, a young girl was hit by a drunk driver on Boulevard Cambrai, down by the docks. Her name was Lucienne Viviers. She was reported missing by her parents, in Paris, last Thursday, just days before Elodie disappeared. If this girl, Viviers, was in Marseilles, then it's entirely feasible that Elodie might be here as well. Part of a . . . consignment. And now, with the dock strike . . .'

Jacquot let out a low whistle. 'That's quite a stretch, if you'll forgive me, madame. Did they know each other? Elodie and Lucienne? Were they friends?'

Madame Bonnefoy smiled. 'It was the first thing I checked, but no. Nothing to link them. Different schools, different neighbourhoods, different . . . backgrounds.' She shrugged.

'And the police know this? The possibility? About the Paris angle? They've made the connection?'

'Of course. I called Chief Guimpier as soon as I heard, to make sure.'

'And what did he say?' asked Jacquot. If his old boss, Yves Guimpier, was on the case, then the investigation would be properly handled. Guimpier was the kind of man who always went that extra mile for one of his own. Examining magistrate or not.

'He didn't say anything,' replied Madame Bonnefoy. 'He's on compassionate leave. His mother is dying.'

'So who's in charge? Peluze . . . Grenier . . . Muzon?' asked Jacquot, thinking of the senior men at police headquarters on rue de l'Evêché. In his opinion, old Grenier seemed the most likely bet to stand in for Guimpier.

'If only,' said Madame Bonnefoy. 'They brought someone in. From Lyons. An old friend of yours, I believe.'

'Old friend?'

Madame Bonnefoy gave him a sidelong look. 'Alain Gastal. Remember him?'

The name took Jacquot's breath away. 'Gastal?' he managed. 'You are joking?'

'I'm an examining magistrate, Daniel. I don't do joking. You should know that.'

'Well, let me tell you right now that there's no way Alain Gastal is ever going to have me on his team, in this or any other investigation. The last time I saw him, on the steps of the Palais de Justice in Lyons, he made it abundantly clear that he would do all in his power to wreck my career in whatever way he could, and take the greatest pleasure in doing so. Not that he hasn't already done a pretty good job of it. That was four months ago. I doubt he's changed his mind.'

'But I'm not asking you to work with him,' said Madame Bonnefoy quietly. 'In fact, I wouldn't have asked you to work with Guimpier either. Or Peluze, or Muzon or any of them. If there's a chance of finding Elodie alive, I don't believe a formal police investigation is necessarily the best way to do it . . . or not in the time we have left,' she conceded, as Jacquot started to disagree. 'I want someone outside the force, Daniel, but someone who knows their way round. Someone I trust. Someone who can sniff about – the docks, the city – without arousing suspicion. Through my office I can get you whatever you need . . . papers, information . . . just name it, and I'll get it. Full support.'

Jacquot started to shake his head at what she was suggesting, wondering to himself if she had thought it through. Did she have any real idea what she was asking him to do? The enormity of the task for one man? It was a hopeless proposition, she must surely know that. The dockers' strike might restrict the movements of merchant vessels from the main harbour, but what of the marinas – La Madrague, Pointe Rouge, the Vieux Port, L'Estaque among others – and the thousands of sailing boats and motor yachts moored in them? He could never begin to . . .

'She could be gone already,' he began, hating to be the one to crush her hope. 'This girl Viviers was killed . . . what? . . . two days ago. The strike only started today. Even if Elodie had been here, she could be on a ship and half-way to Africa by now.'

'Yesterday. The first action started yesterday. In the morning. The first wharves.' Madame Bonnefoy's voice was low, but certain, and her eyes held his. 'I know it sounds ridiculous, Daniel. I know you'll think I'm mad,' she continued. 'But I have to do something. For Elodie. For my sister. For me. I have to start somewhere.' She reached across the table for his hand, her eyes starting to glisten and brim with tears, swallowing hard to keep her voice level. 'So, what do you think, Daniel? Will you do it? Will you go out there and find my niece for me? Please, please, say yes . . .'

Thursday
12 November

10

IT WAS THE SAME DREAM. The same street. The same desperate run. But this time there was something different about it.

Three times Marie-Ange had woken in a cold sweat, a coiling cramp in her belly, unable to make sense of the images, drifting back to sleep as the cramps eased but each time drawn again into the same dream. The final time it began to make sense, and she realised what was different about it now. The perspective had changed. Instead of the girl running towards her, now she was running away from her. Heading down that shadowy, rain-swept side-street towards Boulevard Cambrai.

And Marie-Ange was following her. Chasing her.

Except it wasn't Marie-Ange doing the chasing.

It was someone else.

The previous evening she had returned home from Boulevard Cambrai with a sense of acute frustration. From the moment she had passed the crash site she had felt certain she would make sense of the dream, understand exactly what had happened there. And at first, as she'd retraced the girl's route, that had seemed to be the case. With every step she took – down the side-street, into the zig-zag *traboule* between the warehouses, and out on to that track above the lorry park – she had felt the girl's panic, her desperation, her fear. But in the lorry park, creeping around the parked

41

trucks from Amsterdam and London, from Antwerp, Hamburg and Cracow, her grasp of events had faded. All she'd done was follow a dead-end trail and earn herself a thorough drenching.

By the time she got home, the rain had seeped into her collar and hood, sleeves and boots, and her tights stuck damply to her legs. Running herself a bath, she'd stripped off her clothes and stepped into the hot, scented water, lowering herself down until the bubbles lapped at her chin. For thirty minutes she lay there, going over what had happened, trying to make sense of it, but still got no further than the lorry park. Whatever had happened, whatever had occasioned Lucienne Viviers' desperate flight, had taken place in that lorry park. Had the girl been attacked? Raped? Had she somehow escaped from her assailant and made a run for it? As far as Marie-Ange was concerned, she certainly wasn't dressed for a rainy night. That sodden T-shirt, and barefoot too. And what was a girl from Paris, a sixteen year old from the Lycée Gordonne, doing in a Marseilles lorry park anyway? Had she gone there of her own accord? Or had she been taken there by force?

As she let out the bath water and prepared for bed, Marie-Ange acknowledged sadly that despite her trip to Boulevard Cambrai there were still more questions than answers, more doubt than certainty.

Now, six hours later, with rain gusting once more against her bedroom window, she lay in her bed and stared at the ceiling as the last images played themselves out: Lucienne Viviers stumbling down the centre of the road, thirty metres ahead of her, glancing back over her shoulder with a look of terror on her face. And Boulevard Cambrai looming up ahead through the rain, headlights flashing past the end of the street.

It was now, for the first time, that Marie-Ange registered that the girl was not alone, that someone was chasing her, catching up . . . And as Lucienne Viviers staggered on towards the main road, Marie-Ange sensed the shadow coming up behind her. Heard the scuff of leather soles on cobbles, someone running after her, a man, his panting breaths, muttered curses . . . *merde, merde, merde* . . .

And then Lucienne was out on Boulevard Cambrai and seconds later Marie-Ange flinched as Henri Proche's pale-blue BMW flashed into view and swept her away.

And it was there, in that final moment, in the shifting fragments of her dream, hidden in the shadows, leaning against a warehouse door, that she saw him – just a shape at first – watching it all. A leather jacket, a woollen hat, a chequered Arab *keffiyeh* worn as a scarf, its tasselled ends dangling from his neck as he bent forward, hands on knees and caught his breath.

For a moment, as he straightened up and looked ahead, a beam of light flashed across the man's face and Marie-Ange could see him clearly. Dark, swarthy, his cheeks and chin heavily stubbled, a large fleshy nose, full lips parted over white teeth as he gulped in breath. But it was the scar that caught Marie-Ange's attention, long and white against the dark skin, like a strap securing his woollen hat, slicing a path through the stubble on his jaw from his ear to the point of his chin.

Killer, thought Marie-Ange as the image faded.

Whoever you are, you're a killer.

If the car hadn't hit Lucienne Viviers . . . you'd have killed her yourself.

11

'SHE'S HERE. SHE'S IN MARSEILLES.'

Arsène Cabrille lowered his newspaper and looked at his daughter. They were in his study at the house in Roucas Blanc, one of the city's most prestigious *arrondissements*, Cabrille at his desk, picking at his breakfast tray, Virginie, arms folded, leaning one shoulder against the door to the terrace. Behind her, the view from Maison Cabrille over the Corniche J. F. Kennedy to the distant Frioul Islands was all but lost this morning to low grey skies and a slanting, dancing rain that gusted over the terrace flagstones and spattered against the glass.

Virginie Cabrille had come up from her lodge in the grounds. She was wearing her usual uniform – black and white combat trousers tucked into a pair of high-heeled ankle boots, with a black leather jacket worn over a tight white T-shirt. She was tall for a woman, with a crop of pricily spiked black hair and broad swimmer's shoulders. She could only have been her father's daughter. The same nose, long and pointed; the same mouth, lips thin as a lemon slice; and the same black eyes, still focused on the crumpled newspaper in her father's lap. The front page was dominated by a picture of Elodie Lafour, an inset picture of her parents, and a three column story detailing her disappearance and police efforts to find her.

'Who? She who?' asked her father, who had been reading an inside continuation of the front-page story.

Virginie smiled, nodded at the newspaper. 'That girl . . . Lafour. The one you're pretending not to read about, Papa.'

Her father seemed to give it some thought. 'You think so? Here in Marseilles?'

Pushing herself away from the terrace door, Virginie came over to her father's desk and took one of the two chairs placed in front of it, slinging one leg over the arm and making herself comfortable.

'Either she's dead,' began Virginie, ticking off the first of two fingers, 'picked up by some pervert and presently waiting for a man walking his dog to find her body, or she's been snatched for transport, bound for a sordid little whorehouse somewhere. Or maybe a private clinic where they'll remove vital organs one by one and then dump the body. Although the latter's unlikely. Too pretty for transplants.'

'And what exactly makes you so sure of this?' asked her father, a thin smile playing across his lips. It was exactly the same conclusion he had come to.

'No ransom, Papa. No ransom.'

'Perhaps she's eloped? A boy somewhere . . .'

Virginie shook her head.

'But why Marseilles?' her father persisted. 'If she has been picked up for shipping out, why not from some other port?'

Virginie returned her father's smile with one of her own, equally thin, equally malicious.

'Where better to start such a journey than Marseilles? *La porte du monde*. Please don't tell me you haven't come to the same conclusion yourself?'

Her father shrugged, put aside the paper and worked his thumbs, a tight arthritic pain slicing through the joints. Old age, he thought to himself. Who'd have it?

'So,' he began, glancing at his watch, changing the subject, 'are we ready?'

'Ready when you are, Papa,' replied Virginie with a sigh.

45

12

THE *GARAGISTE* JULES VALENTINE KNEW he was in trouble the moment he rolled up the metal door to his railway-arch workshop in Commanderie and saw the Corsicans standing there. They'd hammered loud and hard enough on the metal roller to fill the workshop with a thunderous din that had Valentine running to open it to stop the noise. And there they were. Two of them. Polished black shoes first, as he bent down to pull up the roller door. Black suits under elegantly tailored black topcoats, black gloves, and a black umbrella apiece. Everything save their crisp white shirts and hard tanned faces as black as the oil on the floor of Valentine's garage.

They didn't ask to come in. When the door had rolled past head-height the taller of the two men snapped his umbrella closed, handed it to his companion then pushed Valentine back inside the workshop.

The radio was blaring, there was old Gideon's Renault van up on the skids and Ibin and Alam, dressed in oily *bleus*, were working on its exhaust. While the first Corsican walked Valentine to his office, sat him down and took up position by the door, his companion approached the two lads in the pit and indicated that they should get up out of it, sharpish. Through the office window, Valentine saw him speak to the kids. Whatever he was saying he certainly had their attention. When Valentine saw him reach inside his topcoat, he was certain the hand would come out holding a gun. It didn't.

46

Instead, the Corsican opened a wallet and slid out a wedge of notes – green ones, the five hundreds. He made Ibin and Alam hold out their hands, dealt them four each, then slid the wallet back into his overcoat pocket.

That was when he took out his gun.

As black as his shoes and his gloves and his overcoat. With a long black silencer attached.

Neat move. Putting the money in their hands first, thought Valentine, as he watched the silenced gun slide between Ibin's legs and then Alam's legs, juggling what was down there. The two of them flinched, eyes wide as oil caps. Then the gun was removed and, without a pause the Corsican swept it up between their heads and blew the radio to pieces, then swung it back down to put out the work-torch hanging from the Renault's back fender. A swift and elegant display. The shatter of lamp glass made more noise than the shot, just a low *phut* that Valentine wouldn't have heard if the radio had still been playing.

Ibin and Alam got the message. They were pulling on their coats and out of there as fast as they could manage it. They didn't quite run. As the Corsican brought down the metal door after they'd scarpered, Valentine knew with absolute certainty that they wouldn't be coming back with the cavalry. And they wouldn't say a thing. Nothing. Not a word.

Unlike him.

Which was why he was sitting where he was, in his undershirt and belted *bleus*, in the company of the two Corsicans.

He knew who they were now. The twins. He'd heard about them. Real *gorilles*. The kind you steered clear of if you had any sense.

And what had he done . . .?

He'd talked. That's what he'd done.

Because now he knew who they were waiting for.

And, with a cold tremor that shuddered down through his thighs, he knew what was going to happen.

Jules Valentine didn't have long to wait.

Or long to live.

13

IF THERE WAS ONE THING that bothered Arsène Cabrille it was his increasing inability to kill. Arthritis, that cruel companion of the elderly, had taken his old hands knuckle by swollen, painful knuckle, starting with his thumbs, which made holding a gun and squeezing a trigger something of a trial. The last time he'd fired his beloved 9-mm Browning *Grande Puissance*, he'd missed his target, the large bald head of Lucas 'Long Legs' Laratour, a small-time runner in Toulon who'd thought he could slip a half-kilo wrap of cocaine off a Cabrille consignment without anyone noticing. The first time Laratour had got away with it. The second time too. The third time he tried it, Arsène Cabrille came knocking on his door. While the elder of the two Corsicans, Taddeus, and his daughter, Virginie, held the man down, Cabrille had drawn his *GP* and waved it menacingly in front of the weeping, pleading man.

Cabrille always liked to play out these kinds of scenes for as long as possible. A kind of signature performance. And in his low, cajoling voice, he liked to talk – taunting and teasing, sometimes suggesting that in future he'd be less generous, giving his victim to understand that this time, maybe, he'd get away with a swift barrel-whipping rather than a 9-millimetre bullet in the brain. That's what Cabrille particularly liked: lulling his victims into a false sense of security, watching the sag of relief in their shoulders. When he finally ran out of things to say, he simply placed the muzzle against their temple and pulled the trigger.

That's what he'd done with Laratour. Except he'd missed. Close range, an inch between muzzle and skull, and he'd missed.

And it wasn't just a matter of getting a firm grip on the pistol or squeezing the damn' trigger either. It was the weight of the thing. His favourite Browning *GP*, with its wooden grip and blued metal, had suddenly become heavy and cumbersome, and his hand weak and clumsy. Seventy-eight years old – with maybe a killing for each of them; he'd have known if he'd kept count – and now it looked like it was over. If it hadn't been for Virginie, he'd have retired to his Mauritian hideaway, found himself a mistress there as obliging and tolerant as the sinuous Cous-Cous and called it a day. Not many of his colleagues had gone so far or been so fortunate, Cabrille knew, sitting in the back seat of his beloved Daimler Sovereign, and settling his old eyes on Virginie.

Genes, he mused, as his daughter played the wheel through her hands, speeding them around the Vieux Port and out on to the Littoral flyover. It was all in the genes. And *grâce à Dieu* for that. Thirty years before, the news that he'd fathered a daughter might have drained the colour from his face, but down the years his little girl had proved herself more than equal to the sons he'd yearned for, the sons who might have followed but never did. His wife, Léonie, had seen to that.

As far as he knew, his only child had made her first kill at the tender age of eleven: the family dog, César. He was old, about to be put down. On the day they were taking him to the vet, Virginie had walked into the kitchen holding a knife, the front of her T-shirt splashed with blood.

'César was my dog, so it was my decision and my responsibility,' she had told her father. 'And . . . I wanted to see what it was like.'

'And what was it like?' Cabrille had asked, amused and intrigued by his daughter's cool.

49

It had taken a moment for Virginie to find the right word. And then, almost wistfully, she had replied: 'Interesting.'

Virginie might never have killed another dog, but Arsène Cabrille knew that she'd made up for it elsewhere. At twenty-three, with a degree in business studies from Sciences-Po, which he had insisted she complete, she'd come back to Marseilles and asked for a job in the family business: drugs primarily, with a healthy measure of murder, extortion, gambling and prostitution as useful, and often associated, sidelines. But there was a condition, she'd told her father. She wanted to be out in the workplace, not behind a desk balancing the books, *s'il te plaît, Papa*.

So, with a raising of his hands and a shrug of surrender, he had given her to Taddeus and his twin brother, Tomas, whom Cabrille trusted above all his *troupe*. The Corsican twins had taken her on, taught her a few useful tricks and after a six-month apprentice-ship, Taddeus had reported back that La Mam'selle was well able to look after herself. A true Cabrille, he'd said. And so his little Virginie joined the firm. It was the proudest day of Cabrille's life. He couldn't have wished for more.

But she was headstrong, too. Impatient with the measured pace of Cabrille operations. She always wanted things to move faster, more efficiently, was always looking to streamline the business. Which was not the way that Cabrille had learned from his own father. *Doucement, doucement*, the old man had told him. *We'll get there in the end, and be safe too. That's the secret. That's the important thing*. And Cabrille had gone along with it, biting his tongue sometimes but always following his father's wishes.

It was not the same with Virginie. He could often feel the tension radiating off her, the impatience, the tongue-biting. Maybe it was just youth, he decided. Maybe she'd grow out of it, learn to control it. And when she did, then she'd be ready to take over. Only then.

On the Daimler's CD player, Charles Trénet's *'Que reste-t-il de nos amours?'* started up and Cabrille smiled. Along with *'La Mer'* and *'Boum'*, it was one of his all-time favourites. Such a smooth voice, that Trénet – smoother, longer, sweeter than Rossi, or Gabin, or Chevalier. The soundtrack of his youth . . . all those old haunts like Cage d'Or on République and Bateau Bleu off Canebière. Champagne in ice buckets, spotlights and sequins, the sweet scent of cigars and *Soir de Paris*. Ah, he thought, those were the days, and he started to hum along, waving a bent finger to follow the beat.

But the fond mood didn't last. Looking past Virginie towards the Joliette docks, he spotted a banner strung up between two dock-yard cranes, bellying in the wind and scrawled with a rain-smeared message of defiance: *Enfin le Mort du Port*.

'So the strike has begun?' he said, Trénet forgotten for the moment, lips now pursed in irritation.

'Tuesday, Papa. The Chamant gate on the Mirabe basin was the last to close,' Virginie replied. 'Now it's stalemate from here to Corbière. Which is good.'

'And why would that be good when we have a hundred-million franc cargo in the hull of *Hesperides* waiting to be unloaded?' asked Cabrille with an icy precision.

'Because, *cher* Papa, if our little girl's in Marseilles, she won't be going anywhere any time soon. That's why.'

Up ahead a truck started to pull out into the fast lane without indicating. Coming up behind him but refusing to brake, Virginie tooted the Daimler's horn and accelerated past with just centimetres to spare. '*Salaud*,' he heard her whisper under her breath.

'And what is so important, so valuable about this missing young lady anyway?' continued Cabrille, not really listening, more concerned by the enforced hold-up of his latest cargo.

'Because, while we wait for the dockers' strike to end we can earn ourselves the same amount – maybe more – finding the girl and making that ransom demand ourselves.'

Virginie wasn't actually thinking about money, but she knew it was a word that her old father understood. She wasn't convinced that he'd quite appreciate the refinements that she had in mind.

'And what makes you imagine her poor parents will have suffi-cient funds to cover such a ludicrous demand?'

Virginie grunted, slanting a look at her father in the rear-view mirror. 'Because, as you will have read in the newspaper, Mama is an heiress and her stepfather is Georges Lafour of Banque Lafour et Finance.'

'An heiress? Banque Lafour?'

'Shoes, Papa. The Bonnefoy *botte*. Her great-great-grandfather supplied Napoleon's army. As for Georges Lafour, he runs one of the most successful private investment banks in the country. And, coincidentally, gave a series of lectures my second year at Sciences-Po,' she added.

'Well, we'd better keep our eyes open then, hadn't we?' said Cabrille, trying to work the ache out of his fingers, knowing there were more important matters on the agenda than some missing girl, though it pleased him to see his daughter so preoccupied with the promise and possibility of profit, even if it was in unrelated fields. And then, 'How much further?'

'A couple more minutes,' Virginie replied. 'Just up ahead.'

On the CD player, '*Que reste-t-il de nos amours?*' came to an end. A second later, Trénet launched into '*Boum*'.

14

ARSÈNE CABRILLE WATCHED HIS DAUGHTER unzip her boots. He was sitting in the back seat of the Daimler which Virginie had thoughtfully driven into Valentine's workshop. He wouldn't have to get out of the car, he needn't even get wet. The CD player was still on, a bouncy accordion accompanying Fréhel on 'La Java Bleue'. The Breton singer added a certain raddled *joie de vivre* to the proceedings, he decided.

Placing her boots together, Virginie got up from the bench and flexed her legs, drawing each to her chest, clasping it with her arms, barefoot now save for a band of white tape around both heels and just above the toes of her right foot. She was still wearing the combat trousers but she'd removed her leather jacket, and her wide swimmer's shoulders stretched her T-shirt. She looked powerful, muscular, highly tuned.

'So tell us about Chief Inspector Gastal,' she began, tugging on what looked like a pair of cycling mitts.

Valentine was standing between the two Corsicans. They had taken off their overcoats and jackets and had made something of a performance of it, carefully draping their clothes over the bonnet of the Daimler. Nice touch, Valentine had thought. Stripping off like that made it so much worse, like there really was going to be a mess. As Virginie approached, the two men reached for Valentine's wrists and pulled out his arms, tugging against each other so that he was crucified between them. And there was nothing he could do about it.

'Gastal?' he asked, as though the name was unfamiliar.

Virginie was lethally fast. Less than a metre from Valentine, she rose on her toes, spun round and, using her hips for added momentum, brought the point of her left elbow slicing across his left cheek. His head snapped back from the blow, but the Corsicans held him fast. When his head rolled forward again there was a trail of green snot draped across his cheek, just a centimetre above a long gash that opened red and smooth, like a second mouth, running from cheekbone to chin. Blood seeped from the wound and flowed down his neck into the front of his *veste*.

Virginie contemplated the result of her handiwork, flexing movement back into her elbow, straightening and bending the arm.

'Never answer a question with a question, *cher* Jules,' she chided. 'It's very impolite. So. Once again. Gastal. Remind me.'

Valentine shook his head and the line of snot followed the blood, slithering down his cheek like a long green worm. 'He's a *flic*. Used to work in Toulon and here in Marseilles – vice, narcotics – but long gone. Up in Lyons the last I heard.' His voice was low and croaky, almost fractured from the blow he'd received.

It wasn't what Virginie wanted to hear. Shaking out her elbow, she suddenly tipped back on her right foot and, with just the merest spring, she brought the heel of her left foot hard down on Valentine's right knee.

In the back of the Daimler Cabrille heard the snap of tendons before the man's voice wailed out in agony: 'Ay-ay-ahhhh-fuckin'-fuckin' sheeeeet!!' He shook his head sadly. Valentine should have known better.

'Please, please, please, *mon petit*,' purred Virginie, walking to and fro in front of Valentine, rolling her shoulders, her neck, getting into her rhythm. 'Such language.' The man was now sagging to the right on an obscenely bent leg. If it hadn't been for the two Corsicans he'd have been down on the ground. But Virginie seemed unconcerned. 'You know as well as I that your little *copain*, Gastal, is right here in Marseilles,' she continued. 'Because the two of you have been seeing rather a lot of each other. Am I right?'

'You're right, you're right. He's back. But I swear . . .'

Whatever Valentine was about to swear, Virginie was not prepared to listen. Twisting back to her right this time, her left foot shot up like a piston and slammed into the man's left shoulder.

Valentine spat out another shriek of pain as the shoulder dislocated with a hollow crunch, the Corsican holding his left wrist adding a few wrenching tugs for good measure. The three of them had done this before.

'What did he want?' asked Virginie gently, circling the three men, retaping the Velcro on her mitts. 'And what did you tell him?'

'The girl . . . the one who was killed. Not anything else! Not you, nothing. *Rien de rien*. Just this girl, that's all.'

Virginie looked over at the Daimler, caught her father's eye.

'Girl?' she asked.

'He wanted to know if Fonton was still around. Wanted to know if he and his boys had her . . . here in Marseilles. I told him Fonton was gone. There were others now . . . working the lines.'

'Others?'

'It's good money. Safe if you get it right. And regular.'

'You got any names for me?'

For a moment Valentine didn't respond, panting out the pain from his knee and his shoulder, licking at the blood and the snot. The Corsican on his left gave his wrist another encouraging tug.

'Santarem . . . Murat Santarem,' Valentine screamed out. 'That's a name I heard.'

'And what is it that this Murat Santarem does, exactly?' asked Virginie, standing in front of Valentine once more.

'He's a fixer,' gasped Valentine. '*Arabe*. Used to run drugs round Toulon, and here in Marseilles. Just a courier. Nothing big. Now I hear he gets girls, passes 'em on. Small time traffic but does okay.'

'And where does this Monsieur Santarem live?' coaxed Virginie, flexing her fingers, cracking the knuckles one by one.

55

Valentine shook his head, and was rewarded with another swipe of her elbow, crunching into his right cheekbone this time. Another spill of blood coursed down his chest.

'It's years . . . I don't know now . . . Could be Toulon. Could be here.' The man was beginning to weep, tears tracking down his bloodied cheeks.

'And that's it? Just this girl?'

'Like I said, it was nothing about the family. I wouldn't do that. Not the Cabrilles.'

Virginie let a smile slide across her features. Nodded understandingly. 'And you're quite sure about that? It was just the girl he was interested in?'

'That's all. On my life . . . I swear to you, on my life.'

Virginie straightened her shoulders and let out a breath, worked her neck. 'Funny you should mention that,' she said, looking back at her father and getting the nod. 'Because, as of now . . . it's over.'

Lifting his head, grunting with the effort, Valentine tried to focus his eyes on her. The last thing he saw was the ball of her hand, mittened fingers curled back, streaking towards his face. There was no time to avoid it. He felt the blow, heard the cartilage in his nose snap, and sensed a cold sliver of bone slide into his frontal lobe.

Jules Valentine was dead before he hit the floor.

15

Paris

SHORTLY AFTER VALENTINE'S BROKEN BODY was tipped into the inspection pit of his Commanderie workshop, Daniel Jacquot pushed open the heavy plate glass doors of La Résidence Camille on the Left Bank of Paris. He had caught an early train from Cavaillon, as agreed the night before with Madame Bonnefoy, and had spent the last four hours going through the Lafour case file which the examining magistrate had brought with her to Kuchnia in the expectation that he would accept her commission – which, of course, he had. The file was dense and on the journey north, chased all the way by the rain, he'd had time for just two read-throughs – from the initial missing person's report timed Saturday evening and the reports of the Parisian investigating officers, to witness statements and background profiles on the Lafour family – Elodie, her mother Estelle and her stepfather Georges Lafour, an increasingly influential adviser in Chirac's administration, according to the sheaf of photocopied newspaper clippings that formed part of his profile's appendix.

It had made interesting reading and the foyer of La Résidence Camille confirmed what the file had noted: that the Lafours were, indeed, an extremely wealthy family. Which made the lack of a ransom demand all the more unusual, and disquieting. If there was no boyfriend, as Solange Bonnefoy had assured him, then murder or possibly trafficking were all that remained.

Brushing the rain from the shoulders of his coat and wiping a hand across his forehead, Jacquot crossed the marble foyer to the concierge's desk, a rich, unlikely summer scent of honeysuckle and gardenia in the air.

'Chief Inspector Daniel Jacquot,' he said to the concierge, now rising from behind his desk to intercept him, a small man given bulk and authority by his topcoat, its generous braiding as warm and golden as the matching gilt mirrors, candle sconces and ormolu *buffets* that furnished La Résidence Camille's foyer. A pair of white gloves was strapped beneath one of his braid epaulettes, and the gold keys of St Peter glinted on his lapel. The man's hair was black, parted high on one side and glistened with pommade, which made him look, Jacquot thought, like a vaudeville performer from the turn of the century, exuding a greasy master-of-ceremonies bonhomie. All that was missing was a curling moustache. 'I have an appointment with Madame Lafour,' Jacquot told him.

'You are expected, monsieur. Please, this way,' the concierge replied, leading him to one of a pair of gilt-caged lifts, hauling back the concertina doors with an oily, rattling *ker-chunk, ker-chunk*. Jacquot wondered how many times the concierge had performed this particular duty. He could probably have done it with his eyes closed: from desk to lifts and back to the desk.

Before stepping in, Jacquot turned to him. 'Your name is Claude Carloux?'

'That is correct, monsieur.'

'And you were the concierge on duty when Mademoiselle Lafour left the building on Saturday?'

'I was, monsieur.'

'*Dites-moi*,' said Jacquot, leaning forward as though wishing to share a confidence, 'did the young lady seem happy to you? Or distracted in any way?'

Despite its size, the Lafour file he'd read on the train had not recorded the mood of the girl on the morning she went missing. Indeed, Jacquot had found it hard to work up any picture of the girl at all, save for her age, her looks, the reports of academic ability from her school. Her music. Her painting. There had to be more.

Carloux frowned. Considered the question. 'Why, she seemed very happy,' he replied. '*En effet*, come to think of it, the happiest I have seen her in a long while.'

'She is not normally so happy?'

The concierge spread his hands and glanced across to the stairs, rising up either side of the lifts to a mezzanine floor. In a softer voice, he confided, 'She is a beautiful young lady, Chief Inspector. It is hard not to notice her, you understand. But sometimes, for someone so young, so pretty, she seems . . . too serious for her years. When she should be full of the joys of spring, *n'est-ce-pas*?' And Carloux turned his eyes to the foyer, nodding towards it as though to suggest that anyone fortunate enough to live at La Résidence Camille could surely have few worries. Then he shrugged, shook his head. 'It is terrible. Poor Madame Lafour.'

'And poor Monsieur Lafour,' added Jacquot with a smile.

Carloux let out a puff of breath. '*Oh, mais oui, bien sûr. Mais* . . .'

'*Mais*?'

'But, I mean, he is the stepfather. It is different, I think.'

Jacquot nodded, as though in agreement, then stepped into the lift and pulled the cage-doors closed.

'Which floor?' he asked through the bars.

'The sixth, monsieur,' replied Carloux. 'Apartment eighteen.'

Jacquot waved his thanks and pressed the button. With a surprisingly swift and silent power the old lift rose away from the foyer, past four floors – four doors a floor – until the cage sighed to a stop on the topmost level. Pulling open the doors, Jacquot paused to examine the control panel. *Ascenseurs Famille Yaeger Orfèvres, 1923*. The real thing, he could see, but given a make-over for the great and the good of La Résidence Camille.

Stepping out of the lift, closing the doors behind him, Jacquot looked around. Like the foyer and floors below, this top floor landing was ludicrously spacious, marble tiled, and furnished in choice

Empire ormolu, its half-dozen gilt sconces and chandelier casting a soft golden light over three large hunting scene tapestries. But it wasn't the space or the furnishings that gave him pause for thought. Up here there were just two doors leading off the landing, not four. Since La Résidence Camille occupied an entire block, it was clear that these two top-floor apartments shared one whole side of the street between them – far, far larger than the sixteen apartments below. According to the case file, La Résidence Camille was the Lafours' pied-a-terre in Paris, their weekend home being further out of the city in Neuilly.

Another world, thought Jacquot, pressing flat number eighteen's doorbell and wondering what he would find inside.

16

A MAID ANSWERED THE DOOR – small, dark, her shiny bobbed black hair pinned into a starched white cap, a Filipino or Malay, Jacquot guessed – and without waiting for his name or asking for identification, she led him down a set of runnered stairs into a formal parquet-floored salon, its four picture-windows and a length of terrace outside looking out over a stepped landscape of leaded mansard roofs to the dome of the distant Opéra and the rain-shrouded slopes of Montmartre. There was little time to take in the view, however, as the maid moved swiftly ahead of him, nor was there any real opportunity to take in what appeared to be a series of separate living areas connected to this central salon, each 'quartier' with its own grand fireplace, each space elegantly separated by folding oriental screens or curtained arches: a small family drawing room with plumper, friendlier sofas and armchairs than the main reception area; a television room with modern loungers and damasked bean bags; and a music salon with silver-framed family photos set out on a grand piano. All Jacquot could say for sure was big money, big influence, before the maid was leaning forward to open double panelled doors. She stood aside, waited till he passed, then closed them behind him.

Apart from a spill of light from a desk-top lamp, the room Jacquot entered was in shadow, outside shutters all but closed on a set of corner windows, their interior blinds steeply slanted and bordered by thick drapes. There was a scent of leather from the desk top, chairs and bookshelves, and an oaky, masculine *eau de cologne*, laced with a lighter, more fragrant note.

'My sister tells me you are the best detective she knows,' came a soft, hesitant voice from the far corner of the room, and a slim shape rose from an armchair placed between the windows. As she came into the fall of light from the desk lamp, Jacquot could see that the voice belonged to a younger version of Madame Bonnefoy – the same proud nose, the same regal air, but the hair longer, much darker and caught in a loose knot, the features sharper, the figure slight and tense. She was wrapped, Jacquot now saw, in a dressing gown, a lushly towelled affair in diamond-shaped blue check with a long narrow collar. It looked a size too big for her, her husband's possibly.

Madame Lafour caught the look as they shook hands, hers like a thin purse of bone. 'Forgive me, Chief Inspector. Recently it is difficult for me to summon the energy to dress. I seem not to have the strength any more.' She did indeed look pale and drawn, eyes red, the skin around them puffed and grey. She seemed as thin and brittle as the tiny hand she had offered. But then her only child was missing, and for five days now this mother had been through a hell unknown to most. Indeed, Jacquot would have been surprised if it had been otherwise.

Releasing his hand, Madame Lafour turned to a silver box on the desk, flipped open the lid and found a cigarette. 'Georges leaves so early in the morning he doesn't see me,' she explained, placing the cigarette between her lips and reaching for a lighter. It was silver, the size of a Pétanque *boule,* and looked just as weighty. Holding it in both hands, she flicked the wheel till the gas caught, then guided the flame to the cigarette. 'All I have to do,' she said, replacing the lighter on the desk with a solid clunk, and picking up an even weightier ashtray, 'is make sure I'm dressed when he comes home in the evening.' She removed the cigarette from her lips and blew a stream of smoke towards the ceiling. Judging by its colour, she didn't inhale. 'And clean my teeth so he doesn't smell the cigarettes,' she continued. '*Autrefois* . . . I am as you see me now. My apologies again, Chief Inspector. Please, take a seat,' she said, pointing to a sofa while she retreated to her armchair, cigarette in one hand, ashtray in the other.

'Please be assured, madame, that you are not alone in this . . . this loss of purpose,' Jacquot began, settling himself. 'It happens very frequently. I have seen it many times. And there are more important things than clothes and dressing, *n'est-ce-pas*? Sometimes, in cases like this, it is enough just to get through the day.'

Madame Lafour blew out another blue stream of smoke. 'And nights. Don't forget the nights, Chief Inspector. They are the worst. While my husband sleeps, I wander. Room to room. Here, the salon, the kitchen. Waiting. Always waiting. And wondering where she is. Praying she is safe, that she will come to no harm.'

'I am sure she will not.'

Madame Lafour sighed. 'You sound like Georges. He is certain she will be found.'

'There is every reason to think so.'

'Really, Chief Inspector? You seem very sure.'

'Call it a feeling, madame.'

'Not very policeman-like,' she replied. 'A "feeling". But I appreciate your kind intention.'

Quietness descended on the room, not even the slightest hum of passing traffic audible, and Jacquot was aware of Madame Lafour steeling herself.

'So, please, ask your questions,' she continued. 'Down to business. Solly called this morning and said I should tell you whatever you need to know.'

'I have read the case notes,' said Jacquot, nodding to the briefcase at his feet. 'There is very little I need to ask.'

'And yet you have come all this way? From Marseilles?'

'*En effet*, Cavaillon. But it is a fast and comfortable service, and not a problem, I assure you. A chance, too, to study the files.'

'And to check out the parents, *n'est-ce pas*?'

Jacquot inclined his head. 'That is a part of it, of course. When you meet the parents, it is often possible to get a clearer picture of the situation, of the people involved, of the person you are looking for.'

Madame Lafour tapped the cigarette against the ashtray in her lap, but did not reply.

'So, tell me. When did you last see Elodie?'

'Friday night. Georges and I came home from dinner. A business thing. Elodie was watching TV. I told her it was late, that she should be in bed.'

'And how did she respond?'

'She asked if she could watch the end of the programme. She said she didn't need to get up in the morning. She had no classes.'

'And you let her?'

'Georges said it would be fine. So I kissed her goodnight. Half-an-hour later I heard her come to bed, but I did not see her. Just heard the door opening and closing.'

'And the following morning? Saturday.'

'I had an appointment with my hairdresser at ten. Elodie was still asleep when I left.' Madame Lafour paused. 'But surely you know this already, Chief Inspector? From the file.'

Jacquot nodded. 'Often, in the repetition, tiny additional details are remembered,' he said softly. 'It is a wearisome process, for which I apologise, but it often produces results. So, Saturday. When you returned from your hairdresser, Elodie wasn't here?'

'That's right.'

'She was going somewhere?'

Madame Lafour shook her head. 'She hadn't said anything. And she had left no note. I was a little cross. Normally she would leave a note. Or call.'

'And your husband?'

'At work in his study.'

'He didn't see her?'

'She would have known not to disturb him. When he is working . . .'

Jacquot took this in, let a silence settle around them. His questions so far had been unprepared, the way he often liked to run an interview. It helped put the subject at ease. Or confused them, made them angry. Sometimes it was a useful game to play. He waited a moment more before continuing. 'I understand that Monsieur Lafour is your second husband.'

'That is correct.'

'Yet Elodie has his name.'

'After her father's death, when we married, Georges formally adopted Elodie. She took his name.'

'And she was happy about that? She didn't mind?'

'She was young, Chief Inspector. Seven years old when her father died. Nine when I married Georges. I doubt she gave it any thought.'

'Your idea or your husband's? The adoption.'

'Mine. It seemed the right thing to do.'

'And your husband made no objection?'

'None, Chief Inspector. He was very pleased. Very proud. As you will have read in your file, he has no children of his own.'

Jacquot smiled, nodded again. 'And recently, madame, there have been no arguments, no disagreements between the two of them? Your husband and Elodie.'

'With Elodie? No, nothing.'

'And you? You said sometimes you get cross . . .'

'About little things, that's all,' she replied, just a shade sharply. 'Nothing more than in any family.'

'Sometimes, madame, at Elodie's age, it can be the smallest thing. So small that to others running away seems inconceivable as a consequence, altogether out of proportion.'

'This is not a runaway case, Chief Inspector. Someone has her. Someone has taken Elodie.' Madame Lafour's voice caught on the name, but she recovered. 'And it's her birthday. Yesterday. She would never miss that.'

'Had you made plans?'

'Since her tenth birthday we have always had lunch at Brasserie Lipp. My husband says their *choucroute* cannot be beaten. After that, Georges returns to work and we go shopping. Two girls. Such fun. Though each year it becomes more expensive, *n'est-ce-pas*? You have children, do you, Chief Inspector?'

'*Non. Je regrette. Pas encore, madame.*'

'Then one day, Chief Inspector, you will know. About the expense . . .' she managed a short little laugh . . . 'but hopefully not the . . . this . . . this horror.' She dragged in a breath and held it, gathering herself again. She may have looked done in, and sounded at the end of her tether, but Jacquot decided there was still a core of Bonnefoy steel there.

'Tell me, please, would you say your daughter was a happy person?'

The corner she sat in was too far away, and too shadowy, for him to see her frown, but Jacquot guessed it was there.

'Happy?' repeated Madame Lafour, as though this was a question she hadn't been expecting. 'Of course, why shouldn't she be?'

'Sometimes, in cases like this, a young person – girls particularly – they hide things from their parents. Something happening in their lives.'

'You're talking about boys?'

Jacquot shrugged, spread his hands. 'It is certainly a possibility. Something to consider. Surely at Elodie's age . . .'

'There are no boyfriends, Chief Inspector. I would know. Nor have there been.' Madame Lafour took a final pull on her cigarette and mashed it into the ashtray, reached out and slid it on to a side table. 'Elodie is, has always been, a studious girl. Shy too. We worry about her sometimes, my husband and I, but Georges says we must give her time, and space. It will all happen soon enough, he says, and when it does she will be gone from us. And our time with her will be over.'

Madame Lafour fell silent. When she spoke again, her voice sounded low and lost. 'Let us hope that time hasn't come already, Chief Inspector.'

17

Marseilles

IT WAS CHIEF INSPECTOR ALAIN GASTAL who discovered
Valentine's body. When his *garagiste* informant failed to phone
that Thursday morning as arranged, Gastal decided to pay a call at
the man's workshop. A personal visit. A little knock-about persua-
sion, the kind Gastal liked, to make sure it didn't happen again, to
let the man know just who was running the show. Striding out of
the squad room on the third floor of police headquarters on rue de
l'Evêché, he called out to Claude Peluze, his number two, to hold
the fort.

He didn't say when he'd be back.

Now that he was boss, he didn't have to.

The ex-legionnaire Peluze nodded, just a bare acknowledgement,
probably only too pleased to have him out of there.

Of course, Gastal knew they all hated him. Every single one of
them on the squad. Peluze, Muzon, Serre, the lot of them. And
Gastal loved it; could almost warm his hands on the glow of loathing
that radiated off every single one of them. The man who'd got
Jacquot sacked. The man who'd had that pony-tailed *poseur* trans-
ferred out of homicide to a no-future posting in the Luberon. And
kept him there for close on three years, quietly putting in a word
of warning whenever requests came through from the authorities
in Marseilles, suggesting Jacquot's return to more active duty.

No bloody way, not the shadow of a chance.

Not if he, Alain Gastal, had anything to do with it.

Stepping out of police headquarters, Gastal jogged through the rain to his car, pulling up his collar, wishing he'd brought a hat. Five minutes later he swung past Cathédrale de la Major, its striped flanks smeared through the windscreen, and, pulling a toothpick from his breast pocket, followed the tram lines west.

Ten days in this city and already he was on top, thought Gastal. Two weeks earlier, he'd been behind a desk in the Lyons headquarters of the *Direction Générale de la Sécurité Extérieure*, tracking freighter movements between Genoa, Palermo and Toulon. Now he was running Marseilles' homicide squad while his old boss was on leave.

'Good cover,' his current boss at the *DGSE* had told him. 'Just sniff around, see what you can find out. You got any *indics* down there?' It was agency slang for *Indicateurs* – informants.

'Not as many as in Toulon,' Gastal had replied, holding out for a longer stint in his old stamping ground. But the Toulon posting had already been assigned. Which wasn't to say that a desk in Marseilles didn't have its compensations, not least the opportunity to stick it to his old comrades from a position of power.

And if Gastal had more snouts in Toulon than he did in Marseilles, there was still Jules Valentine. Within three days of taking over on rue de l'Evêché, he had finally tracked down the *garagiste* to a café-bar called La Toppa on the slopes above the railway line in L'Estaque. It had been an entertaining encounter. Valentine, sitting at the corner of the bar, had done a classic double-take when Gastal sauntered in – couldn't believe his eyes.

'I'm out of it now,' the man had told him when they met up five minutes later in the parking lot outside La Toppa.

'And I've taken holy orders,' Gastal replied, telling Valentine what he wanted: anything on the Cabrille family whose shipping interests he'd been monitoring from Lyons.

The name brought forth even more disavowals from Valentine.

Cabrille? Cabrille? Never heard of them . . . Nope . . . Doesn't ring a bell.

What did ring a bell was the fold of five hundreds that Gastal slipped from his trouser pocket and, licking a finger, started counting, right there in the car park, a dozen regulars keeping a covert eye on them through La Toppa's steamy window. They all knew he was a cop, and here he was, paying Valentine money. Of course, he could have been settling a bill for some body work on his car, but Gastal knew what most of them would be thinking.

So did Valentine.

Keen to conclude this meeting as swiftly as possible, he had then suddenly recalled that he did indeed know of the Cabrilles, and yes, yes, Gastal was right, he did seem to remember something about questionable cargoes.

'When and where?' Gastal had pressed, pushing the money back in his own pocket. 'I want to know the when and the where. *Compris*?'

Valentine had nodded and promised to get in touch.

'You've got till Tuesday,' Gastal had told him. After that, he'd warned, he'd put the word out that Valentine was a grass. *Tant pis*.

And he'd do it, too. He might lose a good snout, but the sooner he got something solid back to the *DGSE*, the better he would look. In Lyons, competition for promotion or preferment was fierce. Keep your head down and you spent your career lunching in the city's *prix-fixe bouchons*. Not that they weren't good. It was just that La Tour Rose and Paul Bocuse were better.

But it wasn't only the Cabrille set-up and the prospect of promotion at headquarters that was lighting his fires. On Tuesday afternoon, waiting for Valentine to get in touch, a call had come through from Madame Bonnefoy, examining magistrate, drawing his attention to the fact that a car-crash fatality on Boulevard Cambrai had been reported missing from Paris the previous week.

So? Gastal had asked.

And Madame Bonnefoy had spelled it out for him. He could almost see her gritted teeth. But by the time she'd finished, he was altogether more attentive. The name Georges Lafour, and the examining magistrate's close family connection with such a man, had galvanised Gastal. He knew an opportunity for advancement when he smelled one, and this particular cherry had Bocuse written all over it. By the time the call ended, Gastal had assured Madame Bonnefoy that the Viviers case was currently his top priority, that he'd already assigned men to check out this particular link, and that he would keep her fully informed of all developments. Anything Madame needed . . . Anything at all . . . Any time . . .

Two hours later, Gastal had cornered Valentine at the same bar in L'Estaque and suggested that, while he was digging up all he could on the Cabrilles, he should also keep an eye out for a missing girl. Elodie Lafour. Was Fonton still around, he'd asked? Or Lousine? Or any of the other traffickers?

Once again, Valentine had promised to find out what he could. And Gastal had given him till this morning to get in touch. Or else.

But there'd been no word from him. Nothing.

If the stupid bastard was jerking his strings, by Christ he'd regret it, thought Gastal as he swung off rue Chatelier and pulled up outside Valentine's garage in the fifteenth arrondissement. He'd do it. He bloody well would. He'd put it around that Valentine was a snout, and leave the man to the sharks.

Five minutes later, after finding Valentine's broken body at the bottom of the inspection pit, Gastal acknowledged that he wouldn't have to bother.

Someone had made quite sure of that.

18

Paris

AN HOUR AFTER ARRIVING AT La Résidence Camille, Jacquot jogged down the front steps, crossed the road just as Elodie had done the week before and found a doorway out of the rain. Huddling into it, he lit up a cigarette and considered all that he had seen and heard. Such a magnificent home, he thought, looking up at the topmost floors of the building opposite. Beautiful furnishings, stylishly decorated. Great wealth, certainly – either from Georges Lafour's financial dealings, or Bonnefoy family trusts. Maybe the two combined. Yet the only room there that had any soul, any heart, was Elodie's bedroom. He had asked Madame Lafour if he could see it and she had called the maid to take him there. She did not want to show him herself, she explained, and Jacquot had understood. Sometimes a parent slept in the missing child's room, sometimes a parent never went near it. It just depended.

Elodie's bedroom was on the floor above the library, with the same corner windows. The shutters were properly closed here and when she opened the door for Jacquot the maid leaned in and switched on the light. The room, as he had expected, was soft and pink and warm, and standing in the doorway he took it in quickly: the bed just short of a double, piled with plump cushions and lacey squares and favourite teddies and assorted furry creatures; a dressing table between the corner windows, with a tilted, necklace-hung mirror;

a rocking chair covered in a tasselled silk shawl; a Sony hi-fi on a chest of drawers with a stack of CDs; a low bookcase within reach of bed and rocker; a pair of ancient armoire doors set into the wall, clearly opening into a wardrobe; the remaining windowless wall blu-tacked with posters of boy-bands.

Stepping into the room, Jacquot had noticed the music stand behind the door, sheet music in place – a tricky Mozart adagio – and noted the violin case. At the dressing table he pushed his fingers through a cut-glass bowl of decorative hairclips and brooches, and at the chest of drawers he riffled through the CDs. Apart from the Mozart and the Chopin, not a single name he recognised. On the wall above the chest were four clip-framed watercolours. He leaned forward, looked at each one: a cream and blue seascape, a vase of budding flowers, a stream running through bare woodland, snow on Paris rooftops. The four seasons, Jacquot had guessed. The same hand too. The same 'EL' in the bottom right corner of each.

Slowly he'd made his rounds, watched from the doorway by the maid. He sat on the edge of Elodie's bed, felt the soft surrender of springs and mattress; opened the armoire doors and leafed through her hangered clothes; pulled out some drawers; then paused to sniff the air – the scent of freshly laundered clothes, soap, shoes, and something . . . something sweeter. Closing the armoire doors he went through into the bathroom and opened a mirrored cabinet above the vanity. A box of plasters, a well-known brand of cream for spots, an unopened packet of toothpaste, and a pack of tampons behind which, almost hidden, was a small bottle of scent. He reached in and lifted it out. Read the label. *Versage*. Sniffed it. Jacquot knew from the advertising posters at the *pharmacie* near police headquarters in Cavaillon that it was a popular fragrance with the young, and it struck him how appropriate a name it was for all the girls like Elodie who wore it. Sixteen. Not quite grown-up, but heading that way.

Coming out of the bathroom, he'd asked the maid if she had tidied the room. She'd shaken her head, Madame had asked her

72

not to clean, *pas du tout*. The room was as Elodie had left it, for the police to examine.

Now, sheltering in his doorway from the shawling drizzle, Jacquot flicked away his cigarette and glanced at his watch.

Time to call Claudine again.

19

Cavaillon

CLAUDINE WAS FEEDING THE SPIN drier with damp clothes from the washing machine when the phone rang. For a moment she was tempted not to take it. It would be Daniel again. Two messages so far. If you could call 'It's me. Are you there? I'll phone you back' a message. Nothing about coming home last night when she was asleep and leaving before she'd woken up. No apology. No explanation. All he'd done was leave a note. He was going to Paris. He'd call.

He had some ground to make up.

Which might be fun, she thought, as she set the spin timer. If the ansaphone didn't cut in by the time she got to the phone, she'd answer it.

It didn't, so she picked up.

'*Oui*? *Allo*? . . .'

'So it's you. The stay-out . . .'

'It would have been nice if you had woken me before you left, that's all . . .'

'You're doing what? . . .'

'This is to do with the call last night? . . .'

'So when will you be back? . . .'

'Don't forget we have lunch with Maddy and Paul on Sunday . . .'

'You had better be, or I'll be cross . . .'

'No, I am not cross now . . .'

'No, I do not have that tone, *s'il te plaît* . . .'

'If you must know I am going out for lunch – with Gilles . . .'

'No, I am not doing the washing,' she said, hunching over the phone, cupping the mouthpiece so he wouldn't hear the drier. He'd seen that pile of laundry and known she wouldn't have been able to resist it.

'What noise? . . .'

'No, it is *not* the spin drier. I told you. I'm seeing Gilles. He'll be here *à l'instant* . . .'

Damn him! Up there in Paris, probably going off to lunch somewhere, and her meekly doing the laundry. She wouldn't give him the satisfaction.

'He's taking me to Scaramouche. Yes, that's right. Scaramouche.' She listened, pursed her lips.

'Okay, okay. I understand. All I ask is that you stay in touch . . .'

'I mean it . . .'

'You promise? . . .'

'Okay then, but be careful, you hear? . . .'

'You had better not or there'll be trouble . . .'

'That's right, trouble.'

20

Paris

JACQUOT PUT DOWN THE PHONE. The third time he'd called since arriving in Paris, but the first time he'd got through. She'd sounded terse at first, put out. Hard to tell if it was game-play or genuine. Bit of both, Jacquot guessed as he stepped from the phone kiosk on the corner of rue Camille and pulled up his collar. He blew out his cheeks with relief. Not as bad as he had expected. Not as bad as he probably deserved. And he'd pitched it just right, kept it loose, got himself out from under. A clean slate. Or at least not as dirty as it had been, he decided, as he crossed place Saint Sulpice, retracing Elodie's last known movements.

His first stop was at the flower stall where he spoke to the *fleuriste* mentioned in the case notes. She was in her sixties, Jacquot guessed, large enough for the apron she wore to tie at the back rather than the front. The tips of her fingers were a grimy green and her make-up as thick as pastry. Yes, she told him, tipping the rain from a bellying awning with a broom-handle, she was the one who had seen the girl. And, yes, she told Jacquot, Mademoiselle Lafour had seemed very happy. 'A spring in her step, Chief Inspector. And about time.'

When Jacquot asked what she meant, she told him. Usually the same tight smile when she passed the stall . . . but suddenly radiant. 'There's a man in her life, you ask me. She may be just fifteen, that's what they said in the papers, but you'd never know it.'

Jacquot asked if she had ever seen Mademoiselle Lafour with a man, and the *fleuriste* shook her head. 'I just know,' she told him, and tapped her nose. 'Only your first man brings out a smile like that. You take my word for it.'

Thanking her for her time, Jacquot walked on, looking to the left for the opening to passage Guillaume. When he found it a few metres further on, between a launderette and a *tabac*, he followed it down the slope, coming out on Carrefour des Quatres Carrosses.

This, he knew from the file, was the last place that Elodie Lafour had been seen, sitting at a café table. Had she been waiting for someone? he wondered. The man that the *fleuriste* had guessed at? It certainly seemed possible. A suitable place to meet, with its bars and cafés, or to start a journey, he mused, glancing around the sloping square. Carrefour des Quatres Carrosses. The place of the four carriages. One of those carriages, he now decided, had been for her and, like Madame Bonnefoy, he felt increasingly certain that it had carried her niece away from here and headed south, up onto rue Raspail, which started over there in the far corner of the square. If the girl hadn't just eloped with a lover only to turn up in a few months time married and pregnant, or deserted and pregnant, Jacquot was now certain that the chances were good that she'd be somewhere down south, in Marseilles, or Fos, or Toulon. With no demand for ransom, and no body yet found, he could only assume she'd be waiting for transport to God knew where. And standing in the rain, watching the hustle and the bustle of the *place*, it suddenly struck Jacquot that he had as long as the dockers' strike to find her. Once the docks were open for business again, she'd be gone. If she hadn't gone already.

He glanced at his watch. Lunch-time. He was suddenly hungry. With more than an hour to go until his meeting with Georges Lafour, Jacquot took a seat beneath the scarlet awning of the brasserie-café Les Carrosses, where Elodie Lafour had ordered her *menthe frappée*, and asked for a menu.

Choucroute, he decided, with the pork knuckle and Montbéliard sausages. And a *ballon* or two of *rouge* to go with it.

77

21

Marseilles

'YOU WANT TO GET SOME lunch?' asked Pascale.

Marie-Ange Buhl had just cashed up after her shift at Fleurs des Quais on rue Francis and was pulling on her coat. It was her half-day, and since the rain seemed to be holding off she'd decided to take another look at the lorry park.

'Next time,' she said. 'I've got so much to get done.'

Her friend and co-worker Pascale gave a moue of disappointment, and Marie-Ange squirmed. It was Pascale who'd got her the job at Fleurs des Quais three months earlier. And it was also Pascale who'd found the small apartment for her up in Curiol. Pascale, whom she'd known since they worked together at Jardins Gilbert in Metz, and Pascale, back there in Metz, who had taught her to drink and smoke and roll a joint. Good, solid, dependable, irrepressible Pascale.

But the lorry park prevailed.

'You meeting someone?' Pascale gave her a suspicious look. 'Is there something you're not telling big sister?'

'You'd be the first to know,' Marie-Ange replied, bustling out from behind the counter, winding a long scarf round her neck, pausing to kiss her friend on both cheeks.

'It's not healthy, you know. Use it or lose it, kiddo. They may be just men, but they sure come in handy.'

'I'll bear it in mind. But right now, I've got to scoot. Tomorrow,

78

chérie, I promise. Bernard's. And the *morue*'s on me.' And with that Marie-Ange was out of the door and heading towards Noailles on La Canebière. Half-way down the slope a dark wedge of low cloud settled over the rooftops and the air grew chill and gusty. Any minute now the rain would start up again, but by the time it did Marie-Ange was rattling west on the Metro heading out to Bougainville. When she got there, the rain had passed and another chill wind brought in the salty tang of the ocean, out there, unseen beyond the wharves and zig-zag warehouse roofs.

If it had been raining, she'd have taken a bus from Bougainville, but the fresh, sharp scent of the sea persuaded her to walk, wondering how far she'd have to go to reach the lorry park, which turning off rue de Lyon she'd need to take. In the event all she had to do was follow the lorries that pulled past her, one wheezing truck after another, turned away from the docks, she decided, and looking for somewhere to park up before working out what to do next. Coming round a bend, Marie-Ange saw the last lorry to pass her indicate left and turn out of sight. Five minutes' brisk walk after that, she saw the park's steel-mesh fence up ahead and, at the bottom of the slope, the lorries drawn up in regimental lines. The previous evening there'd been maybe a dozen trucks parked there, now the space was pretty much filled to capacity.

In daylight, the lorry park looked bigger, maybe two blocks wide by three long. But there was something disorganised and ad hoc about it; it seemed somehow improvised. Which it was. Since Dock Authority rules forbade haulage rigs from parking up on the wharves overnight, the Municipal authorities turned a blind eye when drivers used empty redevelopment sites as somewhere to rest up before or after a long drive. As soon as the building crews turned up to start construction, another vacant lot would come along and the rigs would move on. Better that, the authorities agreed, than lines of lorries parked along the streets, or clogging the wharves.

But Marie-Ange didn't know that. Standing at the mesh fence, looking down at the lorries drawn up in orderly lines, she just felt the place looked unsettled, unregulated, maybe even a little dangerous.

For a moment she debated the good sense of going any further. But it was just a moment. Somewhere down among those lorries, she was certain she'd find something to point the way, take her to the next stage.

She found it sooner than expected, no more than twenty metres from the entrance gate, between the first two rows of lorries: a glint of blue pressed into the packed gravel tread of a lorry's tyre. She bent down and teased it out of the ground, wiped it off, examined it. A hairclip shaped like a coiling serpent, its body enamelled with alternating blue and silver stripes and its eyes picked out in diamanté clusters. It had a feeling of solidity to it, no department-store hairclip picked up for a few francs but a real antique, Marie-Ange decided, turning it in her fingers. Almost Art Deco, elegantly hinged, and with a snappy spring to the clasp.

But it wasn't the weight, or the sinuous shape, or the workmanship Marie-Ange marvelled at.

It was the heat radiating off it.

From the moment she stooped down to lever it out of the tyre tread, the heat just seemed to increase until it settled at a level that was half-way between scorching and left-on-a-radiator hot. Not hot enough to burn a hand, but hot enough to keep it warm. If she'd put the hairclip in her fridge for an hour, Marie-Ange was certain it would still have come out warm to the touch.

It was precisely then, while she was examining the hairclip, standing between two parked lorries, that a familiar silence settled around her, dropping the volume on a nearby cabin radio tuned to a football match. And with the silence came that dry dusty taste in her mouth. Clenching her fist around the hairclip, Marie-Ange closed her eyes and tipped back her head.

Night-time. Rain hammering down. She could feel it on her face, hear it smacking on to the packed gravel. And voices, not two metres distant, in the narrow alley between the rigs. Low, muffled voices. Two men, whispering together – a certain urgency in their tone. Next came the sound of a van drawing up, the engine dying and the rattle of the roller door at the back.

Marie-Ange opened her eyes but it was still dark. Still night-time. Now she could make out shadows passing between the outlines of two trucks – a hurrying and a scurrying, what looked like a small bundle being carried in someone's arms. Then, suddenly, in the darkness and the rain, she heard a stifled scream of pain, a scrabbling over the gravel and something swept past her. Just a shadow, the chill, swirling air of its wake wafting against her, reminding her immediately of the *traboule* off Boulevard Cambrai, that cold draft of Lucienne Viviers, making good her escape.

And here, Marie-Ange was certain, was the place where she had started that run.

Almost immediately, there was a smothered shout of alarm and a second, larger shadow raced past her with the same grunting oath – *merde, merde, merde* – that she remembered so clearly from the side street off Cambrai. Over by the trucks, where the two shadows had sprung from, there was a sense of panic. A hissing, whispered argument. Doors slammed, an engine started up, and one of the two vans swung away with gravel spitting out from under its tyres.

'Hey, *chérie*, you all right? *Tout va bien*?'

Night-time to day-time.

Darkness to light.

Rain to no rain. Just grey scudding cloud moving above the rigs.

Marie-Ange spun round.

A driver was climbing down from his cab. He jumped from the steel footplate and ambled towards her, a big man with a pouched, puffy red face, in cowboy boots and working *bleus*, bib and braces hidden beneath a thick woolly sweater with Tintin's head knitted on the chest.

'No, I'm fine. Just . . . just looking for my cat.' Marie-Ange turned round, left and right, peering under the lorry beside her, even calling out a name. 'Tommi? Tommi? *Viens. Viens.*'

It was a pathetic effort and she knew it, knew she'd never be able to carry it off. And she was right.

The driver shot her an indulgent look.

'Well, why don't you come up to my place,' he nodded back at the cab, 'and you and I can look for your little pussy together?'

Marie-Ange couldn't believe what she'd heard, what he was suggesting, and she felt a flush rise into her cheeks, of shock and then anger more than embarrassment. She might have been asking for it, traipsing round a lorry park, but he had no right to assume . . .

She gathered herself, pulled back her shoulders and looked him straight in the eye.

'In your dreams, Tintin.'

And with that she turned on her heel and walked away, praying he wouldn't follow, the hairclip burning in her clenched fist.

22

Paris

THE OFFICES OF BANQUE LAFOUR et Finance Mondiale were across the river, a block beyond Place des Vosges, a rattling twelve-minute cab ride from the brasserie-café Les Carrosses whose *choucroute*, disappointingly, had turned out to be sharp and sour. Had it not been for the meaty pork knuckle, the brace of Montbéliard sausages, and the two *ballons* of *cru Bourgogne*, Jacquot would have rated his capital lunch a disaster. Next time, he thought, he'd go to Lipp and see what all the fuss was about.

Getting his driver to drop him on rue de Turenne, Jacquot walked the last few drizzling metres to the corner of rue Baranot. It was from here, half-way along a row of elegant Marais townhouses, that Elodie's stepfather ran his banking operations, the name of the bank visible in black italic script on a silver plate beside a pair of glass doors, the glass thick enough to show green around the large brass handle set into each panel. The brass shone, Jacquot noticed. Not a single smudge of fingerprints. He was about to reach for one of the handles when he realised why. With a soft hiss, both doors opened automatically, sliding into recesses.

This was clearly not the kind of bank with a counter, where customers came and went, making deposits, withdrawals, arranging loans – or not the kinds of loan most people contemplated: for a car, a house, a holiday. Instead, Jacquot found himself walking down a panelled, carpeted corridor which opened into a wider foyer. The carpet felt as thick as the glass doors, hugging his boots and softening every step, the wood panelling was light and precious, and the air was filled with the same oaky scent he remembered from the library at La Résidence Camille. Set along the far wall of this foyer stood a long, uplit burr walnut counter, like a hotel reception desk, the grain black-spotted and whorled, its surface sanded paper smooth and polished to a mirror shine. Sitting behind it were two young women – blonde and brunette – both of them smartly dressed in crisp pinstripe suits, business-like and attractive. As he approached the desk Jacquot smiled at them, wished them both *bonjour*, but spoke to the brunette. She reminded him of Claudine, and he always felt comfortable with women who looked like Claudine. He told her his name and said he had an appointment with . . .

'*Mais, oui*, Monsieur Jacquot, we have been expecting you,' she interrupted with the sweetest smile. 'Here, let me take your coat.' In a second she was out from behind the counter and drawing it from his shoulders, peeling it away from him. He turned to face another beaming smile as she folded the coat over her arm and patted it. She would look after it until he returned. 'Monsieur Lafour will see you straightaway,' she told him. 'If you take the lift there, it is the fifth floor. His assistant will be waiting for you.'

Alone in the lift, Jacquot smiled to himself. The bare, minimalist style, the confident and ordered efficiency, the staggeringly pretty girls . . . it was all very impressive. Hushed, swift, controlled . . . like the lift. If you had come here with money to invest, thought Jacquot, everything looked promising. Certainly Monsieur le Président had come to that conclusion.

The doors slid open without Jacquot even realising the lift had stopped. Unlike the reception area, the fifth floor had retained its eighteenth-century proportions. No open space here but a wide landing and a single corridor. There were four large oak doors to each side of this corridor, all of them open, the air between filled with the muted bleep of telephones and muffled voices. A young man in a silk-backed, tightly buttoned waistcoat stepped forward and introduced himself as Monsieur Lafour's personal assistant, Félix. Even without a jacket, Félix looked effortlessy stylish, or maybe as a result of it – a light grey Prince of Wales check, silver linked double cuffs, polished black lace-ups, the easy toss of curly black hair as aristocratic as you could wish for, with a courtier's deference as he ushered the way to Lafour's office. Through the open doors of the corridor they passed along, Jacquot glimpsed marble fireplaces, herringbone parquet, moulded ceilings and computer terminals on ormolu desks, the men in shirtsleeve order like Félix, braces or waistcoats, talking on the phone, looking out of a window, conferring. Two of the rooms were occupied by women. One of them was at her desk, the other was coming out of her office. Silk blouse, pencil skirt, brown hair caught in a tight chignon, a warm spin of scent. Jacquot stepped aside for her and she caught his eye, smiled.

'Et voilà,' said Félix, two steps ahead, reaching forward to open a pair of double doors and waving Jacquot in.

Georges Lafour was standing behind his desk, a weighty slab of glass supported on a chiselled stone plinth. He was on the phone, listening not talking. As far as Jacquot could judge, at first glance, the man was elegantly handsome, almost patrician. Tall, slim, his face smooth and gently tanned, his hands long and thin and expertly manicured, the hair thick and grey and wavy. But as Jacquot drew closer he could see that the skin above his cheekbones seemed to bunch around his eyes, like a chameleon's, the whites almost completely concealed, just the pupils, as round and as black as a shark's, turning on him now and scrutinising him over black-framed bifocals. It was a cold, cruel, calculating look that a perfunctory, pursed smile did little to soften. Like Félix, Lafour was jacketless, his crisp white shirt overlaid by wide green braces that emphasised the narrowness of his shoulders and his stooping height.

Such a difference between them, was Jacquot's second thought. Husband and wife. Mother and stepfather. A suit, an office; a dressing gown and darkened library. The one broken by Elodie's disappearance, the other managing. Managing well. Maybe Jacquot shouldn't have been surprised.

While Félix showed him to a chair, offering a range of refreshments all of which he declined, Jacquot was aware that Lafour followed the performance, acknowledging him with a tilt of the chin when their eyes met, watching as Jacquot took in his surroundings – the four mansard windows behind the desk, a pair of cerise-coloured Warhol screen prints of Elizabeth Taylor, a second set of double doors, what looked like a bronze Maillol nude on a stand – before bringing his phone conversation swiftly to a close. His voice was pitched higher than Jacquot had expected for such a large man – strained and sharp.

'I am sorry, Nicolas. *Il faut m'excuser*. I have a most important meeting and I am late. Please call me later, if you need to. *Oui, oui. Bien sûr. Salut*,' he said and put down the phone. Dismissing Félix with a '*Merci bien*, that will be all', Lafour settled himself in a leather swing chair the same limestone shade as the plinth supporting his desk, and waited until the office door had closed before addressing Jacquot.

'*Alors*. Chief Inspector Jacquot. Another policeman come to cross me off his list.' It was not a question. He smiled and waved one limp, long-fingered hand, to imply there was no need for Jacquot to waste time denying it.

Jacquot remained silent.

'However,' continued Lafour, eyes flicking over his visitor, taking him in, possibly surprised there was no denial, 'my sister-in-law called to say I should see you. My wife as well. Which means you arrive here with two very solid recommendations.' He spread his hands, and managed a smile that was as fleeting as a swift on the wing. 'So, how can I be of assistance?'

'First of all, Monsieur Lafour, thank you for seeing me at such short notice. And, secondly, my sympathies at this difficult time.'

Lafour frowned. 'My daughter is not dead, Chief Inspector. Just . . . missing.'

For a moment Jacquot was taken off guard. He had not expected such an immediate rebuke. Lafour was clearly a man to handle with care. 'Of course, you are right, monsieur. What I meant was . . . I have just come from your wife. Obviously this is a very hard time for you both.'

'Yes it is,' said Lafour, with a note of impatience – as though it could be anything else. 'But let us get on. What do you need to know? What can I tell you that I haven't already told a dozen of your colleagues?'

'To begin with,' said Jacquot, glancing at the Warhols, the Maillol, 'why do you suppose there has been no ransom demand?'

The question clearly took Lafour by surprise. He gave a soft grunt. 'Up until now it is usually me who asks that question,' he replied. 'And when I do, the police tell me it is early days and that we should wait. Be patient.'

It struck Jacquot that Lafour was not the patient type.

Across the desk, he laced his fingers, stiffening them to inspect his nails. 'But if you wish to know my opinion, I can only suppose that Elodie has met up with someone . . . someone my wife and I did not know about, and that she has . . . eloped. Or, possibly, that she has been taken by someone who does not realise who we are. How . . . able we are to answer any demand. If that is the case, then hopefully the newspapers will sharpen their wits, and they will make themselves known.'

Jacquot nodded. It was a reasonable, if limited, take on the situation.

'There is, of course, a third possibility,' said Jacquot.

Lafour levelled his chameleon eyes over the top of his black bifocals. They bored into Jacquot. He knew what the policeman was suggesting.

'I will not . . . That is not a consideration. Elodie is alive. I know it.'

'Have you thought of offering a reward?' Jacquot asked.

'I discussed it with my wife, and we mentioned it to the police. When Elodie did not come home. The second or third day. But they advised us that such a move would cause more trouble than they were able to manage, that it could easily compromise their investigation. Cranks, lunatics, all of whose stories would have to be checked. It remains, however, an option . . . if no ransom demand is forthcoming.' He sounded, for a moment, as though he was formulating a business strategy.

'Tell me, monsieur, how do you get on with your stepdaughter?' Jacquot was careful with his choice of tense.

'I prefer to think of her as my daughter,' Lafour replied shortly. 'She was seven when her father died and nine when I married her mother. She is like my own, Chief Inspector. I love and cherish her.' The black eyes challenged Jacquot momentarily, then blinked away. 'As to our relationship, I would say it is close. Warm. She is a most talented child.'

'Hardly a child, Monsieur Lafour.'

Another black look swung Jacquot's way. 'A child, Chief Inspector. Not yet a woman. There is a difference.'

'Someone else clearly doesn't think so,' Jacquot replied, taking a certain satisfaction in needling Lafour. He could see no good reason to tread gently with the man any longer. 'You suggested that she might have "met up with someone",' Jacquot continued. 'Do you think that is possible? That she could have . . . concealed a . . . such a friendship from you and your wife?'

'I can only hope it is so, Chief Inspector. The alternative does not bear thinking about.'

There was a knock at the door, and Félix popped his head round.

'It's Jürgen. He's coming up.'

Lafour reached for a gold pocket watch on the desk top, snapped it open and looked at the time. 'He is early. Show him to the board-room, Félix.' When the door closed, Lafour slid the timepiece into his trouser pocket and turned back to Jacquot. 'Please, Chief Inspector, do continue. Our German friend can wait.' A curling, self-satisfied smile showed around his lips; his eyes narrowed, like the aperture on a camera lens.

Jacquot felt a shiver of distaste, gritted his teeth.

'When Elodie's father died,' he began, 'how did she take it?'

Lafour gave a grunt of surprise; clearly this was another question he had not anticipated. 'She was devastated, of course. The two of them were very close.'

'You knew her father?'

'I knew of him. Through his work.'

'An architect, *n'est-ce pas*?'

Lafour nodded, flicked at a fingernail.

Through the glass desktop, Jacquot saw him stretch out one leg and point the toe of his shoe. He's bored, thought Jacquot. Time to rattle his cage again. Just because he could.

'And how did Elodie respond to you, when you married her mother?'

Once again, Lafour looked taken aback, and for a moment Jacquot expected the man to turn on him and ask: And what might that have to do with her disappearance, *s'il vous plaît*?

But he didn't. He appeared to give the question some thought, and then a slow smile slid across his features.

'So I was correct,' he said, levelling an indulgent gaze on Jacquot. 'As I suspected, you are here to . . . to take my measure.' The tone was amused, but still icy.

'As I mentioned to your wife,' replied Jacquot with a spread of his hands, 'parents are always a good place to begin. It . . . places the missing person.'

'And, of course, you couldn't have done it on the phone.' It was neither statement nor question. 'You needed to see as well as to hear, *n'est-ce pas*? Well, I suppose I can understand that. Anything that might help get Elodie back . . . So, what was it you asked again?'

'How Elodie responded to you? When you first met her.'

'Warily. Uncertain.' He shrugged as though that should be no surprise. 'She was very . . . polite, I would say. It took some time to gain her trust, to get close to her.'

There was another knock at the door. Félix again. 'Jurgen? . . . I put him in the boardroom.'

This time Lafour pursed his lips as though, now, he really did have to conclude their meeting. He got to his feet, reached for the jacket draped over the back of his chair, and slipped it on with an easy, unhurried grace.

'So, Chief Inspector . . . Jacquot. I regret that now I really must bring our meeting to a close. Since you have had the opportunity to meet me, in order to . . . place Elodie, perhaps you would excuse me?' Coming round the desk, he pulled a thin leather wallet from an inside jacket pocket and slid out a card. 'But if you need anything, Chief Inspector, anything at all, do not hesitate to call me. At any time.'

Jacquot took the card, but Lafour kept hold of it and drew close, close enough for Jacquot to smell the mint on his breath.

'Please find her, Chief Inspector. We want her back.'

And then the card was released. There was no handshake. Lafour gave a short bow of farewell, turned to the second set of double doors that led presumably to the boardoom, and Félix was ushering Jacquot out of the office and down the corridor to the lift.

'A very impressive man,' said Jacquot.

'Monsieur Lafour? *Formidable, oui.*' That toss of his hair, the lift doors opening as they approached. 'How he manages at this terrible time . . .' Félix stood aside. 'As I say, *formidable.*'

Formidable, indeed.

Five minutes later, the plate-glass doors of Banque Lafour hissed closed behind him and Jacquot was standing in rue Baranot once more, pulling up his coat collar. So far that day he had spent four hours on a train to spend no more than an hour with Estelle Lafour and a little less than thirty minutes with her husband. And there was still the train journey home.

But the time hadn't been wasted. He glanced at his watch. Just a couple more things to do before heading back to the station.

23

Marseilles

ALAIN GASTAL CALLED IN THE killing himself and by the time
Claude Peluze and Charlie Serre arrived at Valentine's workshop,
followed soon after by the scene-of-crime boys and forensics, he
had been through Valentine's office and come up with two names:
Ibin and Alam. He'd found them in the desk diary, today's date.
Booked in to do an exhaust job. The van was still up on the skids
above Valentine's broken body. He'd got their surnames from
Valentine's ancient Rolodex, both names on a single card swollen
from use and smeared with grease. Ibin Hahmoud and Alam Haggar.
Phone numbers and addresses.

'Bring 'em in,' Gastal had said, showing Peluze the card.

Now, three hours later, Alam Haggar was sitting in an interview
room on rue de l'Evêché, tapping his foot as though he was in a
hurry to get somewhere. Which he was. Out of there.

Gastal, just back from a fine lunch at Mère Boul', the butter
from a dozen escargots still glistening on his lips and chin, looked
through the glass. Haggar was thin and wiry, bony shoulders
hunched, a mop of black curls crowded over the top of an angrily
pockmarked face. He was wearing a grey hooded sweat-top over
a padded shirt. Because of the table Gastal couldn't see below the
kid's waist but he guessed jeans and trainers.

'Where d'you find him?' he asked, dropping his chin to his chest and letting out a low contented belch.

'At home,' replied Peluze. 'Place Lapeyre, like it said on the card. Told us he was sick. Hadn't turned up for work. Then I found this in his pocket.'

Peluze handed Gastal a fold of notes. Gastal took it, lifted it to his nose, riffled through it.

'Two thousand,' said Peluze. 'That's when he tried to do a runner.'

'What about Hahmoud?'

Peluze shook his head. 'No sign of him.'

Gastal worked his neck out of the collar of his shirt, nodded absently, then headed for the door to the interview room. 'Get me a coffee, will you? Just bring it through.' As he opened the door he heard the smallest, lowest hiss of anger from Peluze. He turned and shot Peluze a look. 'Any problem?'

'No, boss. No problem.'

'Good,' said Gastal, standing by the open door, waiting for his request to be carried out. With a nod, and clenched fists, Peluze went off to fetch the coffee. As the door closed behind him, Gastal slipped the fold of notes into his breast pocket. Oh, how he loved this posting.

And how he loved dealing with little *mecs* like Alam Haggar, who watched him close the door and cross the room, pull out a chair and settle himself at the table. Every move. Dark eyes darting over him. He hadn't even opened his mouth yet and the boy was already squirming. Eighteen, nineteen, Gastal guessed. Turk or Arab, by the look of him.

Gastal took a new cassette out of his pocket, tore off the wrapping and slid it into the tape recorder screwed to the wall.

He pressed Record and looked directly at Haggar.

'Baumettes . . . Baumettes . . . Baumettes,' he said. Baumettes was the notorious prison on the eastern edges of the city. He stopped the tape, rewound it and pressed Play. 'Baumettes . . . Baumettes . . . Baumettes . . .' He pressed Stop, rewound the tape again and pressed Record once more. Loosening his tie, he gave his name, the date and the time.

'So,' he continued, settling back in his chair, 'name, age, address, *s'il vous plaît.*'

'I haven't done anything. And I'm sick.'

Gastal switched off the tape machine. 'I'm not going to ask again, shit-for-brains. Piss me about and I'll break your toes. All I've got to do is say you tried to kick me and hit the table leg instead. It's tried and tested, take my word for it. Understand?' Gastal smiled, pushed the Record button and this time Haggar did as he was told.

'So how long have you been sick?'

'Last couple of days. Just kept my head down.'

'So, no work then?'

Haggar shook his head.

'That's a "no" then,' said Gastal, indicating the tape recorder.

'That's right. No work.'

Gastal seemed to give it some thought. 'So what kind of work . . . when you're not sick?'

'This and that. Whatever comes along. Cars mostly.'

'You know Jules Valentine?'

The name didn't faze him.

'Sure, do some work for him when he needs me.'

'When did you last see him?'

Haggar gave it some thought. 'Couple of weeks back?'

'Is that a question or an answer? How am I supposed to know your fucking schedule?'

'A couple of weeks then. Must be.'

'But not this morning?'

Haggar shook his head.

Gastal knew why. He'd never have managed to get the word out without his voice breaking on it. Gastal pointed at the tape recorder. 'For the record, *Coco* . . .'

Haggar swallowed, gave it a go: 'N-no . . .'

'So you're sick in bed with two thousand francs in your pocket,' said Gastal, pulling out the roll of notes, waving it in front of Haggar. 'Mint fresh. You can still smell the ink on 'em. Lot of money,

93

that. Lot of cash for a pissy little *mec* like you. Drugs, is it? You dealing?'

Haggar straightened up when he heard the words 'drugs' and 'dealing'. Gastal knew he hadn't been expecting that.

'Not me. Not drugs.' The boy's voice was low and urgent, cracking a little.

'So where did it come from? And why did you try and do a runner when my colleague found it?'

'I didn't know he was a cop. He could have been anyone. And I was sick, right? Asleep. Not thinking straight, you know?'

There was a tap on the door and Peluze came in with a mug of coffee.

Gastal looked up at him. 'According to our friend here, you didn't show your badge when you went round to his place. Didn't tell him you were a cop. Is that right?'

Peluze gave Haggar a look. 'I told him. He knew.'

'Okay. So we've got that straight,' said Gastal, smiling at the kid. Then, 'You want a coffee? Some water maybe?' he asked.

The lad shook his head.

Gastal felt a ripple of disappointment. He'd have loved to send Peluze on another coffee run. Especially for the boy. He didn't bother to look round at his colleague. 'That'll be it, then,' he continued, waving Peluze away. 'Now, Alam, where were we?' Gastal took a sip of his coffee. 'That's right. Not working because you were sick. That's what you're saying?'

'You got it.'

'Well, now we got a problem, see,' said Gastal, sliding away the fold of notes into an inside pocket. 'Cos that's not what your friend Ibin is telling us. Ibin Hahmoud? According to him the both of you were at Valentine's garage working on Monsieur Gideon's Renault. This very morning.'

Gastal saw the boy's shoulders slump. Peluze might not have got hold of Hahmoud yet but Gastal had reckoned that bringing up his name was worth a bet. It had paid off. He wondered whether Hahmoud, wherever he was, would have been as much of a pushover

94

as Haggar. He doubted it. It looked like they'd brought the right one in.

'So let's forget your sick leave and talk about the garage, okay? And Monsieur Gideon's Renault. The exhaust, wasn't it?'

Haggar nodded.

Gastal flicked his fingers. 'I need to hear you. It's a tape recorder, not a fucking camera.'

'That's right. Yeah. The exhaust.'

'Okay, so we're getting somewhere at last. Now how long does a job like that take? In your experience. Couple of hours?'

'About that, I suppose.'

'And what time did you start this morning?'

'Eight . . . just after.'

'But you didn't finish the job, did you?'

'No. Monsieur Valentine told us to leave it. Said he'd finish it himself.'

'What time was that?'

'Eleven. Round about. Maybe a bit earlier.'

'And there were just the three of you in the workshop?' Gastal pushed back his chair and got to his feet. He picked up his coffee, and walked behind Haggar.

'That's right.'

'And it was Valentine who gave you the money, was it?'

'Yeah. It was Valentine.'

'For not finishing the job?'

Haggar took a moment or two to answer. 'He owed us. From another time.'

'That's not what it says in his records. Says clearly your pay was up to date. Didn't owe you a *sou*.' Another lie, but worth a try. And once again it paid off.

Haggar said nothing.

'Do you know where Jules Valentine is right now?'

'I dunno . . . The garage? Home?'

'The morgue, Alam. Lying on a steel tray. *Au revoir*, Jules. And it turns out you and Ibin were the last people to see him alive.

95

Which I'd say puts the two of you in a very difficult position. Especially with two thousand francs of his money in your pocket. Doesn't look good, Alam, I'm telling you that.'

'It wasn't his . . . the money!'

'So whose was it?'

Haggar didn't answer.

'You know Baumettes, Alam? You ever been there?'

'No.'

'But you know where I mean, don't you?'

'Yeah, I know.'

'Well, see, if you don't help me along here, Alam, you're gonna get to know it very well, that's my guess. First hand. You and Ibin. Robbery . . . murder. Call it fifteen years, if you're very lucky. By the time they let you out, your arsehole'll be the size of a beer mat.'

There was a long silence, save the rubbery squeak of Haggar's trainer tapping away under the table. He brought an oil-rimmed thumbnail to his lips and started chewing.

Gastal sat down again and waited.

'I never said a thing, okay? You didn't hear it from me,' began Haggar, leaning forward, almost whispering. 'There were these two guys, right? Never seen 'em before. Tough guys. I mean, *vrai dur*, real hard cases. One of 'em takes Valentine to the office, the other tells us to get out from under the Renault. He tells us he wants us out of there, fast. And here's some cash to make sure we never saw them. Counts out two grand each, then pulls his gun. Blows out the radio, blows out the inspection lamp, then tells us he'll do the same to us if he so much as dreams we say anything. Well, we're out of there, Ibin and me.'

'What did they look like?'

'White, shaved heads, dressed in black coats. Big fuckers, I'm telling you. And not locals. A real island accent.'

'Caribbean? Corsican?'

Haggar shrugged. 'Like I say, they weren't from round here.'

'Anything else?'

Haggar gave it some thought. Now he'd spilled the beans, he felt braver, as though keen to help the police in any way. Show how observant he was. And maybe get his money back. Not that he was holding his breath on that one, not with this *flic*.

'When we're leaving, out on the street, there's this car, right, turning out of rue Chatelier? Big limo thing – English. And you don't see too many of those in the fifteenth, right?'

'Model? Registration?'

Haggar spread his hands, remembered the tape. 'No.'

'You get to see who was driving?'

The question caught Haggar; he hadn't thought it through that far.

'Tinted windows,' he managed at last. 'Couldn't see a thing. Too busy getting the hell out of there.' He looked pleased with himself.

And Gastal knew he was lying again. 'So the windscreen's tinted too, is it?'

Haggar's smile vanished. 'It may have been a woman driving. Maybe.'

'Anyone with her?'

'Someone in the back, like she was some kind of *chauffeuse*.'

'And you'd recognise them, right? The two of them in the car, and the *gorilles*?'

Haggar's face fell. He suddenly realised he'd dug himself right in.

'Good,' said Gastal, without waiting for an answer. 'You're free to go,' he continued, switching off the recorder and slipping the tape into his pocket, pushing aside the chair and getting to his feet. 'Only don't go taking any holiday. You try to skip and I'll get you that beer mat to try for size, *compris*?'

Haggar nodded, and watched Gastal head for the door. 'What about my money, then?' he called after him.

Gastal didn't bother to turn round.

'What money?'

24

MADAME BONNEFOY WAS WAITING for Jacquot, as arranged, behind the ticket barrier at Marseilles' Gare Saint Charles. He spotted her at the gate as he stepped down from his carriage and joined the stream of passengers heading along the platform. She stood taller than most of the crowd and was wearing the same coat she'd worn the night before at Kuchnia, wrapping it round herself in the chill night air, her complexion even paler in the harsh station lighting. He passed within a metre of her, almost brushing her elbow, but she failed to recognise him. A dozen steps past her, Jacquot dropped his duffel bag and turned round. She still had her back to him, tipping her head this way and that, peering ahead, trying to spot him. Jacquot felt a ripple of pleasure. It had worked.

With two hours to spare after his meeting with Georges Lafour and before his train left, Jacquot had visited a military surplus store off rue Morzine and kitted himself out with a change of clothes and a rough old duffel bag. He kept the new clothes on and stowed the old ones, along with his briefcase and boots, in the duffel. Two blocks from the station he found a small barber shop and when he'd sat in the chair and the hairdresser had secured the cape round his neck, Jacquot had circled his head and said, '*Le tout, s'il vous plaît.*'

Since this meant the removal of his signature ponytail, it was something of an operation, begun with comb and scissors and finished with buzzing clippers. As he sat in the chair and the onslaught began, Jacquot let his eyes drift over the framed rugby-team photographs and pennants and newspaper clippings that covered every inch of wall space. To his right, high up, there was even a picture of himself, his first and last appearance in the national squad, standing in the back row between Sidi Carassin and Simon Talaud.

'How short?' asked the barber, his eyes catching Jacquot's in the mirror.

Jacquot held up his thumb and bent it. From the knuckle to the top of the nail. '*Comme ça.*'

'Used to be a player with a ponytail,' the barber continued, combing out the hair and snipping with his scissors. 'Forget his name now, but he scored a try you'd *never* forget. Won the match. Against *Les Rosbifs*. That run . . . length of the pitch it was. Mud and guts. Christ, I nearly pissed myself! Never thought he'd make it.'

'Jacquot,' said Jacquot. 'Daniel Jacquot.'

'That's the one. Jacquot. Christ, what a player. And just the one game, wasn't it? Whatever happened to him, eh? Where is he now?'

Jacquot couldn't help but smile.

And now, back in Marseilles, it had been the same with Madame Bonnefoy. She hadn't recognised him either.

He went up to her, stood next to her, like someone waiting to meet a friend, digging his hands into his pockets, hunching his shoulders against the cold. Aware of someone beside her, Madame Bonnefoy glanced round, then turned back to the last few passengers straggling down the platform. Then she looked back at him, more closely this time, and frowned.

'Daniel? Is that you?'

'*À vot' service, madame.*'

'Why . . . Whatever have you done to yourself?' she asked, stepping back to take in the buttoned pea-jacket, the woollen beanie, the speckled roll-top sweater, working boots and thick blue canvas trousers. 'You look like that McQueen fellow, in that film, *The*

Sand Pebbles? And your hair. What have you done to your hair? Your ponytail!'

'All in a good cause, madame. The best cause.'

Ten minutes later, the two of them were sitting in a booth at Bernard's. There may have been an excess of plastic and Formica in this diner-style brasserie midway between the station and the Vieux Port, but the food was good and hearty. Over a shared *brandade de morue*, Jacquot ran through his day, the meetings with Madame Bonnefoy's sister and her husband.

'How was Estelle?' asked Madame Bonnefoy, dipping her toasted bread into the pearly white purée.

'Very tired. Very anxious,' replied Jacquot truthfully. 'But the family likeness was unmistakable . . .'

'She was always much prettier than me,' sighed Madame Bonnefoy.

'And you are entitled to your opinion, madame. All I can say is what I found.'

Despite herself, and despite the horror of a missing niece, Jacquot could see that his companion was flattered, a small smile hovering around the corners of her mouth. But it was for a moment only.

'And Georges?' she asked, abandoning the smile, all business again. 'What did you make of him?'

Jacquot thought back to his brief time with Lafour on rue Baranot. He'd been pleased to get out of that office, to be on the street again. He did not like the man – too smooth, too pleased with himself, too . . . controlling. But he was Madame Bonnefoy's brother-in-law, so Jacquot weighed his words carefully.

'Impressive. Ruthless,' he said at last, the least offensive words he could come up with. 'Almost . . . untouched by it,' Jacquot continued. 'Either he's convinced that Elodie will be found safe and sound, or come home of her own accord. Or – and I am sorry to say this – that he's not . . . unduly concerned.' Jacquot spread his hands. 'It's as if he hasn't got the time for it. I explain myself badly. It's just how he came across. Concerned, but somehow . . . not concerned. I didn't feel any . . . sympathy for him. I should

100

have, but I didn't. He seemed to preclude it. As if his work, his position, were more important. Everything else just lining up in a queue.'

'But you have him in one,' sighed Madame Bonnefoy. 'And you didn't like him, did you?'

'No, madame, I can't say that I did. He is not my sort of man.'

She smiled regretfully. 'Like an icicle sometimes. He infuriates me. I just don't know what my sister saw in him. She was infatuated when they first met, and if you ask me, she's infatuated still. Nothing has changed. It's always Georges this and Georges that . . . But there we are,' she said, dabbing at her lips with a paper napkin. 'Water under the bridge.'

'What about Elodie?' probed Jacquot. 'What does she think of him?'

'She doesn't really say. Doesn't talk about him. I think . . . I think, maybe, she's a little scared of him. He can be very intimidating.'

'And Lafour, is he good with her?'

'From what I have seen and heard, he is very good. Like you, I may not like him very much – too rigid and contained and self-regarding, and . . . creepy, if you ask me. But as a stepfather he seems most attentive. Very protective, too. He really involves himself as much as he can – what she's reading, how she's getting on at school, sport, her friends.'

'Then he hides his concern well,' said Jacquot, as a gust of rain spattered against the window. 'He also . . .' Jacquot paused.

'He also what?'

'It seemed to me that, for him, Elodie is still a little girl. When I would say she clearly isn't. She has pretty underwear, hides her scent, her make-up . . . I would say she is a girl who can keep secrets, who can play a part.'

Madame Bonnefoy nodded, a little distractedly. 'Perhaps. Maybe I am too close . . . I don't see it.'

'Tell me, does Elodie like *choucroute*?'

'*Choucroute*?' Madame Bonnefoy sat back and chuckled, her

101

bruised, sad eyes suddenly sparkling. 'How did that come out? Every birthday, Estelle and Georges take her to Lipp. Brasserie Lipp. For their *choucroute*. It's her favourite thing in the whole world. I like to think it's her Polish roots showing through.'

'So she'd like Kuchnia?'

'She loves it. Adores it.'

For a moment, Jacquot was dumbstruck. 'She's been there? I mean, she's been here to Marseilles?'

Madame Bonnefoy blinked in surprise. 'Of course she's been here. Many times.'

'And the last time?'

'Just a few months back. The first week of her summer vacation.'

'With her mother?'

'By herself. The last two times, she's taken the train by herself. I meet her at Saint Charles, just like I met you.'

'And how long did she stay?'

'A week. That first week. Why?' And then, 'Do you think she could have met someone down here?' Madame Bonnefoy looked stunned. 'I never thought . . . I mean, she went missing in Paris. Not here.'

'While she was here, Elodie did what? While you were working?'

'I took the week off. We were together the whole time. Except the last two days. A pre-trial hearing I couldn't get out of.'

'And what did she do while you were in court? Do you remember?'

Madame Bonnefoy paused, tried to think. 'Elodie was not good in the mornings. It was always eleven before she made it out of bed. Probably because Georges makes her get up much earlier at home. I didn't think it did her any harm to slouch around, so I didn't make a fuss. Most days we started with lunch and then shopped, just . . . walked around. She loved Le Panier, she'd walk there for hours. All those little galleries, the artisan shops. I seem to remember that that was what she did while I was in court.'

And somewhere on those lonely walks, thought Jacquot, or on the train coming south, or going home, maybe Elodie Lafour met someone, maybe she fell into conversation, maybe someone picked her up, paid her some attention. Who could say? What he did know was that he would find out sooner or later.

'So, madame, have you got what I wanted?' asked Jacquot as the waiter brought their bill.

Madame Bonnefoy leant down and drew up her bag from under the seat. She unzipped it, dug in a hand and came out with a large yellow envelope. 'New name, new passport. With a matching union card and maritime service log. *Matelot de deuxième classe*, as requested. The log shows voyages taken over the last four years with references from a dozen skippers and various shipping lines.'

Jacquot took the envelope, sifting through its contents.

'I'm from Rotterdam?' he asked, flicking open the passport and finding his own photo from police files, with unfamiliar details.

'It's as close as we could find – comparable age and height. You were difficult to match, but we managed. Although the hair could be a problem.' She forced a thin smile. In the photo, Jacquot's hair was tied back in a ponytail.

'Let's hope no one asks me anything in Dutch.'

'I thought of that,' said Madame Bonnefoy. 'You may have been born in Holland, but your Dutch father died and your French mother returned to the family home in La Rochelle. How's that?'

'Not bad,' Jacquot replied, putting aside the passport and examining the union card and fold-out maritime service log, both suitably battered and shabby. He wondered how an examining magistrate could have put together such convincing documentation in such a short time. Someone in prison, Jacquot guessed; someone who wouldn't miss their papers. If they ever turned poacher, the magistrates' office would surely lead the police a merry dance.

'It all looks very good. May I ask where you got it?' he asked, pocketing the documents, then reaching into his duffel bag to return the briefcase she'd given him with the Lafour file.

Like the *fleuriste* in Paris, Madame Bonnefoy tapped the side of her nose. 'Just someone I happen to know,' she replied. 'So? What next?'

Jacquot peeled off some notes from a clip and laid them on the table.

'I'll start in the port. Sign up for crew, sniff around. Then the marinas. I'm assuming you booked me in somewhere appropriate?'

'Auberge des Vagues. It's a seamen's hostel. Because of the strike there are a lot of crew around at the moment, so I could only get you a dormitory bed. I hope you don't mind?'

Jacquot got to his feet, reached for Madame Bonnefoy's coat. 'Dormitory's good,' he said, shaking out the garment and holding it up for her. 'More chat, more contacts. Where is it?' he asked.

'Impasse Massalia,' said Madame Bonnefoy, sliding her arms into the coat sleeves and shrugging it up over her shoulders. 'A few streets away from the Chamant and Mirabe wharves. If you like, I can drop you there. Or close by, if you prefer?'

'It's near enough from here. I'll walk. Work in the clothes. Get myself into the part.'

'As you wish,' she said.

Out on the pavement, rain spilling off the diner's awning, a stop-start snarl of traffic beeped its way down to the Vieux Port. She reached for his hand, blinked away tears. 'Good luck, Daniel. Anything you need, just call me.'

'I'll be in touch,' said Jacquot, taking her hand and placing three swift kisses on her cheeks. 'And we'll find her, I promise you.'

25

BY THE TIME MARIE-ANGE got home from the lorry park, flagging down a cab for the journey rather than take the bus or Metro, she was sure of two things. The first was that Pascale sometimes got it right about men. 'Snap back at them,' she'd once told Marie-Ange, 'and the chances are they'll hold off, think twice – if that's possible for men.'

It had certainly worked in the lorry park. The lorry driver with the Tintin jersey had actually taken a step back in surprise when Marie-Ange turned on him, content just to spit out a '*putain*' as she gathered her nerve and her dignity and hurried away.

The other thing Marie-Ange knew for certain was that the serpent hairclip she had found in the lorry park did not belong to Lucienne Viviers.

It belonged to someone else.

Another girl.

Like Lucienne.

Tall, blonde and scared.

But definitely not Lucienne.

Yet somehow connected to Lucienne, she was sure of it.

Did Lucienne have a friend with her there in the lorry park? Marie-Ange wondered . . . Another girl in the same danger? Another girl who, for some reason, was unable to make the run with her friend?

As she held the hairclip in her hands, its warmth seeping between her fingers, Marie-Ange could feel the energy pulsing off it. Keep me. Hold me. Use me. I will show you the way, it seemed to be telling her.

Which was why, after a warming bath, a bowl of soup and a tumbler of reviving *rouge*, she'd slipped the hairclip into her pocket, picked up her car keys and set off for the web of streets around the lorry park, convinced that somehow the hairclip would guide her. And driving round in her battered old 2CV certainly beat walking, she decided. She covered more ground. But for two hours she got nothing from the hairclip. Just its warmth, in the pocket of her jeans, pressing against her thigh.

With the rain drumming down on the sagging stretch of the Citroen's roof and the wipers screeching across the windscreen, Marie-Ange swung from one street to another, street lights flicking past, the warm air from the heater blasting up from under the dashboard. So far she'd covered a four-street radius to all sides of the lorry park, up from Boulevard Cambrai to rue de Lyon and from Avenue Malpense to rue Gujon. Now she was running down a street whose name she'd missed, a combination of warehouses and supply shops, their windows barred, their doors bolted closed – a chandlery, a hardware shop, a carpenter's yard, a gated coal depot.

That was when she saw him, a lone figure coming down the street towards her, picked out in her headlights, hunched against the drifting rain, a duffel bag slung over his shoulder. The collar of his jacket was up and his head was down, a woollen hat glistening with raindrops. In an instant she had passed him, and in that same instant she felt a strange sense of recognition.

Pulling into the kerb, she watched the figure in her wing-mirror, angling her head to keep him in view. After just a few steps, he turned to the left and disappeared.

Without thinking, Marie-Ange engaged reverse and whined back down the street, nearside tyres catching against the kerb as she tried to keep the car straight. A few metres short of the turning she braked to a halt, killed the engine and lights, locked the car and set off after him, now a good fifty metres ahead. Jogging through the rain, she soon narrowed the distance between them, getting close enough for him to hear her approach had it not been for the downpour.

And then he disappeared a second time, ducking through a door to his right.

Marie-Ange slowed to a walk, then slowed even more as she approached the door, its bottom half wood-panelled, its top set with a square of reinforced glass that sent a spill of blue neon light onto the pavement. On a board above the door, in flaking white stencil, were the words *Auberge des Vagues* and in smaller bracketed print beneath, (*Maison des Marins*). A seamen's hostel. Somewhere, she guessed, like the lorry park, for merchant sailors to rest up before joining, or after leaving, a ship. Cheap, anonymous and, like the lorry park, close to the docks.

Stepping away from the pavement and keeping out of the light, Marie-Ange stood back and looked through the glass panel. The man she'd been following was standing at a desk, at the end of a narrow hallway. He'd taken off his woollen hat, dropped his duffel bag at his feet and appeared to be talking to someone. He was large in the confined neon-lit space, with long, wide-set legs, broad shoulders and dark bristle-cut hair. When he leaned forward to sign what was presumably a guest register, Marie-Ange could see the person he'd been talking to. An older woman, with a set wave of dyed red hair and cheeks to match. She wore a thick woollen jacket over her substantial bosom, had a stern, frowning expression, and looked, Marie-Ange decided, as if she'd be able to deal with any damn' sailor-boy looking to cause trouble on her watch.

And that was that. Without showing his face the stranger reached down for his duffel bag, picked up his hat and headed for a flight of stairs to the left of the desk.

Outside, with rain gusting off her hood and trickling into her collar, Marie-Ange wondered what to do next. What was so important about this man that she'd had to stop her car and follow him here? Did she know him from somewhere? Was he somehow involved in the death of Lucienne Viviers? Was it the hairclip leading her on?

There was only one way to find out.

After the street, the hallway was warm and dry, with a welcoming scent of food coming from somewhere. A lot of garlic. And spices. A chilli dish of some kind. There was tobacco in the mix, too, and the smell of wet wool and salt and men's bodies. Like a locker room, Marie-Ange decided, as she made her way down the hallway, its floor made up of lino tiles scuffed down the centre and curled at the edge, its walls pinned with messages and fliers, a plastic-coated sea chart, a ferry timetable, and the details of a local medical centre. All you really needed if you were the seafaring type, thought Marie-Ange, as the old lady came out from her *loge* behind the desk and took up position, fixing Marie-Ange with a long, cool look.

'Men only, mam'selle. Crew quarters here,' she said, her voice low, level and almost menacing – like a zoo-keeper warning that Marie-Ange should come no closer, there were dangerous animals about.

'I just wondered if you could help me, madame?'

The concierge gave her a knowing look then lowered her head, her ruby hair and rouged cheeks picking up the blue tint from the neon tube. I'm listening, her posture said. Tell me something I haven't heard before, from a pretty young girl alone in a seamen's mission.

'The gentleman who just arrived . . .' Marie-Ange began.

A pair of thickly pencilled eyebrows slid up. And?

'I think he may be my husband.'

Husband? Or the father of your child? The old lady knew from long experience that it was more likely the latter. She drew in a deep, disapproving breath, but let out a gentle, resigned sigh. It wasn't the first time she'd heard that story, and she knew it wouldn't be the last. But she still felt it, it still hurt. Sometimes they came with their babies, asleep or crying, bundled up in knitted shawls or blankets, or in buggies that didn't fit in the corridor.

That was the worst. Having to watch them back those buggies down the hall.

Without a word, she leaned below the counter and pulled out the register, licked a finger and flicked through it. When she found the page, she ran a bitten nail (still varnished red) to the last name.

'Muller, Jan. Rotterdam. Didn't sound like a low-lander but he's carrying a Dutch passport.'

'Muller, you say?'

'That's what he's written. And that was the name in his passport,' she replied, going back to the register. 'Date of birth, April the fourth, 1951.' The concierge looked up. 'Bit old for the likes of you . . .'

Marie-Ange turned down her mouth, shook her head slowly, mournfully. 'No. That's not the name.' Then she tried a brave smile. 'And you're right. He's too old. I must have been mistaken. It's not him. I'm sorry.'

The old lady smiled back kindly. 'Next time, *chérie*, eh? Next time perhaps.'

Out in the rain, hurrying back to her car, Marie-Ange felt elated by her performance – far more polished than the one she'd tried earlier that day in the lorry park. But for all her delight – at her nerve, her inventiveness and her success – she still couldn't quite understand what it was all about. Why she should have followed the man in the first place.

This Jan Muller.

Who the hell was he?

And how did she know him?

Because she did.

She was sure of it.

Friday
13 November

26

ELODIE RAISED HERSELF, SLOWLY, PAINFULLY, every movement reverberating through her head as though her brain had broken loose from its moorings and was crashing against the inside of her skull, hammering at the back of her eyes, tightening the tendons in her neck. She felt sick, too. And had been sick; when she swallowed she could taste a fine acid burn in the back of her throat, and the front of her T-shirt had a damp lumpy skin. But she couldn't remember where she might have been sick, or when, or why.

As carefully as she could, Elodie propped herself up on her elbows, one after the other, gently locked her shoulders and squinted into darkness. Staying still, hardly daring to breathe, her dulled senses came into play gradually, like a slowly adjusted focus. Sight should have been next, but there was nothing she could properly identify – just subtle variations of black. Nothing distinct enough to put a name to, though she was increasingly certain she was in a room, the darkest shapes the walls around her. And within those walls, closer to, a number of odd black shapes, like low piles of coal.

Touch was altogether more defined, more real, more intimate – the crusty layer on the front of her shirt, still sticking to the skin of her chest, easing away with a slight resistance as she moved.

The bunched tightness of her jeans behind her knees and between her thighs, and a sense that her clothing had somehow been re-arranged. Then there was the stiff material beneath her that seemed to tip and roll like a tilting deck. Carefully she spread her hands, fingers dancing lightly off a rough buttoned surface. Off a . . . off a . . . a mattress. The word came slowly, but it exactly described what she was lying on. It felt thin and hard but she was grateful for it. Because she sensed the ground directly beneath it. Real ground, earth not flooring. Sloping slightly and lumpy, a cool damp-ness rising off it. She could smell it, too. Earthy, mouldy, like turned soil in a spring greenhouse. The kind of place, she thought, with a strange kind of whimsy, where you might grow mushrooms.

That's when the soundtrack started up, softly, as a rising back-ground, registering on several different levels. An occasional creaking above her head, a soft humming, and somewhere behind her a pattering, tinny sound that she narrowed down to rain on glass. She suspected that if she turned, or tipped her head back, she would see a window, high up on the wall behind her. But she knew that she didn't dare do anything so foolhardy, or her brain would batter against her skull, launching fresh bolts of pain from the top of her neck to hammer and thud at the back of her eyes. At that moment it was enough to believe that the window was there, adding to the picture she was gradually putting together.

Night-time, walls, mattress, a window, the sound of rain . . .

And from the low shapes around her a restless, sleepy whim-pering.

It was impossible to make out any movement, but Elodie sensed that those shapes were alive.

Wherever she was, she was not alone.

But it was too much. All too much.

Her shoulders began to ache, to stiffen, and a deep weariness settled over her. She felt heavy and sleepy and carefully, very care-fully, she lay back on her mattress, closed her eyes and let sleep take her.

27

MURAT SANTAREM SLAMMED DOWN the phone and spat with anger.

That fucking Spaniard!

'Salauds, salauds de la merde, et puis merde encore . . .'

'Tsk, tsk, tsk,' murmured his mother, turning from the sink where she was scrubbing a casserole dish. She smiled at him indulgently. 'There, there, *pauvre p'tit*. Poor baby. Shall I make you a coffee? Would that be better? Your favourite milky coffee? Just the way you like it?'

Murat took a deep breath and slumped across the kitchen table, forehead on crossed forearms, close enough to smell the sour plastic of the tablecloth.

Why did his mother never use the tablecloths he'd given her, he thought, the stiff white damask ones he'd stolen all those years ago from the back of a hotel laundry van? No prizes for guessing. In the wash, of course. If the old lady so much as saw a smudge on the hem from where she'd drawn it out of the airing cupboard then the whole thing would be bundled up and put in the wash. He couldn't remember a single occasion when one of those cloths had actually reached the table. But it kept her happy, put a smile on her face. The bundling up, the washing, the winding of the wet heavy damask through her mangle – only the mangle for the good stuff, she'd say – the airing and drying and eventual ironing. It was a performance, and no mistake.

Like the bastard performance he was having getting things set up with the Spaniard again, after that fuck-up on Sunday night. A real fucking performance, he thought. Because of that *salope* making a run for it half-way through the exchange, spooking the shit out of the Spaniard and his crew. And now that bastard dago was saying he wouldn't do another pick-up till the strike was over. Leaving him, Murat, to look after the cargo, currently housed in the basement below him. And his supply of Zopamyn and Promazyl to keep them quiet running perilously low.

Five days now he'd been left with them. Five goddamned bastard days. When he should have been back on the street checking out the next consignment. Coming up to Christmas was always a good time in his line of work: the shopping, the crowds, the festive spirit. People let their guard down, made mistakes, were somehow more trusting and friendly. And Murat was there, marking them out, always the young ones. On the street, in a shop, a bar. There to be taken and traded. Just another commodity.

And up till last week, Sunday night, it had all been going so well. Two years building the network – France, Switzerland, Germany, Austria, Holland, even Hungary – and refining the operation: the pick-ups, the hand-overs and, most important, staying on top of the rates he paid his boys. All he had to do was make it worth their while, and then some. The Balkan, Milo, took the biggest wedge because he'd been with Murat longest, stayed consistent and covered the widest territory, the rest of them paid on a scale in the order they'd joined. He didn't know whether they all outsourced – Milo certainly did – but he didn't really care so long as everyone worked by the rules, his rules, and they didn't get greedy.

His first take, nearly four years ago now, he'd done by himself. Brought in three, secured in the back of a rental truck, Munich to Marseilles. Turned them over to old Fonton and pocketed a cool thirty thousand francs. With a new van and some cash to invest, he'd brought in Milo to handle Austria and Germany, then that

116

Swiss pimp Jean-Marc in Zurich, Hennie in Bordeaux, and, a year later, Rudo in Budapest and Bernt operating out of Brussels and Liège. Five, maybe six, trips a year, each one starting in Paris which he'd set aside for himself, picking up all the way down – Dijon, Lyons, Valence or Avignon depending on the supply route – till he hit Marseilles with a full load. Never less than six, never more than ten. At twenty thousand a parcel, cash, it all added up. Take out fuel, accommodation, the team's rates, and with a full load he'd walk away with eighty thousand in crisp five-hundreds. Half-a-mill in two years – clear. Sure beat packing the saddle of his old Vespa with quarter-ounce nuggets of Red Leb and two-gramme wraps of coke for the run between clients. These loads might be heavier – and alive – but the work and the payback were way better.

Murat knew he had a good reputation, too. The girls he supplied were class product, once he'd persuaded Jean-Marc to stop passing on his own used goods who were usually so narked they didn't need any tranquillising. And every trip, the process got smoother: the timings, the drops; keeping the age between fourteen and sixteen – the older they got the harder they were to handle; and encouraging the lads to widen their net rather than concentrate on a single area. Spread the risk, he'd tell them. Wide as you like. He was the only one who kept to city limits – but then he was the boss, and he'd always liked Paris.

And all that planning and polishing, that attention to detail, had paid off. Until Sunday when the trip had gone shit-sided. A couple of corkers he'd sourced himself in Paris, the pair from Brussels that he'd taken off Bernt and kept in the van till his final take on Carrosses, the two blondes Milo brought in from Vienna, the Dutch girl from Hennie, and the girl with the big tits from Jean-Marc in Zurich. Eight on a single run from Paris to Marseilles, the last three hand-overs in a service station outside Valence, each perfectly timed and seamlessly executed: Jean-Marc first with Big Tits; Milo forty minutes later with the two Austrians; and finally Hennie coming in from Bordeaux. The whole thing over and done with in an hour-twenty. By the time he got to Marseilles, late Saturday night, Xavier was there, waiting to help move them from van to basement, ready for Sunday's hand-over.

And every single one of them a honey – from Big Tits to the slim little Austrian with the bleary brown eyes. But out of the eight, it was the last take he'd made, the easy one, who was prettiest. Way out ahead . . .

He'd met her first in Marseilles, wandering around Le Panier all by herself: long brown legs, that sundress with the spaghetti straps, the espadrilles bound up her legs. He'd seen her up ahead, followed her a couple of blocks then dodged round Montée des Accoules so he was jogging up the steps as she was coming down from place des Moulins. Bang into her, enough to knock her off balance but not put her on the ground. He'd apologised, picked up her bag and parcels, passed them to her. Asked if she was okay? He was so sorry . . . how clumsy . . . And then he'd looked at her and switched on his smile. That's all it took. The smile, the care, the consideration, the offer of a coffee, the least he could do . . . He'd played the same tune so many times, it was second nature. First nature, if there was such a thing. Had to be. Just . . . a part of him now.

It was over coffee that he'd learned she lived in Paris. Such a coincidence. He was at the university there. Studying fine art. The Sorbonne. They should meet up, have another coffee maybe, go visit a gallery? A date was made. And so it had started.

That was how Murat liked to work it sometimes. No snatch, no bundling of bodies into the back of his Renault van. With his looks and his charm, he simply hooked them, made them fall for him. And then all he had to do was wait for them to come calling. But Elodie had been a tight little thing. In love with love, but not the mechanics. *Une vraie pucelle*. Happy to hold hands and kiss, but when he'd tried anything more she'd closed him out. Told him she wanted to wait. For the right moment. Which just happened to be in the service-station car park outside Valence on Saturday night. Not that she knew anything about it. When the Promazyl he'd added to her Orangina finally took her out, he hadn't wasted a minute getting his hands inside her T-shirt to check out the goods. Up with the bra and two little cherries that puckered to the touch and tasted warm. Right there in the front of the van. And Bernt's girls, and that Lucienne he picked up at the fairground in Clichy, all of them right there in the back of the van the whole time. He'd have finished her off then and there, in the Valence service station, right in the cabin of the Renault van, if Jean-Marc hadn't turned up early with the Zurich girl.

Still, he hadn't moved her on yet so there was still time. If there was one good thing to come out of the current fuck-up with the Spaniard and the dockers' strike, it was surely the prospect of popping that one's little locket. Dealer's perk, he thought, and he felt himself stir. Tonight maybe, after his mother went to bed. Pull her out from the basement and have some fun. Give her a bath, maybe. Tidy her up. Take some time over it.

Murat took another sniff of the plastic tablecloth and raised his head from his forearms. Time to call Xavier, he decided, and see what luck he was having with the tranqs. He reached for the phone again and dialled the number, watching his mother as he did so, yellow washing-up gloves flapping around her bony elbows as she scoured away at a spotlessly clean casserole dish. Time to move her on.

'So what happened to my coffee, Maman?' he asked, knowing it would take another couple of requests before she finally got the message.

'What coffee, *P'tit*?' A troubled expression slid over his mother's features. And then the frown was gone and a smile took its place. 'You'd like a coffee? Is that what you said? Shall I make you one? Your favourite milky coffee? Just the way you like it?'

Turning back to the sink, she started up her humming again just as Xavier came on the line.

'Any news?' asked Murat.

28

DESPITE THE SNORING AND THE farting and the raucous throat-clearing from the two Malays who had turned in first, the dormitory in Auberge des Vagues that Jacquot had been directed to the night before had provided a surprisingly good night's sleep. The metal-framed single bed with its sawdust and horse-hair mattress, hard pillow, rough sheets and thin blankets – tightly tucked between mattress and creaking springs – had put him down as deeply as any anaesthetic. Like his orphanage bed, and barrack-room bed – a hollow, comforting tube to slide into.

Nor had he been expecting such a fine and bracing breakfast, served in a windowless low-beamed basement beneath reception. A basket of torn *petit pain* and warm croissants, tubs of Isigny butter and home-made preserves, freshly squeezed juice, scrambled eggs, a slice of ham as thick as the plate and as much coffee as he could drink, all delivered with a swift but disinterested '*Voilà, m'sieu*' by a thinner version of the concierge. It was better than most of the breakfasts they served in hotels along the Vieux Port, Jacquot decided, against a low hum of conversation from a dozen or so tables set around the room, the rustle of newspapers, the scratch of a match, raised voices and a laugh from the table beside them. And, because he was sitting next to Franco, the meal was topped off with a liberal dose of Calva to wash it all down. By the time he lit up his first cigarette, Jacquot felt like a king.

Franco had been the only other Frenchman in the top-floor dormitory, stretched out on his bed when Jacquot pushed open the door, ankles crossed, both hands cradling a leather-covered Bible. He had a thick broken nose, faded blue eyes and wine-red cheeks. He looked like a drunk, but there was a quiet, scholarly air about him, too, as though his being a sailor was the result of some long-ago misdirection. As well as Franco and the big-bellied Malays, there were two Germans, stripped down to vests and shorts: one playing Solitaire on his bed, the other doing pull-ups on an exposed beam in the dormitory's roof. The room was warm and snug, and smelled of old clothes, sweat and disinfectant, the rain rattling fitfully against two windows in the roof and another two looking down over the street.

The only free bed was next to Franco's, the blue blankets, thin sheets and single pillowslip set out in a neat pile on the bare mattress, each with *Maison des Marins* stamped across it in faded red letters. By the time he'd made the bed and stowed his bag, Franco had dropped the Bible back in his bedside table drawer and declared it *'toute merde'*, followed by a once-over glance at the new arrival: Jacquot. As the beam-pressing German dropped to the floor with bent knees and spread arms, Franco swung his stockinged feet off the bed and started up with the preliminaries. Where was Jacquot from? Which ships? Which line? Which routes?

Rotterdam, he replied, trying to make his french sound a little less Marseillaise, a little more clipped and guttural. *Mayovsky Star*, Crasnova, Russo-Line, Murmansk to Archangel. Industrial piping, motor parts, he added, remembering the last few postings from his log.

'Toute merde,' was Franco's considered take on this information, just as it had been with the Bible. Those Russians, he said. And Archangel . . . just a shithole in the snow. No wonder Jacquot had decided to come south. Except, of course, there was no work right now. The Germans, Franco told him, nodding at the gymnast and

the card sharp, were off down to Fos the following day before the strike reached any further along the coast, the Malays were headed for Genoa, and he himself was taking the train up to Cherbourg to await an Atlantic crossing. Christmas in New York, Miami, maybe Houston.

It was over their breakfast café-Calvas that Jacquot started asking questions of his own, lightly, just in passing.

'*Dis-moi*, how long do you suppose the strike will last?' he began, as though he was maybe reconsidering his options.

Franco shrugged. '*Écoute* . . . these are the boys who started the Revolution, remember? Marseillais to a man. Stubborn bastards, every one of them. So it's reasonable to assume that they'll stick it out no matter how long it takes. But they're greedy too, these Marseillais dockers. And it's the wrong season for striking. After a week standing around in the rain with their bullhorns and their banners, they'll be dousing the braziers and heading back to work, you can take my word on that. But Marseilles is finished anyway, you ask me. And they know it too. Just squeezing what they can out of the old sow while the going's good. Few years time it'll just be ferries to the islands, and all the traffic heading for Fos. So what's your plan? Where you heading?'

'Down south for me – Cape Town, Brazil. See out the winter in sunshine.'

Franco grunted, brought out his flask and splashed more liquor into their coffee mugs.

'Trouble is you never know your cargo . . . know what I mean?' said Jacquot, tipping his mug against Franco's.

'Tell me about it,' he said. 'Two weeks in Genoa, couldn't leave the ship . . . not once . . . 'cos the fucking skipper's carrying.'

'Drugs? Girls?'

'Drugs. No one bring girls in to this coast. From here it's just outward bound. Just the routes you're planning on.'

'Anything I should watch out for? If I decide to stay on and wait out the strike?'

'There's a dozen shipping agents down on those wharves and

122

when the strike's done they'll be screaming for crew. But some're better than others.'

'Any names?'

'Poseidon's good, down on Chamant. Guy in charge's called Yionnedes. Or there's Med-Mer on Arenc, Sud-Agence same spot – *bouf*, there's plenty down there.'

'And the no-nos?'

Franco fixed a look on Jacquot, as though weighing him up. 'There's a couple of Lebanese and a Spanish outfit on Chamant who don't smell too healthy when the sun comes out. Otherwise . . .' He shrugged, gave Jacquot another long cool look, then screwed the top back on his flask of Calva and pushed himself away from the table. '*Alors*,' he said, getting to his feet, looking round the room. 'Time to go.' Then, turning back to Jacquot, he put his hands on the table top and leaned in close. 'A word to the wise, *mon ami*. I shouldn't go saying too much about Archangel – not with a tan like yours. Someone might start to think you're not the man you say you are. And for a low-lander the accent's crap, too. *Toute merde*.'

He straightened back up, smiling. 'Whoever you are, Jan Muller, I just hope you make it home safe.'

29

ARSÈNE CABRILLE EASED HIMSELF FROM his mistress's perfumed bed and made his way slowly and carefully through the warm curtained gloom to the bathroom. He felt light-headed and unsure of his balance, reaching for the bed post and the back of a chair as though he'd just stepped off some wild fairground ride. He knew what that meant and he raged at the injustice of it. Which made his head spin even more.

Closing the door quietly, so as not to disturb his sleeping mistress, he switched on the light and put out a hand for the vanity top, seeing an old man appear before him in the mirror, an old man in red silk pyjamas, with a scrawny brown neck, grey stubbled chin and a ruffled wisp of silvery hair rising from a liver-spotted scalp.

Without thinking, he raised a hand to brush down the hair and felt himself swing away from the mirror as though the floor had tilted beneath his feet like a storm-tossed deck. Quickly he got his hand back to the vanity top and held on tightly until the feeling passed.

What had happened in his sleep? he wondered. What fresh little horror had visited itself on him? He felt it and saw it at the same time: a leaden tightness in his left cheek as though the muscles had shrunk, his mouth open and twisted slightly to the right. He tried to work his lips, but the muscles didn't respond. All he achieved was a soundless snarl. He tried to speak, to say his name, to see if speech might kick-start some response. But the lips didn't move to accommodate the sounds and his tongue flapped like a sail luffing in the wind. 'Arshen, Arshen, Arshen . . .' was all he could manage.

Merde, he thought, knowing he'd never be able to say the word properly. That 'm' sound was sure to defeat him. You couldn't say *'merde'* without putting your lips together. But try as he may, there was no way he was going to pull off that little trick, not with his numbed lips and tongue, and he felt a burst of impotent frustration.

Sometime in the night, he'd had a stroke. He knew it. It wasn't the first, but he knew it was the worst so far. In the weeks or months to come, its effects would either get better by themselves, or he would be stuck with them. Like his drooping left eyelid. That hadn't gone away. *Tant pis*. At least he was still alive.

There was a light tap at the bathroom door. His mistress, Cous-Cous.

'Tout va bien, chéri?' she called to him.

'Call 'irginie,' he replied, a scared old man staring back at him from the mirror. 'Call 'irginie.'

The effort to get the words out filled his mouth with saliva. Without his being able to stop it, a stream of it leaked between his parted lips and spilled down his chin.

He couldn't even say his daughter's name.

30

JACQUOT COULD HAVE KICKED HIMSELF. A tan on a White Sea run? According to the log that Madame Bonnefoy had provided, which he'd checked when he got back to the dormitory, Jan Muller had done two round trips between Murmansk and Archangel in the last nine weeks, and before that had been sailing between Bergen and Hamburg. No way was he going to pick up a suntan on routes like that. And in just a few short hours, Franco had seen right through him. He'd have to get Madame Bonnefoy to find him some warmer routes; in the meantime he'd keep his log to himself and rely on his identity and union cards. And hope the shipping agents he planned calling on weren't as quick or as sharp as Franco.

Now, hunching his shoulders against the rain and digging his hands into his pockets, Jacquot headed down to the port, turning on to Boulevard Cambrai and looking for a way to cross the old coast road. Finally he found an underpass that was scrawled with graffiti and ankle-deep in litter-strewn rainspill, and came out the other side just fifty metres short of the Chamant gates. Huddled under a stretch of green tarpaulin which they'd rigged to the railings as protection from the rain, four strikers stood guard at the dock's entrance, warming themselves around a spitting brazier. On the other side of the entrance, a pair of gendarmes kept watch on proceedings, relying for protection on their capes and plastic-wrapped *képis*.

Jacquot was just wondering how he was going to negotiate the approaching obstacle – the strike crew and the cops – when he heard a lorry swish up behind him, pass by in a cloud of wheel-spray and turn in at the dock gates. There was a flurry of movement as air brakes eased the rig to a final stop and Jacquot could hear voices raised over the rain. Taking advantage of the distraction, he came round the back of the lorry and saw the two *flics* talking to the driver through the open passenger door.

Jacquot darted towards the gate and thought he was through when one of the *képis* turned away from the cab and called him back.

'*Papiers, s'il vous plaît, monsieur.*'

Jacquot dug for the relevant documents and handed them over. The *képi* flicked through them, checked photo to face, and then checked it again.

'You have had a haircut, monsieur. It makes identity difficult.'

Good, thought Jacquot. That's why he'd done it. He shrugged, just the one shoulder, as though it didn't concern him. So what?

'What is your business here?' asked the gendarme, still holding Jacquot's papers, the rain spattering off the plastic wrap on his *képi*.

'Shipping offices. Need to sign on. See if there's any crew needed,' he replied, holding out his hand for the return of his papers.

The gendarme glanced at the outstretched hand, flicked through the papers one last time, then passed them over. 'Through the gate and on your right,' he said, looking over Jacquot's shoulder as the lorry driver worked his revs, released his brakes and started to back away from the dock gates.

Jacquot tucked away his papers, gave the gendarme a half-salute and slipped past him through the gate.

The Chamant wharf was deserted save for three small freighters berthed along the inner quay and two larger merchant ships in the outer basin. Their lights flickered through the rain, but otherwise there was no movement. Normally, the wharf would be humming – fork-lifts, carriage-tractors, balers, stockmen, cranes working on the ships' holds – but this morning there wasn't even a seagull to be seen. Just the sound of the rain and a low passing whoosh of early-morning traffic from the flyover behind him.

Jacquot found the shipping offices beyond the last bale-house, a motel-style two-storey terrace dwarfed by its neighbour, the lights inside gleaming gold against the grey morning light. He started at Poseidon, which Franco had recommended, and asked for Yionnedes. It was a good opportunity to practise his lines and get into character before he moved on to the shadier outfits.

'That's me,' said the man behind the counter. He was tall and slim, mid-forties perhaps, with bristling grey hair and long side-burns. When Jacquot told him what he wanted, Yionnedes turned down his mouth and shook his head. Regrettably there were no openings on offer, he said, but in case anything came up he took Jacquot's name (Muller) and the phone number of Auberge des Vagues.

'Good breakfasts, *non*?' said Yionnedes, noting down the contact details.

Jacquot agreed they were, indeed, very good.

'If the strike goes on any longer, you may be having quite a few of them,' he continued, handing back Jacquot's papers. And then, pointing outside, he said, 'There are other agents here, other ship-ping lines. You might as well get your name down with all of them while you're at it. *Et bonne chance, eh?*'

After calling in and leaving his details with three more agencies (polishing his cover with each visit) Jacquot came to the two Lebanese shipping agents, their offices side by side, whose names Franco had also mentioned. Although all the lights were on, the first office's doors were locked. He peered through the half-closed slats of the blinds but could see no one inside. At the next office, he had to press a buzzer to be let in.

'You speak understand Arabic?' asked the agent in heavily accented shorthand, a toad of a man with wobbling chins, sleeve suspenders and a slick of greasy black hair that curled over a shabby open collar. Jacquot admitted that he did not. The man smiled regretfully and showed him to the door. 'You speak Spanish, you

128

try next office,' he said, as Jacquot stepped back into the rain. 'Who knows?'

Recalling Franco's mention of a Spanish operation, Jacquot moved along to the next office, Ribero Agence Maritime, the name printed on a rectangle of card that had been stapled to the top of the door frame. As he pushed open the door Jacquot noticed that the staples had gone rusty, a brown tracer line along the bottom edge of the card.

Like all the offices he'd visited so far, there was nothing remarkable about the Ribero set-up: a smell of coffee, cigarettes and old after-shave or air-freshener, charts on the walls, a map of the Marseilles waterfront and, through a half-closed door, a back room equipped with a kitchen worksurface, cupboards and sink. In the front office, at one of two metal desks facing each other across the carpet tiles, a young man sat tilted back in his chair, flicking through a magazine, feet up on the desk. The first thing Jacquot noted was his polished fingernails and weighty signet ring, and the fact that he appeared to be better dressed than most of the other agents, neatly turned out in jeans, open-necked white shirt and a blue sweater, the shoes on the desk buffed to a shine, and expensive.

'*Nous sommes fermés, monsieur*,' said the man, not even bothering to look up. His French was good, but the look of him and the accent were Spanish. So was the magazine he was reading.

'But your door . . .'

'*Erreur. Je suis désolé . . .*' he gestured to the door, again without looking up.

'A guy called Franco, at Auberge des Vagues, told me to call by,' said Jacquot, trying to muster what he hoped was passable Spanish. *Un hombre que se llama Franco, del Albergue des Vagues, me a dicho que lo visite.* If the Arab next door wanted an Arabic-speaker, then this fellow might be impressed if he had a handle on Spanish.

'Franco? Franco Delavera?' This time the man put down his magazine.

Jacquot shrugged. 'Just Franco,' he replied, dropping back into French.

Another voice broke in. 'If you're a friend of Delavera, you can fuck off now.'

Jacquot turned to see a second man – broad shoulders, big hands, with a sharp unfriendly glint in his eyes. Unseen till now, he'd come through from the kitchen. He was drying his hands on a ragged strip of towel.

'Just a man I met,' said Jacquot. 'Talking, you know? He told me to come down here to sign up for crew.'

'It's okay, Citron. I've got this,' said the Spaniard. Levering his expensive shoes off the desk he gave Jacquot the once-over, a long look, head to toe, then back again. 'Where you from, *marin*?'

Jacquot told him Rotterdam, not Cavaillon.

He gave this some thought. 'You got papers?' he asked.

Jacquot brought out his passport and union cards, offered them.

The Spaniard nodded at Citron who stepped forward and took them, flicked through them.

'You got a log?' asked the Spaniard.

'Back at the hostel.'

'You got a good tan working out of Rotterdam,' said Citron, handing back his papers.

'I get around,' replied Jacquot.

'There still that bar down Delfshaven?' asked Citron, with a half-smile, as though testing him. 'On Schanstraat? Cleo, is it?'

This time Jacquot shrugged, as though such a place would be of no interest. 'I'm at sea. Who knows? Who cares? It's the work I'm interested in.'

The Spaniard considered this, then nodded as though Jacquot had said the right thing. 'So how come you're here? Right now, with the strike, all the crews are heading down to Toulon or up to Fos.' The Spaniard gestured through the door, further up the coast. 'Northern ports too.'

'Too many birds, too few worms,' replied Jacquot. 'Another week and I'll be front of the queue when the docks open down here.'

130

'So what'll you do between time?'

'Whatever I find. I'm easy. It's been a lean few months.'

The Spaniard nodded. 'You look like you can handle yourself. Am I right?'

'If I have to,' replied Jacquot.

Citron didn't move, didn't take his eyes off Jacquot.

The Spaniard smiled. 'Auberge des Vagues, you said? That's where you're staying?'

Jacquot nodded. 'Anything comes up, just let me know. Anything at all.'

'Yeah, sure thing. I'll let you know,' said the Spaniard and, with a final long look, he swung his feet back on to the desk and reached for his magazine.

31

ALAIN GASTAL SAT IN AN unmarked car chewing on a sugared length of *chichi-fregi*. The coil of browned dough was still warm, his fat lips were coated in sugar and its sweetness filled his mouth. They served something like it in Marseilles – a kind of French take on Spanish *churros*. But if you wanted the real thing – or an equally delicious chick-pea *panisse* – you had to come to L'Estaque and sniff out one of the small kiosks with their tubs of bubbling oil.

But Gastal hadn't just made the journey from Police headquarters for the *chichi-fregis*, much as he liked them. He'd come to find himself a new snout. At Bar-Café La Toppa, in the heights above L'Estaque. This was where he'd collared Valentine, and now the man was dead. Maybe the two were unconnected, but maybe they weren't, and someone in La Toppa had seen them together and been telling tales out of school. It could have been anyone putting Valentine down, for any number of reasons, but after his little talk with Alam Haggar, Gastal favoured the Cabrilles. The two *gorilles* in matching outfits, an English limo in the Fifteenth, a woman driving, and someone in the back. And the Cabrille family didn't take too kindly to anyone getting chatty with the *flics*. Or, if it wasn't the Cabrilles, maybe it was someone holding the girl. This Santarem character Valentine had mentioned. Whichever, Gastal considered it a win-win situation. Either a lead on the

Cabrilles, or on the girl. Or maybe both. And a new snout into the bargain, now that Valentine had been retired. Right now, it was the only way to go.

Pushing the last piece of *chichi-fregi* into his mouth, Gastal balled up the newspaper cone it had come in, tossed it on to the back seat and set about licking his sticky fingers before brushing the sugar off his tie. He looked at his watch. It was coming on for midday and he'd been sitting there for an hour. He'd wait as long as it took.

To make his mark, Gastal had come out to La Toppa the previous night and taken up position across the street from its parking lot. He knew what he was looking for and didn't have long to wait.

At a little after 10 p.m. two kids had come out of the bar and hurried into the parking lot's shadows. Gastal was out of the car as fast as he could manage and waddled across the street, pulling out his service Beretta and coming up on them between two parked cars. With the rain pelting down, the dealer and his customer didn't hear a thing until Gastal put his pistol to the dealer's head. 'Police. Blink and you're dead,' he'd said, then turned to the kid. His mouth hung open and his eyes were out on stalks. In his hand was a roll of notes. Gastal relieved him of the roll and waved him away. '*Casse-toi*, *petit*, or you'll get the same. Go on, beat it.' The kid didn't need any further encouragement. He spun on his heel and legged it across the lot.

When they were alone, Gastal had pushed the dealer into a doorway, caught hold of his wrist and twisted it round. When he had the nark on tiptoes he tapped the muzzle of the Beretta against the man's elbow. 'Have you any idea how it feels when a bullet mashes through this? And the damage? Believe me, you don't want to find out.'

That was all he'd had to do to get just what he wanted: a name, a description, a regular at La Toppa, someone connected. The dealer didn't have to think twice about it. Lévy, he'd said, Marcel Lévy.

'He likes his lunches, does Marcel,' the dealer told Gastal. 'Tall, fat, not a lot of hair. Somewhere in his fifties. Drives a Solex and sits by himself in the window.' But he'd been unable to supply an address.

Nor had police records when Gastal ran a check that morning. No current address listed. But there was a mug shot, a set of finger-prints and a good long rap-sheet going back to Lévy's late teens, small stuff most of it, but a spell at Baumettes in the early eighties for assault. Since then, nothing. According to records the man was clean.

And that's who Gastal was waiting for, back at La Toppa again and occupying almost the exact same parking spot he'd taken the night before, listening to a slow rain drum on the roof of his car, waiting for the lunch crowd to assemble, and for Monsieur Lévy to make an appearance.

It didn't take long for the man to show, swinging into La Toppa's parking lot on a sagging Solex that looked a couple of sizes too small for him. Drawing up outside the bar's steamy window, Lévy hauled himself off the saddle, kicked the bike back on its stand and hurried inside. From the car, watching through the rain and two sets of smeared glass, Gastal saw him drop down at a table in a corner of the lit window and snap open a paper. Ten minutes later, the first of three courses and three *demi-pichets* was served to him. And with every course Gastal's irritation mounted, wishing he'd bought another cone of *chichi-fregi* and wondering whether he could chance a quick trip to the kiosk down on des Canes.

Gastal had pretty much decided he could make it there and back before Lévy finished his lunch, and was reaching forward to start the car, when the man got up and slid some notes on to the table. A moment later he pushed out through the door, pulled up his collar and hurried to his bike.

Out in the street, Gastal started up the Renault, hoping Lévy would head back the way he had come. If he didn't, Gastal realised he'd have to turn the car and risk losing him in L'Estaque's warren of narrow back streets where that sagging Solex would have the advantage over the Renault.

But luck was on his side. Without bothering to stop at the entrance to La Toppa's parking lot, Lévy spun out into the road and headed back the way he had come. Before he'd reached the corner Gastal was on his tail, noting with satisfaction that Lévy's Solex had no rear-view mirrors on its handlebars.

Keeping a reasonable distance between them, he followed Lévy and the Solex down chemin du Marinier, approaching the entrance to the railway tunnel as Lévy braked for the turn at the other end. Hunched behind the wheel, Gastal decided it was just as well they were going downhill. If he'd been following Lévy uphill, the Solex would have been doing a quarter of the speed and it would have been impossible to tail him. As it was, the bike was getting ahead of the Renault on the slope, swinging round into Chemin de la Nerthe as Gastal came out of the tunnel. For a moment the Solex was out of sight and Gastal put on a bit of speed, enough for the Renault's back end to slide out on the rain-slicked surface, but enough for Gastal to glimpse the Solex turning down Traverse Mistral towards the port. Another few moments and he would have lost his man.

At the bottom of Mistral, just before the coast road, Lévy slowed and steered his bike up on to the pavement, freewheeling to a stop outside a chandlery shop. When Gastal drove past, Lévy was pulling out a key and letting himself in through a glass door. Lights went on.

Open for business, thought Gastal, and parking the car on the next block, he walked back up to Lévy's shop.

'Can I help you, monsieur?' asked Lévy as Gastal wandered down the aisle to the counter.

'I'm sure you can,' he replied, reaching into his jacket pocket and pulling out a knotted plastic bag. 'Here, catch,' he continued, and lobbed it over the counter.

Lévy instinctively reached out and caught it. By the time he'd opened his hand and seen what he was holding, Gastal was plucking it away from him.

'And that will do very nicely to begin with,' he told Lévy,

holding the four-ounce polythene bag of coke by its knotted end and dropping it back into his pocket.

'I think you will agree, Monsieur Lévy, that life just took one of those nasty little lurches . . .' Gastal smiled, bringing out his badge and laying it on the counter. 'At least, for you it just did.'

32

THE DINER BERNARD OFF RUE Tapion was humming when Marie-Ange and Pascale pushed through the doors for a late lunch. Given a choice, Marie-Ange would have spent the ninety minutes behind the wheel of her car, cruising the streets of Arenc, Chamant and Mirabe with the hairclip in her pocket, keeping an eye out for a man called Jan Muller. But she'd promised Pascale that lunch was on her, at Bernard's, this very lunch time, and there was nothing she could do to get out of it. And besides, Pascale was a friend, she owed her, and if that meant listening to a ninety-minute mono-logue on the latest man in her life then so be it.

There was a no-reservations policy at Bernard's – first there, first served – which meant that coming late they'd had to wait ten minutes under the rain-tapping awning outside before it was their turn to be seated, both of them ordering the *morue* without bothering to look at the menu.

Reaching for her cigarettes, Pascale lit up and started in on Jean-Charles. He was a beast, she said, but just a fabulous lover. Marie-Ange made all the appropriate noises but her attention was elsewhere. Ever since she'd picked up the hairclip in the lorry park, she'd been waiting for something to happen. But so far nothing had, save for her certainty that the hairclip belonged to someone Lucienne Viviers had known, someone connected to her in some way, someone in trouble. And now that hairclip was in her pocket, pressing against her thigh. It was then, scooping out the last of her *morue* with a toasted *pain*, that she realised Pascale was no longer listing the questionable talents of her latest lover.

'I don't know how they can bear it,' she was saying.

'How who can bear what?' asked Marie-Ange.

'Why, those poor people. You know, the ones in Paris. Their daughter is missing. It was on the news this morning. And look, there, in the paper, there's the story.'

Marie-Ange looked over where Pascale was pointing, to the rack of newspapers set out for lone diners. Beneath a headline about proposed tax cuts was a photograph of a man and a woman standing on the steps of what looked like an apartment block.

'She's been missing since last week,' continued Pascale. 'No word from her. No ransom. Here, take a look,' she said, pulling the newspaper from the rack and handing it to Marie-Ange, 'while I powder my nose . . .' She gave Marie-Ange a conspiratorial wink. 'You want some? It's a little present from lover boy. Only the very best.'

Marie-Ange smiled and shook her head. '*Non, merci. Pas pour moi*. You should know that by now. A drink, a cigarette, a spliff now and then. That's all for this little lady.'

'You don't know what you're missing, *chérie*,' said Pascale, and reaching for her bag, she headed off for *Les Filles*.

To pass the time, Marie-Ange unfolded the paper and looked at the photograph of the couple in Paris, then read the caption. *Monsieur et Madame Lafour whose daughter, Elodie, has been missing since Saturday, make a plea for her safe return. Full story, page three.*

Pascale was right, thought Marie-Ange, examining the parents' faces. How could they possibly cope with such a terrible thing? Their daughter taken, maybe dead. In the photo the mother looked as though she hadn't slept for a week, her eyes dark and haunted but her lips set in a stiff, severe line, holding everything in. Her husband had his hand up, as though trying to quieten the mob of photographers gathered around them.

138

Without thinking, Marie-Ange opened the paper only to reel back as a strong scent blasted off the page. *Versage*. The scent *Versage*. Coming off the newsprint, as though the page had been soaked in it. She recognised it immediately, a popular scent with young girls – Marie-Ange had used it herself – but could see no reason for it being there. Had there been some promotional gift from the manufacturer tucked between the pages? Had some girl spilt her perfume on it?

And then she felt a stir of recognition. In the centre of the page was a photo of the missing girl, Elodie Lafour. A formal studio shot by the look of it. She wore a light green cardigan draped over a darker green button-down shirt and she was holding a leather-bound book in her lap. She looked about fourteen, with blonde hair secured by a hairband and a sweet uncertain smile directed at someone off-camera. But it wasn't a happy smile, Marie-Ange decided. It was a smile for the photographer, for show, like her mother's tight lips in the photo on the front page; something held back, something hidden behind it.

For a moment or two Marie-Ange examined the photo, let her eyes range across the girl's features, tried to place where this increasing sense of familiarity came from. And then, with a jolt, she had it. The hairband across the top of the girl's head. Blue, enamelled, and wavy. She couldn't see the ends tucked away behind the girl's ears, but Marie-Ange had no doubt they would be a serpent's head and tail.

Just like the head and tail on the matching clip in her pocket.

And the perfume . . . *Versage*.

Like the reek of Cognac and beer that had come off the page when Marie-Ange had read the newspaper report about Lucienne Viviers.

There had been no promotional gift between the pages.

No accidental spill.

It was Elodie Lafour.

Elodie Lafour, she was certain, wore *Versage*.

33

'*BON DIEU*, DANIEL, YOU LOOK like a tramp. And who the fuck took your scalp?'

Shaking his head, Jean-Pierre Salette, the Vieux Port's former harbour master, wadded some bread, took a swipe at the last of the cheese on his plate, and shoved the lot into his mouth. Jacquot had found him at his usual corner table in Brasserie Clément, on the corner of Rive Neuve and rue Calisto, a crumpled copy of *L'Equipe* on the banquette beside him and the *demi* of *rouge* in front of him almost empty. His face and hands were deeply tanned, the hair a salty rug of spikey white, and his eyebrows as black as ebony splinters. Everything he wore – work trousers, crewneck jumper and plimsolls – was as blue and faded as his eyes which he now settled on Jacquot.

'Work,' said Jacquot, pulling out a chair.

'Near six months and not a word,' continued Salette, looking him over, still chewing away on the bread and cheese. 'Is that the way to treat an old man who's kept you out of trouble all these years . . . kept you on the straight and narrow?' He swallowed the bread and cheese and indicated the empty *pichet*. 'The least you could do is order more wine. Or do you want me to die of thirst?'

'Already done,' said Jacquot, smiling at the waitress as she put down a fresh *pichet* and took away the old one. 'I asked for it on the way in.'

'Now I know you're on the scrounge. Softening me up. I may be old but I'm not stupid.' Salette indicated with a wave of his index finger that Jacquot should pour the wine. 'Come on, out with it. What is it you want this time?'

From the very start, after that first dinner with Madame Bonnefoy, Jacquot had realised he would need help. And he knew that Salette was the man to provide it. The old *loup de mer* might have surrendered his desk at the *Capitainerie* to a younger man but there wasn't much that happened in the Vieux Port that he didn't know about, or else find out about if he had a mind to. And there was no one in the world Jacquot trusted more than his father's old shipmate, the man who had taken the young Jacquot under his wing when his father was lost at sea and his mother murdered.

And so he explained everything: the missing girl, the likelihood that she might be in Marseilles awaiting transportation, and the job he'd been given of finding her. Outside the police. On his own. Under cover.

'Easier to get round,' he explained. 'I go looking for her as a cop, they'd spot me a mile off. I need to be in there, a sailor, looking for work. One of them. It's the only way. Which is why I look like this . . . signing on as crew, sniffing around.'

'They take you?' Salette let a grin steal over his features. 'You're looking a little out of condition, if you ask me. Must be all that soft living up country. I'd have thought that girl of yours, Claudine, would have kept you in better shape.' There was a glint in the old man's eyes. 'She didn't strike me as the kind of woman who's going to like a man fattening up . . .'

'There's been no complaint,' replied Jacquot, remembering the ache that had accompanied his wood-chopping just a few days earlier and his struggle with the log basket. 'Of course, the tan doesn't help.'

Salette narrowed his eyes, let them range over Jacquot's face and hands. And scalp. 'Don't tell me. You got papers saying you're on northern routes?'

Jacquot nodded.

141

'You *flics*,' chuckled Salette. 'It's a miracle you catch anyone.' The chuckle broke into a laugh that made him catch his breath, then cough. He reached for the *pichet*, refilled his glass, took a slug. 'So what do you need?' he asked, after drowning the cough and getting his breath back.

'Where to start would be good?'

Salette gave it some thought, working gnarled brown fingers across a white stubbled chin. Jacquot could hear the rasp.

'Well, you've got your work cut out, and no mistake,' he began. 'A half-dozen ports within spitting distance of this table and a lot of traffic.' He tipped his head towards the Vieux Port. 'A couple of thousand craft tied up right there, and more along the coast.'

'Just what I needed to hear,' said Jacquot, pulling a pack of cigarettes from his pocket and lighting up.

'But it's not all bad,' the old man continued. 'Take away the *pointus* and the fishing skiffs out there, and you'll be down to maybe a thousand craft of one sort or another – sail, motor. If, like you say, there's a bunch of these girls being moved then you can discount the smaller vessels. No room, see. Below decks. So now you're down to a few hundred, but of those there'll be no more than fifty lived in . . . full-time, you understand. And this time of year, in weather like this, maybe no more than ten or fifteen. The rest'll be pretty much wrapped up for the winter.'

Jacquot nodded at this swift and confident appraisal, relieved that his companion was giving the problem due consideration, and felt for the first time a trace of hope that the job was maybe not as daunting as he'd feared.

'There's another thing,' said Salette, emptying his glass and smacking his lips as Jacquot refilled it. 'There may be a lot of boats out there, but there aren't many sailors, if you know what I mean. Not the kind who'd set sail in this kind of weather. It's been pushing a force seven out beyond the islands and you'd need a good skipper to see you through that. Since it started up, I can count on one hand the boats that have come and gone. And I know 'em all.'

'What about the other marinas?' asked Jacquot. 'Madrague? Pointe Rouge? L'Estaque?'

'The same story. L'Estaque's a possibility, *c'est certain*. But the others . . .' Salette shook his head. 'Too small – port and boats both. Too difficult to get your girls aboard and keep 'em there. Someone would notice. And where are they going to go, anyway?' he asked with a shrug and a wave of his hands, wine tilting in his glass. 'Most of them haven't got the range . . . haven't got the specs to make a long trip. You ask me, it's the freighters you need to keep an eye on. Like you're doing. Get *les petites* into a container, haul 'em aboard with food and water, and you're pretty much home free. A week's sail and you're half-way across the Atlantic, or port hopping down the African coast. In the meantime, they'll likely be somewhere ashore. That's what I'd put my money on. A warehouse or basement somewhere, with a skipper and crew that know how to look the other way when they come aboard.'

'What about another port? With the strike on, would they take them to Fos or Toulon?' Jacquot thought he knew the answer, but he wanted Salette to confirm it. He stubbed out his cigarette and waited.

The old harbour master gave it some thought, then shook his head. 'If they've got a system, they'll stick to it. They won't change things. If the girls are here for transport, yours included, that's what'll happen. They'll go from here, using whatever means they've got in place. Far too tricky to set something up at the last moment – some other ship, some other port. Even if they've got to keep the girls till the strike ends.'

'That's what I reckoned,' said Jacquot.

'So what do you want me to do?' asked Salette.

'Just keep an eye open, ask around.'

'Where're you staying? Up in Moulins?'

Place des Moulins had been Jacquot's home when he'd worked in Marseilles. Since the move to Cavaillon, he'd rented the place out, leaving it under the watchful eye of his concierge, the formidable Madame Foraque.

143

Jacquot shook his head. 'Auberge des Vagues. On Impasse Massalia.'

'So you'll have Madame Boileau looking after you now?'

'Is that her name? I didn't know.'

'An old trout, but a big heart. You'll be eating well, that's for sure. Her sister does the cooking. *Incroyable*. They make their own conserves. And there's a brother, Luc, with a smallholding up round Bouilladisse – chickens, pigs. They smoke their own ham, you know . . . *délicieux*. Tell the old girl I still think fondly of her,' he said, with a lewd wink. 'In her day she was quite a performer.'

'And how do you suppose I can do that when my name is Jan Muller and I'm half-Dutch?'

'And you think she believed you? Take my word for it, Madame Boileau's got a nose for bullshit and she'll sure have smelt it on you.' Salette leant forward and sniffed dramatically. '*Boufff*!' he declared, turning his head away. 'Unmistakable.'

'Well, thanks for that, old man. That's really made me feel good.'

Salette shrugged. As if he cared. 'So how long are you going to be here?'

'Until I find her. Or the strike ends. Whichever comes first.'

'I'll have a word with the Brotherhood. We're meeting up Sunday, if the weather breaks. The usual place. Why don't you join us?'

'If I can, I will.'

Salette considered this. 'So . . . Sunday it is, then.'

34

EVEN UNDER LOW GREY SKIES and through a soft mist of rain, the Druot Clinic's four-floor cube of white stucco and tinted blue windows on a tree-lined side-street off Avenue du Prado had a sleek, summery look to it. As she slid her vintage Porsche roadster into an empty space in the parking lot, Virginie felt her spirits rise. Locking the car, she hurried up the front steps into the building, automatic doors swishing open for her, a glitter of raindrops tumbling from her coat as she swung it off her shoulders and shook it on to the marble tiles.

It was Cous-Cous who had called her. The old man was feeling unwell, she had reported, her voice low and timorous. There was a possibility that Monsieur Arsène had suffered a small *attaque* sometime in the night, Cous-Cous continued, and what should she do?

Virginie had done it all for her. After telling her father's mistress to get him dressed and ready – there was nothing to worry about, it was fine, Virginie assured her – she had phoned the Druot to have an ambulance despatched, giving Cous-Cous's address as the pick-up point.

At no point did Virginie consider going to her father herself. This was not the first time the old man had suffered a stroke and been taken to the clinic, and she knew the drill. It would take at least twenty minutes for the ambulance to reach the small fisherman's cottage that her father had bought for his mistress in Endoume, and a further twenty for the paramedics to check him over. It would then take at least as long again to make it back to the Druot with their patient. Even if Virginie had been there to meet him, there would have been no time for anything beyond 'Papa, Papa', before his trolley or wheelchair was whisked into a lift and the old boy was taken for tests. Those tests, Virginie knew from experience, could take anything from one hour to three, and it was for this reason that, after calling the clinic to start things moving, she had turned back to her lover to continue what Cous-Cous's call had so cruelly interrupted.

Now, some four hours later, Virginie strode across the clinic's entrance hall and headed for the lifts. From her many previous visits she knew where to go. Top floor, one of two balconied suites overlooking the green expanse of Parc Borély. As she stepped from the lift she wondered which it would be: 407 or 408.

Let the numbers do the talking, she decided. She was a qualified accountant after all, and numbers had a purity she respected.

If it's 407, the old boy lives.

If it's 408, he dies.

'Ah, Mademoiselle Cabrille, *bonjour, bonjour*,' called the senior ward sister at the nurses' station. 'Your father is fine, just a little woozy. He's in four hundred and eight. At the end of the corridor, to the right.'

Virginie smiled and carried on walking, down the corridor and around to her right. She knocked lightly at the door to 408, pushed it open and slid inside.

The first thing she did was flick down the corridor blinds. Then she went over to the bed and leant down to kiss her father's forehead. It was difficult not to recoil from the smell of old wrinkled skin, wine-sour breath and the cheap perfume of that whore Cous-Cous.

'Papa, Papa, Papa. Did that naughty little Cous-Cous give you bad dreams?' she whispered, drawing back from the bed.

146

She watched her father's eyes flicker open and turn to her, roaming over her features until finally they settled and focused on her. As soon as they did, the old man frowned.

Was he trying to remember who she was? thought Virginie.

Or did he know exactly who she was . . .

. . . and what she was about to do?

35

MARCEL LÉVY KNEW THAT HAVING his prints on a bag of cocaine was bad. But he knew that providing *les flics* with information about the Cabrille family was infinitely worse. Look at old Valentine, dead in his workshop. La Toppa had been full of it that lunchtime. Beaten to a pulp, Toni, the barman, had told him. Torn limb from limb, Janni, the pretty little waitress had said. And the Cabrille name written all over it, that's what La Toppa's regulars all agreed. Him included. Which meant that Valentine had likely been blabbing about the family. And the Cabrilles had got to hear about it and dropped by his workshop for a chat. Because when the Cabrilles came knocking on your door, that's what usually happened – a bullet in the back of the head from the old man, or a more extended interval of pain if that sadistic little bitch, the daughter, and her two Corsican cronies were involved. Which, judging by Toni's lurid description, they had to have been.

And now it looked like the same cop was leaning on him to take Valentine's spot. Playing catch with that bag of coke. Just to reel him in. Lévy felt a shiver start up in his shoulders and drop to his guts.

Merde alors, what a fucking mess.

What was it the cop had said? A nasty lurch, that was it. 'I think you will agree, Monsieur Lévy, that life just took one of those nasty little lurches . . .'

No fucking kidding.

But what to do about it? What to do?

After the cop had gone, sauntering out of the shop, whistling lightly, Lévy had locked the front door and switched the sign to *Fermé*. Taking refuge behind his counter, he'd pulled out a stool and sat in the shadows, his beady grey eyes on a level with the drawer of the cash register, reviewing his options. It hadn't taken him long to realise that he didn't have any. That fat slob of a cop would work his balls till they scraped the ground, and then toss him to the dogs. Or in this case, the Cabrille family, in whose activities – surprise, surprise – the cop had been particularly interested. Anything he could find out about the family, the cop had said – ships, cargoes, movements.

But it wasn't just the Cabrilles he was interested in. He had also wanted to know about Fonton and Santarem and anyone local involved in the trafficking game. Lévy wondered if it had anything to do with the missing girl in Paris. They'd been following the case up at La Toppa, and most of the regulars had been surprised there'd been no demand for ransom. The Lafours? A family like that? With their kind of money? Well, whoever had her could demand millions. On the other hand, they also agreed, it didn't take a genius to work out that if there was no ransom, the girl was likely dead or en route somewhere. There'd been hours of speculation as Toni stood behind his bar and polished his glasses, but as far as Lévy could remember there'd been no mention of Marseilles or any local involvement.

Sitting there in the shadows, by the till, he wondered now if Santarem did have the girl and didn't know what he was sitting on – a good grafter but thick as pig shit when it came to the bigger picture. All his brains in his face. Maybe he'd give the lad a call. Old times. How're things going? And whatever he found out he could pass on to the cop; give him Santarem rather than risk the Cabrilles.

A sudden squall of rain battered against the window, and brought

149

him round. Despite the twisting in his gut, he knew now what he had to do.

Play smart. Play for time. And cover his arse.

And the only way to do that was to talk to the Spaniard.

150

36

ON THE CHAMANT QUAY, IN the offices of Ribero Agence Maritime, Guillermo Ribero was ready to call it a day. With the docks shut down by the strike there'd been little he could gainfully do, but when you worked for the Cabrille family you kept your sheet clean or you paid the price, Cabrille-style. And with Citron hanging around, always on the look-out for a way into the family's favour, it was best to put in the hours, even if all he'd managed to do was flick his way through a pile of magazines and sign up a single sailor for possible crew. Big son of a bitch who looked like he could handle himself, and didn't seem too bothered what jobs he was asked to do, someone who might just come in handy for the Santarem handover. If the strike ended that weekend, which was what Citron had dropped by to tell him, Citron's father being the dock union boss, then he could do with some extra muscle. He didn't want any more mistakes, nothing to jeopardise his pitch.

Guillermo had run the Cabrilles' shipping interests for four years, quietly and efficiently servicing a fleet of twelve mid-weight freighters working Mediterranean, Atlantic and West African routes. At any one time, three of the fleet were usually engaged in illicit trade, namely drugs, particularly cocaine, brought in from stop-over ports like Freetown, Accra and Libreville. Transhipment of cargo in those lawless ports was a hazardous business but worth

151

the effort. Better one of the Cabrille fleet arriving in Marseilles or Toulon, Genoa or Palermo, from one of these West African ports than docking direct from Brazil or Venezuela. The proof was in the pudding. Not a single hiccup in four years. And that included his own private cargoes, outward bound from Marseilles on Cabrille vessels, and the family none the wiser.

Guillermo and Murat Santarem had been doing business on the side for two years now, since Fonton threw it in, and Guillermo was making a considerable amount of money by providing Santarem with the means of getting his merchandise out of the country, and selling on down the line. And until the previous week everything had gone without a hitch. That girl making a run for it on Sunday night had brought home to him the problems that could arise, and as he washed up coffee cups in the kitchen behind the office he decided the time had probably come to ease himself away from Santarem. The man was getting sloppy and that worried Guillermo. After this last pick-up he'd find himself another source, move on.

Of course it wouldn't be easy making the break. Santarem would threaten to shop him to the Cabrilles, try to blackmail him into continuing. But Guillermo knew that the time had come to cut loose from the man. Before there were any more problems. Before the Cabrilles got to hear about it. Maybe he'd have that sailor who'd dropped by that morning go pay a call on Santarem and show him the error of his ways. The man looked like he could handle that kind of work.

Guillermo was switching off the office lights and about to punch in the security code when the phone rang. For a moment he wondered whether he should leave it, but some instinct made him put down his overcoat and take the call.

It was Marcel Lévy, in quite a state by the sound of it. A cop called Gastal had paid him a visit, wanting to know about the Cabrilles, Lévy told him. 'Thought I'd better let you know, see what you think . . . maybe pass it on? Anything I can do for the family. Just let them know I'm happy to do whatever they think is appropriate.'

152

Guillermo assured Lévy that he would pass on the information and put in a good word for him, for which Lévy had sounded suitably grateful, and then he put down the phone. Pulling out his chair, Guillermo sat down, reached for a cigarette, and in the half-light, smoked it to the filter.

Santarem and the runaway girl; now Lévy and the *flics*. Two years earlier it was Lévy who had introduced him to Santarem, and Lévy was the kind of man who kept his memory, if not his body, in perfect order.

It was all getting a bit too close, Guillermo decided. For a moment, just a moment, he felt a flutter of unease in his guts, a nervous twitch.

Time to offload the dead weight, he thought to himself.

Time to clear the decks.

And get in first.

He reached forward and picked up the phone, dialled a number.

'It's Guillermo,' he said, when his call was answered. 'I'm at Chamant.'

As usual, he was told to hang up and wait. Which was the way the Cabrilles liked to do things. One time he'd waited two hours before the call-back. Tonight, it was just a few minutes over the half-hour.

'I thought you should know,' he told his contact. 'There's a man called Marcel Lévy been talking to the cops. Some guy called Gastal. About the family, so I heard. He runs a chandlery, Marin Azur, out L'Estaque way. On Mistral. That's right, Traverse Mistral. No problem.'

Twenty minutes later, Guillermo pulled out through the dock gates and headed home with a smile on his face.

37

THE DEATH OF ARSÈNE CABRILLE in room 408 of the Druot Clinic caused a kind of shocked disbelief among the duty nursing staff on the fourth floor and, in the hour that followed, amongst the clinic's administrative team who came from their various offices on the ground floor to offer Virginie their deepest sympathies and heartfelt condolences.

Such a man . . .

Such a loss . . .

It had begun with Virginie's scream.

'I leaned over to kiss him and . . . he just looked up at me and smiled and closed his eyes,' she told the nurses who came running to her father's room. She repeated the same story to her father's physician, to the Head of Admissions, and to anyone else who came within range. Two hours later, that same Head of Admissions helped Virginie to her car and personally drove her back to the family home in Roucas Blanc. Like everyone at the clinic, he told her, he was stunned and appalled by her father's sudden and tragic passing. Of course, he demurred, as Mademoiselle Cabrille probably knew, sometimes, regretfully, this kind of thing happened with stroke victims . . . like earthquakes, *n'est-ce pas*? he'd said. Always the aftershocks . . .

And Virginie had nodded and sniffed and thought of her finely placed thumb in that tented hollow between her father's neck and shoulder, *Dam Têe Nâng*, the black place, a pressure point she'd learned about from Taddeus, which effectively blocked the supply of blood to the brain. It had taken just moments for the monitor beside her father's bed to register the attack – a sudden, danger-ously increased pulse-rate, excessive electrical activity in the brain – and just a few moments more to show a green flatline for both functions.

Dead in eight seconds. She had never done it faster. Standing back from the bed, she'd dusted her hands, composed herself and then screamed.

He had had it coming, of course – his lack of imagination, his old-fashioned ways – and for months now she'd been playing with the idea. But it was the girl, Elodie Lafour, that had stiffened her resolve. She couldn't miss this one, wouldn't miss this one. Yet despite that *garagiste* Valentine saying that the Lafour girl was all the cop Gastal had been interested in, and despite the death of another young girl reported missing in Paris just the previous week, and despite the fact that no ransom demand had been made – the implications of which should have been clear to a blind man – her father had refused to be swayed. If Virginie wished to pursue it, he had told her on the drive home from Valentine's workshop in rue Chatelier, then she could do so only after a more pressing busi-ness interest – the security of the merchant ship *Hesperides* and its cargo – had been successfully concluded. And that, as far as he was concerned, was an end to it, chopping the air with that gnarled old hand of his to indicate the discussion was over. That was how he had wanted it. And that was how it would have gone had it not been for that timely phone-call from Cous-Cous, just the perfect opportunity to arrange *un petit coup de famille*.

At no time had Virginie felt the least shred of guilt at having so coldly disposed of her father. If that nurse had said room 407 and not 408, she'd still have done it, she acknowledged now. For symmetry's sake, as much as anything. As she started searching through the drawers in her father's desk, the only things on her mind, besides Elodie Lafour and the ransom demand she'd soon be making, were the pleasing *symétries* attached to his murder. A decade earlier he had drowned Virginie's mother, Léonie, in the swimming pool. Her mother's crime? Sleeping with the family lawyer, a man who had subsequently had his testicles removed by Taddeus, and his moustachio-ed top lip scissored off by Tomas, the two items then wrapped in plastic and posted to his home address. The rest of him they'd taken on to the family's yacht, weighted with chains and dropped into the bay.

Now it was her father's turn to die, at the hands of his daughter, albeit for the lesser crime of standing in her way.

Frankly, Virginie decided, there wasn't much difference between her father and her old dog César. Another satisfying parallel. Though she had felt love for the animal she had felt also a compulsion to take responsibility, to spare the beast further misery. And to do it herself. Her dog. Her job. So it had been with her father.

And then to kill him in the very clinic that he had endowed in memory of the wife he'd murdered, giving it her maiden name and using it, along with an increasing number of other hospices and private clinics, as a fail-safe means of laundering their other businesses' excessive cash profits . . . why, there was yet another, pleasing *symétrie*.

And never, ever again would she have to endure Charles Trénet singing '*Boum*' or '*La Mer*'. It was worth it just for that, she decided as she crossed to her father's drinks tray and poured herself a large scotch. Coming back to the desk, she sipped her drink and felt a buzz of warmth and power. Of all the spirits, whisky had that effect on her. Warming, comforting, but most of all enabling. A couple of scotches and she felt as if she ruled the world. Which, since pressing her thumb into her father's neck, was pretty much the case.

She put down her drink and was reaching for her father's desk diary when there was a knock at the door.

'*Oui. Entrez*,' she called out, not bothering to look up as Taddeus and Tomas came into the room.

The two men took up position in front of the desk, just as they would have done with her father. Neither wore a jacket, but each sported a black armband on their white shirtsleeves.

'It is sad news,' said Taddeus.

'*Trés triste*,' his brother, Tomas, agreed.

If they suspected anything, it was impossible to tell.

'He was old,' said Virginie softly, as though age was the killer and not her. 'It was his time. Regrettable, of course, but there you are. *C'est la vie. C'est le mort*. But there is business to attend to,' she continued.

'First, the girl . . . Elodie Lafour. I want her found, fast, before the docks open for business. Bring in whoever you need, but make it happen,' she said, settling a look on the twins, who stood with legs apart, hands behind their backs, their shaven heads shining in the lamplight. If she had any feelings for anyone, she decided, it was for these two men before her. Not that she would ever let them know that.

But Virginie wasn't finished. 'And while you're doing that, I want that raddled old whore Cous-Cous out of Endoume.' She tapped a wad of documents with her fingernail. 'I have checked – the house is not in her name. Give her time to pack her bags, then drive her to the Sofitel. Two weeks and she's on her own. *Compris*?'

'*Oui, Mam'selle. Pas de problème*,' replied Taddeus, then he raised his hand, cupped it over his mouth and coughed softly. There was something he wanted to say.

'Is there anything else?' asked Virginie, recognising the signal.

'It seems that *flic* Gastal is getting busy.'

'Gastal?'

'Apparently he's been chatting with one of Valentine's mechanics. There's two of them worked there. Arabs, both. A friend saw one of them leaving police headquarters yesterday. He'd been there a couple of hours. I wondered if you had any instructions?'

Virginie didn't need to give it much thought. Who'd miss him? Some Arab? She reached for her drink, swilled the whisky around in the tumbler. 'Set an example,' she said. 'And make it the pair of them, just in case. Anything else?'

157

'Tomas had a call from the Spaniard. It seems one of his contacts is also getting pally with this Gastal. A guy called Lévy . . . runs a chandlery out L'Estaque way. Same brief. Anything he can get on the family.'

Virginie took a gulp of her whisky and felt a warm pulse of excitement.

'Take him out too. Time to let people know there's a new boss in town.'

It was then that she remembered something.

'*Attendez*,' she called out, rummaging in her bag. She pulled out a key ring and flung it across the desk. Taddeus reached out and caught it.

'I forgot. There's a young woman at the lodge. In the bedroom. Please release her and give her what she's owed.'

'How much should we give, mam'selle?' asked Tomas.

Virginie smiled, 'Whatever you think appropriate for her pains. I shall leave it to you.'

The two brothers smiled. An unexpected treat.

'*Merci, mademoiselle*,' they said, almost together.

38

MURAT SANTAREM WAS WATCHING TV in his mother's salon when Xavier called by.

'You see the story in the newspaper?' asked Xavier, dropping the latest edition on to Santarem's lap. 'That girl in Paris. It's the same one, isn't it? You've got her downstairs.'

'So what if I do . . . who cares?' asked Santarem, switching off the TV and picking up the paper. He scanned the headlines, looked at the picture of Elodie Lafour, then put it aside.

'So she's worth a bit, I'd say.'

'She's already taken.'

'You gotta be kidding! What do you get . . . twenty from the Spaniard? A girl like this, you're talking millions.'

'I got customers, Xavier. I got a core business. I don't go changing the goalposts. I do what I do. I do what I know. That's good enough for me.' He was pleased with the way he'd said that, and ran the words through in his head once more. *I do what I do. I do what I know.* Yeah, he liked the sound of that.

Shaking his head, as though he couldn't credit it, Xavier flopped down in a chair beside the TV, looking sour. 'Man, it's just a phone call. A pick-up. And we're out of here.'

'It's not going to happen. I spoke to my man and the exchange is on for this weekend; word is the strike's going to wind down.

Seven girls. That's the deal. And I'm not going to him and saying, "Oh, sorry. There should have been seven, but now there's only six." If it goes wrong again, there'll be trouble. And blood.'

'We could bring him in on it,' suggested Xavier. 'Tell him what we got down there. Divide it three ways – there'd still be a stack of it. We wouldn't have to work for the rest of our lives. Retire some place, free and clear.'

Santarem gave him a look. 'We do it my way. That's all there is to it. Understood? Now, what about those sleepers? Our guy come up with anything?'

Xavier clenched his teeth, balled his fists. For a moment he wanted to reach out and throttle the man, but he took a few deep breaths and calmed himself.

'I said, has our man . . .'

'Tonight,' said Xavier, interrupting him. 'It's arranged.'

39

WHEN JACQUOT TURNED INTO IMPASSE Massalia and saw the spill of blue neon from Auberge des Vagues' front door, he felt a weary sweep of relief. And disappointment. All he'd managed to do his first day on the job was have his cover blown by Franco, sign up with what felt like every shipping line agency between the Vieux Port and Corbière, call in on a dozen or so freighters moored along the wharves' inner basins, and note down the registration details of the blue Seat parked outside Ribero Agence Maritime. Hardly an Olympic performance, he decided. If it hadn't been for his meeting with Salette – and the old man's assertion that at this time of year and in this kind of weather the marinas were an unlikely bet, but that he'd call up some old friends, put the word out – Jacquot would have ranked his first day an exercise in futility. But you had to start somewhere, he thought, and then remembered Madame Bonnefoy saying the same thing. It was just like every other investigation he'd ever been involved in. You started with so little but, gradually, things came into focus, began to make sense, take shape. It was like building a wall. You started with one small brick, and then you added another and another. It was the way these things went. You carried on. You built the wall.

Right now, as Salette had observed, a merchant vessel seemed the likeliest bet, and both men knew that the dockers' strike was the one advantage Jacquot had. If it hadn't been for the strike, someone could have put Elodie on a ship and sailed her out of there before he'd done up his laces that morning. But while the strike was on, there was still a chance of finding her somewhere. He had maybe another forty-eight hours before the dockers' demands were met or they simply gave up and went back to work.

Pushing through the hostel's front door, Jacquot clomped down the hallway and headed for the payphone at the bottom of the stairs. Beyond the reception desk he could see Madame Boileau's shadow on the other side of the frosted glass door that led to her private quarters. When Madame Bonnefoy came on the line he turned his back on the desk and brought her up to date, putting as positive a spin on it as he could – his work along the wharves, signing up with the shipping agents, and how his friend Salette had promised to keep his eyes and ears open on their behalf.

'There's not much that happens in these ports without Jean-Pierre getting to hear of it,' explained Jacquot. 'His network is . . . *formidable*. He also suggested that the nineteen freighters laid up on the quays waiting for loading and unloading be thoroughly searched before being allowed to leave port. It would give us a little more time.'

'And be hell to implement,' said Madame Bonnefoy. 'As you well know, Daniel.'

She was right. He did know. Apart from ships being notoriously difficult to search, every shipping line involved would be threatening law suits before they set foot on a companionway. He was clutching at straws, he knew it. He just needed more time.

'Tell me about this shipping agent you mentioned. The Spanish one. Could he be involved, this Ribero?' asked Madame Bonnefoy hopefully.

'There was just something, madame. I can't explain it. A feeling that there was more to him, more to his operation. Who knows? But if you can find me an address, or any kind of record, then we move to the next step.'

It was then, after Madame Bonnefoy promised to get everything

162

she could on this Ribero, that Jacquot made his request for a more convincing log to explain away his tan.

'How stupid of me,' she said. 'I didn't think . . .' She was clearly upset by her mistake, immediately concerned and contrite – as though she had let the side down. He could hear the irritation in her voice. '*Quelle stupide! Je suis ... . stupide.*'

The call ended with Madame Bonnefoy promising to get hold of new, more plausible papers, and making a request of her own: 'And do please call me Solange,' she told him. 'Madame Bonnefoy sounds so stiff and severe.'

With promises to get back to each other the moment either of them had something to report, they ended the call.

Turning to replace the phone on the hook, Jacquot was startled to see Madame Boileau leaning against the counter. Quite a performer in her time, Salette had told him. Looking at her now, Jacquot was hard pressed to see it. There was a harshness about her face which had set in deep grim lines. But he detected an under-current of gentleness, too, in her old grey eyes.

'With everyone checking out, there are rooms free, Monsieur Muller. If you want to have one of your own. Same rate,' she told him.

He shook his head. He was quite happy staying in the dormi-tory, he told her, heading for the stairs.

But she wasn't finished with him. 'Any luck at the docks?'

'Not today, but maybe tomorrow,' he replied, his foot on the first step, hand on the rope banister.

She shrugged her shoulders, spread her arms. '*Les docks. C'est autre monde, n'est-ce pas*? It is different from the real world, *non*? All on its own. People come, people go . . .' She shot him a look. 'Is this your first time in Marseilles?'

There was something in the way she framed the question – so light and conversational – that it brought Jacquot up short. Had she seen through him too? What was it Salette had said about sniffing out bullshit?

'Two or three times,' he replied. 'Why do you ask?'

'On the phone just then, your French was good. Not many low-landers have that Marseilles tone. I thought you must have spent some time here, *ça, c'est tout*.' And she smiled archly.

Up in the dormitory – every bed stripped down to its bare mattress save his – Jacquot was still kicking himself. First Franco seeing through him, and now letting his cover slip in front of Madame Boileau. If she'd seen his log she'd probably have said something about the tan as well. As he tugged off his rain-soaked clothes in the empty dormitory, he wondered how much she had overheard? Had he mentioned any names during the phone call: Salette? Madame Bonnefoy? Elodie? Had he given anything away? He couldn't for the life of him remember now, but acknowledged that if he was going to get anywhere in this investigation he'd have to play a smarter game than he had done so far. The next time he called Solange Bonnefoy, he'd find another phone, or keep up his low-lander accent if Madame Boileau was within earshot. It had been a careless slip, and he should have known better. Going undercover, he decided, as he reached for a towel and headed for the showers, might be a good way to track down a missing girl, but keeping up that cover was a great deal harder than he had imagined.

40

MARIE-ANGE SAT IN HER car on the corner of Impasse Massalia, listening to the rain bounce off the canvas roof, keeping an eye on her wing and rear-view mirrors, waiting for the mysterious Monsieur Muller to make an appearance. She didn't know for sure whether he was still staying at Auberge des Vagues, or whether he had moved on. But so far, the prospect of facing that concierge again, to find out one way or the other, had put Marie-Ange off a return visit. Later, she would do that later, if he hadn't shown up in – she glanced at her watch – another hour.

After her lunch with Pascale at Bernard's and seeing that story in the newspaper, Marie-Ange had spent the entire afternoon in a haze of uncertainty and indecision. There was no doubt in her mind that the hairclip in her pocket belonged to the missing girl from Paris, Elodie Lafour. And she was equally certain that Elodie Lafour had been in that lorry park when Lucienne Viviers made her escape.

That she was still alive.

And somewhere close by.

But what to do about it?

By the time she'd rolled down the metal blind at Fleurs des Quais, Marie-Ange had decided there were two options open to her. Either she should go immediately to the police and show them the hairclip – and the matching hairband in the newspaper photo

– and tell them where she had found it. Or she should keep the clip and use it to find Elodie herself.

Of course, if she went to the police, she'd have to decide whether or not to let them know about her dreams, her 'moments'. The slim possibility that these disclosures might add weight to her evidence was heavily undermined by the fact that the police might attach even less importance to the hairclip because of them. Over the years, Marie-Ange had learned that policemen were somehow hot-wired to dismiss anything . . . psychic. They simply couldn't accept it. She might be able to offer references – the detectives in Metz and the Luberon whom she had 'helped' in the past – but she knew she was just as likely to be shown the nearest door.

Marie-Ange also knew that even if they did believe her – and in her experience it was a very big 'if' – there was still a proce-dure to be followed, a bureaucratic by-the-book protocol: questions would be asked, statements would be taken, endless hours sitting at a table saying the same thing over and over again to different people. It didn't happen like it happened on TV. When you dealt with the real police, things took their own sweet time. And time, she was certain, was in short supply.

Most of the afternoon, too, she had tried to come up with some plausible explanation for Elodie Lafour and Lucienne Viviers actu-ally being in that lorry park in the first place, trying to think what could have caused Lucienne to run, and Elodie to drop or throw or lose her hairclip – or have it torn from her head during some dreadful, deadly attack.

And both girls from Paris, reported missing within days of each other. Had they been friends? Had they planned something together? Were they running away? Or had they been kidnapped? Two of them? At the same time? And why had the *flics* not connected the girls as she had done? Surely they could put two and two together – Lucienne and Elodie both reported missing in Paris in the same week, then Lucienne run over by a car on Boulevard Cambrai. Then again, maybe not.

Which was why, by the time she arrived home, Marie-Ange had

decided to go her own way for now. And if she hadn't got anywhere by this time tomorrow, well, that's when she would go to the police and show the clip and tell her story.

In the meantime, there was this Jan Muller to check out on Impasse Massalia, as good a place as any, she'd decided, to start her evening's wandering. This man she'd just glimpsed the night before. From Rotterdam.

Something about him. Something familiar.

But who was he?

Did she know him?

Did he have something to do with the missing girls?

She was so lost in her thoughts that she didn't see the man until he brushed past her wing-mirror. The sound, the snapping contact, made her start. For a moment she couldn't think what had happened, and then she saw the bent mirror and a figure hurrying on through the rain, the man from the night before, she was sure of it – the stooped shoulders, hands plunged in pockets – striding away from her. It was him, Jan Muller. She was certain.

Pushing open the car door, Marie-Ange stepped out into the rain, opened up her umbrella and started after him. He was a fast walker, she thought. Half-walking, half-running, she tried to catch him up, now a good fifteen metres ahead, turning into rue Pythéas and rapidly increasing his lead.

She gave up the half-and-half pace and started jogging, cutting down his lead.

'Monsieur,' she called out when she judged herself close enough to be heard over the rain. 'Monsieur? Monsieur?'

But still he hurried on, as though he hadn't heard her.

'Monsieur Muller,' she called now, louder this time.

Without thinking, close enough now, she reached out to grab his sleeve.

41

GLOWING WITH WARMTH AFTER A piping hot shower, and dressed in dry clothes, Jacquot set out from the hostel, pulling up his collar, digging his hands into the pockets of his jacket and hunching his shoulders against the rain. His day wasn't over yet. There were a couple of bars he'd spotted on his travels that looked like good places to hang out and pick up the gossip. He was heading in their direction when he heard a voice call out.

'Monsieur?'

It was a woman's voice, and for a moment he thought it might be Madame Boileau coming after him. But this voice was not hers, altogether more gentle, tentative. He decided to walk on, as though he hadn't heard anything over the pelting of the rain, or didn't realise that he was the 'Monsieur' being addressed. He was just a sailor, didn't know anyone, just waiting for the strike to end before taking a ship somewhere.

But it didn't work. The voice came again, more persistent this time – 'Monsieur? Monsieur?' – and he could hear footsteps, a younger woman's lighter, quicker footsteps coming up behind him.

And then the voice came a third time, breathless, uncertain, spoken at the very moment that a hand closed on his arm.

'Monsieur Muller?'

Reluctantly, he turned. A woman. A familiar face under the brim of an umbrella.

There was a moment's confusion and then a slow, dawning recognition. For both of them. In the shadowy darkness, with rain spitting down between them, Marie-Ange Buhl and Daniel Jacquot looked at each other.

And then, almost together, with Jacquot just a fraction slower, they said, 'You.'

Marie-Ange started to laugh, the rim of her umbrella dipping down to cover her face, rain spilling off its taut black slopes.

'I knew . . .' she began, tipping the umbrella back over her shoulder, gripping its handle with both hands as though for support. 'I knew there was something . . .'

'It's been a long time, Mademoiselle . . . Buhl,' replied Jacquot, the surname slipping in from somewhere, the Christian name just out of reach, as he remembered his investigations in St Bédard the past summer. The two of them huddled over a table at Mazzelli's bar on the *place*. The Martner case, an innocent man accused, an innocent man arrested. Marie-Christine . . . No, Marie- . . . Marie- . . . Marie-Ange. That was it. Marie-Ange Buhl.

It was then, standing there in the rain, each of them wondering what came next, that they both thought the same thing.

What is he doing here?

What is she doing here?

Marie-Ange was first to break the silence. 'I saw you yesterday evening,' she said. 'I realised I knew you from somewhere.'

'Then you had the advantage of me, mademoiselle,' he replied, wondering where and when she might have seen him. He'd certainly not seen her. 'I'm so sorry. It took me a moment . . .'

'St Bédard,' she said, thinking he still needed help. 'The Fontaine des Fleurs. The Chaberts.'

'That's right, I remember now,' he replied, smiling, rain streaming down his face. He wiped it away with a hand. 'But what . . .?'

'What am I doing here? All dry under my umbrella, while you . . . Here, you take it. We can stand under it together.' She handed

169

it to him and he took it, raising it to cover his own head, but trying to keep it over hers too. It brought them closer, sheltering together under the drumming rain.

'There's a bar up ahead,' he began, for want of something to say. 'If you're . . .' He was going to add '*If you're not doing anything*', but realised how stupid it would sound. He remembered too, at the same moment, how unsettled she always made him feel. Not exactly uncomfortable, more . . .

'I have a car back there,' said Marie-Ange, pointing over her shoulder, the way they had come.

'The bar is closer . . . If that . . .?'

She shrugged. 'Then lead the way, Chief Inspector,' she said, and taking his umbrella elbow, drawing close to keep out of the rain, they hurried down the street, both grateful for the opportunity to gather themselves, covering any awkwardness with exclamations about the downpour, followed by the familiar dance of precedence under the narrow awning of Café-Bar Dantès, its door pushed open by Marie-Ange, held open by Jacquot, the umbrella shaken, and closed behind them.

They saw at once that every stool in the bar, every table and booth was taken, a low smoky haze hanging over the crowd and barely stirred by three ceilings fans. There were more men than women and a few curious looks settled on Marie-Ange and Jacquot as he led her across the room to the bar. He imagined they looked an unlikely pair – twenty years between them, surely? He in his thick canvas trousers, working boots and pea-jacket, his woollen hat and close-cropped hair; she with her shiny cap of black hair, just as he remembered it but a little longer now, her perfect oval face and finely-set features, her slim figure in belted leather jacket and black cotton jeans over heeled boots. Then he remembered where they were, a couple of streets away from the docks of Marseilles, and it struck him that they probably weren't that unlikely a couple – only most couples like them usually headed off for a room somewhere to complete their business. The thought brought an unexpected flush of heat to Jacquot's stubbled cheeks and he

170

was grateful now for his tan. It was just the same; she still somehow managed to rattle him.

As he scooped up a pair of glasses and a bottle of white wine from the bar, he felt her nudge him, heard her whisper '*Voilà*', and saw her head across the room as one of the booths was vacated. Jacquot followed, nodding thanks to the people leaving, squeezing into the banquette opposite her, pushing aside empty glasses and bottles, brimming ashtray, crumpled paper napkins, to place their own bottle and glasses.

'So,' he began, making himself comfortable on the warm red plastic, intending to take the initiative. But that single word was as far as he got.

'Muller? Monsieur Muller?' asked Marie-Ange. 'What happened to Jacquot, and the ponytail, and the poli—?'

He held up the bottle. 'Wine?'

She noted the swift interruption, looked around, and nodded.

He poured. Both glasses, hers first. As he did so, a waitress came to the table, set down a plate of olives and a basket of bread, and removed the remains of the last occupants.

Marie-Ange leaned forward. 'I'm sorry . . . I didn't mean . . . Are you working? Is that why you've cut your hair?'

And then she paused, knew what he was doing there.

The same thing as her.

Looking for Elodie.

It made her smile.

'*Santé*,' said Jacquot lifting his glass and tilting its edge against hers. The wine was tart and bitter, strangely astringent, but satisfyingly fresh. 'And you . . .? You live in Marseilles now?' he asked.

'Working. Like St Bédard. Another flower shop, off La Canebière.'

Suddenly knowing what he was doing there, prowling the streets in his clumsy disguise, gave her an edge and she played it, wondering how long it would take him to realise they were working on the same case. She took another sip of wine, and watched him.

Jacquot nodded and the two of them were silent for a moment.

171

He looked across at her, sipping her wine, her eyes catching his, her lips curving into a smile. A very beautiful girl. Or rather, woman.

'I came back to St Bédard after the arrests,' Jacquot began, 'but you had gone.'

'Job done,' she replied.

He couldn't decide whether she meant her stand-in job at the Fontaine des Fleurs, or the job of hunting down the killer of the German family.

'Monsieur and Madame Chabert were coming back from Lyons,' she continued. 'The trial was over. It was time to move on.'

'I wanted to say thank you. For the help . . .'

She smiled, sipped her wine again, waited.

'And after St Bédard, you came here?'

Marie-Ange nodded. She was starting to enjoy this. He still hadn't made the connection; he was still trying to work it all out. 'I'd never eaten a real bouillabaisse,' she said.

'So you travel the country in search of regional specialities?' said Jacquot with a smile.

'And sometimes in search of other things, Monsieur Muller,' she teased, keeping her eyes on him. She could see now that he was catching up, starting to put it all together, the last few pieces of the jigsaw. She decided to put him out of his misery. 'Elodie Lafour,' she said, and saw his expression change, a look of swift, stunned surprise, his face lighting up with sudden understanding.

'You know about her? You're . . .?'

'Looking for her, that's right. Like you. Because she's here, somewhere.'

Jacquot was careful with his words. 'You know that? Or you . . . feel it?'

'You should remember, Chief Inspector . . .'

He held up a warning hand. 'Daniel. Or rather – Jan.'

'Jan then, though you don't look like a Jan. But as I was saying, you should remember that with me the two are very much the same. Knowing and feeling.' And leaning forward, lowering her voice, she told him how she came to be there, sitting in the booth with him – the dreams she had had of Lucienne Viviers running down the street, the photo and the story in the newspaper about her death, tracing her back to the lorry park, the sense of threat and escape, of being chased . . .

'And Elodie?'

'They were together. Elodie was there too, I'm sure of it,' she said, reaching into her pocket and bringing out the hairclip. She passed it to Jacquot. 'I found it in the lorry park. Where it all happened. It's hers, Elodie's.'

Jacquot turned the clip in his fingers. 'It could belong to anyone . . .'

'It's hers,' said Marie-Ange, low and fierce. 'It's hers, believe me. She's here somewhere, and close by.' And she looked around the bar as though she might see Elodie sitting at a table.

Behind him, Jacquot felt a draft of chill air and heard the Bar Dantès's front door open and close.

Marie-Ange heard it too, and looked over his shoulder.

Her eyes narrowed, then widened, her lips parted as though to speak, and in an instant her face drained of colour.

42

'ARE YOU ALL RIGHT?' ASKED Jacquot, glancing over his shoulder to see what she had seen, what had startled her. A man had come in and was brushing the rain from his jacket. He waved to a friend at the bar and went over to join him, two friends meeting up for a drink. He was thick-set and swarthy, his face darkly stubbled, a black and white checkered *keffiyeh* scarf wound around his neck and tucked into the collar of his jacket.

Jacquot turned back to Marie-Ange. 'Do you know him?'

She leant forward, elbows out, almost cowering over the table. For a moment she looked frightened, as though the man might recognise her, drawn too close to danger and wanting to be clear of it.

'He was in my dream,' she whispered at last. 'I'm sure of it. The man chasing Lucienne . . . *Le même* . . .'

Before the affair in St Bédard, Jacquot would have been as doubtful, as sceptical, as the next man – at the blatant improbability of such a coincidence, this figure from a dream coming into the bar where they sat, greeting a friend, sitting down with him and falling into conversation. But Jacquot knew better now. He remembered the time they had spent together in the Luberon, and had experienced at first hand the strange gift this woman possessed.

'If it is him,' confided Marie-Ange, 'and I am sure it is, he will have a scar . . . like so.' She drew a finger in a slanting line down the side of her face.

'Stay here,' said Jacquot, shuffling himself along the banquette and getting to his feet. He pulled a ten-franc note from his pocket and crossed to the bar.

'Some change, boss?' he asked, proffering the note. 'For the cigarette machine.'

The barman took the money and turned to the till. As he rang it open and sorted through his change, Jacquot glanced over to the end of the bar where the two men were still deep in conversation. The one in the checkered scarf had his back to Jacquot, elbow on the bar. All Jacquot could see was his companion – blond hair cut short at the sides, a thin moustache, eyes that darted to left and right, even catching Jacquot's, lingering for a moment then moving on.

'*Voilà*,' said the barman, tipping a handful of coins into Jacquot's palm. 'The machine's in the corner, over there.' He nodded along the bar, towards the two men, and Jacquot saw the cigarette machine behind them, almost hidden beside a rack of coats. It was a lucky break; now he could go to the machine and, on his way back, get to see the other man's face.

Sorting through the coins, he made his way down the bar.

''*Scusez–moi*,' he said, sliding past the two of them. The one with the scarf leaned into the bar without looking at Jacquot, giving him just enough room to squeeze past. At the machine, he fed the coins into the slot, selected his brand and pulled out the drawer. In no rush, now directly behind the blond man, he turned back to the bar and slid the wrapping off his cigarette packet. Crumpling it up, he leaned over the bar and tossed it into a bin.

And there was the scar.

Just as Marie-Ange had described it.

An old scar, white, not pink and puckered as he had imagined, slanting through the dark stubble on the man's right cheek.

A chill passed through Jacquot.

'*Pardon, je m'excuse*,' he murmured, squeezing out past the two

175

men, giving Scarface a nod of thanks and a smile that was not returned.

As he headed back for their table, Jacquot felt a quiver of excitement. Earlier that evening, on his way back to the Auberge des Vagues, everything had seemed to conspire against him – his cover, his search, the seeming impossibility of the task he had taken on. Yet now, here, just a few hours later, things were suddenly slotting into place. You had to start somewhere. And soon enough the wall started to take shape.

Back at their table, Jacquot confirmed that the man did indeed have a scar on his cheek.

'I knew it. I knew it,' whispered Marie-Ange, as though this vindicated her. 'So what do we do now?'

'We wait and we watch,' said Jacquot.

43

XAVIER WAS IN NO MOOD for a chat or a beer. He wanted the meeting over and done with. It was going to be a busy night. There was a lot to do. He felt a hot, racing surge of adrenaline. Now was his chance, he thought. If Murat didn't want to join him, then tough shit. Things, he'd decided, were going to change.

But Petitjean, the dealer with the downers, had other ideas. Before Xavier could object, he had ordered a round of beers and was chattering away like a sparrow on speed. Xavier could see the carrier bag by the stool, its sides sharply angled by the boxes inside, knew the deal was done. But he still had to pay, still had to get hold of the goods and get out of there. And everything, it seemed, was conspiring to make him impatient and irritable: the line of coke he'd taken before coming out for the meet, the rain and getting soaked, the close fuggy atmosphere of Bar Dantès, the crush of regulars, the tinkly treble sound of the jukebox pumping out a bad selection of warped soul, and the endless, infuriating push and shove of people trying to get to the cigarette machine.

Finally he'd had enough. He downed his beer, pulled out the envelope that Murat had given him and slid it across the counter to Petitjean whose darting eyes latched on to it almost as greedily as his hands. The envelope was spirited away to God knows where and the bag unhooked from the toe of his boot and passed over.

It was done. Xavier was slapping Petitjean on the back, pulling his scarf round his neck and, finally, thankfully, pushing through the front door, out into the rain.

With every step he took, his determination increased. Murat was a pussy. He might have put together a reasonable business and honed the run, but he didn't have the balls to expand. Somehow, by chance, he'd picked up a girl who was clearly worth a bundle, but he refused to play her, didn't see the bigger picture, the opportunity. But Xavier did. And he knew it would be madness to let Elodie Lafour slip through their fingers. His fingers.

Since Xavier had spotted the story in the newspaper, and put two and two together, his brain had gone into overdrive. What would she be worth? he wondered. Ten, twenty, maybe even thirty million francs? The parents were clearly loaded and for sure would be only too happy to dish out some cash to get their precious little girl back. Either they'd put up a reward for information leading to her return, or Xavier would give them a call – spell it out for them.

But right now, he had to get the girl. If Murat wasn't going to play ball, he, Xavier, would have to play it for him. Once the girls were tranqued up, he'd move in and take her. And if Murat objected – which he was sure to do – well, maybe the time had come for the two of them to go their separate ways.

So preoccupied was Xavier with his planning that it was only as he turned into rue Jacobe and hurried towards the old abattoirs that he sensed someone behind him, maybe fifty metres back, following him. At the next block, waiting for a car to pass before crossing the wider rue Ginot, he glanced behind him, as though checking for other traffic, and saw a hunched figure coming after him, slowing down now. It was the slowing down that rang all the bells, something timed, something deliberate, pace matched to pace; the way the man dug his hands into the pockets of his pea-jacket, kept his head down, rolled his shoulders against the rain.

It was the pea-jacket that Xavier suddenly placed.

The man at the cigarette machine. Back in Bar Dantès.

Cop. No question, thought Xavier, increasing his pace. Probably someone from narcotics working that piss-artist Petitjean. And here he was with enough class-A to see him banged up in Baumettes when the world was just about to become his oyster. It was then, with a lurch in his guts, that another possibility struck him – that whoever it was might be looking for the missing girls. If that was the case, then they'd worked fast. As Xavier quickened his step, he tried to think how the cops could have come so close, so soon. It wasn't possible, not that quickly, he decided.

But just thinking it made him realise how little time he had to get things organised. If he was going to take the Lafour girl, he'd have to move fast.

And get rid of the *flic* on his tail.

If he'd been anywhere but rue Jacobe and these ill-lit side-streets he'd have waved down a cab and got the hell out of there, left the cop well behind. But few cabs came to this part of the city. He'd have to wait for the rue de Lyon before that became any kind of option.

And with a bag-full of tranqs in his possession . . .

There was only one thing for it.

44

JUST AS JACQUOT HAD SAID, he and Marie-Ange waited and watched. With his back to the two men, Jacquot relied on her for a commentary.

'He's just passed something to the blond man,' she told him. 'And now Blondie's giving him a carrier bag. He's getting up. They're both going. They're at the door. They're shaking hands . . .'

Jacquot pulled out some money and slid the notes under the ashtray. By the time he and Marie-Ange reached the door, the two men had parted.

'You follow Blondie, I'll take Scarface,' said Jacquot. 'We'll meet back at your car. If I'm not there, wait for me. I'll do the same. It's the Citroen, right? The Deux Chevaux?'

Marie-Ange told him it was. 'Take care,' she called after him, and he waved a hand back at her. Thirty metres ahead, she saw Scarface pass the turning for the hostel and head on towards rue Jacobe with Jacquot following. Opening up her umbrella, she turned to the right and followed Blondie down rue Pythéas.

As Marie-Ange hurried after him, careful not to get too close, she wondered at meeting Jacquot again and acknowledged that his unexpected appearance had given her a lift. And after working with him on the Martner case, she knew she wouldn't have to go through the testing rigmarole of persuading a *flic* that her powers were real, that she could provide a failing investigation with the impetus it needed. But there was also Jacquot himself, the man. He may have been a good bit older than her, but she felt a strong attraction to him. She seemed to recall he had a wife or girlfriend, though. She tried to remember, sifting through her memories. But then, up ahead, she saw Blondie cross the road and registered a change in the man's pace. There was a line of cars parked on the far side of the street and as he crossed the road she saw him reach into his pocket and pull out a set of keys. A moment later he was getting into an old Audi. Its lights were switched on and the engine revved. With a few swift turns of the wheel he was out of the space and driving away, with Marie-Ange just close enough to get the registration. Repeating it over and over, she searched through her pockets for a pen and paper, found them and scribbled the number down.

By the time she got back to her car, there was no sign of Jacquot so she opened it up and sat behind the wheel. He'd be back, he'd said. She should wait for him there, he'd told her. But the longer she sat there, rain pelting down, the more uncertain and anxious she became. She looked at her watch. Just twenty minutes had passed since they'd split up at Bar Dantès. Something was wrong. She was sure of it.

Something was wrong.

45

WHOEVER HE WAS AND WHEREVER he was going, Scarface was in a hurry. For three blocks he stayed on rue Jacobe, heading in the general direction of the old abbattoirs, with Jacquot holding position a good fifty metres back. Occasionally a car passed, its lights glittering through the slanting rain, but otherwise the street was deserted.

Did Scarface have a car? Jacquot wondered. If he did, it seemed strange that he should have parked so far from the bar, especially in weather like this. And what was in the carrier bag? Jacquot had seen his fair share of drug deals go down and this had looked as good an example as any. An anonymous bar, a casual meeting, the swift, discreet exchange, the parting of the ways. And if there were drugs in that bag, what kind would they be? Whatever he was carrying, it was no small amount, the carrier bag swinging heavily in the man's hand, bumping rhythmically against his leg. And where was he headed with them? Somewhere within walking distance? Or was he looking out for a cab, or heading for the nearest bus stop or Metro? With a bag of drugs, the latter looked unlikely. But if he found himself a cab, the game would be up, the quarry lost.

As he walked, Jacquot couldn't help but feel a sense of elation. In just a few short hours everything had suddenly turned around. He was actually doing something, following a man Marie-Ange had pointed out to him, a man she believed had something to do with Elodie Lafour. And Jacquot knew enough about Marie-Ange's 'feelings' to take them seriously.

Up ahead, on the corner of rue Ginot, Scarface paused to look left and right before crossing the road. Traffic was light in these side streets and the precaution seemed strange. Jacquot wondered whether the man suspected he was being followed, but there was still a reasonable distance between them and Jacquot had made no move to cross the street after him, keeping to his side, staying parallel and now only fifteen metres back. It was then, having crossed the road, that Scarface suddenly darted around a corner. One minute he was there, the next he had vanished.

Jacquot realised that he'd been made, and the prospect of losing his quarry overtook what should have been a professional duty of care, a cop's instinctive sense of caution. Instead, Jacquot picked up his pace and jogged across the road, breaking into a run as he came to the corner and turned it.

The first thing he realised was that the road ahead was empty.

No one there.

No sign of Scarface.

Either he'd reached his destination and had gone into one of the houses . . .

Or . . .

Jacquot knew at once it was too late to do anything, his neck actually presented for the blow as he hurried past, shoulders hunched, head down.

No chance to protect himself, beyond the slightest, reflexive feint away from the shadow which suddenly flashed out from a doorway and . . .

46

THE PAIN IN THE BACK of Jacquot's head was gigantic, a great throbbing ache that seemed to pulse outwards in rolling waves of blackness, gathering at a point directly between his eyes. It felt as though his skull had been split open, like one of the logs he'd been chopping back at the millhouse. Opened up from the back of his neck to the crown of his head. It hurt even to breathe.

Carefully, he opened his eyes, squinting, and took stock. He was lying on a bed, in a small room, the wall in front of him papered with flowers, the walls to either side just plain plaster, painted a light orange colour, blistered here and there, darkened in places by damp. He knew at once that this was Marie-Ange's room, and Marie-Ange's bed.

The moment he realised where he was, the rest came flooding back. Hurrying round that corner to catch up with Scarface, so carelessly off his guard. And then that numbing, crashing thump to the back of his head. It was a long time since anyone had put Jacquot down and he'd forgotten just how painful it could be. In the movies, on TV, they shook their heads, rubbed their necks and got on with it, as though nothing had happened. In real life it was different.

Of course, he was lucky. In that part of town it could as easily have been a knife. And he'd walked, or rather run, right into it.

184

He remembered seeing Scarface turn off rue Jacobe and had put on a spurt of speed so as not to lose him. He'd come round the corner, looked ahead, seen nothing, and then . . . a shadow in the doorway, that blinding blow . . . and he was on the ground . . . distantly aware of his pockets being rifled, a kick in the ribs, then the sound of footsteps hurrying off.

He couldn't say how long it was before Marie-Ange was there, shaking him awake on the pavement, trying to lift him into her car, driving him to her apartment. The trundling of tyres over cobbles, the spooling glow of passing streetlights, the bucketing turns, the gear-changing straights, that coughing, screeching two-horse engine.

There was a gentle knock at the door, and it opened slowly, a shaft of yellow light slanting across the painted wall. It was Marie-Ange.

'How are you feeling?' she asked, setting down a bowl of water on the bedside table, squeezing out a flannel. 'You've got some colour back, thank goodness. For a while there, I thought I should just drive you straight to the hospital despite your telling me not to.'

'I'm glad you did as you were told,' whispered Jacquot, each word hammering at the back of his eyes. 'Jesus, it hurts.'

'It's a nasty bump. Here,' she said, folding the flannel into a band and placing it gently on his forehead. He closed his eyes at its coolness and felt the side of the bed sag as she sat down beside him. 'There was no bleeding, just a terrible lump. I put on arnica and some Tiger Balm. It was all I could find.'

'How did you get me here? By yourself?'

'You weren't a dead weight. You managed to stand. Getting you into the car was the hardest. Once I was here, I got Monsieur Bardot at the bakery to help me up with you. I said you were my uncle, that you'd had too much to drink. I'm not sure he believed me.' Marie-Ange gave a gentle laugh. 'You've ruined my reputation.'

'I'm glad it wasn't you.'

'So am I.' She leaned forward, turned the flannel. 'Was it Scarface?'

185

'Had to be. There was no one else around. He must have spotted me following him. I'm sorry I lost him.'

'Don't worry. We can find him.'

Jacquot frowned. Even that small movement brought a swell of pain. 'How?' he managed. 'How can we find him?'

'His friend . . . Blondie? I took his car registration.'

The realisation that they were still in with a chance was a blessing. He asked Marie-Ange if she had a phone and, when she brought it to the bedroom, had her dial Solange Bonnefoy's number. Taking the receiver from her, he listened to the ring tone, first at Madame Bonnefoy's office and then at her home, leaving the same message. He kept it brief.

'It's Muller here. I have another car number for you to check. French plates . . .' He took the scrap of paper Marie-Ange handed him and read it out. 'You can reach me at the hostel . . .'

'You're not going anywhere,' whispered Marie-Ange, 'give her my number,' and told it to him.

Jacquot repeated the number then broke the connection. As he handed her the phone he remembered something: hands tugging at his pockets. 'Was anything taken?' he asked. 'Was I robbed?'

'Your wallet and papers were beside you on the pavement. There was still money in your wallet, and some coins lying round on the pavement. Which means, Monsieur Muller, that if he wasn't after your money, if it wasn't just a mugging, then he wanted to stop you following him. Which means he must have something to do with Elodie.'

But Jacquot wasn't listening.

'Nothing else? You didn't find anything else?'

Marie-Ange frowned, shook her head.

'Then he's got my gun,' said Jacquot, and with a grunt of pain he levered himself off the pillow, feeling for the first time the bruising ache in his side where the man's boot had connected with his ribs. 'I've got to . . .'

'You've got to do nothing, monsieur. So . . . the gun is gone. There is nothing you can do about it now.' She gave him a look. 'Well? I'm right, aren't I?'

Jacquot would have nodded if he'd been able to. Instead, realising that what she had said made absolute sense, he eased himself back down on the pillows. 'Yes, you're right.'

'And you are staying right here,' she said, leaning forward to plump the pillows gently. 'I've already made up the sofa. If I'm gone when you wake up, just help yourself to some breakfast. But right now you need rest. Even if I do want to stay up all night and talk about it.' She smiled down at him. 'But I'm glad we've met up.'

'So am I,' said Jacquot, surprising himself. 'So am I.'

And he smiled, closing his eyes.

Saturday
14 November

47

ELODIE COULDN'T REMEMBER FALLING ASLEEP, but
suddenly she was waking up again. Stiff and aching, but somehow
not as dulled and disoriented as she had been. Lying there, she
tried to remember what had happened, tried to take stock.

She was in a cellar, on a thin mattress, on an earth floor; it was
still dark and it was still raining. And she was not alone.

That much she knew in a matter of seconds.

The next thing she focused on were her clothes. What she was
wearing. Jeans, T-shirt, socks, her favourite woollen jacket. She
was dressed, but not properly dressed. There were clothes missing,
she realised. Clothes she no longer had. Her Converse sneakers –
gone; her leopard print rucksack – gone; the belt from her jacket
– gone; and the cashmere scarf she'd taken from her mother's
dressing room – also gone.

She remembered her mother's dressing room. Suddenly. Stealing
in there for the scarf. She could see herself pulling out the drawer,
sliding out the scarf, winding it round her neck.

And then everything came back to her very quickly. In a rush.

Leaving the apartment, hurrying down rue Camille, waiting at a
café table, waiting for . . . Murat.

Murat.

The name came to her like a bright, blinding light.

191

Murat. Murat. Murat.

But the light didn't last long. It darkened. And Murat, her Murat, the man of her dreams, darkened with it. No longer the Murat she met for coffees and *menthes frappées* . . . the Murat who took her for walks in the park, the Murat who had held her hand in the cinema, who had kissed her there, for the first time. In the cinema's warm, velvet darkness. Across the arm-rest. A proper kiss.

Not that Murat.

That Murat, Elodie now realised, was gone.

And though she might not have been quite able to credit it at first, though it squeezed her heart to think it, it didn't take long for the truth to settle in.

Murat didn't love her.

Had never loved her.

Everything he'd ever said to her had been a lie.

He'd just used her. Betrayed her.

Murat. Murat.

With surprising clarity now, Elodie remembered the last time they'd been together, the journey from Paris to wherever she was now. South certainly, that's how they'd left the city. Rattling along the Autoroute du Soleil: Fontainebleau, Auxerre, Chalons, the tunnel lights in the hills above Lyons. Heading for Nice, that's what Murat had told her. They would spend a week in Nice – he had some business to attend to there – and then they'd cross the border into Italy. A holiday . . . Just the two of them . . . There was a place he knew . . . She could call her mother from there, she remembered him telling her.

But the further they travelled, the quieter he had become. Increasingly moody, impatient with her . . .

She was sure she must have said something to upset him, but the more she tried to cheer him up, the more distant he became. Maybe a grunt in response, that was all, the countryside sliding by, darkness gathering, headlights coming north, flicking past them, tail-lights curving south like a long red serpent.

Until . . .

It was night-time, she remembered – Saturday night, however long ago that was. And she was hungry. They'd parked up in a motorway service station north of Lyons, before the tunnels. He'd taken her to the rest-rooms, then gone to buy baguettes, an Orangina for her and a Red Bull for him. He was waiting for her when she came out of the rest-room, took her back to the van and they drove on, eating the baguettes, drinking . . .

And that was all she could remember. Headlights, tail-lights and a smothering darkness settling around her – more immediate, more powerful, than sleep.

She'd been drugged. She'd been kidnapped. There was no other possible explanation.

Kidnap. Hostage. Ransom.

The words slid into her head and made themselves comfortable.

Murat had targeted her, seduced her, then trapped her. And right now, he'd be making his demands. So much money and you can have your daughter back.

Because Murat must have known that her mother and step-father were rich, that they would pay, that they could afford whatever he asked. And Murat would have known it, she now realised, because he'd made it his business to find out. And she had told him. Either directly – where the family went on holiday, the cars they drove, the chauffeur for her step-father. Or indirectly – her clothes, her manners, her accent, the private school where he sometimes came to meet her after class.

And if he was making ransom demands, he had clearly found out where she lived. She might always have met up with him in a museum or a gallery or at a café, never at her home on rue Camille, but it would have been easy enough for him to follow her after one of their dates.

Thinking of home made her think of her mother. And thinking of her mother made Elodie sob out loud.

Oh, Maman, Maman . . .

But then another thought lodged in her head. Something that stopped the tears and the sobbing.

193

Maybe there was no ransom.

Maybe Murat didn't know she was rich, or if he did he didn't care.

Maybe there was some other reason he had taken her.

Maybe he had something else in mind?

He was Arab, she knew that. From a wealthy family in Saudi Arabia, he'd told her. Not that she could believe that any more. So perhaps he was going to sell her – turn her into a white slave? She'd read the stories in the newspapers, seen the documentaries on TV.

Which might explain why she was not alone down here in the cellar.

She pushed herself up on one elbow and looked around. Five or maybe six shapes around her. Softly snoring. Whimpering. Restless. Starting to move about.

Were they girls like her? Other girls Murat had seduced and trapped?

But there was no time to give it any more thought.

Somewhere above her, Elodie heard knocking. A distant rat-a-tat.

Then stockinged feet shuffling along what must have been a hallway, the sound of locks being turned, of bolts being pulled back, a door opening, voices. Bolts and locks again, more footfalls passing directly overhead.

Straining her ears, Elodie tried to make out what was being said. But the voices were muffled. All she could say was that, judging by the tone of the voices, there was some kind of argument going on.

But she wasn't prepared for what came next.

48

IT WAS PAST MIDNIGHT WHEN Xavier got to Murat Santarem's place.

'You've taken your time,' said Santarem, opening the front door just a fraction, looking up and down the street as Xavier slipped past him. 'You get the sleepers?' he asked, bolting the door.

'I got 'em,' said Xavier, going ahead of him, down the hall to the kitchen.

'Go quietly, the old lady's just gone to bed,' whispered Santarem, shuffling after him.

In the kitchen, Xavier had the carrier bag on the table and was tipping out the various packets.

'They still quiet?' he asked, nodding to the floor and the basement beneath.

'One or two are beginning to stir.'

'They eaten yet?'

Santarem shook his head. 'I was hanging on for you. We need to get things going.' He tore open one of the boxes and emptied the contents – maybe twenty blue pills – into a mortar. 'Here,' he said, handing Xavier the stone pestle. 'Get crushing. Maman left a stew – we can use that.'

Xavier made no move to take the pestle. He just looked at it.

'Here,' repeated Murat, pushing the pestle against his arm. 'Take it. Get moving, or they'll be up here asking to call their mothers.'

'*You* get moving,' replied Xavier, pulling out a chair and sitting down. 'But I'm out of here. With that girl. If you don't want to go that route, cashing in on her, fine. But I do. And I'm taking her with me.'

Santarem's shoulders slumped, then seemed to straighten. 'Are you fucking with me?'

'Yeah, I am,' replied Xavier, playing the end of his *keffiyeh* through his fingers but keeping his eyes on Santarem.

Santarem was quick as a striking snake. But Xavier was quicker. As Santarem swung back the stone pestle and hurled it at Xavier with all his strength, he ducked to the right and the spinning pestle took a piece out of the wall behind him. When he sat up, he had Jacquot's gun in his hand.

The sight of the gun stopped Santarem in his tracks.

'Where the fuck did you get that?' he asked, stunned by the appearance of the weapon. 'You gotta be kidding me?'

Xavier shook his head. 'You had your chance.'

Santarem spread his hands, gave a big shrug, his eyes flicking between Xavier and the gun. 'Hey,' he said. 'Whoa there!' He chuckled a little.

Xavier saw the change in him. Suddenly the hardness had gone. This was not the man who had thrown the pestle. The gun saw to that.

Santarem pulled out a chair and settled himself at the kitchen table. Time to talk now, to negotiate. He could handle that. 'So, we do it your way,' he said, with an easy smile. 'Hey, no problem.'

Xavier gave it some thought. Even lowered the gun.

Santarem saw the move and relaxed.

'You know what?' Xavier smiled at him. 'I don't think so.'

Reaching across the table, he buried the snout of Jacquot's Beretta against Santarem's chest and pulled the trigger. The sound of the gunshot may have been muffled but it still filled the room.

Santarem rocked back in his chair from the force of the shot, but his knees, catching under the table, brought him tipping back, his face smacking down on to the plastic cloth.

As the echo died away, a voice called from above, 'Murat? My boy? Is that you?'

49

THE CORSICAN BROTHERS, TADDEUS THE elder, and Tomas, had had a busy night. After taking care of the bound girl in Virginie's bedroom – asleep when they entered, but awake soon enough, her eyes wide as they set about her, teeth chewing the gag, limbs thrashing uselessly against the restraints – the two of them had dumped her body down a manhole in a side-street off République then driven over to Valentine's workshop in the Fifteenth. Forcing the lock on the metal grille, they'd searched the *garagiste*'s office by torchlight, and found what they were looking for, just as Gastal had done before them, in Valentine's desk diary and Rolodex. Half-an hour later, they parked outside Alam Haggar's home on place Lapeyre and waited.

At a little after eight o'clock, dressed in jeans, trainers and hoodie, Alam jogged down the steps of his apartment block. He was swinging his leg over a Vespa, rocking it off its stand, when Tomas came up behind him and tapped him on the shoulder. When Alam turned and saw the man who not two days before had pressed the barrel of a gun against his testicles, the same man who had probably done for his boss Valentine, his face turned white and he tried to kick the scooter away from him and make a run for it. But Tomas was too fast. He sidestepped the tumbling scooter, caught the sleeve of Alam's hoodie and brought him up short.

'Hey, hey, hey. *N'inquiète pas*. Don't fret,' Tomas had said, and smiled encouragingly. '*Tiens, tiens*. Hold on,' he continued as the lad struggled to pull free. 'We need your help, that's all. And it'll be worth your while, I promise. More than before, hunh? What do you say?'

The soft tone was persuasive. Alam eased up, relaxed. He wasn't going anywhere, and he knew it.

'Come on then. It's cool. No problems. Just some help is all. We need some muscle. A couple of hours, no more,' said Tomas, even letting go of Alam's sleeve and bending down to pick up the scooter, set it back on its stand. 'And afterwards, when the job's done, we can drop you wherever you need to be. How's that? Limo service,' he said, nodding towards the black Volkswagen where Taddeus sat at the wheel. When Alam looked in his direction, Taddeus nodded, smiled, raised a hand from the steering wheel.

If the lad had still wanted to run, it should have been then. His last chance. That was the moment for it. And he'd have made it; he'd have got away and lived to tell the tale. But he didn't. As Tomas had judged correctly, the gentle approach, the winning words, the promise of money, even stooping to pick up the scooter, had convinced their target there was nothing to fear.

'Yeah. Okay, I guess. What's the job?' the lad had asked.

Again the friendly, confiding tone. 'Just a small job, won't take more than a couple of hours, less if we're lucky. But we'll need to pick up your chum. We'll need the two of you,' said Tomas.

Five minutes later, Taddeus was driving them up rue Saint Pierre, Tomas in the front passenger seat, Alam behind – free to jump from the car if he felt like it. But the thought never occurred; he didn't think about it, not at any of the stops they made at traffic lights and intersections, passing up the western edge of the Saint Pierre cemetery or looping down beneath the A50 autoroute before heading up into Saint Loup where Ibin still lived with his parents. Nor, at any point, did Alam pause to wonder how the two men knew where he lived.

When they got to Ibin's, they made Alam get out and ring the doorbell, the two of them staying in the car. Ten metres ahead they watched an older woman open the door – Ibin's mother – and then the other boy dodged past her, shouting something back at her as he waltzed Alam away from the door, out into the rain, and back up the street towards the Volkswagen. That was when Alam pointed out the Corsicans. At first Ibin had taken one look and, like Alam, turned to make a run for it. But, like Tomas, Alam had held him back, whispered in his ear.

A moment later, a suspicious scowl on his face, Ibin was sitting beside his friend in the back seat, Taddeus was pulling out into traffic and Tomas was sliding a cassette into the player. As they headed south, down through Pont-de-Vivaux and Capelette towards Prado, with Ella Fitzgerald crooning her way through 'Summertime', 'Manhattan' and 'Blue Moon', Tomas explained what they wanted. They were headed for their workshop, he told the boys. He needed them to keep watch while he and his brother loaded up some stuff. By the time they reached their destination, a narrow unlit *impasse* one street back from the rocky waterfront of Maldormé, the two boys were up for anything.

As they got out of the car, Tomas pointed to the end of the alleyway. 'We need one of you there,' he said, 'and one of you down there. If you see anyone coming, just radio it in. Here, come on into the workshop and I'll get you kitted up with the walkie-talkies.'

And that was it. As they stepped into the brothers' workshop, relishing the prospect of walkie-talkies and some well-paid adventure they could crow about to their friends, bending under a metal grille much the same as the one at Valentine's garage, they were as good as dead. Five minutes after that grille was back in place, Taddeus had Ibin tied to a chair, while Tomas set to work on Alam.

Ibin didn't see a thing after Tomas broke his friend's leg. He squeezed his eyes shut and prayed, grunting in terrified alarm when he heard Alam's second leg get broken, and then both arms.

After that, Taddeus took over and it was Ibin's turn.

By the time the Corsicans got to L'Estaque, it was after midnight. They cruised past Marcel Lévy's chandlery store and twenty metres further on they parked their car and walked back up the slope. All the lights were off in Marin Azur's interior and the place was locked up for the night. In less than thirty seconds, Taddeus had the door open and both men were inside. In the back office, Taddeus switched on the light, rifled through the desk drawers and found what he was looking for. Holding up Lévy's business card, he lifted the phone and dialled his home number.

When Lévy came on the line, Taddeus introduced himself as Inspector Monque of the local gendarmerie. He apologised for the lateness of the hour but went on to explain that there had been a break-in at Marin Azur, and could Monsieur Lévy please come down to the shop?

Twenty minutes later, Lévy arrived to find Taddeus standing by the counter. He knew in an instant that this was no Inspector Monque and realised equally swiftly who it really was.

The Spaniard had fucked him. That fucking Dago had fucked him over!

When he turned to run, Tomas stepped out from between a rack of roping and stood in his path. One hour later, they dropped Lévy's body behind a stand of recycling bins on rue Bandini, just as they'd done with Alam and Ibin on the Corniche road out past Fausse Monnaie.

Acting on information supplied to them by the recently deceased Monsieur Marcel Lévy, the two brothers then returned to their car, drove down to the promenade and turned left, back towards town, cutting off the Littoral at La Joliette and winding up into Saint Mauront, cruising past Murat Santarem's house and peering through the slow intermittent drizzle at its curtained windows. There were no lights on and the house was far enough away from the nearest streetlight to guard its secrets – a black, shadowy façade, two floors, a low pitched roof, an attached garage, and what looked like a basement beneath the steps leading up to the front door.

Thirty metres on, around a corner, Taddeus parked their car. Opening umbrellas, they made their way back to the house. Without breaking stride, they pushed open the gate, walked up the path and jogged up the front steps.

50

INSIDE THE HOUSE, MURAT'S MOTHER had woken up to find herself lying on the kitchen floor. She couldn't for the life of her remember how she had come to be there, nor how long she had lain there, nor how she might have sustained her injury – a throbbing lump the size of a plum on the side of her head which she examined with shaking fingertips. All she knew with any certainty, as she reached for the basement door handle and struggled to her feet, was that her old limbs ached something dreadful, and that lying on the floor was not a good idea for a lady of her age.

It was years since she'd taken a drink, but she seemed to recall that this was how she'd felt when she'd had too much, a few too many *jaunes* down at Bar Chat with Murat's father, or an *eau-de-vie* with her neighbour Pauline, both long gone, God rest their bones. The symptoms were all there: a throbbing headache, a certain unsteadiness putting one foot in front of the other, and a wincing sensitivity to light, making Madame Santarem screw up her eyes as she made her way to the sink for a glass of water, noting as she did so that her son was also asleep, head on the table. What had they been doing to get themselves in such a state? she wondered. When there was so much work to be done, for goodness' sake. Their guests to be fed and watered, the buckets in the basement to be emptied. More of Murat's lovely girls come to stay, sleeping

202

down there, regaining their strength. Seven of them this time. *Les pauvres*. Such sad lives, Murat had told her. Deprived, abused . . . terrible things had been done to them. Unmentionable. She remembered him shaking his head as he told her of the horrors these girls had endured. And how he had rescued them, how he was going to save them, how he would send them away somewhere safe. Her son's kindness made her mother's heart flutter with pride. Maybe later, after supper, if any of them were still awake, she'd read to them, down there in the basement.

Humming to herself, but otherwise making as little noise as possible so as not to wake her son, Madame Santarem set about preparing the girls' supper, putting the *daube* to heat in the oven, scraping potatoes, finding a saucepan, water, salt. *Et voilà*. There, that would do it, she thought, and she pulled out a kitchen chair, smiled at her sleeping son, and blessed him for his kind heart and generous spirit. A saint . . . *vraiment* her boy was a saint.

Some time later – the kitchen clock said 2.20 but she didn't believe it – she heard the water in the saucepan begin to bubble. The sound made her frown. What was it she was cooking? Ah, yes. Potatoes. For the girls. Their supper. And there in the oven, she could smell it already, a *daube* to go with them. But there was one more thing she had to do, she was sure of it. Something she had to prepare, since her son was still sleeping. She looked around the kitchen and wondered what it was.

The answer was right in front of her, on the table. A mortar, filled with those little blue pills. The job that her son usually did. Vitamins for the girls. Since Murat was sleeping, she drew the mortar towards her and looked around for the pestle. She needed the pestle to grind them down, so she could season the stew with them, flavour the water they would drink. But she could see no sign of it.

Where had it gone? she wondered.

What should she do?

Think, think, think.

A spoon . . . why, she could use a spoon. Of course, just perfect.

Spoon, spoon, spoon, she repeated, so she wouldn't forget what it was she was looking for, going through the various drawers until she found the one with the cutlery, and a spoon, just the right size, and brought it back to the table.

But by the time she sat down again, made herself comfortable, she had lost the thread, wondering what she was doing with a spoon in her hand.

It was exactly then that she heard a gentle tapping at the front door.

That boy, Xavier. That's who it was. Murat's friend. Come to help her with the stew.

She looked down at Murat, sleeping so peacefully. She'd have to tell Xavier not to make any noise. She didn't want anyone waking up her son until he was good and ready. Exhausted he was, all that work, the responsibility . . .

Another knock at the front door. A rattle of the doorknob.

'*Alors, alors. J'arrive*,' she called out, putting down the spoon and getting to her feet. Across the kitchen and down the hallway she went, humming happily to herself.

51

CLAUDE PELUZE LOOKED AT THE two bodies. They'd been lodged behind a bank of recycling bins on a wide stretch of pavement outside Fausse Monnaie. Save for the hands and the faces they could easily have been mistaken for a pile of old clothes dumped on the ground because there was no more room in the bins. A seagull had been at work on the topmost of the two bodies, a strip of cheek already removed, squirts of gull shit caking the shoulders of the second body. It was the gull, tugging at the flesh, that had caught the attention of a room-service chef returning home after her shift at Hôtel Caron on the Corniche. She was currently sitting in one of the gendarmerie patrol cars that had turned up following her call.

Even with the cops there, the seagulls were still patrolling. Yellow eyes stern and watchful, heads flicking to left and right, they rode the damp breeze or strutted impatiently to and fro across the pavement, feathers ruffling, watching for any opening.

Peluze turned away and walked over to the parapet while one of the Police Nationale boys ran some tape round a lamp-post to isolate the crime scene. Out on the Corniche road, tyres swishing over the shining surface, a few early drivers coming in from Prado and Roucas Blanc and Montredon slowed to take a look. Peluze watched their curious faces turn as they passed, trying to see what had happened.

If they had seen what he'd just seen they'd never have slowed down, he thought. Or maybe they would.

Leaning against the parapet, looking out to sea, he pulled a pack of cigarettes from his pocket and lit up, cupping the flame on his Zippo against a drift of rain coming in from the Frioul Islands. Just a couple of kilometres offshore, they showed up in the dawn light like humped grey whales, an inshore swell breaking against their rocky sides in a lacy white spray. Snapping down the lid on his lighter, Peluze slipped it back into his pocket, took a deep drag on his cigarette and turned as a scene-of-crime van pulled up on to the kerb. He went over and briefed the man in charge.

One by one other squad cars turned up, lights flashing or unmarked. The boys in the unmarked cars were from rue de l'Evêché – Serre and Grenier, first, followed by Muzon and Laganne. Each of them took a look at the bodies then joined Peluze by the parapet.

'Any ID?' asked Grenier, one of the longest-serving officers on the squad. 'Anyone know 'em?'

'The one with no cheek, Gastal had him in yesterday,' said Peluze, flicking away his cigarette half-smoked. He watched it hit the roof tiles of a house below the parapet and roll away in the streaming rain. 'Name of Haggar. Alam Haggar. The other's probably his chum. They worked at Valentine's, over on rue Chatelier. Couple of grease monkeys is all. But it looks like someone had it in for them.'

It wasn't long before Gastal arrived.

'Here comes the *crapaud*,' said Muzon, and they turned to watch their boss drive his car up on to the pavement and lever himself out of the driving seat. There was, indeed, something toad-like in Gastal's appearance: the bowed legs, the hunched shoulders, a complete absence of neck, slightly protuberant eyes and a pelt of black hair as thick and as short as felt napping, that came to a point in the middle of his low forehead. He wore a tight, three-piece suit the colour of dry mustard, a blue shirt and a bold red tie that would have been happily hidden by the waistcoat if the waistcoat had been buttoned up.

Peluze felt the muscles in his shoulders tense. 'Christ, I hate that little fucker,' he muttered.

'You and everyone at l'Evêché, *mon brave*,' Muzon muttered back, managing a tight little nod of greeting when he caught Gastal's eye. 'And not just because he dresses like an Englishman.'

'So, what have we got?' asked Gastal, shouldering his way past the scene-of-crime boys and glancing down at the bodies. He frowned as though he recognised something.

'Your two lads,' said Peluze. 'Looks like Haggar and his side-kick, Ibin Hahmoud. Judging by the angle of the bodies, I'd say their arms and legs have been broken. Then they got a bullet apiece in the back of the head. One slug came out through the mouth, the other through an eye. Nothing for ballistics, but judging by the exits they'll be heavy calibre from a serious piece.'

Before Gastal could say anything, there was the squawk and hiss and static of another report coming in from Despatch. Grenier went over to his car and took it. A moment later he came back to the group.

'We got another one,' he said. 'Over at L'Estaque. Same kind of MO. Broken legs, broken arms, and a bullet in the back of the head. Very nice.'

'They got a name yet?' asked Gastal, feeling a shiver of certainty.

'Lévy. Marcel Lévy. Runs a chandlery near the marina. It was his wife who found the body.'

Gastal tossed back his head, set his eyes on the low cloud above and made a series of 'pah-pah-pah' sounds that set his chins trembling and made him look even more like a toad.

Shit, he was thinking. He must be getting close, really getting under someone's skin good and proper. Valentine, the two kids who'd worked for the *garagiste*, and now Lévy?

Forty-eight hours. That's all it had taken.

And the name Cabrille was written all over it.

207

52

JACQUOT WOKE TO THE SMELL of roses. He was sure it was roses – warm, soft and velvety. If the smell had a colour, that colour, he decided, gently working his neck against the pillow, would be pink. Dark pink roses, turning to red at the tips of their petals. Like the roses on the wallpaper at the foot of the bed.

For a while he didn't move, not daring to lift his head from the pillow, just flicked his eyes around the room, noting only a weak pulsing behind his eyes and a tension in his shoulders. In shuttered daylight, he could see an old armoire on his left, its wooden panels dark and polished, a dressing-table set against the rose-patterned wallpaper and between two half-shuttered windows, and a chest of drawers on his right – pine by the pale look of it, and nowhere near as grand as the armoire. Sparse furnishings but unmistakably feminine, all the props of a woman's bedroom there. A satin, dragon-embroidered wrap on a hook behind the door, clothes left over the back of the dressing-table chair, scarves and belts hanging from its mirror frame, and candles everywhere – big fat church candles on the chest of drawers, a nest of them in all sizes in the blackened fireplace. And the smell of roses, drifting off the quilt and pillows. And from another room, the distant humming of a clothes drier.

It was then, with a jolt of alarm, that Jacquot realised his shirt and his trousers had been removed, just his shorts remaining. And he couldn't remember having taken them off himself.

Oh, *Dieu*, he thought, and forgot all about the roses – and the injury to the back of his head. He sat up in bed too quickly and groaned. As much at the prospect of Marie-Ange Buhl having undressed him as the great wave of hangover headache that now took revenge for that sudden, unwise movement, making him squint with the pain.

Slowly, stiffly, he swung his legs out from under the duvet and planted them on the bare tiled floor. From there, with many further grunts and groans, he managed to get to his feet and straighten up, his head feeling twice its normal size and weight, his neck and shoulders as pliant as a slab of rock.

There was a message for him on the kitchen table, propped between a tube of arnica and a jar of Tiger Balm.

I am at work, Fleurs des Quais on rue Francis.
I have left you some medicine, and the car keys.
It's a green 2CV in case you can't remember.
She's called Rosie, by the way.
Please be kind to her.
P.S. Your trousers and shirt are in the drier.
Je m'excuse. *You were soaked through.*

But there was no time to mull over the previous evening – meeting up with Marie-Ange, being undressed by her, and spending the night in her bed. Back in the bedroom he heard the phone ringing. He got there as the ansaphone clicked on. He grabbed up the receiver and pressed the Stop button.

'Monsieur Muller?' It was a woman's voice, but not Marie-Ange's.

'*Oui, c'est moi*,' he replied.

'Béatrice Nalon, here. Madame Bonnefoy's assistant. She is in court this morning, but has the information you requested. She suggests you meet her for lunch on rue Breteuil.' If the message sounded odd – like some war-time code – Béatrice Nalon showed no sign of it.

'That is fine,' said Jacquot. 'Tell her I will be there. Thank you.'

53

AS HE WHISKED UP A bowl of eggs and set a buttered skillet to heat on the stove, Xavier reflected that his first instinct had been spot on. Jan Muller, the man who'd followed him from the Bar Dantès the night before, the man he'd floored on the corner of rue Jacobe, was a cop. As sure as eggs are eggs, he thought, tipping the mix into the skillet. There'd been nothing in Muller's wallet to suggest he might be, and his seaman's papers in their grubby plastic case had looked authentic – soiled, salt-sticky in the rain, many times folded and unfolded; the real thing. But the gun was another matter.

Xavier had found it in the left-hand inside pocket of Muller's pea-jacket. An easy reach for a right-hander. Going for a wallet, coming out with a gun. Xavier had pulled it out and turned it in his hand, rain spattering off it. A slim, blue-black Beretta 92G, the three-arrow maker's mark in the middle of the grip, ten rounds in the magazine, one chambered. It was slickly maintained, a little scuffed round the muzzle, and pleasingly weighted in the hand.

That gun was the clincher. All the sailors Xavier knew carried knives, or else the rope-bound lead cosh he favoured. Not one of them carried a gun. And the Beretta 92G, as Xavier also knew, was a *flic*'s gun. Service issue.

Jan Muller, if that was his real name, was a cop. Had to be. And working undercover. No question. Most likely narcotics, and most likely tailing Petitjean. Which meant that Petitjean would have to be dealt with. Silenced. The dealer knew Xavier's name, even knew where he lived. Soon as he could manage it, he'd pay a call down Montredon and deal with it. Yesterday he'd have stuck Petitjean with a blade, or laid in with the cosh. This time he had a gun.

As he flipped his omelette and shuffled the skillet, Xavier acknowledged that finding the gun had changed everything, given him the edge, the impetus he needed, that extra lick of confidence. He'd never owned one before, never carried one, and feeling its weight in his pocket as he headed off for the meet with Santarem had given him a real buzz. Guns were serious, guns got the job done. Now that he was moving up in the world, it was time he had one. And now he did.

Switching off the electric ring, Xavier slipped the omelette from skillet to plate, sat at the table and started eating, just knocked out by how easy it had all been, how everything had fallen into place. Not that killing Santarem had been a part of the plan. It just . . . happened. When that pestle whistled past his head, he'd reached for the gun without thinking, an instinctive self-defence. And he recalled the sense of triumph he'd felt as he'd levelled it on Santarem. The look of surprise on the other man's face. The sudden turning of the tables. The way the gun changed the perspective, directed the action.

It had been a good feeling – pure, powerful, irresistible – and as Santarem pulled out that kitchen chair, switching on that smile, flashing those even white teeth, Xavier had simply reached forward, stuck the barrel into his chest and pulled the trigger . . .

Just because he could.

And because a part of him suddenly wanted to.

And it had been . . . just staggering. Feeling the gun buried in Santarem's chest kick back in his fist, hearing the muffled report, watching that chair flip back and then slam forward, Santarem's face smacking down on to the table.

In-croy-able.

212

After that, it was a stitch. Once he'd checked Santarem was a goner, he'd pulled the stew from the oven, ladled out a portion and roughly crumbled two of the blue pills and one of the yellows over it. He'd been filling a bottle with water when the old lady finally made it down from her bedroom and came into the kitchen. She saw the gun, saw her son flat out on the table, a pool of blood already gathering around his stockinged feet, but Xavier could tell that she didn't quite know what to make of it.

No need to kill her, he thought. Mad as a bag of snakes anyway. So he put her down with a tap on the temple from the butt of the Beretta.

Down in the basement, flicking a torch from face to face, it hadn't taken him long to find Elodie.

'I'm a policeman. I've come to get you. Here, eat this, drink this,' he'd told her, squatting beside her, supporting her as he helped spoon the food into her mouth, washing it down with the water. Hell of a mess, but he'd managed it, felt her drift away.

Ten minutes later, he'd steered her up from the basement and through to the garage where he bundled her into Santarem's van, pushing back the passenger seat so he could fit her into the footwell, where she wouldn't roll around or be seen. Thirty minutes later they were back at his place and right now she was in the spare room upstairs, sleeping like a baby, breath burbling gently between her lips.

All he had to do now was make a phone call. Long-distance. Name his price. The Lafour home might have been ex-directory, but he'd had no difficulty obtaining the number for Banque Lafour.

Finishing the omelette, Xavier reached for his cigarettes, lit up, and took a long contemplative drag.

Or maybe not. Maybe he should forget the ransom demand and just sit tight till Maman and Papa reached for their wallets and offered a reward? For information leading to the safe return of their daughter. So much easier to pull it off then. Spin them a good story, play the hero, collect a cheque. Maybe not as much as a ransom demand, but a safer bet. And now that he had the tranqs he could

213

easily handle the girl for another day, maybe even two. And it would give him time to get his story right. How he found her in the street, recognised her from the newspaper . . .

No, he decided. He'd hold on to her.

There'd be a reward.

He just knew it.

And the way his luck was running . . .

54

'AT KUCHNIA,' SOLANGE BONNEFOY EXPLAINED, 'the menu changes every day. One starter, one main, a dessert. Lunch, dinner, the same. No choice.'

The examining magistrate and Jacquot were sitting at the table they'd occupied the last time they'd met at Kuchnia, its rooms just as crowded, the same soft susurrus of whispered talk, the same rolling clatter of cutlery and crockery. The coat-racks were as fat and unmanageable, the lady with the pink swollen forearms manned the counter with her customary efficiency, and the white-jacketed waiters were just as old and thin and stoop-shouldered as Jacquot remembered them.

'Wednesdays, of course, you know about,' continued Solange. 'Mushroom soup and goulash. But if it's Tuesday, you come for *Bigos* and *Kotlet Schabowy*. Or on Thursday it's pea soup *Grochowka* and stuffed beef *Zrazy*. But it doesn't matter, it's always good. Today, Saturday, it's *Barszcz*, or Borsch, followed by *Golonka*,' she said, shaking her head as their waiter approached with a soup tureen, indicating instead that he should serve Jacquot. 'I just hope you are hungry.'

'Very hungry,' he replied as he watched the beetroot soup spill like creamy blood into his white china bowl.

And just a little nervous, too. This was not, he knew, going to be an easy lunch.

It had taken Jacquot a long, painful time to get himself cleaned up and dressed at Marie-Ange's apartment. Bending down to retrieve his trousers and shirt from the clothes drier had been the first real hurdle; getting into them the second. Then it was into the bathroom, carefully dousing his face at the basin, drying himself on a towel that also smelled of roses, and looking for a spare toothbrush but not finding one. Rather than use hers, standing alone (he noted) in a china mug, he had squeezed the toothpaste on to a finger and gently worked it round his gums, finishing with a sluice of antiseptic mouthwash. Thirty minutes later, after resisting the impulse to snoop around the apartment, he'd taken the car keys and locked up.

And all the way there, he'd wondered how Solange Bonnefoy would react when she heard what he had to tell her.

They had arrived at Kuchnia at almost the same moment, Solange just ahead of him, the two of them hurrying through the rain. He'd caught up with her at the door, seen the advocate's white cravat as he helped her off with her raincoat.

'Court on a Saturday?' he'd asked.

'Ceremonial. A swearing in for the new *Juge des Affaires*. A horrible little man called Barreau. He'll make life a misery for all of us. But there we are . . .'

By the time they were shown to the table, she'd somehow managed to remove the white tie without him noticing, leaving her in an elegantly cut black suit with a now open-necked black shirt.

'So,' she said, as Jacquot started in on his soup. 'Down to business.' Unzipping her attaché case, she slid out a sheet of paper and passed it across to him.

'Two registration numbers. Two names,' she began. 'The Spanish plates belong to a Guillermo Ribero, born Gerona 1962. According to his work permit he runs a maritime agency on Chamant, and has an address in Vauban. An apartment block. Not too smart, not too shabby. No record. Clean. Spain and here. The other plates – the French ones – belong to a Christophe Petitjean who does have a record. Small-time stuff – a domestic, handling stolen goods, and

216

two counts of possession – but none of it big enough to put him away. The last address we have for him is out in Montredon. It's all there,' she said, tapping the sheet of paper with a finger 'So tell me – what do Señor Ribero and Monsieur Petitjean have to do with Elodie?'

Briefly, Jacquot explained once again how he'd visited Ribero's office and just . . . felt something. A whisper of suspicion, nothing more. (Marie-Ange would have been proud of him, he thought.) Taking the car registration had simply been an instinct, he told her. Something to follow up. 'Just a hunch at this stage. Maybe a lead, maybe not.'

'And Petitjean?' asked Solange. 'What about him? Where does he fit in?'

Jacquot tipped his bowl and took the last spoonful of soup. This was where it was going to get tricky.

'He's a drug dealer. And we think he may be involved in trafficking,' replied Jacquot, laying down his spoon.

'We?'

There was a moment's pause as the waiter appeared with another tureen. As with the goulash on Wednesday, the red-stained soup bowl was used for the stew, ladled out in steaming chunks. Jacquot leaned over the bowl, breathed it in. Whatever *Golonka* was – a rich stew of pork belly by the look of it – it smelled delicious.

'It'll be hot. Take care,' warned Solange, as their waiter withdrew and Jacquot reached for his spoon. 'So who's this "we"?'

'There is someone I want you to meet,' he replied, blowing on his first spoonful before tasting it. It was, just as she'd said, scaldingly hot. But Jacquot got enough of a mouthful without burning his lips or his tongue – a rich meaty taste that filled his cheeks – to know that he was going to enjoy *Golonka* very much indeed. Even if he wasn't going to enjoy the conversation that would now accompany it. 'Her name is Marie-Ange Buhl,' he continued, reaching for the *pichet* of rouge to refill their glasses. 'She works in a flower shop on rue Francis. Which is why she couldn't make lunch. But she said she would drop by later, for coffee.'

217

'She's a flower girl?' Solange looked confused. 'And how exactly . . .?'

Jacquot took a swig of wine, cleared his mouth. 'I met her in the summer. In the Luberon; a case I was working on,' he said, trying to put off the moment, but knowing there was no avoiding it. 'She . . . she has certain talents.'

Solange raised an eyebrow. 'Talents?'

'I'm afraid there's no easy way to say this. And I know . . .'

'Out with it, Daniel, for goodness' sake. You're making me nervous.'

'She's . . . a psychic.'

Solange sat back, frowning, as though she hadn't heard him properly, didn't quite understand. 'A psychic? Is that what you said?'

'She has these . . . powers. She . . .'

Solange began to shake her head, eyes narrowing, lips thinning, as though Jacquot had tried to swing some lame alibi past her. 'Please tell me you are joking, Daniel. Please don't tell me that we've got so little chance of finding Elodie alive that we're resorting to shams and charlatans. That's why I called you. To make a difference. And . . . and you bring me a . . . soothsayer, for Christ's sake?'

The rebuke was swift, and stung more than he'd imagined. He'd known, of course, that she wouldn't like it but he'd underestimated the depth and force of her desperation.

'I promise you, Solange, this girl is no sham, no charlatan, no soothsayer. I have seen her at work, and I . . . well, I trust her. And where I am right now, having her around means a considerable amount to me.'

Solange let out a low, mournful sigh, lifting her napkin to wipe at her mouth though not a morsel of food had passed her lips, using the move to dab at her eyes as well. 'I'm sorry, Daniel. It's just . . .' She took a deep breath and steadied herself.

'I know. And I understand. But I want you to meet her all the same. There is something . . .' Jacquot looked up, smiled. 'But I will let you find out yourself. *Elle arrive maintenant.*'

And there she was, Marie-Ange, being led to their table, slim

218

enough to glide between the diners, smiling brightly when she saw Jacquot, but looking hesitant too. When he had called her that morning and told her to meet them there, she'd sounded nervous.

Don't worry, she won't eat you, Jacquot had told her. But now, as he introduced the two women, he wasn't so sure. The examining magistrate stiffened her back and gave Marie-Ange just the shortest of smiles.

'Mademoiselle,' was all she said.

And as she settled in her chair, Marie-Ange shot Jacquot a look.

'Some coffee, young lady?' Solange asked, politely. 'Something to eat? Maybe a slice of *Makoweic*? It's a poppy-seed cake.' Her smile was almost a wince of good manners, and wafer-thin patience.

Marie-Ange shook her head. 'No cake, thank you. But coffee would be wonderful. Very black, very strong, please.'

Solange nodded to the waiter, who'd been listening, and he withdrew.

'So, Mademoiselle Buhl. According to my friend, Daniel, you have something to tell me.' Her voice was brittle as a brandy snap. It was a tone she used in court. Jacquot had heard it many times.

'*En effet*, something to show you, madame,' replied Marie-Ange, opening her tote bag and bringing out a small wrapped object. Putting aside her bag, she unwound some tissue paper and held out her hand.

The blue enamelled hairclip.

The moment she saw what it was Solange gasped, then gulped in air and sat back in her chair, eyes wide, as though she had just been punched. The next moment she darted forward like a magpie after something shiny, and snatched the hairclip from Marie-Ange's hand. She turned it over, held the underside to the light to check its provenance, that it wasn't some other serpent hairclip.

'Where did you get this?' she demanded, as though Marie-Ange might have stolen it.

'Here,' replied Jacquot. 'In Marseilles.'

55

WHILE JACQUOT SCOOPED UP THE last of his *Golonka*, Alain Gastal felt his appetite drain away. At this particular lunch, on Quai du Port, taken alone at a heavily-draped corner table in Le Mirador's main dining room, Gastal had ordered *escargots*. *La douzaine*. Provence's very own *petit gris*, the 'little grey', raised on thyme and myrtle leaves before purging. A glistening pile of shells stuffed and served, *à la provencale*, in a pock-hollowed porcelain dish that swam with hot butter, fragments of garlic and speckled green shreds of parsley. On any menu, snails were Gastal's *plat du choix*. And always he would start with the dozen, before moving on to meat or fish, though it wasn't uncommon for him to stay with snails and order a dozen more. Even a third serving was not unknown.

At Le Mirador that lunchtime, the first eight *petits gris* he'd seen off with cheery despatch, one a minute, dabbing up the juices with a piece of bread, ignoring the silver spring clamp in favour of his own thumb and middle finger. It was an old trick of his, and there was nothing that put him in a better mood. After puncturing the base of each shell with the nail of his index finger, he'd place shell to red lips and suck loudly – the flesh, the sauce, *le tout*, bursting into his mouth.

But the ninth *escargot* was not as accommodating as its predecessors, its shell thicker, tougher, more stubborn. In the end he had to reach for the tiny fork and dig around for the flesh inside. It was as he pulled the snail clear, dangling from the fork's tip like a piece of dripping black snot, that Gastal's appetite suddenly vanished. Putting down fork and snail, pushing away the porcelain dish, he reached instead for a dusty bottle of ten-year old Cornas from the slopes of the upper Rhône to drown his sorrows.

In just two days he had lost Valentine, Lévy and the two Arab kids – though they didn't amount to much. Which left him with nothing. Not a single snout to hit on, not a single lead to follow up beyond an English limo and a woman driver in a part of town where English limos were thin on the ground. If he didn't get his act together *tout de suite*, he could kiss goodbye to Paul Bocuse and long lunches in La Tour Rose.

Worse still had been the news in that morning's newspaper. Arsène Cabrille dead. A stroke at home, followed by a heart attack at the Druot Clinic. A three-paragraph story at the bottom of the front page, with a longer, follow-up piece on the obituary page that noted his birth in Ajaccio, his upbringing in Marseilles, the tragic loss of his wife, Léonie ('never replaced in his affections'), before going on to list the man's achievements: his shipping interests, his trading empire, his hospices and health-care clinics, and his long-standing patronage of the Opéra – without once approaching the meat of the matter: the drugs, the prostitution, the racketeering, the extortion that had contributed to his business success. The closest the piece came to a raised eyebrow or pointing finger were adjectives like 'colourful', 'energetic', 'respected' – which easily translated for those in the know, like Gastal, into 'cruel', 'lethal' and 'feared'. Now that the man was dead, Gastal would have expected the obituarist to have been braver. But the last line explained any reticence. 'Arsène Cabrille is survived by a daughter.' Gastal sighed, poured the last of the Cornas and signalled for *l'addition* with an impatient click of greasy fingers and a cursory wipe of his chin.

His low spirits stayed with him all the way back to headquarters on rue de l'Evêché, in the lift to the third floor, and down the corridor to the squad room and his office beyond.

221

Where everything changed.

'Boss?' called Peluze, as Gastal passed between the desks.

He turned, lifted his chin in Peluze's direction to indicate he was listening.

'You've got a visitor. I put her in your office to wait.'

Gastal frowned. 'Visitor?'

'Mademoiselle Carinthe Cousteaux. She said it was important.'

56

CARINTHE COUSTEAUX WAS DARK ENOUGH for her scarlet lipstick to look more luscious than it might have done on a woman with a lighter complexion. This was the first thing that struck Gastal as he pushed open his office door and the woman sitting at his desk turned to look at him. Between the door and his desk he took in the rest: late forties, maybe sliding into her fifties, dark almond eyes expertly mascaraed and shadowed, a lustrous sweep of black hair that would have reached past her shoulders if it hadn't been secured in a neatly netted chignon, long crossed legs, black stockings, black high-heeled shoes, and a black satin topcoat and skirt that suggested a busty, voluptuous figure beneath. She looked as though she was on her way to a funeral, or fresh back from one. When she held up a hand for him to take in greeting, the movement was accompanied by the heavy oily links of a gold bracelet clunking down her wrist to disappear into her sleeve. The sound – expensive, alluring – and the scent from the glove, and the faintest returning pressure from her fingers, were enough to secure Gastal's attention.

'So, mademoiselle, what is it I can do for you?' he asked, releasing her fingers and going round his desk, pulling in his stomach as he did so and squaring his shoulders, aware that she was scrutinising him keenly, as though considering a purchase.

'*Mais non*, monsieur. It is what I can do for you,' she replied. Her voice was pitched low, exotically accented, a playful murmur that came from the back of her throat, ladened with promise and intrigue. There was also a smile to accompany this offer, and a glimpse of pink tongue and glistening white teeth, and they drew from Gastal a sudden and unexpected lurch of desire, as though Carinthe Cousteaux was suggesting something that had nothing to do with police matters. She may not have been in the first dew of youth, but her presence was electrifying.

Gastal spread his hands, as though to suggest he couldn't possibly imagine what she might be referring to, but as he settled back in his chair he hoped he made it quite clear that he was in no hurry to have her state her business and leave. On the contrary . . . Her next words hit him like a thunderbolt.

'I am a close friend of Monsieur Arsène Cabrille. You may know of him?'

'*Mais bien sûr*,' Gastal managed, clearing his throat, tasting garlic from his *escargots*. 'And I was so sorry to read . . .'

But she waved aside the condolence, revealing between the buttoned edge of her glove and jacket cuff a warm brown wrist. 'And so was I, monsieur, but not so sorry that I feel any sense of disloyalty in coming to see you now. It is not Monsieur Arsène who brings me here. *Pas du tout*. Rather,' she continued, shifting her shoulders with a shivering distaste, as though trying to dislodge something from between her shoulder blades, 'it is his daughter, Virginie.'

If that name had tasted of something bad, foul, dead, Gastal couldn't imagine seeing a more pained expression on the lady's face. He nodded, though he could think of no reason to do so, a small flicker of interest starting up in his gut. 'And how is that?' he asked when Mademoiselle Cousteaux showed no sign of continuing.

'You must understand, *cher* monsieur,' she began, 'that Arsène and I were very close. We have shared a great deal together. Indeed, it was in my house, our home, that he suffered that dreadful *attaque*.

And it is from that house that *she* has now sent me. His daughter. And her father not two days dead. Out, with all my belongings, my memories, helped along by her thugs.'

'But how exactly can I be of assistance, mademoiselle? In what appears to be really nothing more than a domestic . . .' began Gastal, already scenting a new source of information, but playing down his interest.

'As you may know, Chief Inspector, the family Cabrille is not without its little secrets. Out of respect for Arsène, out of love and loyalty, I have kept my own counsel, turned a blind eye to many of the things I have seen and heard when maybe I should have . . .' That smile again, soft and scolding. 'But now, now that Arsène is gone, now that I have been so cruelly used, it is perhaps the time to . . .'

Gastal leaned forward, a thin smile stealing across his lips. Glancing over her shoulder, he spotted Peluze in the squad room talking to Laganne. 'One of you,' he called out, 'some coffee for the mademoiselle . . .'

57

NOW JACQUOT KNEW FOR CERTAIN.

Elodie was there.

In Marseilles.

The hairclip confirmed it.

Or if not Marseilles, then L'Estaque, or Montredon, or Madrague, or any of the city's outlying fringes, and more than likely near the coast, close to water, waiting to be shipped away.

As he and Marie-Ange dropped down towards the old port in her 2CV, he felt a stir of excitement. Things were really beginning to move now.

'Did you believe me?' asked Marie-Ange, as he skirted round Quai des Belges. 'When I showed you the hairclip?'

'It helped when Madame Bonnefoy recognised it,' he said with an apologetic smile. 'I'm a cop, Marie-Ange. I like proof. We may work on hunches a lot of the time, but somewhere along the line we need something tangible, like a hairclip.'

'So what are we going to do now?'

'I'm going to drop you at Fleurs des Quais, and then, with your permission, I'm going to borrow your car.'

'To do what, exactly?'

'To pay a call on your friend, the one from last night. Blondie.'

'And find out what he knows about Scarface?'

'That's correct,' said Jacquot, rattling the 2CV over a set of tram-lines and onto a stretch of cobbles that set up a dull, corresponding pain in the back of his head.

'You'll let me know what happens? It's my car, after all.'

Jacquot drew up at the flower shop. 'I will let you know what happens. I promise.'

'I finish at six. You can pick me up.'

Caught off guard, he demurred. 'I can't say when . . .'

'Six will be fine. That gives you easily enough time. Or you can't have the car.' Before he could do anything, she reached across and slipped the keys from the ignition. 'There. Now what are you going to do?' she asked, and gave him a triumphant look.

With a smile, he gave in. 'Six o'clock then. Or thereabouts.'

'Six on the dot,' she said, handing him back the keys. 'Or I'll call the cops and report the car stolen.'

With a wave and a crunch of gears, Jacquot pulled out from the kerb, joined the traffic and headed back the way he had come, turning off along Rive Neuve, accelerating past the sloping grey walls of Fort d'Entrecasteaux and out on to the Corniche, feeling good – almost noble – that he'd resisted the impulse to snoop in Marie-Ange's apartment. He would have felt ashamed now had he done so.

Yet he had to admit the impulse was still there. To find out about her. To understand her. To know her better. Just a few months earlier they had spent some time together, and he tried now to remember what he had learned. It was slim pickings. Back then she had worked for an agency – he couldn't remember the name – and maybe she still did, moving around the country to work in flower shops or nurseries, filling in for absent staff, or owners who were taking a holiday, or attending court like the Chaberts in St Bédard. She came originally from Alsace, he recalled. Had worked with the police there, in Metz. Murder tricked out as suicide, some-thing along those lines, and she had seen through it. Or rather, pointed the police in the right direction.

As for St Bédard, the part she had played in the investigation had started, he remembered, with letters, anonymous letters that had echoed his own misgivings about the case, from Ile-de-France, from Brittany, from Poitou-Charente – letters from the various garden centres and florists where she'd worked before coming to the Luberon. And that's where they'd first met, at a murder scene, introducing themselves where blood had been spilt. On that first occasion she had talked to him of orchids and he could recall the easy familiarity with which their full latin names had trickled off her tongue, the guided tour she'd given him in that distant hot-house, and her gentle flirting.

That first time they'd met she'd been out riding and was wearing jodhpurs, a scent of grass and sun and horse and flowers drifting off her. Not easy to forget. Such a pretty girl, he thought. No, he reconsidered, not pretty, beautiful. Quite simply beautiful. And single too. No ring on her finger. No sign of a man in her life. Nothing male in her apartment, no photos on the fridge or the dressing-table. (It wasn't snooping to notice such small things, surely?)

For a moment Jacquot felt his age, and a regretful flush of dis-appointment that she was beyond his reach. He was too old, for God's sake. He could be her father – just. And anyway there was Claudine, who meant more to him than . . . But still, *Dieu*, he was a man too, he had eyes and a pulse, and Marie-Ange Buhl was one of the most beautiful creatures he had seen, stood close to, touched. He'd even slept in her bed . . .

And, truth to tell, he had to admit he'd never really got her out of his head. Not since St Bédard. The way she'd just left like that – no forwarding address, no contact number. Just . . . gone. Out of his life. He'd felt bad about that. Not cross, just . . . unsettled. And a few months later, here she was again. Back in his life.

By now Jacquot had reached Montredon and was looking for the apartment block where Christophe Petitjean lived, checking the address Solange Bonnefoy had given him. He found the place at last, a sixties housing block, its four balconied floors set on concrete pillars, the space beneath used as a residents' car park. Since he didn't have a card to raise the barrier, he had to park two streets away and walk back in the pelting rain.

He checked the bells for one marked 'Petitjean' but found only 'Christophe'. Fourth floor. He didn't ring, just put his shoulder to the glass entry doors and gave a shove. It had worked before and, with a complaining glassy shriek from the automatic lock, it worked again.

There were six doors on the fourth floor, reached along an open walkway with fine views of the chalky hills rising above Montredon. Another block was currently under construction across a patch of weedy open ground. Just the fenced foundations were in place, but given the slope of the land it was clear the current view would be lost when the building was completed.

Petitjean's was the last door on the walkway. He answered Jacquot's knock in T-shirt, shorts and a dressing gown. He looked as though he'd just got up which, given his night-time activities, wasn't all that surprising. His blue eyes looked weary, his blond hair stood up in tufts, and the only thing that looked bright about him was a sparkling diamond ear stud.

He was just about to ask who the hell his visitor was when Jacquot slammed his fist in the man's face. Petitjean staggered back and crumpled on to a low sofa, his hands clutching his bleeding broken nose.

58

CHECKING THE WALKWAY AND CLOSING the door behind him, unable to tell whether his knuckles hurt more than his head, Jacquot wasted no time in getting to work. In short order, and with very little opposition, he'd hauled Christophe Petitjean off the sofa and on to a kitchen chair, binding his legs and arms with the man's dressing gown cord and a couple of belts he found in the single bedroom – a mess of newspapers, coffee mugs, pizza delivery boxes and old clothes strewn about a tumbled, grubby bed. When he was satisfied that his prisoner was secure, Jacquot went behind the breakfast bar, filled the kettle with water and switched it on.

'You want a coffee, man, all you gotta do is ask,' said Petitjean, coming round, tipping back his head and snorting up the blood. He knew he was in trouble, and he knew there wasn't much he could do about it.

'It's not for coffee,' Jacquot told him, and pulled out a chair for himself, sitting in front of Petitjean. 'Just think of it as encouragement.'

Petitjean frowned.

'So let's start with last night. Bar Dantès. You and your chum.'

'Bar Dantès?'

There was a click from the kettle in the kitchen.

230

'Hey, you know what? That kettle's fast. The water's already boiled.'

Petitjean watched Jacquot go to the kitchen and lift the kettle from its base. The water was bubbling, spitting from the spout. Jacquot came back to Petitjean and poured a stream of it on to his bare knee.

'*Merde!* What the fuck're you doin', man?' he screamed, trying to buck the chair and himself away from the boiling water.

'If you don't answer my questions, I'll do it higher up.'

'You a cop? What is this?'

'Would a cop do this?' asked Jacquot, and he spilt some more scalding water on to the other knee.

'Okay, okay. Jesus Christ! All right. Bar Dantès . . . I was there. Meeting up with a friend.'

'And the friend's name?' Jacquot poured another stream of boiling water between the man's feet, letting it spatter and steam off the lino floor.

'Xavier something. That's all I know. Xavier . . . He works for Murat.'

'Murat?'

'Murat Santarem. Lives up on Bandole, with his old mother.'

'And what did you sell this Xavier?'

'Drugs, of course. Drugs.'

'What kind of drugs?'

'Hey, man, just drugs, you know? Some hash, some coke . . .'

'In a carrier bag?' Jacquot shook his head and smiled, reaching out to angle more water on to the inside of Petitjean's thigh.

'Okay, okay. Some other stuff, too. Zopamyn. Promazyl. A few boxes.'

'And they are?'

'Tranqs, downers. Strong stuff. Benzodiazepines. Bennies, you know? Prescription stuff.'

'And what do they do?' asked Jacquot, already with a pretty good idea what they'd be used for.

'Hey, man, they put you out. Like a light.'

Jacquot felt a beat of excitement. He was closing in. He knew it.

'And what would our friend Xavier want with something like that – and in that quantity?'

'Hey, I supply. I don't ask questions.'

'He a regular customer, this Xavier?'

'Now and then, this and that.'

'You know where he hangs out?'

Petitjean squirmed against his bindings. Jacquot raised the kettle.

'One time I delivered to a place in the Fifth. Rue Artemis?'

'And what about this Murat? He a customer too?'

Petitjean nodded. 'Every month or so, the same stuff. Bit of blow now and then. Xavier usually does the pick-up.'

'So the drugs are for Murat?'

'Yeah . . . maybe. I dunno.'

'You got a number for Murat? Up on Bandole.'

'Shit, I sell drugs, man. I don't read meters, you know what I'm sayin'?'

'Describe him.'

'Tall, good-looking guy. Arab, right? Mid thirties. Black curly hair. Great smile, you know?'

'You got a phone number for them?'

Petitjean shook his head. 'Like I say, I'm a dealer. They phone me. I deliver. *C'est tout.*'

Jacquot nodded, pushed back the chair and took the kettle back to the galley kitchen. 'You got any of those drugs here – the Zopamyn and Promazyl? The hash. Maybe some coke?'

Petitjean seemed to perk up, as though he sensed a sale. 'In the bedroom, under the bedside rug. There's a loose board.'

Five minutes later Jacquot was back in the kitchen with two supermarket carrier bags packed with an assortment of pills, hash, grass and what appeared to be wraps of cocaine.

He emptied out the bags of coke and grass on the floor around Petitjean, stacked the pillboxes in a pyramid on the breakfast counter, then picked up the phone and dialled a number.

'What you doin', man?'

'Calling some friends,' he replied. And then: 'Police Nationale? I just found a load of drugs. Everything. A huge amount. And a dealer to go with them. He's in a pretty bad way, I'm afraid . . .'

'Oh, man,' wailed Petitjean, as Jacquot gave them the address and put the phone down. 'Oh, what you go and do something like that for?'

'To save a young girl, you little piece of shit!' And before he could even think about what he was doing Jacquot swung at Petitjean a second time, sinking his fist into the man's cheek, loosening teeth with a satisfying crunch and sending him tipping backwards in his chair.

Working undercover certainly had its advantages, he thought as he closed the door behind him.

59

THE TALL POINTED RAILINGS IN the wrought-iron gates of the Cabrille mansion in Roucas Blanc were bound with swatches of black and purple silk, the lowest branches of the lime trees that lined the drive were hung with black and purple pennants dripping tearfully in the rain, and the sills of each window of the stuccoed villa from which Arsène Cabrille had run his empire were similarly embellished. On each panel of the double front doors was an oval wreath of black-sprayed laurel collaring the tightly packed heads of a hundred white rosebuds, and standing in the driveway was a glass-sided hearse, its etched-glass sides spattered with raindrops, four purple-plumed black stallions whickering and pawing at the gravel.

Guillermo Ribero had never seen anything like it. Here was death as drama and spectacle, grief on a grand scale: something he had only seen on television before – the funerals of De Gaulle, Princess Diana. As he climbed the steps to the pillared portico, past a group of frock-coated undertakers in sashed top-hats sheltering from the rain, and stepped through the front doors, Guillermo wished he'd thought to put on a dark suit rather than the tan leather jacket he was wearing. He hadn't expected such a send-off for that old cutthroat Cabrille, and had limited his mourning dress to a black armband and thin black tie.

The summons to Maison Cabrille had come a little before midday. Guillermo had been at his quayside office, going through arrangements with Citron and the skipper of the *Hesperides*. It now looked certain that the strike would be over by Sunday and Citron reported that the Chamant quay, where their freighter was moored, had been set for unloading first thing Monday morning. Dope off, girls on. All being well the ship and her new cargo would sail Monday night, or Tuesday morning at the latest. Within a month Guillermo's bank account would be bulging again, but right now there was a lot to be done, and not much time to do it. But when had it ever been any different in Marseilles, or in his line of work?

The most pressing of his problems was Murat Santarem. Despite a dozen phone calls there had been no answer. If he couldn't finalise arrangements for an exchange, the deal was off and Murat could sing. Guillermo would leave it a few months, then find someone else to provide the goods.

When the phone rang on his desk Guillermo had expected to hear Murat's voice, finally returning his calls. Instead it was one of the Cabrille boys – Tomas, Taddeus, one or the other – to let him know that Virginie Cabrille wanted to see him.

For a second or two Guillermo had felt a frisson of dread. He might never have met the lady, but he knew as well as anyone what La Mam'selle was capable of; when it came to handing it out, rumour had it that the Corsicans were school kids in comparison. But following that initial chill there came, too, a sense that he was safe. If they'd wanted him killed, it would have happened here in his office, or on his way home, or in his bed. Not at Maison Cabrille where he was asked to present himself that afternoon, to talk about the family fleet and future cargoes. A new boss was always trouble, of course, but as the time for the meeting drew near Guillermo had persuaded himself that things would continue as they always had done. In the four years he'd been handling the Marseilles end of the Cabrilles' trading fleet, there'd never been a single set-back in the smooth running of the operation. Hundreds of millions of francs worth of A-list merchandise passing through his port, his offices, and never so much as a sniff or a whisper from Customs or Gendarmerie.

Guillermo had met the old man on just two occasions – a gallery opening on rue Grignan and a race meeting at Parc Borély – a sly cadaverous-looking bastard if ever there was one, with flinty pirate's eyes, sunken cheeks and scalpel-cut lips. But this was the first time he'd been summoned to the house. As one of the Corsican brothers crossed the hallway to greet him and show him through to the main salon, Guillermo straightened his tie and rolled his shoulders. Double doors were opened and the Corsican ushered him through into an Empire-style salon.

A fire had been lit in the marble hearth and the room smelt of resin and woodsmoke. Virginie Cabrille stood beside the fire, taller than he'd expected, dressed in a black trouser suit, her short black hair parted to one side like a choirboy's. Her hand, when she offered it to him, felt strong and cold.

'It is kind of you to come,' she said, sliding her arm through his and leading him to a pair of high-backed battened chesterfields. She took one, he the other. Through the window and across a terrace Guillermo could see white waves crashing silently against the stony shores of Château d'If and the Frioul Islands.

'I am only sorry that it is in such sorrowful circumstances, mademoiselle,' replied Guillermo, taking in the old oak panelling, the damask drapes, a dusty pink Persian rug that revealed only a narrow border of floorboards, and a large ormolu desk set beneath a group of Corsican landscapes. The old man's study, for sure, the style and furnishings too old and weighty for the slim young woman sitting opposite him.

As he made himself comfortable, Guillermo felt an unexpected surge of confidence. Suddenly at ease, with an increasing sense that this was more than just a planning meeting, he suspected there were surprises in store for him. Promotion, perhaps. His record surely spoke for itself, and now the new boss was recognising his past efforts and rewarding them. He was right.

'My father held you in high regard,' she began.

'I'm very flattered that he should have thought so, mademoiselle. I just do my job as best I can,' replied Guillermo, lowering his eyes modestly but letting them stray, as he did so, across the buttoned swell of her jacket. God, he thought, she was a sexy woman. She reminded him of Madonna: haughty, hard . . . but evil too. He'd heard someone say that she liked girls, exclusively, but he couldn't believe it. If it was true, it was a tragedy.

Virginie nodded, smiled again. There was a ring with a diamond the size of a date on her right index finger. She played the gold band that held it with her thumb, fingers held stiff, nails polished but not lacquered, short but not bitten. 'As for me, it was made clear when Tomas, here, told me about your phone call. That tittle-tattle Lévy.'

Guillermo spread his hands. 'It does not do to have such men around, mademoiselle. I would have dealt with him myself, but felt that you should know what was going on. That you should decide the best course of action.'

'Which is exactly what we have done. And why, *cher* Guillermo, it is time to recognise your loyalty, and your contribution, and move you on in the organisation. My father would have left you where you were, of course. That was his way. "The operation is working, don't rock the boat" would have been his view. But I am not my father. I believe there are more profitable and imaginative ways to utilise skills such as yours.'

'It is kind of you to say so, mademoiselle.'

'But who should replace you? In such a sensitive position.'

Guillermo sucked in his breath, as though such a question would take some consideration, and let it out in a comfortable sigh, rather pleased that his opinion should be sought, his opinion valued. This was inside track, as close as he'd ever come, and the prospect of more meetings such as this, at this level in the family, filled him with a pleasing warmth.

'There is Citron,' he began. 'Louis Citron. A Marseillais born and bred. He knows the docks. I have brought him on slowly, introduced him to the right people . . . I have no doubt he would be loyal to the family.'

'Citron? Citron? Isn't his father a union boss?'

'That's correct, mademoiselle. A good contact. Solid.'

Virginie turned to the two Corsicans who had stayed by the door during this exchange. 'Do you know this Citron family, Taddeus? Have we had dealings?'

The older twin gave it some thought, but shook his head.

'So, you think this Citron could take over?' she continued.

Guillermo gave a nod. 'Yes, I would say so,' he replied.

'The *Hesperides*?'

That woke Guillermo up. 'The *Hesperides*, mademoiselle? But it is in port already. It unloads on Monday.'

'But he could do it?' Virginie continued. 'This Citron. He could handle things?'

Guillermo had time only to spread his hands before she began speaking again.

'Because I have another job for you.'

'Another job?'

'I want you to help me find someone.'

'Find someone? Of course, if I can . . .'

Virginie smiled. 'I believe you know a man called Santarem? Murat Santarem?'

60

THE NAME LANCED INTO GUILLERMO'S guts like an icy
blade. All the confidence and ease he'd felt just drained away.
'Santarem?'

'He is a local trafficker. Girls.'

Guillermo started to shake his head. 'Santarem . . . Santarem. No,
mademoiselle, the name is not familiar.'

Virginie looked surprised. 'But how extraordinary. According to
Monsieur Lévy, you do. He was quite insistent on that, was he not,
Tomas?'

Over by the door, the smaller of the two brothers inclined his
head. 'Yes, he was, Mademoiselle.'

Virginie turned back to Guillermo, settled a forgiving, understanding smile on him.

His heart was pounding. What had that little shit Lévy gone and
said? How much did he know? What had Santarem told him? Jesus
Christ . . . Jesus Christ . . .

'Now, Guillermo, I understand your loyalty. I understand you
are a man who values discretion. And that is good. Very good. A
friend like you is a friend indeed. But the fact of the matter is that
this Santarem has something I want.'

'Something you want?' he managed.

'That is correct.'

'A girl?'

'*Exactement*. A particular, special girl.'

Guillermo nodded. This was going way above his head. He felt more than a little adrift. But his heart-rate had begun to steady, which was good. Maybe Lévy hadn't known anything. Hadn't said anything.

'The problem I have is that this Santarem is dead,' continued Virginie.

'He's dead?'

'Like Monsieur Lévy. And the girl I want to find is missing. Someone else has her now, and I need to know who.'

Guillermo felt his pulse-rate pick up. No wonder there'd been no reply to his calls.

'So, does this Santarem character have an accomplice? A partner? Someone who might have done this? Someone who knew the value of the girl he was holding?'

Guillermo was thinking furiously. Xavier! It had to be Xavier. It was time to shift the spotlight away from himself.

'Xavier Vassin. I believe Santarem and he work together.'

'And where can we find Monsieur Vassin? And, hopefully, the girl?'

Guillermo remembered the house where Xavier lived. He and Santarem had been there once – a party. 'The last I heard he lived up in Saint Luc, rue Artemis. I don't remember any number but I seem to recall that the front door was painted green. And the gate too.'

'Excellent,' said Virginie, getting to her feet. 'Good, good.' She glanced at her watch and took a breath. 'So, tell me, Guillermo, would you like to see my father?'

The question took him by surprise. A firm 'no' would have been his answer of choice. But now, he judged, was not the moment to do anything that might upset his new boss. He got to his feet. '*Mais bien sûr*,' he said, as though it was only appropriate he should be invited to see the old man for the last time and pay his respects.

Once again, Virginie took his arm and led him to a set of doors on the right of the fireplace. One of the Corsicans was ahead of them and opened the doors.

They entered a small library, Guillermo and Virginie, the doorway wide enough for them to pass through side by side. The Corsicans followed and closed the doors behind them.

Across the room, in front of another marble fireplace, was a stepped catafalque draped in black silk, with an open mahogany coffin set upon it. Two giant candles, rising from a nest of canna lilies, burned at either end, filling the room with a thick, funereal scent.

Virginie led him up the steps and together they looked down at the still, icy features of Arsène Cabrille, his head resting on a cream silk pillow, his grey hair neatly parted just off centre. He was dressed in a shiny black suit, white silk shirt and tie, his long, scrawny neck too shrivelled now to fill the collar. A rosary was fixed in his clasped hands.

'Such a small man, for such a large coffin, *n'est-ce pas*? So much room.'

Guillermo frowned. He turned to Virginie with a questionning look.

'I'm not sure . . .' he began.

But it was as far as he got.

Guillermo hadn't heard Taddeus come up behind him, but he felt the prick of the needle in the side of his neck and pulled away from Virginie as though he had just been stung.

He raised his hand as though to swat away an insect, but suddenly there was no strength, no ability to continue the movement. His arm fell back to his side and his eyes closed. His legs trembled and buckled, and he slumped back into Taddeus's arms.

Passing the syringe to his brother, Taddeus stooped, slipped an arm behind Guillermo's knees and lifted him up. With a small grunt, he hoisted the Spaniard over the lip of the coffin and rolled him in on top of the body of Arsène Cabrille.

Looking down at the pair of them, Virginie smiled. Sometimes it wasn't enough just to kill. Sometimes you had to make it special.

The following morning, after a short funeral ceremony at Cimetière Saint Pierre, Guillermo Ribero, 36, of Gerona, Spain, would wake up in his shared silken bed and realise where he was.

And start screaming and hammering . . .

Virginie smoothed her hand across the polished wood. '*Adieu*, Papa. *Adieu*, Guillermo.'

Reaching up, she lowered the lid. 'You can screw it down now,' she said to the twins. 'Then call in the undertakers.'

61

MARIE-ANGE BUHL PULLED DOWN the roller blinds of Fleurs des Quais with a staggered rattle, tidied up the shop's warm, flower-scented interior and, at a little after six o'clock, suitably wrapped against the weather, stepped out into a cold pattering rain. A few minutes later she was standing in the bus shelter on rue Francis, looking out for her 2CV and Daniel Jacquot.

Already the day had ended and streetlights and car headlights shimmered off the rain-slicked street, the low belly of the clouds glowing a thin orange from the lights of the city below. A bus drew up at the shelter and wheezed to a stop. Its double doors opened and the people waiting in the shelter tramped on, shaking umbrellas, brushing themselves down. Marie-Ange let them pass, stayed where she was.

The driver looked down at her. '*Vous venez?*' he called out, with a lift of his chin.

'*Non, non. J'attends un ami, merci.*'

With a nod, he reached for the lever, pulled the folding doors closed and hauled on the steering wheel, pulling away into the traffic on rue Francis.

Un ami, un ami, she thought wistfully. She supposed Jacquot was. Not just a policeman. Not just an acquaintance either. Not any more. She had, after all, removed his trousers the night before

– they'd been soaking wet, dirty; she couldn't possibly have let him sleep in them. But by then he was past caring, unable to help, fallen into a deep sleep. So she'd unbuckled his belt, loosened his zip and tugged the trousers down by the waistband, trying to keep her eyes on the wall above the bed as she did so, praying his shorts didn't pull down with the trousers. And as she worked on him she'd hummed, as though she was simply performing some familiar domestic duty. Of course, his shorts had shifted, as she'd tugged the sodden trousers over his hips, and her eyes, despite her every best intention, had been drawn to that broad, firm stomach and the cord of black hair that disappeared into the band of his shorts. It had been a struggle, retaining her sense of propriety and protecting his modesty. And all the time, he lay there with his eyes closed, a great heavy man, on her bed, hers to do with as she wished.

Saturdays were always busy at Fleurs des Quais which meant that, apart from their brief time together at Kuchnia, she'd had little time to think about him. Now, standing there in the bus shelter, she made up for it. Apart from the shorn hair, he was just as she remembered him. The same green eyes glinting behind curling black lashes, caught in a tracery of wrinkles, the depths of which, while he slept, showed as thin pale lines against his tanned skin. Of course, the clothes he was wearing were different – cheap, working clothes – but she could recall the jeans, the clean open-necked shirts, and soft tan loafers he'd worn that summer past in St Bédard. Anything less like a policeman, she couldn't imagine. But he was, and she had to remember that. She had also to remember that there was another woman in his life. She was sure of it. There may have been no wedding ring but she remembered him wanting to buy an orchid for someone's birthday. Someone special.

As she leaned against a Metro map of Marseilles framed in a side panel of the bus shelter – already filling up again, the crowds pressing in under its roof rather than stand out in the rain – she wondered if that someone was still around, or someone else, someone new. He certainly didn't strike her as the kind of man who spent too much time on his own, but she had to admit there was something . . . isolated about him. Quiet, a little introspective, as though the soul of him, the heart, was somehow out of reach, or at the very least hard to find. A natural loner.

There was a tinny beep-beep from the kerb, but at first Marie-Ange failed to register it.

'You taking a bus or would you like a lift?' a voice called out. She recognised it immediately and spotted its owner, passenger door open, leaning out into the rain and beckoning her over. She made her '*Scusez–moi*s, *merci*s, and *s'il vous plaît*s as she pushed through the crowd and hurried over to the car. She was aware of envious looks, either for the man who was picking her up, or the fact that she would not have to wait for the bus which even now was drawing up behind them, flashing its lights to move Jacquot on. She didn't look back at the queue but sensed the general envy turn to resentment as the bus was unnecessarily delayed.

With Marie-Ange praying that Jacquot wouldn't stall her car on the slope and delay them even more – Rosie could be temperamental if her gears weren't properly meshed – they finally pulled away and joined the traffic heading up rue Francis.

'So, how did it go?' she asked, noting a graze on the swollen knuckles of his right hand. 'You've been fighting. Are you okay?'

'We have some names,' Jacquot replied, waving away her concern. 'Santarem. Murat Santarem. And your friend last night . . . Scarface? He's called Xavier, and works for Santarem. He was buying drugs for him at Bar Dantès. Tranquillisers. Sedatives. Strong ones. Your guess is as good as mine why he might be needing them.' He turned and gave her an encouraging smile, saw the light of excitement in her eyes. 'We also have a couple of addresses,' he continued. 'This Santarem character lives on rue Bandole, a few streets away from the docks. And Xavier's on rue Artemis.'

'Where to first?' asked Marie-Ange.

'The boss, Santarem. I hope you've brought the hairclip. Since we don't have any house numbers, we might need it.'

'Couldn't we just knock on a door and ask a neighbour for

directions?' asked Marie-Ange, warmed by that 'we'. 'Sometimes that works just as well.'

Jacquot glanced across at her. 'Are you always so practical and sensible?'

'Only when I have to work with the police,' she replied.

62

IN A PERFECT WORLD, JACQUOT wouldn't have made that six o'clock pick-up on rue Francis. He would have driven straight to rue Bandole and checked out Murat Santarem by himself. But he had to admit that he was pleased to have Marie-Ange along, to have the company. And the more time he spent with her, the more certain he became that she'd be able to look after herself in a tight spot. There was something naturally calm, something contained and independent, about her. And practical too, of course.

'Rue Bandole,' she called out, pointing ahead. 'Over there on the right.'

Jacquot indicated and turned up a gently sloping road with a dozen houses to either side, small stuccoed villas set in their own cramped gardens, two-storey, tiled steps up to narrow verandahs and shadowy front doors, with what looked like a basement level below each verandah. Some of the gardens had palm trees, one of them a dark, malevolent-looking monkey tree. But all of them appeared tidy and well-kept, in proper suburban style.

'It's that one,' said Marie-Ange in a whisper.

Jacquot glanced at her. 'Are you okay?'

'I'm fine. Fine,' she replied, but there was a dryness to her voice, a tremor in her shoulders. 'That one,' she said. 'Your side, with the closed shutters on the ground floor. There, do you see it?'

So much for knocking on a door and asking directions. She had known which house it was immediately, and he had no doubt that she was right.

'I see it,' he said, noting the darkened windows when every other house had lights on somewhere. But he carried on driving. At the top of the street he turned to the right and pulled in a couple of metres along rue Cardin.

'You stay here, I'll just go . . .'

'*Non, non, non*. I am coming too. If Elodie is there, it will be better for her if I am there, to have a woman . . .'

Jacquot sighed. 'Okay, okay. But you do exactly as I say, *compris*? Everything. And no argument.'

Marie-Ange smiled, crossed her heart. 'It's a deal.'

'Are you sure you're up to it? You seem . . .'

'I'm fine,' she said again, buttoning up her coat and reaching for the door handle. She wasn't, but she wasn't going to let him know that. 'It was just . . .' She shook her head, as though words were hard to find. 'I wasn't expecting anything, but the moment we turned into the road, something . . . I don't know. All I can say is that there is danger there, and . . . something wrong. The house just . . . leapt at me. Almost as if it was barring the way, didn't want me there. It was a little strange, you know?'

Jacquot didn't know, but he nodded. 'Just so long as you're all right. Do you want to rest a moment?'

'No. Let's go,' she said, pushing open the door and climbing out of the car. 'Let's do it.'

As they turned the corner, back into rue Bandole, Jacquot felt Marie-Ange slide her arm through his. He didn't know whether she had done it to steady herself, because she needed support, or because she thought it might look more natural, in case someone in the house was looking out into the street. Just some couple walking past – going to a bar, to the cinema, out for the evening. If he'd thought about it, he might have done the same, but she had beaten him to it.

Keeping to the opposite side of the street, walking slowly despite the slope and the drizzling rain, they had longer to check out the house. No lights, no movement, the only house on that side of the street showing no sign of life. Watching it through the corners of their eyes, they walked on to the bottom of Bandole, then crossed the road and walked back up.

'The garden gate's open,' whispered Marie-Ange.

'And the garage door,' added Jacquot as they drew closer, the house only ten metres ahead of them now, close enough for them to make out the dark hollow of a garage and the garden gate standing a few inches ajar. They hadn't noticed that from the other side of the street.

A few steps further on, without any hesitation, as though they had reached their destination, Jacquot turned in at the gate, with Marie-Ange following behind. Together they climbed the steps and he rang the doorbell. There was no answer. He tried the bell again, longer this time, gave the door a couple of knocks, but no sound came from inside the house.

'Why don't we try the garage?' asked Marie-Ange. 'Maybe there's a connecting door.'

There was, indeed, a connecting door. And it was unlocked. Without making any sound Jacquot pushed it open and looked down a narrow passageway that smelt of cheap cooking oil and stale vegetables. There were no lights on and it took a moment for his eyes to grow accustomed to the darkness – on the left a washing machine and spin-drier, a cabinet freezer, and on the right a drying rack for clothes. At the end of the passage was a door. Placing his feet carefully and quietly, feeling for the movement of floorboards as he let his weight down, he crept towards it, wishing he had his gun.

Pausing at the door, he held up his hand to keep Marie-Ange back. But she came up right behind him and reached for his arm. He could feel her hands shaking.

'It's not good,' she managed. 'There's something not right . . .'

'It'll be fine,' he said. 'Just stay here. I'll be back for you.'

63

AS JACQUOT EDGED OPEN THE door, the smell of cooked food grew stronger. But there was something else too ... other scents he recognised. The sharp carbon reek of cordite mixed with something heavier, more pungent. He reached out his hand and felt for the light switch. His fingers found it and, taking a breath, he pushed it down.

A click, a buzz, a blinking strobe of blue light from a neon tube in the centre of the ceiling that sent shadows flickering around the room. A kitchen, just as he had guessed. And then the light caught and held and the neon hummed into life, blue turning to electric cream.

At once the shadows stopped racing and the room settled into its shape and form. Through the angle of the door he could see oak-fronted wall cupboards, a porcelain kitchen sink and wooden draining board, the corner of a kitchen table with two chairs, and a bulging black bin liner set beside what appeared to be a back door, waiting for someone to take out to the trash. There was a saucepan and casserole dish on the stove, an open cutlery drawer, a yellow plastic cloth on the kitchen table, and from where he stood he could see a bowl of fruit, an ashtray, a teaspoon, and a mortar with blue pills in it. The same pills, he was prepared to bet, that Xavier had bought from Petitjean.

It was then, stepping round the door, that Jacquot saw the body. A man. Head on the table, cheek to the cloth, hair spilled over his face, arms hanging down past his legs. He could have been sleeping, but Jacquot knew a corpse when he saw one – the slump of muscle, the heaviness, the punctured vital presence – confirmed by a deep dark puddle clotting beneath the table.

Jacquot drew closer, watching where he stepped, and brushed aside the long, curling black hair, touched the man's neck. Cold and hard, his eyes closed, his lips parted, a pale steely colour that made the white teeth look yellow, almost a smile in the two-day stubble. Young, maybe mid–thirties, and strikingly good-looking. He moved around the body, looking for the killing wound, and found it under the man's left arm – clean to the heart, the blood soaked through his T-shirt and cream linen trousers. Jacquot touched the bloodied cloth – sticky, nearly dry, the material stiffening.

It was then that he spotted a glint of brass on the edge of the puddle of blood. He reached down and picked it up, tipped it to the light. A shell casing. On the base, set around the dent from the gun's hammer, were the letters ber/g/gn. He slipped it into his pocket.

'There's another body,' said Marie-Ange. She hadn't waited, as she'd been told to do, but had followed Jacquot into the kitchen. Her voice was low, measured, as though she wasn't surprised by her discovery, not in any sense shocked. She was standing by the sink, looking at the back door.

Taking care not to stand in the blood and trail footprints around the kitchen, Jacquot went over to her and looked down at what he had first thought was a bag of rubbish. As he drew closer, opening up the angle between them, he could see now that he'd been mistaken. It was a woman. An old woman in a dark-blue dressing gown, crumpled in the doorway, her legs tucked under her, hands in her lap, her thin fingers curled. Santarem's mother, more than likely. The head had fallen forward, the greying hair gripped in coloured plastic rollers that had earlier looked to him like items of rubbish at the open end of a black bin liner. Jacquot went down on his haunches, noted the exit wound at the back of the skull, and tipped the head back with his index finger under her chin. In the space between her eyebrows was a small black-rimmed hole, a thin dried trickle of blood trailing down the side of her nose. There was also a dark bruise on her temple, as though she had struck her head against the corner of the work surface as she fell.

Jacquot didn't need any forensic team to give him the basics. The chill flesh, the drying blood, the stiffness of the bodies. A day dead. The pair of them. Sometime the previous night, he reckoned.

Jacquot got to his feet and looked around the walls. He found what he was looking for. A splintered hole in the side of a wall-cupboard, dressed in dark red, with drying shreds of grey tissue and bony splinters caught in it. She'd been shot right there, close to the cupboards. The bullet had gone straight through the old lady's head, taking fragments of skull with it, and lodged in the woodwork. But there was no misshapen plug of lead filling the hole. This bullet had been prised out and the casing picked up, pocketed, taken away.

A professional hit, no question, thought Jacquot.

He looked back at the other body. A body shot. Ejected casing left at the scene. Not so professional.

'Mother and son,' said Marie-Ange. 'She was not well. She was . . . confused. She . . .'

But Jacquot held up a finger, silenced her.

From behind an understairs door, which looked like it led down to the basement, came a soft scuffling sound. Once again Jacquot wished he had a gun.

For a moment there was silence, so deep they could hear the soft battery-driven tick of the clock on the wall and the whisper of neon. Then it came again, further away this time, and what sounded like muffled voices.

Stepping up to the edge of the door, Jacquot waved Marie-Ange to one side, out of any possible gunshot range, then he reached for the handle. He turned it slowly, tried to open the door, but it was locked. Releasing the handle, he reached for the key, felt the lock roll back and come to a rest. This time the door opened with a gentle squeak.

The warm, airless stench was immediate, a sinuous stream coiling up out of the darkened staircase and spilling into the kitchen. It was enough to make Jacquot step back and Marie-Ange cover her mouth and nose. It was clear there was something bad, something rotten, down there in the darkness. And alive. With the door open, the scuffling grew louder, attended by whispers, a frightened whimper and soft sobbing.

Jacquot put his hand inside the door, found a switch but no light came on. He looked around the kitchen, saw a torch hanging from a hook and snapped it on, the thin beam of light piercing the darkness beyond the basement door. He took the stairs carefully, bare wooden steps that creaked under his weight, breathing through his open mouth all the way down. At the bottom, wood gave way to bare earth that was soft beneath his shoes and smelled sweetly of vomit and urine. He swung the torch beam around the basement, shadows spinning away from four vertical wooden beams that supported the floor above. And there they were, huddling in a corner at the far end of the basement: pale dirty faces, wide frightened eyes, filthy hair.

'It's okay,' he called out, trying to make his voice soft, encouraging. 'I'm a policeman. You're okay.'

Behind him, Marie-Ange came down the stairs. She slid past him, looked at the huddle of girls in the far corner and whispered, 'You sort out upstairs. I'll go to them.'

64

THANKS TO GUILLERMO'S DIRECTIONS, Taddeus and Tomas had no trouble finding Xavier Vassin's home. They spotted it straight away, a narrow two-storey box of a house, with green garden gate and green front door, set in the middle of a sloping line of houses. Each property was divided by creeper-covered wire fences and narrow alleys, a shallow flight of red-tiled roofs dropping down just one side of the street, a basketball court and two residential blocks on the other side.

As the Corsicans edged their black Volkswagen into a space twenty metres down from the house, the streetlights in rue Artemis blinked on, one by one down the slope, a soft rain drifting on the breeze past the glowing goldfish-bowl lamps. It was still early, too early for them to make a move, so they settled down to wait. There was no discussion between the two men. When Taddeus killed the engine he reached into the VW's door pocket for his copy of Montaigne, opened it, found the page and angled it to catch the light from the nearest streetlight. Tomas, meanwhile, folded his arms and settled into his seat, his eyes fixed on the house with the green gate. Exactly fifteen minutes later, Taddeus put down Montaigne and Tomas flipped open the glove compartment and pulled out a book of crossword puzzles. Always general knowl-edge. And he never needed to fill in the spaces. Once he had the answer, the word or phrase was there in his head. He'd finish a crossword in less than an hour and there wouldn't be a mark on the page.

The two brothers waited patiently, for more than two hours, as life on rue Artemis began to slow: the last of the street's Saturday workers coming home on foot or by car, double-parking if they couldn't find a space; the younger kids called in first for their supper and bed; the older kids hauled off the basketball court not long afterwards. It was only when all was quiet that the two men stirred – crosswords and *pensées* put aside.

Taddeus found some breath freshener and sprayed it into his mouth. Chewing the taste into his cheeks, he put the aerosol away and, in a simple reflex, raised a hand to his left armpit, as someone else might check for their wallet. Tomas did the same.

It was time to go to work.

Out on the pavement, the two men put up their umbrellas and parted company. Tomas walked up the street and Taddeus walked down, coming back together in the shadow of a white Renault van. With a final glance around, Taddeus eased open the gate and started up the short path. There was a single curtained light on the ground floor but nothing in the upper rooms.

At the front door, Taddeus turned to his brother. 'Montaigne says that the greatest happiness we can know comes from a liberation of the soul.' It was the first time either of them had spoken.

'Is that so?' replied Tomas, lowering his umbrella, shaking it out and standing it against the wall.

Taddeus did the same, then leant forward, ear cocked to the green door.

Behind it, somewhere in the house, came the unmistakable sound of running feet.

65

ELODIE LAY ON THE BED waiting for him, whoever he was, chill with a trembling fear but coiled tight with a desperate determination. She wasn't going to kill him – or at least she didn't intend to. What she wanted to do was hurt him or knock him off balance just long enough to make her escape. The man downstairs, the man holding her prisoner, thought she was drugged. But she wasn't. Not any more. All she had to do was make that advantage work for her. Because it was the only advantage she had. That, and the small pair of nail scissors she'd found under a chest of drawers in her room and now clutched in her hand.

As far as she could tell, she had been locked away in this tiny single bedroom from darkness to darkness, a passage of time she had measured by the brightness of the pinprick holes in the metal blind rolled down on the outside of the locked window. And in that time she had slowly but surely regained her senses. She still ached from the drugs she'd been fed, and her limbs felt soft and floppy from lack of exercise, but she was finally starting to think straight.

She might not have been able to say exactly how long it had been since she'd climbed into the passenger seat of Murat's van on rue Raspail, but she knew it had been long enough for her to start smelling. Her blonde hair was greasy and lank, her teeth thickly coated in a soft velvet mat, and her skin so filthy that when she rubbed her fingertips along her arm, the dirt rolled away in grimy black balls. She had never gone so long without a bath or a shower, and to make matters worse she felt horribly constipated, slow and fat and bloated. She'd also been badly bitten by whatever bugs had inhabited the mattress she'd been dumped on in that cellar, her legs and arms, face and neck – any patch of bare skin – reduced to a rough, itchy swelling of hard spots and crusted heads where she'd scratched too enthusiastically.

But there was nothing she could do about any of that now – the smell of her body, or the foul taste in her mouth, or the itching, or the bloating, or the dull echo of a headache. What she had to do now was concentrate on getting out of there. The next time he came to check on her or feed her, hopefully leaving the door open behind him as he'd done the last time he'd looked in on her, she was going to stab him and make a run for it, maybe even slam the door on him and lock him in if she had enough time.

All she had to do was wait. And be brave. And hold her nerve. If she didn't, there was no telling what might happen to her.

It had begun the night before – the sound of raised voices somewhere above her, followed by a muffled gunshot. Her first thought had been that they were being rescued, that the police had come for them, and there in the darkness she had felt like shouting out: 'I'm here. We're here. We're down here.'

But something had made her stay silent, some sixth sense, as the basement door creaked open and a figure came down, flashing a torch around, moving from one girl to the next. She could hear his voice, gentle, persuasive – 'Elodie? *Es-tu* Elodie?' – but she'd stayed silent, suddenly not sure. Why was he asking only for her? And then it was her turn – 'Elodie? *C'est toi*?' He was close enough for her to smell his breath on her face – beery and stale. And in the torchlight she'd seen the scarf, and the scar, and from somewhere she felt a dim distant sense that she had seen him before. He was one of them. She was sure of it.

But there'd seemed little point in not responding so she'd nodded her head, pretending to be more dazed and confused than she was.

And suddenly he was sliding his arm round her and helping her sit up, whispering to her in the torchlight – he was a policeman, she would be home soon, with her parents, everything would be fine.

And for a moment she'd wanted to believe him, wanted to believe he was telling her the truth, that he had come to rescue her. But then he had a bowl of that horrible stew in his hand, and a bottle of water, and he was telling her to eat, to drink, she needed to get her strength back. And she'd known then, for certain, that he was lying, that he wasn't a policeman, that he hadn't come to take her home, and that if she ate or drank anything he offered her she would go to sleep again.

So she'd pretended to take the food, to eat it, to swallow, but as he spooned it into her mouth she had coughed and choked it out unseen, into her hand, smearing it along the edge of her mattress. And then, after only half-a-dozen mouthfuls, she'd brushed the spoon away, and let herself go loose.

Now, lying on her bed in the darkness, with the scissors clenched in her fist, nerving herself to attack him and make a run for it, Elodie listened for sounds from below. For most of the day she'd heard the distant chatter of a radio station, then a hi-fi playing rock and roll, but now there was the canned sound of laughter from some TV game show. And, for the last twenty minutes, the smell of cooking. She was sure of it. He was getting her something to eat. If only to feed her more drugs.

Any time now, she thought, any time now . . . and a moment later the TV went off and she heard a thomp-thomp-thomp as he came up the stairs.

And there he was, pushing open the bedroom door, carrying a tray, a shaft of light from the landing spilling in behind him.

She held her breath, waited, fist tightening on the scissors, watching through half-closed eyes as he approached the bed, bent down to put the tray on the bedside table. And as he did so she swung her arm up with all the strength she could muster and plunged the scissors into his side, heard him grunt with surprise and stagger sideways, and the tray crash to the floor.

But she didn't wait to see what damage she might have caused. She was up, struggling off the bed, racing for the door as best she could, the first time in days that she had properly moved her legs, suddenly a dangerous and unexpected liability, thin and weak and clumsy beneath her as though they belonged to someone else. But at least she was moving, getting somewhere, through the open bedroom door and out on to a landing, no time to lock him in, the stairs to the right and just ahead of her.

In a jerky, jumping, downward rush she bounded down to the ground floor. Into a low-lit salon, a muted TV flickering in the corner, posters on the wall, a single leather armchair, a low coffee table, a long ratty sofa covered in throws. Past a small kitchen area and breakfast bar. Where to go? she screamed to herself. Which way now? How did she get out of there? And then she spotted the hallway and knew where to run.

But he was coming after her. She could hear him crashing his way down the stairs, lumbering through the salon, stumbling over the furniture. As she turned into the hallway, she chanced a look back, just an instant, to see how close he was, how much time she had, whether she could get to the front door, open it and get out of there before he caught up with her, praying the door wasn't locked, praying she was far enough ahead. And there he was, charging after her, one hand pressed to his side, a red stain spreading over his white T-shirt, his face clenched with pain and rage.

And gaining on her.

Closing on her.

But it didn't matter.

Suddenly the front door burst open, and two men stood there, close enough for her to collide with one of them, falling at his feet.

Elodie's heart sank. He hadn't been alone after all. He did have back-up. And here they were, just as she was trying to make her escape.

Or were they police? Was this another rescue?

There was no time to think. The man she'd run into scooped her up, and as he did so she saw his companion reach into his coat and bring out a gun. She watched his arm snake past her and distinctly heard two low popping sounds.

Phut. Phut.

And from somewhere behind her she heard a stunned, pig-like grunt and the sound of a body crashing back on to the hallway floor.

It was over in seconds.

'Are you okay?' asked the man holding her. He had lovely blue eyes, honest, kind, caring. He was clean-shaven and his breath smelt minty. And he was dressed well, in a suit and an overcoat that felt soft and warm and expensive even if it was wet.

'Are you the police?' she asked.

'Something like that,' he said, and smiled.

And she felt just the tiniest prick in the side of her neck.

66

IT TOOK NEARLY TWENTY MINUTES to coax the girls from
Murat Santarem's basement, six of them, clinging to one another
and squinting as they stepped into the kitchen light. As far as
Jacquot could tell, greeting them at the top of the stairs, handing
out blankets which he had stripped from the beds upstairs, they
ranged in age from fourteen to sixteen. None of them had shoes.
Two of them wore dresses and one was wearing what looked like
part of a school uniform – a white shirt, knee-length grey socks
and a pleated skirt. The remaining three wore jeans. Each of them
had a name written in felt-tip pen on the front of their blouse or
T-shirt: Ilse, Wanda, Elise, Anna, Marga and Kris.

Smiling kindly, Jacquot directed the girls to the salon where he'd
put out jugs of water and milk and whatever food he'd been able
to find: some bread, cheese, biscuits, a bag of mixed nuts and
raisins, some olives, a bunch of grapes, a couple of oranges, and
some bananas. There'd have been apples, too, from the fruit bowl,
if they hadn't been plastic, and stew from the casserole if it hadn't
had an odd taste. Probably laced with the ground-up pills from the
mortar, Jacquot guessed.

As well as sourcing blankets and food, he had also dealt with
Santarem and the old lady, covering their bodies with a pair of
damp tablecloths he'd found in the washing machine, so the girls

wouldn't see them. They looked like icebergs floating on the blue lino floor; it wouldn't have taken much to make out what they really were, but there wasn't anything Jacquot could do about that.

Marie-Ange was the last one up from the basement.

'She was here,' whispered Marie-Ange, breathless with excitement, as they followed the girls down the hallway. 'Elodie. Here, in this house. She was here. They told me.'

Jacquot nodded. It made sense, with these other girls held in the basement, but that didn't mean he wasn't astonished just how quickly they'd managed to track her down. And, judging by the bodies in the kitchen, only a few hours behind her.

As he ushered Marie-Ange into the salon where the girls had set to on the food, he realised that he shouldn't have been too surprised. Not with Marie-Ange at his side. If they hadn't bumped into each other . . . If they hadn't gone for that drink in Bar Dantès . . . If she hadn't spotted Scarface . . . well, he'd likely still be wandering around the docks by himself, looking for a lead.

But where was Elodie now? he wondered. Did Xavier have her? Or the other killer? Which of them had got to the house first?

'So what did they tell you?' he asked.

'Just that she was here. A girl called Elodie. And that a man came to get her.'

'When?' asked Jacquot, peeling the skin of an orange for one of the girls.

'They can't remember. One said an hour ago, another said yesterday.' Marie-Ange shrugged. 'They're still a bit out of it. According to the Swiss girl, the guy who came for her said he was a policeman too.'

'They're not French then?'

Marie-Ange shook her head. 'These two,' she said, nodding to the girls nearest to them, 'Ilse and Wanda, are from Austria – Vienna and a place called Kirkshof; the Swiss girl, Elise, is the other side of them.' Marie-Ange turned to the facing sofa. 'The other three, over there, are from Belgium and Holland. According to the Belgian girl, Marga – the one you just gave the orange to – he shone a torch around and asked for Elodie. Apparently he gave her some food and water then took her away, locking the door after him. There was gunfire too.'

'Before or after he came to get her?'

'Before, she thinks.'

'How many shots?'

'Just the one.'

Jacquot smiled. 'You asked?'

'It seemed a good question.'

'Any description?' he asked.

'You know what it's like down there. Even in daylight it'd be too dark. There's only one tiny window and it's been painted out.'

'He had a scar, monsieur,' came a tiny voice. It belonged to the Austrian girl, Ilse, in the pleated skirt. She might have been answering a question in a classroom. 'Like this,' she continued, and drew her finger down her cheek.

'Xavier,' said Marie-Ange.

Jacquot nodded. 'And he'll have used my gun to kill Santarem.'

'Not the mother, too?'

Jacquot shook his head. 'Two different guns. Two different killers.'

'Two? How do you know?'

'I just know, believe me . . .' If she'd pressed him for a reason, he'd have shown her the shell casing in his pocket. And told her what the letters – ber/g/gn – stamped on its base signified. Brand: Beretta. Model: the 92G. Issue: Gendarmerie Nationale.

'It wasn't just the man with the scar,' piped up another voice. It was Marga, the Belgian girl. She was lanky and blonde with a sour-looking mouth and sharp *banlieue* accent. 'There were two more come afterwards,' she continued.

Jacquot looked at Marie-Ange and smiled a told-you-so smile.

'Men or women?' he asked, turning back to Marga.

'Both men.'

'And what did they look like?' asked Jacquot. Whoever they were, they were the ones who had killed the old lady.

The girl shrugged. 'Dressed in black, is all I can remember. They came down like the other one and asked for this Elodie. Didn't bother with any "Police" crap . . .'

'And when was this, *s'il vous plaît*?'

Marga shook her head, shrugged helplessly. 'Not sure,' she replied. 'A couple of hours ago? I don't know. Could be more.'

'And what did they do,' asked Jacquot, 'when they discovered she was gone?'

'One said *merde*.' It was Ilse, the Austrian girl, again. She seemed to take a childish relish in using the word, as though it was not normally a part of her vocabulary, forbidden at home and at school, but here she could say it with impunity.

'And that's it?'

Marga nodded. 'Brought some water down for us. Then locked us in again.'

Jacquot pushed back his cuff and looked at his watch. A little before nine. He knew there wasn't anything more he was going to get from the girls so he excused himself and left the room. Out in the kitchen he went to the phone and dialled the emergency services, requested an ambulance and gave Santarem's address. 'Six girls. In trouble. Need help,' was all he said before ending the call and pulling the plug. Back in the salon, he found a socket by the TV and reconnected the phone. Then he turned and put it on the table between the two sofas.

'I'm sure there are people you will want to call,' he told them. 'Your mothers and fathers. To let them know you're safe . . .' Quite unexpectedly, Jacquot felt his throat tighten. He nodded, rather than risk saying anything more, and indicated the phone. Marga was the first to grab it.

As she dialled her number, the others crowded round. Over their heads, Jacquot caught Marie-Ange's eye.

She came over to him.

'I called the emergency services,' he told her. 'We need to get moving.'

'Get moving where?' she asked.

'Rue Artemis. Where our friend Xavier lives. Or lived.'

264

67

'YOU THINK HE'S DEAD?' asked Marie-Ange, hurrying along beside Jacquot as they left the house and started up rue Bandole.

'I'd say it's a very good bet,' he replied. 'He got here first, probably last night, used my gun to kill Santarem, then took the girl.'

'But why?'

'Maybe he was getting greedy. Wanted her all to himself. Since Santarem hadn't put in a ransom demand, it stands to reason he either didn't know who he had down there, just one of a load of girls he was shipping out, or he couldn't be bothered to play her.'

'Play her?'

'Go for the ransom. Money. Big money. But Xavier must have known, and by the look of it he did want to play her.'

'What about the other two men who came later?'

'That I don't know. But whoever they are, they're professionals. Either working for themselves, or hired by someone to find Elodie. Which means that right now they'll be looking for Xavier. Or they've already found him.'

'How would they know about Xavier?'

'Your guess is as good as mine. Maybe the same way they knew about Santarem. Or maybe the old lady told them, before one of them dropped her. But if they do know about him, and where he lives . . .'

As Jacquot and Marie-Ange reached the corner of rue Bandole and turned on to rue Cardin they heard the distant, wailing rise and fall of sirens. By the time they were back in the 2CV the flashing blue lights of an ambulance were coming up fast behind them, the vehicle swinging left up ahead and down into rue Bandole. Before they could get away, two blue squad cars from the gendarmerie came racing past, one of them missing the turning, but the other just making it. By the time the driver of the first squad car had reversed and made the turn, two unmarked units, coming from opposite directions, squealed around the corner after it.

Unmarked. The boys, thought Jacquot. And he wondered who they'd be. Peluze? Grenier? Muzon? Or maybe even Gastal. According to Solange Bonnefoy he called her almost every day with some update. He'd certainly have an update for her after this little find, thought Jacquot, if not an altogether comforting one.

When the road was finally clear, Jacquot started up the 2CV, pulled out and drove across the top of rue Bandole. As they passed the turning, he and Marie-Ange looked back at the Santarem house. Half-way down the street, the road was blocked by a scrum of emergency vehicles and flashing lights. Already a couple of gendarmes in capes and *képis* were running tape around the scene, from one streetlight to another. It would be the same further down.

'Do you have a city map in the car?' asked Jacquot, as he followed rue Cardin down to the Littoral.

'Under your seat,' she told him.

Jacquot reached between his legs and felt around for the book. He found it and pulled it out, handed it to Marie-Ange.

'Look up rue Artemis,' he told her. 'If I remember correctly it's somewhere in the fifth, around Saint Luc.'

'You'll have to pull over,' she told him, 'under a streetlight, so I can read the index. The print is so tiny, it's just impossible.'

Jacquot checked his mirror and pulled over, close to a light.

'One day there'll be a machine in cars,' said Marie-Ange, as her finger dropped down the first column of the index. 'You say where you want to go and it will tell you how to get there . . . Ah, here it is. And we are lucky. Just the one. Rue Artemis, in the Fifth, off . . .' she turned to the map page and followed the grid references, ' . . . Boulevard Saint Clément. You know where it is?'

'Now I do,' replied Jacquot, and he took off again, past the docks and up on to the Littoral access ramp. 'It's not far but we'll have to hurry. We may be too late to help Xavier, but right now we have to keep ahead of the *flics*. Young Marga is sure to tell them about us, and where we were headed.'

For the next few minutes they drove in silence, past the layered Romanesque flanks of Cathédrale de la Major, down on to Quai du Port, up La Canebière and into the Fifth. At the bottom of Boulevard Saint Clément they were brought up short at a set of traffic lights, the wipers swishing away the rain.

'It was a wonderful moment, wasn't it?' said Marie-Ange softly.

'What moment was that?' asked Jacquot. 'You mean, finding them?'

'Of course, that. But giving them the telephone, that was the real moment. Did you see their eyes? Even the hard one, Marga.'

'I didn't know what to say . . .'

'I saw that too,' she said, gently. 'For a policeman, Monsier Daniel Jacquot, you're just a bit of a softie.' Taking off his trousers had made her brave, she decided.

He acknowledged she was correct, thinking to himself that when a woman has taken off your trousers without you knowing anything about it, there's not much point putting on an act.

Finally the lights changed and four blocks on they turned off Saint Clément, pulled into rue Artemis and did exactly what they had done before, driving the length of the street, parking the car around the corner and coming back down on foot.

Unlike rue Bandole, it was a rougher neighbourhood, this part of the Fifth, and the road was badly pot-holed and dimly lit, the line of small block-built properties on one side of the street set behind waist-high walls, many of them spray-painted with graffiti. In an attempt to make the street a little more attractive, the local council had planted trees along the pavement. Only stumps remained, none higher than a metre, any branches ripped off.

As they walked back down the street, Jacquot examined each of the houses they passed. There were sixteen in all, bracketed by a tyre fitters at one end and an all-night launderette at the other, with nothing to distinguish one property from the next, all of them ill-kept and tawdry. Refuse bins stood by front doors, with two of the twenty or so cars along the street wheel-less and up on bricks. When they reached the launderette, Jacquot and Marie-Ange stood beneath its awning, the strong smell of washing powder and the warmth of clothes driers seeping through the glass doorway. There were a couple of old women sitting inside on the benches, reading battered copes of *Pointe de Vue* as they waited for the machines to do their work for them. In the old days, Jacquot knew, they'd have taken their dirty clothes down to the baths on Boulevard Saint Clément.

'What do you think?' asked Marie-Ange.

He shook his head. 'I just don't know. None of them stands out. They all look like the kind of house where a low-life like Xavier might live, but we can hardly go knocking on every door. Did you . . . feel anything? Was there anything that caught your attention?'

'Nothing like Bandole. Nothing immediate . . .'

'But?'

Marie-Ange shrugged. 'It may be coincidence, but there's a van half-way down – the white one? There was something about it, something . . . I don't know. Something . . . familiar.'

Jacquot peered up the street. He'd been so busy checking out the houses that he hadn't paid much attention to the cars parked along its length. He could see the van now, partly visible behind the car parked in front of it. He thought of the empty garage at the house on rue Bandole. It was just about high and wide enough to accommodate a van like that, a van that looked as though it could quite comfortably accommodate the six girls they'd found . . . or eight even, if they counted Lucienne and Elodie.

'Let's go back and have another look,' he said, taking Marie-Ange's arm. 'Only this time we'll keep to the road, put the van between us and the houses.'

It was late and there was no traffic as they walked back up the street, just a cat streaking across the road through the rain. The van had been parked facing up the street, coming from the same direction that they had, driver's side to the street, passenger door closest to the pavement. The first thing that Jacquot noted was the registration.

'Paris plates,' he said to Marie-Ange, 'and in good condition for this part of town.' He cupped one hand and peered through the driver's window – the passenger seat pushed way back, sandwich wrappers, an empty bottle of Orangina, an old newspaper.

'And it has a roller-tailgate, not doors,' said Marie-Ange. 'You lift it up, pull it down. Like at Fleurs des Quais. It makes a rattling sound. That's the sound I remember from the lorry park. In my dream,' she added, a little more softly.

She glanced at Jacquot. He'd left the window and was leaning down, running a finger along a deep scratch over the rear wheel-arch.

Jacquot straightened up and a smile of satisfaction slid across his lips. Detective work – joining the dots, building the wall; he loved it.

Marie-Ange frowned. 'What's so funny?'

'Remember the garage on rue Bandole? There was a scrape of white paint along the left-hand side of the door-frame. At just about that height,' he said, pointing to the scratch he'd been examining. 'I'm not a betting man, but I'd say we have found Monsieur Santarem's van and that Xavier used it to bring Elodie here, either in the back, or, more likely, bundled up in the passenger footwell where he could keep an eye on her, and get her out quick into one of these houses.' He peered around the back of the van. 'But which one? You got any ideas?'

Marie-Ange shook her head. 'I'm sorry,' she said, quietly. 'I just don't know.'

It was then that Jacquot spotted something. Through the rain. Something that shouldn't have been there. The house one down from the van. With a green gate set into the low wall, a beer can stuck between the railings on the top of it, and what looked like a front door not quite square in its frame, an odd spill of light falling on the steps. But what he'd spotted was a wisp of black smoke.

'Quick,' he said, pointing. 'The house there . . .'

And he was gone.

68

BY THE TIME MARIE-ANGE came round the back of the van, Jacquot was already through the gate and sprinting up the path. She raced after him, reaching the narrow porch in time to see that the door was off its top hinge and the hallway beyond was filled with smoke, coiling like a black snake along the ceiling and being sucked through the open doorway. She wasn't certain whether Jacquot had barged it open himself or if he'd found it like that. All she could see was his outline up ahead, pulling his jacket off and wrapping it round his head as he disappeared into the house. Pulling off her own jacket and plugging it against her mouth, she pushed through the front door and followed him, down a smoke-filled hallway. The first thing she saw, through watering eyes, was a body sprawled against the wall, almost hidden under a rack of coats. But she didn't stop, just hurried after Jacquot, through an archway to the right and into a small galley kitchen, the ruby glow of an electric stove plate radiating heat and colour through the smoke.

'Get some water,' he shouted, wrenching out the wall-plug for the electric cooker and knocking a skillet pan off the top of it and on to the floor. A boiling black spiral of smoke poured off the pan, filling the kitchen with the hot stench of burning food.

Marie-Ange didn't waste a second. Snatching up a kettle, she emptied the contents on to the skillet and the black smoke turned into a billowing, scalding hiss of steam. On the other side of the kitchen, Jacquot leaned across the sink and flung open a window, fanning away the smoke with his jacket.

With a through-draft from kitchen window to front door, the smoke and steam soon cleared, the tiled kitchen floor puddled with blackened water, the skillet in the middle of it still hissing and ticking.

'Another few minutes and we'd have been too late,' said Jacquot, holding up a scorched drying cloth, its singed edges still smoking, before dropping it into the puddle. 'Or someone else would have smelled the smoke and come running.'

'There's a body,' said Marie-Ange, putting the kettle back on its stand.

'There is? Where?'

'The hallway. You went right past it.'

Jacquot stepped over the skillet and went to take a look. 'I didn't see it,' he said, dropping down on one knee. It was Xavier Vassin, his eyes wide with shock, a neat hole in the centre of his forehead and a second hole in his left cheek. Jacquot lifted the head, felt the sticky, bony edges of a single large exit wound, and looked up at the coat rack above the body. A cream cotton windcheater was spattered with blood at about head height. Getting up, Jacquot started working through the coats. He found what he was looking for soon enough. The two high-impact bullets may have hit their target within a few centimetres of each other, but Xavier's bony skull had deflected their trajectory and spread the spent slugs much further apart. The first had torn through the windcheater and lodged in the wall, but the second had sheared away to the left and taken a gouge of plaster out of the cornicing. He reached out, put a finger to each of the holes, then looked around the floor of the hallway. No curled, flattened shells in the plaster, and no shiny brass shell casings either. Just like the kitchen cupboard on rue Bandole.

Going back to the body, Jacquot examined the spill of blood on the front and side of the man's white T-shirt. It seemed strangely localised – with no apparent connection to the bullet wounds – and he pulled up the man's shirt. Just as he'd thought. No bullet, this, but a jagged wound, probably a stabbing, an inch above the top of his jeans. It wouldn't have killed him, but it would have bled like an open tap and hurt like hell, and sooner or later Xavier would have had to get it treated.

After searching the ground floor – just the blackened kitchen, a cramped salon poorly furnished, and a squat lavatory by the back door – the two of them climbed the stairs. On the landing Jacquot found what had caused Xavier's wound, a pair of bloodied scissors, the blades curved for cutting fingernails, small enough to fit into a purse, just lying on the carpet.

She tried to make a run for it, he thought.

Elodie must have found those scissors somewhere, and stuck them into Xavier – when he came up to feed her or check on her.

Plucky girl, thought Jacquot. A true Bonnefoy. Her aunt – and her mother, too – would be proud of her.

He passed the scissors to Marie-Ange, and looked around the landing. Three closed doors. The first door he pushed open led to a bathroom – plastic shower curtain, one toothbrush, a pair of trainers in the bidet; the second concealed an untidy pit of a bedroom at the front of the house, bed unmade, clothes littering the floor, the whole room thick with the airless smell of a man who didn't care too much for ventilation; but in the third room, at the back of the house, was a single bed, its thin blue counterpane rucked and ruffled, its pillow dented, a tray of food spilled on the carpet.

Jacquot stood in the doorway and could almost see the action playing out in front of him. Elodie's lunge from the bed, the girl clearly no longer drugged but pretending to be asleep as Xavier bent down to put the tray on the bedside table. And then she was off that bed, scrambling past him for the door, while a stunned Xavier groped to find his wound, realised what had happened and turned to give chase.

Which of them, Jacquot wondered, had thrown the scissors to the landing floor? Was it Elodie? Or had she left them sticking in Xavier's gut, for him to pull out and cast aside?

But before she'd got very far, probably before she made the stairs, Xavier was after her, oblivious to his wound, desperate to stop her reaching the front door and running out into the street. A door which suddenly sprang open as his two killers shouldered it off its hinges and dealt with everything – Elodie and Xavier.

At rue Bandole they had been hours behind the action. But here it was ten or fifteen minutes. No more than that. Any longer and the place would have been ablaze. He wondered about the time-frame, the loss of headway? Had the killers not known where to come after hitting the Santarem place? There was no other explanation. But some time after hitting rue Bandole, they'd found out and followed up.

'She was here, wasn't she?' said Marie-Ange quietly, the scissors in her hands.

'Oh, yes, she was here,' replied Jacquot, turning from the doorway. 'But where is she now?'

It was then that they heard the first siren.

Marga, back at rue Bandole. She'd have told the police where he and Marie-Ange were headed. He could almost hear her. 'They said they were going to rue Artemis . . .'

Jacquot could have kicked himself. He should have kept his mouth shut or at least waited until they were out of earshot. And learnt his lesson; it was Madame Boileau all over again.

'Time to go,' he said, as a car squealed to a halt out in the street. 'Come on, out the back. *Allons-y*. We'll have to make a run for it.'

69

ALAIN GASTAL WAS NOT IN a good mood.

The day may have begun badly with the loss of his latest snout, Marcel Lévy, but the appearance of Mademoiselle Carinthe Cousteaux in his office had changed all that. If Gastal could have picked a better informer he couldn't imagine it. A woman of a certain age, a once trusted confidante, motivated by that greatest of all persuaders. Not fear, but revenge. A woman who had been unceremoniously dumped by the new management, given just a few hours to pack her things, and driven to the Sofitel where a stand-ard room had been laid on for just two weeks. There was no need for him to coax, or threaten, or scare, no need to play the heavy to get Carinthe Cousteaux talking. She wanted to talk. Was happy to do it. And for more than two hours, in Gastal's office in Police Headquarters on rue de l'Evêché, that's exactly what she had done.

For the last four years, maybe twice a week, Monsieur Arsène Cabrille had shared her bed in Endoume, and during that time there wasn't a great deal she hadn't learnt about the man and his operations. And remembered. Things he'd said to her, told her about, let slip; things she'd heard him say on the phone or in his sleep even. Her insurance policy, she told Gastal. Just in case. And her recall was prodigious, nothing less than an insider's guide to Monsieur Arsène Cabrille and his various operations. Everything from his clinics, care homes and hospices to his construction companies and trading fleet, the thing Cabrille loved most, a dozen mid-sized freighters and their occasional illicit cargoes – cocaine and heroin usually – never more than two- or three-hundred-kilo bales concealed in otherwise legitimate ten-thousand-bale loads. There was even a ship in port that very moment, she'd told him, and though the name escaped her now, she'd assured him that she would remember it in due course.

And Gastal had lapped it up, having to hold up his hand and stop her occasionally when he had to change the tape, so he wouldn't miss a thing, the only real disappointment the way she shook her head when he'd asked about the missing girl, Elodie Lafour. It didn't ring a bell, she told him. Cabrille hadn't mentioned it. She was sure of it.

And all the time, Gastal had watched her, couldn't take his eyes off her. Those scarlet lips, those soft almond eyes as black as treacle, the silky crossing and recrossing of her legs, the occasional shifting of her shoulders that seemed to set into movement the great and glorious juxtaposition of her breasts.

Nearly three hours after finding her in his office, Gastal thanked her for her help and her time and, rather than have one of the squad take her back to the Sofitel, he'd offered to drop her back there himself. The least he could do. And she had seemed delighted at the prospect, the personal service, and when he suggested en route that maybe they should stop somewhere for a drink, or a light supper, she had seemed equally happy to accept, switching on a warmth of attention and flood of compliments that washed over him like a scented wave. With as solid a certainty as a man can possess, he was sure that within the next few hours he would be opening the front of Mademoiselle Carinthe Cousteaux's blouse and helping himself to its contents.

But it was not to be. After a nightcap in the Sofitel bar, the lights of the Vieux Port twinkling through a rain-smeared picture window, just as he was about to suggest that maybe they would be more comfortable in her room, as if reading his mind, the lady mentioned

276

that ten thousand francs would be a suitable . . . an appropriate gesture of goodwill on his part.

She'd said it with a confiding smile, her fingers brushing across the tops of his thighs, and it had taken more than a few seconds before Gastal quite understood what it was she had just told him. If he wanted to sleep with her, then he'd have to pay. Not that he was unused to the exchange of money before sex. But this time he'd been appalled. The very thought of it! Five thousand he might have managed, but ten was out of the question. And he'd been so certain . . . had no idea . . . Fuming with anger and indignation, but holding on to his temper, for this was a snout not to mess with, he had made his excuses and left with as much dignity as he could muster. Back in his car, he slammed the steering wheel with his fist, elbowed the door and swore low and long. It was exactly then that he heard a police despatcher call in an all points on six girls in a house on rue Bandole.

By the time he arrived the place was overrun with paramedics and an emergency victim-support unit seeing to the girls, while four of his squad stood talking it over in the kitchen.

'She's not here, boss,' Laganne had told him, chewing on a tooth-pick. 'She was, but someone took her.'

And now, an hour later, stepping aside as the body of Xavier Vassin was loaded on to a stretcher and manoeuvred down the hallway on rue Artemis – the name and address provided by a Belgian girl called Marga at rue Bandole – there was still no Elodie.

Gastal swore under his breath. He'd been so certain they'd find her – that *he'd* find her – so sure of it, as he'd spun across town towards rue Bandole and then on to rue Artemis, that he could almost taste the *raviolis* of foie gras and truffles at Pierre Orsi.

But he was getting closer. He knew it. He could smell it. Vassin was the man who'd snatched Elodie from Santarem – an accom-plice, maybe, who'd grown too greedy, that was the way Gastal read it. And the two *gorilles* who had got to rue Bandole next and had tracked him down here, put him down and taken the girl, were probably the same ones who'd done Valentine and his boys, and maybe Lévy, and maybe even the same ones who'd removed Mademoiselle Cousteaux from her Endoume love nest to a guest room in the Sofitel. In which case it seemed reasonable to suppose that Virginie Cabrille might also be after the girl.

What he couldn't figure out was who the man and the woman were, the ones who'd come in third at rue Bandole, the ones who'd thoughtfully covered the bodies of Murat Santarem and his mother, and, by the look of it, done the same at rue Artemis – the doused fire, the stove plug out, the thrown skillet.

'We've got a gun!' called Grenier, breaking into his thoughts, holding up an evidence bag. 'In a kitchen drawer. Beretta. Looks like service issue. Maybe one of ours.'

Gastal frowned. 'Call it in. Get it matched. Ballistics. And prints too. Like, yesterday,' he added, when Grenier just pocketed the bagged gun and strolled off with a nod in his direction.

Christ, sometimes he hated them more than they hated him.

70

TWO MEN, DRESSED IN BLACK. Two professionals, in Jacquot's opinion, given the ruthless efficiency of their killing style. Everything measured. Precise. No slugs, no casings. Nothing left to point to them at the house on either rue Bandole or rue Artemis, nothing to give them away save the slick style of the murders.

If Jacquot had been investigating these killings as a duty cop, he'd have rung every doorbell there and then, hustled friends and neighbours out of their beds, and started asking questions. Did anyone see anything? Hear anything? Tonight? Last night? The last seven days? Cars? Faces? Strangers? But he was working under-cover. Proper police procedure was not an option here.

'It's like we're right back at square one,' said Marie-Ange, quietly, hopelessly. They were sitting at a table in Bar Dantès where, twenty-four hours earlier, she had first spotted the man in her dreams: Scarface. Xavier. Xavier Vassin. It was well past midnight, but they weren't the only customers.

'On the contrary,' said Jacquot. 'We are much further along, much closer. At Santarem's house we were maybe a day behind Elodie, but at rue Artemis maybe just a few minutes. *En effet*, if we had gone there before rue Bandole we might even have Elodie with us right now. But we didn't. Sometimes that's how it is.' He shrugged, glancing across at his companion. For a woman who'd

279

seen three dead bodies in the last four hours, Marie-Ange appeared remarkably composed, if a little downhearted.

'So close, but so far,' she replied, stirring her *menthe frappée*. 'I don't know why I ordered this,' she continued. 'It tastes horrible.'

'However it tastes,' said Jacquot with a smile, 'it's worth remembering that a *menthe frappée* was the drink Elodie ordered before she disappeared.'

This information brought a fleeting smile to her face. 'Really? Then that's the reason. I couldn't understand why I asked for it. It just popped into my head. And I was worrying that I was losing my way. Not being any help. Not being able to tell which house . . .' She looked down at the table and shook her head, her hair falling forward like a pair of wings. 'And now we've hit a dead end.'

'I promise you we haven't,' replied Jacquot, taking a sip of his coffee and following it with a slug of the Calva he'd ordered to accompany it. 'Police work,' he continued quietly, 'investigations like this, well, it's like building a wall. Each case the same. Never varies. Just stone after stone, one on top of the other, until . . .'

'Until it all comes tumbling down,' she interrupted miserably.

'*Non, non, non. Pas du tout.* Look how far we've come since the last time we sat here. We know that Elodie is in Marseilles. We know that she was probably picked up by Murat in Paris, in his van with the Paris plates. We know that she was brought here with other girls, six of whom are being looked after by the emergency services, and even now being reunited with their parents. We identified Scarface – Monsieur Xavier Vassin. Established that he worked with this Murat Santarem, trafficking these girls, and we tracked them both down – first one, then the other. And now we know that Elodie is with two men, professional hit men, either working on their own account or, more likely, for someone here in Marseilles. Someone big. Someone who can afford to bring in professionals, or else employs them right here. And it's the latter I'd go for. Those two men in black are Marseillais, for certain.'

'And how exactly do you work that out?' asked Marie-Ange, her eyes wide, stunned by Jacquot's take on what she saw as complete failure.

'*M'écoute*. They knew their way round town. They knew where to go. How to get there, do what they had to do, and get out of there. And they'll have been looking just as long as we have. Maybe longer. Which suggests they have a base, somewhere safe, here in the city. Somewhere they can go without arousing suspicion – so rule out a hotel.'

'What's our next move then?'

Jacquot looked at his watch.

'We sleep on it. It's been a long day.' He pulled the car keys from his jacket pocket and pushed them across the table. 'Take the car. Get yourself home. I'll call you in the morning.'

'But what about Elodie?'

'She's safe,' said Jacquot.

'Safe?' Marie-Ange started shaking her head as though Jacquot had just suggested the monarchy would soon be returned to power, as though, finally, he had lost his senses.

'Safer than she's been all week,' he continued.

'And how exactly do you figure that?'

'Up until now, mademoiselle, we've been working against the clock. The dockers' strike, the threat of transportation, God knows what else. But now Elodie Lafour's not going anywhere. She's become too valuable. A real commodity. And very soon, believe me, there's going to be a hefty ransom demand.'

Jacquot picked up his glass and slugged back the last of his Calva, signalling for the tab.

'As of tonight,' he said, pulling out his wallet, 'the game changes.'

Sunday
15 November

71

EVERYONE WHO SAW IT THAT early Sunday morning held their breath. After ten days of low cloud and drenching, chilling rain there was blue sky, just a patch of it, out at sea, beyond the domed tower of Fort Saint Jean. Enough to make a sailor's shirt, the fisherwomen on the Quai des Belges remarked one to another, pulling their shawls tight as a crisp breeze shivered over the water.

But it didn't last. The clouds might have moved on and the rain might have stopped but a wide bank of fog rolled in from the Marseilles roads and Golfe du Lion, high grey sails over a churning black sea. You could see its silky fingers stealing through the mouth of the Vieux Port, passing down the *pannes*, row after row of moored craft softened in shape and line. Streets shortened. Tall buildings lost. Church bells dropped an octave, as though clappers and rims had been baffled in blankets.

By ten o'clock the cemetery of Saint Pierre was appropriately shrouded, scarves of fog trailing through the trees, blunting the tips of the sentinel cypresses, the ringing of chewed bits and the stamping of hoofs and the impatient whickering of the plumed horses that had drawn Arsène Cabrille's hearse and led the cortège along the cemetery's gravelled paths, distant and hollow, muffled in the grey gloom.

The Cabrille family had not lived in the city long enough to have a family vault on one of the better avenues. Instead, a plot of land beyond the Porte Rampal, in an angle of the cemetery walls and screened by a semi-circle of shrubs and cypress, had been purchased from the authorities and set aside from its neighbours by a length of black anchor chain strung between two ancient cannons sunk into the ground. Inside this plot, beneath the trees, stood a limestone plinth, its stepped panels carved with tilting masts and billowing sails, snapping flags and pennants, coiled ropes and storm-tossed barques – source of the family's fortune – its topmost decoration an oval cartouche with Baroque flourishes in which the words *Famille Cabrille* had been sternly incised.

In the lawn below this plinth stood three gravestones: those of Arsène's father, Giulio; his mother, Mariana and a newer, cleaner stone for his own dear wife. Beside the later Madame Cabrille, Arsène's own flower-bedecked casket rested over an open grave, the mounds of earth tidily camouflaged beneath green sheets of plastic turf. Standing in front of the casket, head bowed, hands clasped, listening to the final round of blessings, Virginie covered a yawn by pretending to dab away a tear. Behind her, ghostly figures in the fog, stood her father's mourners, all dressed in black, most of the women veiled, four of the city's most feared crime bosses attended by their wide-shouldered retinues, along with assorted family friends, well-wishers, directors of the Druot Clinic and three members of the Opéra board all looking distinctly uncomfortable in such notorious company.

If only they knew, thought Virginie. All of them gathered here on a Sunday morning to pay their respects, not only to a man they knew and feared and universally loathed, but also to a shifty, second-rate, cheating little hoodlum called Guillermo Ribero. Standing so close to the casket, she wondered what would happen if poor Guillermo woke up now, realised where he was and started hammering on the padded satin sides of the coffin. Or maybe poked a finger out, like a tiny pink worm, through the vent holes that Tomas had drilled below the casket's lid. Now there would be an exquisite moment, Virginie decided, timing his return to consciousness to the very last minute, the very last second, and she leaned closer, listening keenly for any sound. But there was nothing, just the shuffling of restless feet and a rasping stir of gravel as the priest closed his missal and the service came to an end.

And then she gave a little start, felt a shivering flicker between her thighs, as a thin whining began from the far side of the grave where an electric lift mechanism had been discreetly placed. The casket trembled slightly as the lift's gear engaged, one of the wreaths shifted, and then slowly, smoothly, it began its descent between the draped astro-turf. When it reached the bottom, Virginie stepped forward, took a black gloveful of earth from the silver trowel a sacristan was offering her and cast it on to the box, the loose dirt dancing off the wood.

'*Adieu*,' she whispered, the smile hidden behind her veil. '*Adieu, les deux*.' And she turned away to join the other mourners, walking with them to the line of limousines waiting to carry them away. When the last outlines had faded into the mist, their footfalls a soft distant crunching, a small bulldozer concealed behind the trees started up, its rubberised caterpillar treads making little noise as it headed for the mound of earth beside the grave and lowered its scoop. In six deft moves, swinging back and forth between pit and pile, the grave had been filled by the time Virginie reached her limousine.

Tomas and Taddeus stood beside it.

'Did you get what I wanted?' she asked.

Taddeus nodded, dug into his pocket, pulled out a wrap of paper and handed it to Virginie. Carefully she opened the wrap, looked at the hairclip. 'Very pretty,' she said. 'Just the thing. And she's safe?'

'Quite safe, mam'selle,' replied the elder brother. 'She should be waking up any time now.'

'Like someone else we know,' replied Virginie, slipping the hairclip into her small clutch bag and sliding into the back of the limousine.

Taddeus and Tomas nodded their agreement.

Ten minutes later, as the cortège passed between the last of the mist-shrouded trees on the Grande Allée and turned through the cemetery gates on to rue Saint Pierre, Guillermo Ribero opened his eyes, blinked and wondered where he was.

72

THERE WAS A PHONE MESSAGE and a package waiting for Jacquot at the front desk when he made it down to a late breakfast at Auberge des Vagues.

Madame Boileau delivered them both.

'You know a man called Salette?' she asked, as Jacquot passed her desk, one gnarled hand on the package, the other clasping the ends of her woollen shawl.

Jacquot was taken aback. He thought for a second or two before answering, frowning as though the name was not immediately familiar.

'Salette?'

'Jean-Pierre Salette. The old harbour master,' she said, looking at him suspiciously.

'I seem to remember the name,' he said, not wishing to be more exact.

'Well, it seems he remembers you. Said there's a ship you may be interested in. Called *Brotherhood*.'

Jacquot nodded. 'Sounds encouraging,' he replied, remembering what Salette had told him the last time they'd met.

'They say the strike's ending today,' continued Madame Boileau. 'Back to business.'

'Then perhaps I won't need this Monsieur Salette.'

Madame Boileau looked doubtful. 'Use every contact you have is my advice. And you can't go wrong with a man like Salette. I've known him years. An eye for the ladies, and a nose for the sea. As good a man as you'll find.'

Jacquot agreed with every word, but gave no sign of it bar a thoughtful nod. As though this was a judgement worth considering, and he was grateful for the recommendation. He was about to move on when she slid the package across the desk.

'This came as well. Last night. By courier. You were back too late for me to hand it over personally, but I didn't want to leave it out for you.'

Jacquot took the package, thanked Madame Boileau and headed down to the basement canteen which was humming with a loud, raucous crowd of seamen, of every age and size and shape, a dozen chattering languages under a cloud of cigarette smoke, every bed in his dormitory and every room in the hostel taken as word had spread that the strike was about to end. He looked round for Franco, wondering whether his new friend had gone north or had come back to Marseilles. There was no sign of him, no familiar faces, so he helped himself to coffee, found himself a table, ordered eggs and ham and pastries, and opened the package Madame Boileau had given him. A sailor's log suitably curled and aged and stained – Mediterranean routes this time, rather than Baltic. And a note from Solange Bonnefoy, clipped and precise, giving nothing away. *Apologies for the delay. They say the strike is ending. Any progress?*

For a brief moment, Jacquot felt a twist of guilt. As soon as he finished breakfast, he'd call her, bring her up to date. He should have called the night before but it was late when he got back to the hostel, and he was too tired to do anything but fall into bed and sleep, waking only briefly when the first early risers started moving around the dormitory. As for the strike ending . . . well, it didn't really matter any more. Whether it ended or continued made little difference now. He might keep his disguise, would certainly continue to work undercover – Gastal would never allow it any other way – but, as he'd told Marie-Ange in the bar the night before, the game had changed.

Sometime soon there would be a ransom demand.

A price set.

An exchange arranged.

He had no doubt that Elodie was alive.

The question was, for how much longer?

73

ALAIN GASTAL WAITED UNTIL THE last mourners had moved off before coming out of the trees. He'd arrived twenty minutes before the service, flashed his badge at the grave-diggers, and watched the service from behind the bonnet of the earth-mover.

As the mourners had assembled, gathering at the graveside, Gastal whistled softly at the line-up. They were all there, criminal royalty every one of them: René Duclos, head of the Duclos family from Toulon; Jean-Claude Rachette, also known as 'Hachette' the Hatchet, after his favoured means of punishment; Guy Ballantine, whose grandfather had established the family's fortune by swindling the Gestapo out of fifteen million francs; and there, in the wheelchair, a rug tucked round his long-lost, machine-gunned legs, Patric 'Le Papa' Polineaux, the *parrain* of all *parrains*, godfather of all godfathers.

They weren't alone, of course. Standing around them were the heavies, every one a *gorille* who'd cut a throat just to see how far and how high the blood would spurt. Dozens of murders between them, maybe hundreds, not to mention drug running, prostitution, racketeering, extortion . . . and not a single night spent behind bars. All of them in black topcoats and shiny black suits, white shirts and thin black ties. They looked as if butter wouldn't melt.

And standing apart from the mourners, in a slim black pencil skirt and double-breasted black jacket, gloved and veiled, Arsène Cabrille's only child, his daughter Virginie. Educated at all the best schools in Marseilles and Paris, and finished at the prestigious *Institut d'Études Politiques de Paris*, otherwise known as Sciences-Po. Oxford, Cambridge, Harvard and Yale rolled into one. No one did it better than Sciences-Po when it came to equipping its graduates with the means to make it in the world. In France, you didn't come better educated than that, borne out – as Gastal knew – by two of his contemporaries at the *DGSE*, both of whom had studied at Sciences-Po, both men taking promotions that should have been his. Not even Arsène Cabrille's fabled wealth and fearsome influence could have secured his daughter a place there. She had done it on her own. And not so much as a parking ticket to her name.

As he watched her dab at her eyes, standing just a few metres away from him in the clinging fog, as the priest flourished a sign of the cross over the descending casket, Gastal wondered just how much she knew, how much of her father's operations she'd been privy to?

Though he couldn't prove a thing – beyond a string of flimsy coincidences and the testimony of snouts no longer around to back up his case – Gastal had no doubt that Arsène Cabrille had been behind the murders of Jules Valentine, his two young mechanics, and Marcel Lévy. And he was equally sure that this Santarem character and his mother and Xavier Vassin had also been despatched by the family. Seven murders in just four days. But did Virginie know about any of it? If she was working for the family, as rumour had it, was it in some legitimate corner of the empire isolated from the real action? Or did she have her finger on the trigger? There may have been a woman in that English limousine in Chatelier, but was Virginie Cabrille the woman in question?

There was only one way to find out.

He would call on her.

He would look her in the eye. And he would know. One way or the other.

And if she was involved in those murders, if she did have Elodie

Lafour squirrelled away somewhere, and if she did decide to ransom the girl – or damage her in any way – he would climb up on to her shoulders, and the shoulders of those smirking Sciences-Po bastards back in Lyon, and grab the promotion that was his due. *Bocuse, j'arrive*.

As the earth-mover swung into action, Gastal stepped up to the grave and watched the first scoop of earth tumble down, rattling on to the wooden lid of Cabrille's casket. As he listened to the dull thumping of earth on wood, and then the soft shuffling of earth on earth, he removed a wad of chewing gun from his mouth and pressed it against the new headstone waiting to be set above the grave.

Bon débarras! Good riddance, *connard*, thought Gastal, and he plugged his hands into his pockets and ambled off into the fog, unaware that ten feet below him, under three tons of limestone scrag, Guillermo Ribero had finally woken up, realised where he was and started to scream, his fists drumming against the wooden sides of the casket, his polished fingernails scrabbling and tearing at its satin upholstery, and the brittle ribs of Arsène Cabrille snapping one by one under his squirming, frantic weight.

But there was more to come that Sunday morning.

Back at police headquarters the squad room was buzzing when Gastal arrived, all the boys called in on Sunday to sort out the mess from the night before. When they saw him the buzz subsided.

'We got anything on that gun yet?' asked Gastal, eyes fixing on Grenier who'd found the weapon at Xavier Vassin's home and been tasked with its identification.

Grenier took a deep breath, pushed through some papers on his desk as though he was looking for the details when he knew them already. He looked up, glanced across at Peluze and Bernie Muzon.

'Well?' pressed Gastal, catching the glance and sensing that something was up.

'Yes, boss . . .'

'And?'

'Initial tests indicate that the bullet that killed Murat Santarem was fired by the gun found in Xavier Vassin's kitchen.'

'And the gun belongs to . . .?'

Grenier took another breath, rubbed the palm of his hand across his stubbly scalp. He didn't want to do this, but he had no choice.

'Jacquot, boss. Daniel Jacquot.'

For a moment there was silence as Gastal took in this piece of information. And then he began to laugh. A chuckle first, a shake of the head, and then he took a deep breath and really laughed, held his sides and rocked on his feet.

'Oh, yes,' he said, wheezing with the effort of speaking. 'Oh, yes, oh, yes, oh, yes.'

74

'SO WHERE AM I TAKING you?' asked Marie-Ange, peering over the steering wheel, trying to make out the road ahead through the curtaining fog.

'Somewhere special, I promise,' replied Jacquot. 'Just head for the Corniche. You're doing fine.'

She'd picked him up shortly before midday, as arranged on the phone, on the corner of place de Lenche and rue Caisserie. The walk from Impasse Massalia had done him good, opened up his muscles, his mind, filled his lungs, the fog thick enough for him to risk turning down rue de l'Evêché, scuttling past police headquarters, head sunk into his collar, but not so deep that he couldn't glance up at the patchwork of lit windows on the upper floors. Sunday morning and all the boys at work, thought Jacquot, trying to make sense of what they'd found at rues Bandole and Artemis.

'How did you sleep?' asked Marie-Ange. 'You looked exhausted. You must have been out like a light. And how's your head?' The questions tumbled from her. Jacquot sensed she was feeling nervous.

'Just about in one piece,' he replied, pressing his foot against the floormat – had she seen that Renault coming out from the right? She had. The 2CV slowed. He eased his foot off the imaginary brake. 'What about you?' he asked. 'Any dreams? Feelings?' he added.

She shook her head. 'I'm sorry. Nothing.'

It was the one thing she had hoped he wouldn't ask. If only because she'd have to say no. No dreams. No silences. No dusty taste. She knew the reason, but didn't feel she could tell him. Not about her monthly cycle, about how her 'moments' usually coincided with this time of the month. And truth to tell, she didn't want to tell him, would have been crazy to tell him. If he knew there'd be no more dreams, no more 'moments' for the next few weeks, she'd be superfluous. He'd thank her and that would be it. He'd go his own way because she could no longer help. That was the way policemen were. So she kept quiet.

There was something else that bothered her too. Something much more unsettling. If she was eased out of the investigation – the continuing search for Elodie – she wouldn't be around him any more. And for reasons she couldn't quite articulate, she didn't like the prospect of that at all. The last two days had been special. Meeting up with him again, working together, both of them following the same trail. As she double-declutched and second-geared her way round the bend into rue des Catalans she quietly breathed him in, sitting there beside her: the warmth of him, from his walk; the dampness of the sea fog on his pea-jacket; the sharp scent of soap – not perfumed, but strong and clean; and the rich aroma of tobacco clinging to him. People always said how they hated the smell of tobacco. Not Marie-Ange. She might not smoke that much, but she loved the rich dark scent of it on a man. Cigars, pipes, cigarettes, it didn't matter. It suited them. Suited him.

'Do you mind if I ask you something?' she asked, not taking her eyes off the road.

'Go ahead.'

'I mean, when you do what you're doing, working undercover like this, how do you manage it? Or rather, what does your family . . .' she took a breath, peered ahead as though she had seen something ' . . . what does your wife think about it all? Being away from home. The risks. Or don't you tell her?' She gave a little chuckle, as though to lighten the mood, and hoped that her questions had come out the right way. Despite her best intentions, she found she needed to know if he was married. Or had a girl-friend. There was no ring on his finger, but then he was working undercover – another man, another history.

Jacquot, looking ahead, was silent for a moment. 'I am not married,' he replied. 'Not yet, at any rate.' And then, leaning forward, pointing, 'Here, the next turning to the right. Do you see it? There.'

And that was that. Whether he recognised her questions for what they were, and was using the directions to sidestep her probing, or had not really been listening, she couldn't say. What she did feel, as she pulled up at the end of the narrow *impasse* that Jacquot directed her to, pointing out where to park in front of a ten-foot high wall of rock, was that she still didn't have the whole story. A man like him, he couldn't be alone, surely? Or maybe he was. He'd just told her he wasn't married, but what did he mean by 'not yet'? That he was about to be? Any day now? Or 'not yet' as in not at all? She was certain there'd been someone in his life back in St Bédard, but was she there still?

The questions buzzing around in her head stopped the moment Marie-Ange opened her door and stepped from the car, as the scent of the sea flew into her nostrils, filled her head. Sharp, salty, raw and briny. She closed her eyes and drew it in.

'Are you okay?' asked Jacquot, coming round the back of the Citroën, past its slanting boot. 'You're not . . .?'

'Having one of my moments? *Mais non, je regrette*.' She looked up at him and smiled. 'It's just the smell. The sea. It's so strong, so . . . glorious. Where have you brought me?'

'Like I said. Somewhere special. And to someone special, too. Over here,' he said, and putting a hand into the small of her back, exerting the gentlest pressure, he directed her to the right. Five steps on he leant ahead of her, his chest brushing her shoulder, pushed open a slatted gate and waved her through into a narrow stepped passage that cut through the rock. 'When you get to the end, turn left,' he said from behind her, 'but watch your footing. If the waves are high, it can get slippery.'

At the end of the passage, Marie-Ange did as she was told and stepped out on to a broad platform of rock set between the sea and the high buttressed edge of the Corniche maybe fifteen metres above them. Because of the fog, the sound of passing traffic was distant, muted, and the sea, invisible, somewhere below and to her right, did no more than slap and suck and gurgle lazily at the rocks and fill the air with its scent. As far as she could judge, she was in a small cove on the Malmousque Head, somewhere along the rocky shore between Vallon des Auffes and the bay of Fausse Monnaie.

She was about to turn and ask Jacquot, when a rough-sounding voice shouted out: '*C'est toi*, Daniel? Are you here at last?'

75

'*C'EST MOI*, SALETTE,' said Jacquot, stepping past Marie-Ange as a figure loomed out of the fog – not as tall as Jacquot, she could see, as the two men embraced, but powerfully built, filling every centimetre of a thick blue roll-neck sweater, his trousers a stiff and stained cream cotton, leather sandals buckled at the heel and slapping against the stone. He was older, too, this Salette. Much older. Old enough to be Jacquot's father.

Turning back to her, Jacquot made the introductions and Marie-Ange felt her hand taken in a great warm paw and lifted to the old man's lips, her knuckles close enough to brush the stubble on his chin.

'Marie-Ange, Marie-Ange! Even in this poor light, and with these old eyes, I can see that you live up to your name,' he told her gallantly. '*Et bienvenue, chère mademoiselle*, to the headquarters of *La Confrérie des Vieux Pecheurs et Autres Hommes de Gloire*,' he continued, turning his back on Jacquot, sliding his arm round her waist and drawing her forward. 'We meet here, the Brotherhood, every Sunday, fog or no fog. But when it rains or the sea is high we adjourn to a small *boîte* back across the Corniche. Otherwise you find us as we are, as it should be for men like us.'

As far as Marie-Ange could make out, still stepping carefully through the gloom, these so-called headquarters comprised nothing

300

more than a number of split-cane panels lashed to four iron girders sticking out from the face of the rock, unused remnants of past road construction, she guessed. The leading edge of this lean-to, makeshift roof was hung with a string of bare low-wattage bulbs, like a poor man's Christmas decoration, and dimly illuminated beneath it were four foldaway metal tables drawn into a square and set with plastic stacking chairs. As she came in under the cane roof, Marie-Ange could smell the woody scent of burning vine cuttings and made out a griddle set against the rock face, its bed of embers glowing a faint orange against the stone.

'*Mes confrères*,' called Salette, guiding her forward. 'Allow me to introduce our guest for today, Marie-Ange.'

There was a scraping of chair legs as three men, old fishermen by the look of them, rose just far enough from their seats to let it be known that they understood the niceties, sitting back down with a murmur of, '*Mam'selle, bonjour, bienvenue.*' Two of them were playing backgammon at a corner of the table-square, a third had obviously been sitting with Salette before they arrived, while a fourth, working at the griddle, turned to wave a greeting. She couldn't help but wonder how many women ever came here; not many, she would have guessed.

'That's Bruno there, by the grill,' continued Salette. 'And L'Abbé drinking all my *pastis* while I'm meeting and greeting, and over there Laurent, the net-maker, and Philo, the scholar. Fishermen all.' Salette pulled out a chair and waved Marie-Ange into it, pulled out another for himself, but left Jacquot to find his own. 'We take turns to cook, mam'selle. Today, I regret to inform you, you'll have to suffer Bruno's poor offerings. *Je m'excuse.*'

But as Marie-Ange soon discovered, there was nothing for Salette to regret and nothing for Bruno to be ashamed of. As soon as they were settled, after she'd been poured a tumbler of wine – it was either that or *pastis* – Bruno waved a square of sail-cloth over the tables, laid out a dish of diced tomatoes and red onions, a basket of toasted bread and a saucer of garlic cloves. Wishing her *bon appétit*, Salette showed the way, rubbing the toast with the garlic and using it to scoop up the tomatoes and onions. By the time the dish had been wiped clean, Marie-Ange could smell fish grilling, skin sizzling, and the scent of rosemary drifting through the fog. The next instant Bruno was serving them a pair of sardines each.

'Don't worry,' explained Salette. 'They come in pairs. Any more than two, as Bruno will happily tell you, and the fish go dry and cold. By the time you finish these, the next two will be along, just as fresh and as sharp and as hot as the first. Brought in this morning they were, by our brother, L'Abbé.'

Across the table L'Abbé nodded and smiled, not a tooth in his head. '*Le plus frais. Rien de mieux.*' None fresher. None better. And he raised his tumbler in a toast.

'They look delicious,' she said. 'And your china. It's so pretty,' she continued, running her finger over the faded blue faience. 'And so clean. Such a shine.'

'Our very own dishwasher, Marie-Ange. *La bonne mer.*' Salette nodded to a square lobster pot dragged up to the griddle and already filling with dirty dishes. 'Before we go, we put the pot over the side for the sea to do a woman's work. A week later, it's as clean as you see it now. And everything as safe as can be.'

'It doesn't seem like there's too much risk of a burglary here,' she noted, looking around. As far as she could see there were only three ways to reach this hidden place – with a key to the padlocked gate, by boat, or by rope, abseiling down from the Corniche.

Salette laughed. 'In this city, it pays to take precautions,' he said. '*Mais alors, mademoiselle, il faut commencer*, or Bruno will be back with the next sardines.'

While she set to on her fish, lifting the fillet from the bone with a crinkling of blistered skin, Salette turned to Jacquot and Marie-Ange quickly realised that this wasn't just a social visit.

'So how's your girl?' asked Salette. 'Any news?'

Jacquot, with a mouthful of sardine, shook his head, swallowed and then proceeded to run the old man through the last couple of days – Petitjean, Santarem, Vassin – and explain the current state of play.

'Just as well she got taken then,' said Salette. 'Soon as the strike's done, sometime this afternoon so they say, the big ships'll be queuing up to get in and out. And then she really would have been gone for good. You'd never have found her.'

'Any thoughts?' asked Jacquot, nodding his thanks to Bruno as the old boy shuffled two more silvery-brown sardines on to his plate.

'All I can promise is that me and the boys will keep an eye out. L'Abbé lives out at L'Estaque, Bruno at Montredon, Philo at Pointe Rouge and Laurent at Madrague. They know what's going on. Not much'll get past us. But I'm afraid that's it. Ask a few questions, keep an eye out. There's not much else we can do,' admitted Salette.

The last of the sardines were brought to the table, and Bruno sat down to join them. He was a big man, like Salette, but bald as a *boule* with a tanned scalp and sun-scorched eyes.

'You said there were two men in black, that right?' he asked.

'That's it,' replied Jacquot. 'In and out. Shot the mother. Then dropped this Vassin – two to the head.'

'And no casings, you said? No shells?'

Jacquot shook his head. 'Nothing. Close enough, and heavy enough calibre, to go clean through.'

'Professionals, got to be,' said Salette.

Bruno reached for some bread, smeared it across Salette's plate. 'No shortage of those around,' he said, chewing and swallowing. 'Not in this town.'

'That's the problem,' said Jacquot. 'Where to go next.'

'If it's professionals,' continued Bruno, 'and the girl's still here in Marseilles, I'd guess it'd have to be one of the families. The *Milieu*.'

'*Milieu*?' asked Marie-Ange, sitting back from her empty plate. 'You mean gangsters? Underworld?'

'Forget *Borsalino* and Jean-Paul Belmondo, mam'selle,' said Bruno, turning to her and reaching out his hand to grasp her arm and shake it affectionately. 'When it comes to *Les Familles*, you have to think hotels and new developments, construction contracts, tailored suits and boardroom tables. City council too. Nowadays it's all legit. Or tries to be.'

'There are five or six, at least, who could handle this kind of thing,' said Salette.

'Rachette, Ballantine, the Polineaux, Cabrille,' said Bruno, ticking the names off his fingers. 'You hear the old man died, by the way? Cabrille. Big do up at Saint Pierre this morning, putting him to bed. All of them there, like as not.'

'I didn't know,' said Jacquot, trying to recall what he knew of the Cabrille family. 'What'll happen now? A carve up?'

This time it was Philo, the scholar, who chipped in. 'Not if his daughter's got anything to do with it. Bright and shiny, clean as a whistle, but just as nasty as her father so I've heard. I'd guess the other families will keep their distance. For now. See what happens.'

'Maybe I'll take a snoop around,' said Jacquot. 'Until there's a ransom demand, there's not much more I can do.'

'Not a bad idea,' said Salette, getting to his feet and gathering up the plates, holding up his hand when Marie-Ange made to help. 'Now that Bruno has done his worst, Marie-Ange, it's time for the cheese, which I can vouch for, on account of my supplying it.'

While he gathered up the plates, walked to the edge of the platform and flung the bones into the sea, Jacquot leaned forward.

'Good lunch?'

'I think it was the most beautiful, the most wonderful meal I've ever eaten,' she whispered. 'The tomatoes, the fish, the fog, the sound and the smell of the sea – so close . . . Just magical.'

'And the company, of course,' said Jacquot.

'That too. They're all so lovely, so kind. It's just . . .' She frowned, suddenly looking anxious. 'It's just, I feel guilty somehow. Us here, and Elodie still missing. With those killers. I mean, shouldn't we be doing something?'

Jacquot shrugged, poured them some more wine. 'There's nothing much we can do right now. All we have are two men who took Elodie from rue Artemis. We don't know who they are, where they've come from or where they've gone. Maybe they work for one of the families, maybe not. But for the moment Elodie is safe. That's how it works in cases like this. And in my experience that's how it will stay until a ransom demand is made. Tomorrow probably. That's when it'll start again.'

Later, when the wheel of cheese that Salette had supplied was reduced to rind and crumbs and straw packing, the long mournful hoot of a ship's foghorn rolled over them from somewhere along the coast, down around the docks. It held for five long seconds and ended in two short blasts.

Salette glanced at his watch. 'Four o'clock. Just when they said. The strike over.' Pushing himself away from the table, he got to his feet. 'And lunch, too, *mes amis*. Now it is time for us old men to lower the lobster pot and get quickly to our firesides and a warm armchair before the chill sets in.' He shivered with a 'Brrrr', and said: 'Breeze is getting up, and cold too. Soon get rid of this fog . . .'

And so they said their goodbyes, Bruno lowering the stacked lobster pot into the sea, L'Abbé, Philo and Laurent folding the tables and stacking the chairs, and Salette seeing Marie-Ange and Jacquot safely back to the cut in the rock. As she went ahead, Salette caught Jacquot's arm and held him back, drew close.

'You be careful, boy,' he said with a wrinkled, stubbly grin, 'and I'm not talking kidnap and bad guys.' With a pincer-like fix of finger and thumb he squeezed Jacquot's arm. '*Une vraie ange, n'est-ce-pas?* Just remember, you already have an angel of your own.'

76

MAYBE IT WAS THE BREEZE that Salette had sensed, or maybe it was the chill that stole across the city that late Sunday afternoon. Whatever the reason, the fog had thinned considerably by the time Marie-Ange and Jacquot climbed back into the 2CV and headed through the lanes of Malmousque and up on to the Corniche.

'Where to now?' she asked, glancing across at Jacquot. He was looking through the side window, elbow pushing up the flap-up pane of glass.

'If you could drop me in town, anywhere near the top of rue Grignan, that would be great.'

'Rue Grignan?' she repeated, waiting for a gap in the traffic, then turning left.

'That's right,' replied Jacquot, too quickly. 'Madame Bonnefoy . . . She has an office on Cours Pierre Puget, near the Palais de Justice.'

Marie-Ange knew at once that he was lying, and didn't need any special powers to tell her so. She felt cross, and let down. The warmth had suddenly gone from him. There you are, she thought, you're out of the loop already. What was it he'd said, just the previous evening? *The game changes*. How right he was.

With the fog clearing and Sunday evening traffic light it didn't take long to reach town, but neither of them spoke, the rough whine of the Citroën's ancient engine and the rattling of its loose exhaust filling the silence between them.

'How's that?' she said, pulling up at the corner of Grignan but not bothering with the handbrake. She knew she wouldn't be there long. The footbrake would do.

'*C'est parfait, merci bien*.'

'Thank you for lunch. I enjoyed it.'

'And so did I,' he said. 'I'll tell Salette.'

She paused a moment, wondering whether she should ask what was on her mind. Thought, dammit, there was nothing to lose. 'What was it he said, by the way, when we were leaving? He held you back. Was it something about Elodie?'

Jacquot frowned, shook his head. 'Not Elodie, no. Just something about the Families. To be careful.' He reached for the handle, swung the door open. 'I'll call you tomorrow,' he said.

'You'd better,' she replied, and gave him a smile that was hard to hold.

With a tug and a heave he was out of the car, slamming the door closed and bending down to wave at her through the window. She let off the footbrake and started down the hill to the Vieux Port, the shivering shape of him growing smaller in the rear-view mirror. She looked ahead. A light rain had started up and tapped against her windscreen. He'll get wet, she thought, switching on her wipers. Serve him right.

But if Jacquot had imagined she was going home – not that he'd thought to ask what she might be doing – he was badly mistaken. She still had an ace up her sleeve, and realised that if she wanted to keep in with him then now was the time to play it. At the bottom of rue Fort, she checked her watch. It was getting dark and there were still drifting shreds of fog about, but it wasn't far to go, and it wasn't too late, even for a Sunday. With a glance in the mirror, to make sure he wasn't still there, wasn't still watching, she indicated left, turned on to Rive Neuve and headed back towards the Corniche. Ten minutes later she turned left up Avenue du Prado at the statue of David and sailed through all the lights along that broad, straight boulevard, one set after another, as if they recognised the car, as if they knew she was coming, and where she was going.

As she crossed Boulevard Michelet and headed east out of the city, Marie-Ange had a feeling they probably did.

77

SOLANGE BONNEFOY DID INDEED HAVE an office on Cours Pierre Puget, one street up from rue Grignan, its rear windows overlooking the long pool of the Palais de Justice. But Jacquot did not have a meeting with her that Sunday evening. As he watched the 2CV freewheel down the slope towards the port and cough into gear, Salette's final words rang in his head like a clarion call.

You already have an angel.

In the two days since she'd caught his arm on rue Pythéas, Jacquot suddenly realised how deeply Marie-Ange had drawn him in, how swiftly she'd worked a kind of warm, gentle magic on him. Deliberately or not, he couldn't say for sure. But draw him in she had. And old Salette had seen it, taken him aside and given him fair warning.

Burrowing his hands into his jacket pockets, Jacquot watched the 2CV a moment longer, then set off down the street, relieved to be away from her – from her magic – but feeling, too, the weight of her absence, the emptiness it entailed, just the dreary prospect of a solitary Sunday evening in November, with the rain starting up again, stretching ahead of him.

What to do? he thought, nearing the centre of town. So many options when he'd lived here: long Sunday lunches that turned into suppers, new friends turning into lovers, parties, music, shopping.

But now, working this case, a knock on a friend's door, just passing by kind of thing, simply wouldn't work. Too much to explain – the hair, the clothes.

And then he remembered Claudine – and the Sunday lunch with Maddy and Paul that he'd promised to be back for. He'd forgotten all about it, forgotten to call her, to let her know that he was fine, but wouldn't be able to make the lunch. He felt a stab of guilt. *Dieu*, he'd be in for it now! He started looking round for a phone booth, saw one on the corner of rue Paradis and ducked into it. He shovelled around in his pockets for change, found the right coins and dialled the number – the first time, he realised, that he'd called her since Paris. As the rain spat against the plastic cover of the booth, he heard the ringing in their millhouse kitchen. He could see the room, smell it: bread baking, coffee perking, garlic; the tilting shelf of cookery books, the old beams, the bound bunches of herbs; her paint-brushes standing in solvent on the window-sill above the sink, a jug of flowers on the table, a bowl of fruit. The more he thought about it, the more he missed it. And her. Yet no one answered. She wasn't there. Finally the ansaphone clicked on. Her voice, when it came, was sweet and immediate. '*Il y a personne ici à ce moment, mais laissez vos détails, s'il vous plaît . . .*' All those sibilant 's' sounds. That smooth whisper of hers. He could almost taste her. But that's all he got. Her soft voice sounding so close, but so distant, followed by an abrupt beep.

'It's Daniel. I'm fine. Sorry about lunch, and sorry I haven't called. It's been a . . .' He paused, not certain that the usual work excuses would cut it. 'But it's going fine. No need to worry. Not long now and I'll be back. You be good. Love you.'

Twenty minutes later, feeling as lonely as the first girl at a party, Jacquot carried his bucket of popcorn into the middle row of Cine Luxe's big-screen theatre and settled down for two hours of *Godzilla*, his choice of movie decided by the presence in the cast of Jean Reno, one of Jacquot's favourite actors. Not such a bad way to pass the time, he thought. And in the flickering darkness, whenever Reno was off-screen, he thought about Claudine and Marie-Ange and

310

Elodie. Like driving at night, Jacquot had learnt that the darkness of a cinema was a good place to think things through. And when the film ended he'd make his way back to Impasse Massalia, his dormitory bed at Auberge des Vagues, and get in a good night's sleep.

78

WHILE JACQUOT LOUNGED IN HIS cinema seat, picking at his popcorn and planning his next moves, Marie-Ange pulled off the autoroute and followed the signs for Aubagne. A pretty little sleeper suburb enclosed by a sprawl of new building, it huddled under the soft rain below the twin bulks of Monts Garlaban and Saint Baume, now just shadows looming above the rooftops, black slopes outlined against the low yellowed belly of the clouds.

All she had was the name of a street in the old quarter, but she found it within minutes, without a single wrong turn, as though she'd been there a dozen times before. Or been led there. And being a Sunday there was no shortage of parking space. So she parked. Because she knew she was close. Though Marie-Ange had never called on Agim Zahiri, she knew it was just a short walk now. Even the rain had eased off.

Agim Zahiri had come into her life at Fleurs des Quais, no more than a month after Marie-Ange stepped off the train at Gare Saint Charles and started work in Marseilles. One quiet Wednesday morning, alone in the shop on rue Francis, she was on the phone advising on a complicated order for wedding bouquets when she felt a sudden warmth, as though a beam of heat had been directed at her. When she looked up there was a big black woman standing in the doorway, arms filled with bunches of flowers that she'd selected from the display racks on the pavement. She wore an extravagantly knotted turban whose printed pattern, black birds on a canary yellow background, was repeated in the folds of cloth wrapped round her body. She looked like a ball of sunshine, Marie-Ange decided as she put down the phone. Somewhere in her middle- or late-fifties, Martiniquaise or Guadaloupienne, Marie-Ange had guessed. Wrongly on both counts, as it turned out; Agim Zahiri was Senegalese. And closer to seventy.

'*Alors, quelle surprise*,' the woman had said in a lilting sing-song voice, sailing across to the counter and laying down her flowers, clucking her tongue against the roof of her mouth like a big mother hen. 'And a very good morning to you, child,' she'd continued. As though she'd known Marie-Ange since the day she'd been born, as though she knew all about her.

Which, of course, she did.

'Surprise, madame?' Marie-Ange had asked as she took the flowers and began to wrap them.

'Oh, don't you go and be so coy, young lady,' Agim Zahiri had chortled, big brown caramel eyes twinkling with mischief. 'I am sure you know exactly what I mean.' And taking a pencil and a scrap of paper, she had written down her address. 'There are times when those with the sight needs to clean their spectacles, *n'est-ce pas*?' She'd pushed the piece of paper across the counter, paid for the flowers and left the shop, calling over her shoulder, 'You'll know when you needs me. I'll be waiting.'

It hadn't taken Marie-Ange very long to work out exactly what Agim Zahiri was talking about, but she hadn't done anything about it until tonight. And there, up ahead, on a side-street off rue Gachiou, stood the lady herself, looking out of her front door, waiting for Marie-Ange. Just as she'd promised all those weeks ago at Fleurs des Quais on rue Francis.

'Brrrr, but it's cold!' she said, hugging herself, and then opening her arms to hug Marie-Ange. 'I thought you'd be here earlier,' she chided, closing the door behind them. 'A night like this,' she continued, giggling mischievously, 'I've made us some *chocolat chaud*. You likes that, I think.'

And for the next two hours the two of them sat in Agim's kitchen, just as bright and colourful as its owner: the yellow lampshades, the blue and white plastic table cover, the tall green candles and the short black ones, a rainbow rug on a red-tiled *tomette* floor, cushions in tiger stripes and leopard spots. And from her new friend Marie-Ange learnt a little more about the strange talent she possessed.

'The older you gets, the more you sees,' Agim told her. 'When I was younger, just the time of the month, that's all it was. Like I thinks it is with you . . .'

Marie-Ange nodded, cupped her hands round her hot chocolate, sipped and listened.

'. . . those were the only times, back then. Just dreams that would wake me up dead of night, make me sweat with the cold fears. Or these big silences . . .' she spread her arms and circled them to show just how big the silences were '. . . just descending and, and . . . isolating me from all the world around me. So that I could peek into that other place, see something others couldn't. But now, *alors*, let me tell you, there's no stopping it. All the time. *Oufff*, but it can be exhausting! Then again,' she continued, untangling the knot of bangles on her wrists, 'you do get to meet some interesting people.'

'Like me?'

'The moment I walked into that shop, there you was. Like a light shining. And I knowed. Instantly. Two of a kind. And there's not many of us round about. You not alone, I'm telling you, but you gotta look.'

The hot chocolate had been quickly demolished and Cognacs poured, peanuts shelled. Memories, tales, histories swapped.

'We like fortune tellers, you and me and people like us,' said Agim, 'but without the crystal ball. The past and the future. Some see just the one, some the other, and some, like you and me, we can see the both. It's all there for us, to see what we see.'

314

'I'm not good on what's coming,' said Marie-Ange. 'It's usually what's happened with a link to the present. Or people. Sometimes I can look at someone and just . . . know something about them.'

'An' that's how it starts, child. That's how it begins,' said Agim. 'Like, lookin' at you now, I knows about the man in your life. There is one, isn't there? Tall, he is, a rough, rugged sort of fella. Big and strong. Not beautiful, no film-star looks, but . . . mesmeric all the same, *hein*? And when you see him, your insides just start churning. Something about him . . . His eyes maybe, the size of him, his presence. The kind of man you wants in your bed, to curl up against.'

Agim saw the blush rise on Marie-Ange's cheek and let out a laugh that set her chins and chubby arms shaking. 'There you go. There you go. Plain as day. And right now, *ma petite*, you're just a very few centimetres . . .' Agim measured the distance between thumb and forefinger '. . . from falling badly, badly in love with him. Or maybe you already have. But you listen up, child,' she continued, 'don't you show your hand. Not yet. Not for a long while maybe. Now is . . . now won't work. And maybe never will. Only time can say.'

Agim settled back in her chair and aimed a long, level look at Marie-Ange. 'But I tells you one thing, for sure and certain, that there is something big linking the two of yous. Something strong, very strong. And I don't think yous ever be able to break free from him. Or him from you.' She stopped talking, nodding her head up and down slowly, as though there was more she knew but wasn't telling. 'But enough of that, enough of all that. Tell me, how you getting on with the girl?'

'The girl? Elodie? You know about Elodie?'

'I knows!' laughed Agim. 'Course I knows. Soon as I seen the picture in the paper. The girl who died.'

'That's why I came. What I was going to ask.'

'And I knows that too, child.'

Marie-Ange paused, frowned. 'But when you saw that picture, didn't you want to do something about it?'

Agim smiled at her. 'Why? I knew I didn't have to. I remembered my little girl in the flower shop.'

Marie-Ange's heart was beating fast. 'So . . . do you know anything? Can you help me . . . help us?'

'I knows she alive, child. And I knows she safe.'

Marie-Ange couldn't help but smile. Just what Jacquot had said. But maybe there was more. 'Is she here in Marseilles?' she asked.

'Maybe. Somewhere close and that's for sure. But why don't you show what you brought me? In your pocket there. That might help.'

For a moment Marie-Ange didn't understand what Agim meant.

'The clip you found. A hairclip, ain't it?'

Stunned, Marie-Ange dug into her pocket and pulled out the blue enamelled serpent. Agim took it, shuffling it around in the darkly lined palms of her hand, as though it were hot.

'Yes, I right for certain.' *Serre-tan* was how she said it. 'Alive. And, yes, close by.' Now Agim pressed the clip tight in her hands, one fist held inside the other, thumbs tapping against her lips. 'But she in a strange sort of place. A strange kind of room. The walls . . . The walls aren't straight. And the windows are small, and the curtains too. There's a noise as well, like . . . *mmmmmmmhhhhhhh* . . . Something like that.' Agim frowned, as though trying to put the picture together, trying to make sense of whatever it was she could see. But suddenly the frown turned to a smile, as though something had come to her. 'This house where she is has a name . . . Léonie. I didn't have that before.'

Then the smile faded as swiftly as it had come, wiped away. Agim opened her hands, cupped the clip. 'But wherever she is, that girl is in very dangerous company. Not just criminal dangerous, I means evil dangerous. Someone, someone . . .' Agim shuddered, seemed suddenly lost for words.

'Man or woman?' prompted Marie-Ange.

Agim laid the hairclip on the table, pushed it around with her finger, shaking her head. 'A woman. There's men around, too. Bad men. But it's a woman at the roots of it. And she's young, certainly.'

Serre-tan-mon. 'And cruel, even more certainly. Oh and cold, cold as night,' shivered Agim, wrapping her arms around herself. 'Whatever you do, child, you take good care . . . You be very, very careful . . .'

79

ALL WAS QUIET IN THE study of Arsène Cabrille save an occasional spattering of rain on the terrace windows, the squeak of a chair and the rustle of paper. At her father's desk, its tooled leather surface lit by the silver spill of a desk-lamp, Virginie sat back in the shadows and contemplated her handiwork. She had used two sheets of paper and worn white kid gloves while she wrote. The notepaper and padded envelopes were cheap brands found in stationery shops throughout France, the pen a simple Biro.

It hadn't taken long to write the covering letter, nor had it taken much time to compose the message that accompanied it. In a funny sort of way, she thought to herself, she'd been writing it for years, in her head.

Now the moment had come, and she had written it for real.

For her lover, Nathalie Plessin. For justice and revenge. For pleasure and pain.

On the first sheet of paper, just four lines written in small capital letters:

DO AS YOU ARE TOLD OR SHE'S DEAD.
WHAT YOU CHOOSE TO DO AFTERWARDS
IS NO CONCERN OF MINE

It was signed:

AN OLD FRIEND

The message that accompanied this note, also written in small capitals, was longer. A single paragraph of instructions followed by five more paragraphs, fifteen lines in all.

But she hadn't finished yet.

Leaning forward, Virginie reached for two fresh sheets of paper and wrote a second letter in the same neat little capitals, just as she had done before. So he wouldn't be able to ignore it; to pretend he'd never received it. This was Virginie's fail-safe, her back-up, to make sure her instructions were properly followed.

The second letter read:

CHÈRE MADAME
I HAVE NO DOUBT THAT YOU WILL WISH
TO SPEAK ABOUT THIS MATTER WITH YOUR HUSBAND

Then she copied out the message on a second sheet, word for word, remembering Nathalie as she did so. Her lover's smile, the fall of blonde hair, the way she kissed, the scent and softness of her body, the strange and special tastes they shared. And how it had all ended.

When Virginie finished writing, she slid the two letters, with their identical messages, into the padded envelopes. Both envelopes carried Paris addresses, and into one of them she dropped the girl's hairclip.

When it was done, she sat back once more in her father's chair and felt a pleasurable warmth spread through her body.

Oh, how sweet revenge.

Just two short letters. That's all it took.

How sweet and simple was that?

She knew, of course, there'd been other ways to do it. A visit from Taddeus and Tomas was usually enough to effect a satisfactory conclusion when someone crossed her. But something had always held her back, some sense that the best revenge needed time . . . time to refine its power and sharpen its edge. And she'd been right. Oh, how she had been right. She didn't even need to be there, to see him open the letter, to see his fear, to feel his pain. She felt it now, just looking at those two envelopes, and was warmed by it.

She called in Taddeus.

'I have a job for you,' she said, sealing the two envelopes and pushing them across the desk to him. She was still wearing the kid gloves. Taddeus saw them and reached into a jacket pocket for a handkerchief before picking them up.

'*A vot' service*,' he replied.

'There is an Air France flight to Paris in just over an hour,' Virginie continued. 'Tomorrow morning I want you to deliver these packages to the addresses on the envelopes. Get yourself a motor-bike helmet. Look like a messenger. There's no need to wait for any reply.'

Monday
16 November

80

'YOU KNOW A MAN CALLED Jacquot, don't you?'

It was Jean Davide, one of a group of cloaked crow-like coun-
sellors coming down the glistening steps of the Palais de Justice,
gowns and briefcases held over their heads as they hurried through
the rain to their cars. Solange had just arrived from her offices on
Cours Pierre Puget and was coming up the steps. Davide parted
company with his colleagues and ducked under her umbrella; she
was tall enough, and held it high enough, for the shorter Davide to
do so with ease. They were close, too close for Madame Bonnefoy's
liking, for Davide had a way of looking at her, an insinuating manner,
that made her feel uncomfortable. There was something cold and
wet and fish-like about him, as though he'd just been plucked from
the ocean. Clammy, that was the word. Already late for a client
interview in the holding rooms beneath the Palais, Madame Bonnefoy
wouldn't have put up with such a close intrusion if she hadn't heard
the name Jacquot.

'Jacquot? Daniel Jacquot, up in Cavaillon. Yes, why?'

'Signed a warrant for his arrest last night,' said Davide, Adam's
apple rising and falling behind his advocate's collar like a pale
walnut on a string. 'According to Chief Inspector Gastal at headquarters, he's here in Marseilles, not Cavaillon, and his gun's been
picked up as a murder weapon. His prints all over it. Gun and

cartridges both. I'm afraid Gastal was quite insistent. There wasn't much I could do but oblige.'

There was a great deal he could have done, Solange knew, but he clearly hadn't. Working defence, Davide had a professional loathing for cops; anything he could do to put them down he would. A policeman fingered as a possible murderer? Too good to miss. And if said policeman happened to be a friend of a leading prosecutor then so much the better.

'Good of you to let me know,' replied Solange, distantly, as though there was no real interest for her in the issuing of such a warrant. 'And now, Jean, you really must excuse me,' she said, and lifting the umbrella away from him she continued up the steps, pleased that he looked a little disappointed by her reaction.

The first thing she did when she reached her chambers, however, was put a call through to Jacquot at Auberge des Vagues. She caught him as he was leaving.

'Apparently there's a warrant out for your arrest,' she told him. 'It appears you've mislaid your gun . . .'

She listened as he explained how he'd been mugged, that it had been taken from him.

'And I suppose you're going to ask me to find you another one . . .'

She nodded, 'I thought as much. I'll see what I can do. There's a small Supermart at the corner of place de la Bergasse. Meet me there at midday.'

With that she cut the connection and dialled another number.

'Chief Inspector Gastal? It's Madame Bonnefoy at the Palais de Justice. A word, if you please. In my office.'

81

JACQUOT SAW THE 2CV as he left the hostel and started down the street, a salty chill catching his bare neck. He pulled up his collar and headed over to the car. He came round the passenger side, tapped on the window and opened the door. With an arm on the roof, he peered in.

'I phoned the shop. You weren't there,' he said.

'I called in sick,' replied Marie-Ange, covering her wariness from the day before behind a mischievous smile, but pleased to hear that he had tried to contact her. 'Took the day off.'

'Are you ill?' As soon as he said it, he knew how stupid it sounded. Of course she wasn't ill. She wanted to come out to play. And if she wanted to play, she'd have to be available.

'Not at all,' she said. 'But I thought you might need a car. Only, the way you drive her, I'm not letting you behind the wheel again. So you see? You've got to take me along. Or walk.'

'Not in this weather, mademoiselle. So thank you,' he said, dropping down into the passenger seat, folding his legs into the cramped footwell and adding to his sense of discomfort. For, on the walk back from Cine Luxe the night before, after leaving another message on Claudine's ansaphone, he'd decided to clear up any misunderstanding there might be between him and Marie-Ange. About him not being married. As though there was no one in his life. It was a stupid thing to have said, not fair on the girl or Claudine, and he felt ashamed that it had taken Salette to point it out to him.

As they turned out of Impasse Massalia and headed down to Boulevard Cambrai, he cleared his throat and started on the speech he'd been rehearsing since getting up that morning. 'Marie-Ange,' he began. 'There's something I need to say, in case there's been any misunderstanding. It's just . . . I don't know if I made it clear or not. You see there is someone . . .' But he got no further.

'I understand, don't worry. It's not a problem,' she said briskly, acknowledging that something did, indeed, need to be cleared up, yet surprised by how calmly she took the news, that there was someone in his life, confirming what Agim had told her the night before. 'But there's something I have to tell you . . . So where do you want to go?' she interrupted herself, coming up to the Cambrai turning.

'Left at the lights and into town,' Jacquot replied, feeling a weight lift from his shoulders and relief course through him. Honesty was always best, and he felt pleased that he had acquitted himself honourably, if a little tardily. 'I have a meeting with Solange Bonnefoy at midday. There's something I need to pick up,' he added, 'so why don't we get ourselves some *café*-Calvas at Samaritaine. Do you know it? On the corner of . . .'

She shot him a look. Samaritaine was probably one of the city's best-known cafés.

He caught the look, laughed. 'Okay. Okay . . . So, tell me. What's this information you have?'

'It can wait till Samaritaine, if I don't get lost,' she said, and straightening her back she cut her way through the Vieux Port traffic, slotting the Citroën into an empty space off République. Five minutes later, shaking off the rain, they found themselves a corner table, their view of the Quai des Belges and the Vieux Port strangely warped by the plastic window panels in the café's crumpled, side awnings.

'So are you going to tell me or must I beg?' asked Jacquot, their knees knocking together as they settled at their table. 'You have something to tell me? Some information?'

A waiter appeared and Jacquot told him what they wanted. After the waiter was out of earshot, Marie-Ange leant forward. 'Elodie is alive and in Marseilles, or close by,' she began.

'Which we kind of knew . . .' Jacquot suggested warily.

'And she is being kept in a strange-shaped room: the walls aren't straight, there are small windows, and there's a kind of background sound, a kind of *mmmmmmmhhhh*.' She hummed it, just as Agim had done.

'Which could make it pretty much anywhere in Marseilles, Marie-Ange. Old buildings – and you'll have noticed we have a few here in the city – mean old walls. Bent, curved, leaning, even falling down, some of them . . . And small windows? Look at any loft, or basement. And as for that hum, well, it sounds very like traffic to me. Or maybe an air-conditioning unit . . .'

'In November?' she shot back, clearly put out that he hadn't responded more positively.

'Okay, I hear what you're saying. But listen, I'm not against you here. And if it sounds like I'm shooting it all down, it's because I have to. It's what we do. The police. Sometimes we have no choice. There are always . . . interpretations, and we must keep an open mind.'

Jacquot pulled a pack of Gauloises from his pocket, tapped out two of them and offered the pack to Marie-Ange. She took one of the cigarettes and held it, he noticed, like someone who wasn't really a smoker, at the very end of her fingers.

'But how exactly do you know all this? The room? The sound? That she's close by?' he asked, lighting her cigarette, then his own. 'A dream?'

'Let's just say I know. But I can't explain.' She blew out the cigarette smoke with a little *puh* and held the cigarette high and away from her. Definitely not a smoker, thought Jacquot. 'I also have a name,' she continued, 'though you'll probably tell me it's not much to go on.'

'A name would be good.'

'This house, wherever it is, has a name. Léonie.'

Before he could say anything, the waiter returned with their coffees and Calvas. When he slipped the till receipt under the ashtray and turned to go, Jacquot held him back, asked for a phone directory.

'Business or residential?' the waiter asked.

'Business,' Jacquot replied.

'*Bien sûr. Tout de suite, monsieur.*'

'Well?' said Marie-Ange, sniffing her Calva and sipping it cautiously. 'What do you think? About the name? It gives us something to work on, don't you agree?'

'The name of a person would be better, but it certainly narrows things down,' he replied.

'There is also the possibility that Elodie is being held by a woman. A very dangerous woman,' continued Marie-Ange, recalling Agim Zahiri's warning the previous night. 'We should take care.'

Jacquot nodded. 'In cases like this, it always pays to take precautions. You are hardly a saint if you kidnap a young girl . . . ah, *monsieur, merci beaucoup*,' he said, as the waiter returned to their table with a directory. 'So, "Léonie". Let's see what we have.' He riffled through the pages, found L, ran his finger down a column. 'Four Léonies listed in Marseilles: Léonie Stoves; Léonie Dry Cleaners; Léonie, a *corsetière* on rue Saint Ferréol; and Léonie Chiens, a dog's beauty parlour in Endoume. Do you have a pen and some paper?'

She reached into her tote and found what he wanted. Taking the pen and paper from her, he noted down the addresses then flicked on through the directory to M, ran his finger down a page, shook his head. 'Just the one: Maison Léonie – a fashion outlet in Le Canet.' He turned back to the beginning of the directory. 'And under "Casa" . . . nothing.'

Jacquot closed the directory and put it on the table. Pocketing the slip of paper and handing back her pen, he picked up his Calva and smiled encouragingly. 'So, let's drink to Léonie, whoever and wherever she is. And then find her.'

82

HESPERIDES. THAT WAS THE NAME of the ship.

Hesperides. Hesperides.

The name she couldn't remember, the name her policeman friend had been so keen to learn. Mademoiselle Carinthe Cousteaux was pushing through the glass doors of Galerie Duchamp on rue Saint Ferréol when the name just came to her. Out of the blue. There she was, planning how to spend the ten thousand francs she had taken from Arsène Cabrille's wallet in the minutes before the paramedics arrived, when the name just popped into her head.

The moment her shopping was finished, she decided, the moment she'd done spoiling herself with a couple of new outfits and maybe a few hours in the Galerie's new treatment spa – a massage, pedicure, manicure, facial – she'd call that sweet little policeman and let him know. And maybe, if he behaved himself, she might lower her price. Then again, he might be so pleased that she had finally remembered the ship's name, he'd decide that the full amount was now a reasonable investment. And didn't the gendarmerie pay informers? Surely she'd heard or read that somewhere. And didn't they sometimes, in really important cases, provide a new identity, a new life? Perhaps, if she was smart, she might have them set her up in Nice or Menton, a small villa on the coast, or up in the hills where it was cooler, to entertain her gentleman callers.

But Mademoiselle Carinthe Cousteaux was not alone on her shopping expedition. From the moment she'd left the Sofitel hotel in a city cab, a slim wiry individual known to those who hired him as Le Stylet, the Blade, had been following her. No one knew his real name, but everyone in the business knew his speciality.

Mademoiselle Cousteaux's first stop was the Parfumerie counter where she spoke with an assistant, finally settling on some L'Occitane bath essence, body lotion and a small bottle of her favourite perfume, Guerlain's *L'Heure Bleue*. She paid in cash, Le Stylet noticed, and then she moved on, stopping here and there to admire this, to finger that, to speak with the counter staff – a woman of means, idly passing the time as others worked.

And every step of the way Le Stylet shadowed her, coming close enough to smell the tester scent that she'd sprayed on her wrists in Parfumerie, dropping back far enough to take in the easy, luscious swing of her hips as she walked down the aisles.

But it wasn't any appreciation for a fine figure of a woman that drew his interest. What he needed to know was the height and the weight of her, and the possible dampening, deflecting thickness of the fur coat she wore. And, when the moment arrived, where best to aim his attack. How many blows. And how she might fall after contact. He didn't want to trip over her, or be held up, or have her turn and grab him for support. He had to do it, and be out of there. Strike fast, strike lethally, and disappear. That's how Le Stylet worked. And that's what clients like Virginie Cabrille paid him for.

By now, the aisles of Galerie Duchamp had started to fill with mid-morning shoppers. Which was what Le Stylet had been waiting for. A crowd. The killer's friend. Not just women, but men, too. Which was also good. He didn't want to be the only man around when the moment came.

Quietly, he closed once more on his target, idly twisting his left wrist and forearm, as though shaking loose a tight watch strap. But he wasn't wearing a watch. Instead, buckled to the inside of his forearm, was a thin leather holster, spring-activated, containing the single steely tool of his trade. He'd seen it first in the film *Marathon*

Man, and its action had intrigued him. A perfect weapon. So discreet. So . . . effective. As he twisted his wrist, he felt the blade slide out of its housing, slip into the palm of his hand and lock into place, its braided T-bar handle fitting snugly into his fist. With his arm at his side and the crowds around him, it was simply not possible to see the fourteen-centimetre carbon-steel stiletto gripped between his index and middle fingers.

And there she was, just a few metres ahead, talking with yet another sales assistant who was laying out a number of scarves on the counter and keen to conclude a sale. But her customer would have none of it. With a shake of her head Carinthe Cousteaux moved on, towards the escalator leading to the first-floor fashion department.

Trying to do what he had to do on a moving staircase was not, Le Stylet knew, an option. He'd be trapped, nowhere to fade away. He had either to reach his target before she stepped on to the escalator or follow her up to the next floor which, he knew from earlier scouting, was not as crowded as the ground-floor area.

He had to reach her before she put her hand on the rail, in the crowd of people waiting to step on to the escalator. He drew closer, closer, part of the scrum of shoppers, until he was right behind her, close enough to feel the warmth of her, the brush of her fur coat against his knuckles.

This was it. The perfect moment. The perfect spot.

In less than three seconds Le Stylet slid the blade into the small of her back, feeling the steel scrape past the spine. And then it was out, his hand now darting to left and right to plunge the dagger into her sides, a few soft centimetres above the ledge of her hips.

Carinthe Cousteaux felt little more than a bump when Le Stylet's blade went into her back, as though another shopper had jostled her, was pushing up behind her. There were two more bumps, followed by a sharp swift pain like a pinching in the small of her back, and she was about to turn to remonstrate with whoever it was pushing up against her so rudely and impatiently, when she felt her legs go cold and numb.

331

She was no longer able to feel them, or her arms.

Just the cold, the numbness.

But the momentum of the crowd carried her on towards the escalator, until it was her turn to step on to the metal tread and reach for the moving handrail. Pressed forward by the crowd behind her, but unable to move her legs or arms, she did neither. With no one to support her, she simply fell forward, slumping on to the steel risers.

The last thing she saw was the stitched seams in the heels of the shoes of a woman on the step above her, and the last thing she heard was someone behind her calling out, 'Madame, madame, are you okay?'

And someone else saying, 'I think she's had a heart attack.'

And then a third voice: 'Someone, help! Stop the escalator!'

But no one could find the emergency button and thirty seconds later Madamoiselle Carinthe Cousteaux arrived on the first floor as a bundle of fur and bags, the hem of her coat trapped in the side of the moving escalator, a stream of blood pulsing down her legs and dripping on to the steel stairs.

By the time the escalator was finally brought to a stop and she'd been pried loose, Le Stylet was ducking out of the rain into a café on the corner of rue Saint Ferréol and rue Vacon.

Job done.

83

AFTER LEAVING CAFÉ SAMARITAINE Jacquot asked Marie-Ange to drive back towards the docks. Before they started on their list of Léonies, he explained, there was just one last matter he needed to follow up. The name had come to him that morning, he said. Señor Guillermo Ribero. Ribero Agence Maritime on the Chamant wharf. He had met him the previous week, Jacquot told Marie-Ange. And there was something about him . . . He'd feel better after he'd followed it up. Either something would come of it or he could cross Ribero off his list.

A tattered rain-weighted banner still hung from a couple of cranes, but the brazier was no longer in place at the Chamant dock gates when they pulled in, just a black ring of soot and charcoal to mark where it had stood. Not even the rain had yet managed to clear it away. Stopping at the gate, Jacquot showed his sailor's log and union card and was waved through.

A few minutes later, Marie-Ange parked in a space outside the shipping offices and Jacquot was out of the car, running through a fresh gusting rain to the end of the block. As he drew closer he could see that Ribero's blue Seat was not parked outside and that the office was still in darkness.

After trying the lock and peering through the window, he went next door to the Lebanese shipping agent he'd also called on the

333

week before. The wobbling chins, the shirtsleeve suspenders and the greasy black hair curling over the man's collar were just as they had been, but the agent gave no sign that he remembered Jacquot.

'If they'se not open for businesses, they'se not open, m'sieur,' said the agent.

'When did you last see Monsieur Ribero?' Jacquot asked.

'He was in, maybe Saturday. Then again . . .' the man rubbed his chin '. . . maybe not.'

It was clear to Jacquot that he wasn't going to get any kind of useful answers but he persevered.

'Does he often close up like this? On a Monday morning? Strike officially over?' Jacquot asked, wondering whether a roll of notes might loosen the man's tongue – not that he had any money to offer.

'Who can say? I do not lives here.' The Arab shrugged; it was not his concern. And then he smiled, a long, low smile, his eyes hooding over. 'But he is young man, eh? Not like you and me. Maybe he has girlfriend or boyfriend who keep him warm in bed.' The man chuckled, and his chins trembled. 'He pretty boy. You see him too, you understand.' He gave Jacquot a knowing look. 'Me? I say boyfriend. He in bed with boyfriend, I say. Maybe back today, maybe not. Maybe boyfriend not want him to leave.' The phone on his desk started ringing and he reached for it. 'And now, m'sieur . . .'

84

GASTAL CAME OUT OF MADAME Bonnefoy's chambers on Cours Pierre Puget with his teeth clenched tighter than a clam. He couldn't remember being in such a rage, not since . . . not since the Palais de Justice in Lyons when that Chabert case had been snatched away from him at the very last minute. By that *espèce de merde* Jacquot, no less. Gastal's bosses in Lyons hadn't liked that at all. Not one little bit.

And now Jacquot was at it again. Working undercover on the Lafour case, in a private capacity for Madame Bonnefoy. That's what the examining magistrate had told him when he called by to see her, explaining that Jacquot had lost his gun after being put down by Xavier Vassin (three cheers for him, thought Gastal, wishing he'd been there to see it – maybe add a kick or two of his own), and that the arrest order he, Gastal, had obtained through Jean Davide's office would be rescinded forthwith. Madame Bonnefoy would vouch for Jacquot if and when it was necessary to do so.

Reaching his car, Gastal flung himself in behind the wheel and spat out a torrent of abuse. The night before he had gone to sleep thinking how it would feel to apprehend Jacquot himself, dreaming of a shoot-out in which Jacquot went down. Now, thanks to Madame Bonnefoy, the *connard* could operate with impunity; there was nothing Gastal could do about it. He had tried to explain, of course, that having someone working undercover could seriously compromise the operation he himself was running. But Madame Bonnefoy would have none of it. When he saw her shoulders square and that gleam in her eye harden to a steely glint he knew he was on dangerous ground. 'Live with it, monsieur,' she had told him sharply, showing him to the door, the implication quite clear that she valued Jacquot's input and skills and chances of success a great deal more highly than his own. Which had made him madder still.

But he was closer than she imagined. Just steps away, he was certain of it. He'd already called *DGSE* for an update on the Cabrille fleet's status and had established that three freighters were currently berthed in Marseilles and slated for unloading later that day. Of course, just being a Cabrille vessel didn't necessarily mean it was carrying contraband. Sometimes the questionable cargoes came in with other shippers. The Cabrilles liked to play the odds. Nothing was predictable with them. Until he had the name, one that Mademoiselle Carinthe Cousteaux had promised to try and remember for him, his hands were tied and the possibility of making a fool of himself was greater than he dared risk. Search the wrong ship and he could kiss goodbye to any chance of promotion.

Starting up his car, Gastal pulled out into the traffic without bothering to indicate, accelerated down to Rive Neuve and swung left for the Sofitel. It was time for another chat with Carinthe Cousteaux.

Rain was rattling off the palms surrounding the Sofitel forecourt as Gastal parked. A doorman stepped forward to redirect him to other parking facilities but he flashed his badge. Park it for me, *connard*, or leave it where it is, his look said.

Inside Gastal strode towards reception, gave his name and asked for a call to be put through to Mademoiselle Cousteaux's room. As soon as he said the name, he saw the receptionist falter.

'Is there a problem?' asked Gastal.

'*Un moment, s'il vous plaît, monsieur,*' the receptionist replied. She went over to a colleague and whispered in his ear. The man looked at Gastal and acknowledged him with a short nod. He said something to the receptionist and then came over.

But before he could say anything, Gastal saw Peluze and Serre step out of a lift. Not bothering with the manager, he went over to them, a nasty feeling bubbling up in his guts.

'What are you two doing here?' he asked, squaring up to them.

'Your lady from Saturday, Mademoiselle Carinthe Cousteaux, was murdered this morning at Galerie Duchamp,' said Peluze. 'Stabbed three times. They found her hotel key in her bag. We came here to check her room out.'

'*Merde alors*. And?'

'Nothing we can find of any interest. Just a room. Booked for two weeks. Maids have been in and done it over. Spick and span.'

'Whose name? The reservation?'

'Hers,' replied Peluze, thankful that he'd thought to check.

'Any witnesses in the shop?'

Peluze shook his head. 'Looks like a professional hit,' he said. 'A load of people around, but no one saw a thing. One minute she's shopping, the next she's down.'

85

Paris

MADAME ESTELLE LAFOUR WAS STILL in her dressing gown when the maid tapped lightly on the door of the library at La Résidence Camille. She had settled there after breakfast – a pot of strong coffee, a buttered crust of *petit pain* and three cigarettes – and hadn't left her chair.

'*Entrez*,' she called.

The maid entered with a bob of her head and went over to Estelle. 'This has just been delivered. The messenger said it was urgent.' She offered the envelope and Estelle took it from her, spilling ash on her gown as she reached for it. 'Thank you, Marie. *C'est tout.*'

After the maid had gone, Estelle put out her cigarette and examined the packet. The envelope was padded, weighty, her name and address written in black capital letters, the single word *Urgent* in the top right corner underlined three times.

With a sigh, she pushed her forefinger into the sealed flap, tore it open and pulled out two sheets of paper.

She read the letter first. Just three lines. Short and concise. But she read it again, trying to make sense of it; then a third and a fourth time. Putting it aside, she reached for the second sheet. This took her longer to read, to take in. As she did so a frown settled across her forehead and then her breath caught. Tears filled her eyes and she started to shake her head. '*Non, non, non, c'est pas possible . . .*'

And then she remembered the envelope's weight; there'd been something else inside. She reached for it, tipped it over into her lap, and Elodie's hairclip came tumbling out.

Across town, in a fifth-floor boardroom on rue Baranot, Georges Lafour was taking his Monday heads of department meeting – planning the week ahead, assigning duties, outlining targets – when his eye was caught by the gentle swell of Déanna Gombert's breasts as she leaned down to retrieve notes from her attaché case. She was four places away from him on the right of the boardroom table, but that single, slight exposure was like a beacon, holding his eye as his assistant, Félix, went through the social stuff – lunches, dinners, guests, contacts.

Gombert was head of Banque Lafour's Far East acquisitions programme, in her mid-thirties, and attractive in a prim, efficient, short-blonde-hair-and-Chekhov-spectacles sort of way. This morning she was wearing a mauve silk blouse tucked into a tight pencil skirt. It was the loose opening at the top of this blouse that had attracted Lafour's attention. He had never really thought of Mademoiselle Gombert in any kind of sexual context but he could see now that, naked, she might well be a remarkable sight. As she leafed through her case, he noticed a thin red strap and followed it down into the shadowy pull and tug of her breasts. But she was staff. Madness. Utter madness. Unless, of course . . . He allowed himself a moment's distraction.

It was then that his secretary, Monique, came over the speaker phone.

'Monsieur Lafour. Your wife on the line.'

'Thank you, Monique,' he said, and guiltily pressed the flashing red light rather than pick up the receiver.

His wife's voice, sharp and bitter and filled with hatred, spat through the boardroom.

'You shit, you shit, you shit . . .' she managed before her husband was able to snatch up the receiver and silence the speaker.

Around the table a dozen faces looked on in astonishment, stunned by the outburst. And even though the speaker phone was now off, those executives closest to the head of the boardroom table could still hear what Lafour's wife was shouting down the line: 'You damn well better do what they say!' she screamed at him. 'Or I'll do it for you. You hear me? You hear what I'm saying, you bastard?'

86

Marseilles

AFTER CALLING AT RIBERO AGENCE Maritime and at Ribero's apartment block in Vauban, it took Jacquot and Marie-Ange the rest of the morning to check out the five addresses he had found in the directory listed under the name 'Léonie'. They found the first, a wholesale fashion outlet called Maison Léonie, on a small trading estate just a short distance from the Littoral behind the rain-swept sidings of Gare du Canet. This time Marie-Ange did the call-in but came back within minutes, shaking her head as she hurried through the rain.

'Just a small office,' she told Jacquot. 'Racks of clothes in one room, and a dozen women at sewing machines in another. As far as I could see there was no basement and no loft. Nowhere hidden away. Nowhere to keep Elodie without somebody noticing.'

It was the same story with the other Léonies. The stove shop, Léonie Fourneau, was empty and had a rental sign in the window; the *corsetière* on rue Saint Ferréol was *strictly by appointment only, mam'selle,* just a small reception area and various fitting rooms on the fourth floor, Marie-Ange reported back. And it was no different at the dry-cleaners, Pressing Léonie on rue Castellane, or at Léonie Beaux Chiens in Endoume. Not a single one of these businesses looked a likely hide-out for whoever had snatched Elodie Lafour from rue Artemis.

It was just as Jacquot had expected, the unrewarding tedium of police work – a slog around town with no return save names crossed off a list.

'What now?' asked Marie-Ange, as they followed the Corniche road back into town, crossing the viaduct over the tiny fishing cove of Vallon des Auffes.

'My meeting with Madame Bonnefoy,' he replied. 'Here, take the next right, now a left, that's fine. A shortcut,' he explained, as they swung along Avenue de la Corse and place Corderie and a few minutes later dropped down into place de la Bergasse.

Jacquot spotted Solange immediately, standing under the awning of a supermart, its sloping corner premises set with a stepped display of fruit and vegetables. She was wearing a belted mackintosh over her court robes and carried a briefcase and umbrella. She did not recognise the 2CV, despite Jacquot's wave as they passed.

Marie-Ange parked in a side-street and watched Jacquot cross the square and disappear inside the grocery store with the magistrate. Five minutes later, Madame Bonnefoy came out alone and set off up the street towards Cours Pierre Puget. After a few more seconds, Jacquot appeared, carrying a small bag.

Back in the car, he checked for passers-by then reached into the bag and brought out a gun and a box of cartridges. He pulled out the clip from the pistol grip and fed in ten shells. Pushing it back into the pistol, he pumped a round into the chamber, removed the clip once more and added another shell.

Sitting behind the wheel, Marie-Ange might have been watching a card sharp, eyes wide as she tried to follow the Queen of Hearts. Or, in this case, the practised ease of Jacquot's click-clunk, click-clunk gun handling.

'Do you think you'll need it?' she asked, as though she couldn't believe he ever would.

'This is Marseilles. And I'm a policeman. I might not like them,' he said, with a sad smile, 'but it is a comforting companion when I'm tracking down people who would probably kill us without a second thought – like you or me buying a newspaper or ordering a coffee.' He emptied the box of remaining shells into the bag and slotted it on to the dashboard shelf, sliding the gun away into the inside pocket of his pea-jacket.

'Where to now?' she asked.

'Lunch. Salette. He called this morning. Bruno's got something for us.'

Marie-Ange gave him a look. 'Is there ever an investigation in Marseilles that happens without lunch?'

'None that I'm working on,' replied Jacquot.

87

AFTER LEAVING THE SOFITEL, Gastal drove just three streets before he saw the sign and pulled over. A neighbourhood bar – a few tables in the window, a zinc counter set with three stools, football pennants hung like a pelmet above the shelves of bottles, a stale sandy scent of sea and cigarettes. He was still so incensed by his meeting with Madame Bonnefoy and the loss of Carinthe Cousteaux that he found it hard to spit out the word 'Cognac'.

The barman – shirtsleeves rolled up, arms heavily tattooed, thick neck and hairy wrists hung with clunking gold chains – raised an eyebrow at his customer's abruptness but set a glass on the counter and poured the measure requested without comment. At that moment, if anyone had said anything to Gastal, or not done what he wanted, on the double, he'd have bunched his fist and thrown it. He knew it; and the barman had probably known it too. Gastal would have hit anyone. Anything. Very hard. He was just so damned furious, so seething, so boiling with rage, that it wouldn't have taken much to set him off. The barman had been lucky to get away with that raised eyebrow.

Gastal was so hot with anger that the Cognac he tossed back had as much effect as a shot of cold milk. He tapped the glass on the counter and another measure was poured. He waved his hand up and down – a larger measure. And quick about it.

Taking up the Cognac, Gastal hoisted himself on to a stool, rested his elbows against the bar and looked through the rain-smeared window. He sat like that for some time, eyes fixed on the traffic sluicing along the Corniche, unblinking. Then he tossed back the drink, left a handful of change on the bar and hurried back to his car.

As he started up the engine, he decided he felt a great deal better. Finding that bar and getting himself a drink had been a first class idea. Given him the time and space to think.

And now he knew what he had to do.

88

CHEZ HUIT WASN'T A RESTAURANT that appeared in any guidebook, the number eight referring to its position half-way down a sloping line of houses in the old quarter of Le Panier, overlooking a narrow rectangle of the Vieux Port. There was no sign outside its front door to indicate that these were business premises, and that a dozen tables – all *doublettes*, big enough for just two – filled the cramped ground-floor salon and terrace. The elderly widow who owned the house and kept kitchen was called Tant'Anne, and every lunchtime, from Monday to Friday, she welcomed a shifting band of salty regulars and their guests. Salette was one of these regulars, and Jacquot and Marie-Ange his guests. Because of the rain and a troublesome breeze, the terrace doors had been closed and the available tables reduced to just six, two of which, with Tant'Anne's permission, Salette had pushed together to make room for his party.

Salette had clearly been caught off guard at the previous day's lunch, dressed in a rough and ready collection of week-old clothes. When he stood up from the table in Tant'Anne's to greet them, taking Marie-Ange's hand to kiss, Jacquot could see that the old fellow had gone to some effort to look more presentable for this meeting. He had shaved the chalk shading of white bristles off his chin, leaving his face more tanned than it had appeared the day before, his thick thatch of curling white hair was somehow more tutored than normal, and the old blue sweater and cream canvas trousers he always favoured now looked fresh and clean.

The three of them had made their way through a dish of sliced fresh vegetables dipped into Tant'Anne's legendary *anchoïade* and had seen off the best part of her chicken couscous when Bruno, the old harbour master from Montredon, came bustling into the room and made his way between the tables, pausing to shake a hand here, nod a salute there. In his other hand he carried a sheaf of papers.

After more hand-kissing and greetings when he reached their table, Salette's old friend settled himself and passed the papers to Jacquot.

'I thought it might be useful, Daniel. A list of vessels berthing or departing port in the last seven days. Pleasure craft, that is. Fifteen metres and above. Sail and motor, just in case. Between Montredon and L'Estaque. I realise your girl's maybe held somewhere else now, but you never know.'

Jacquot felt a lurch of disappointment as he leafed through the sheets – columns of names, berthing quays, times of departure, ports of call, estimated times of arrival. The previous week he'd have been delighted to get his hands on such a list, but with Elodie no longer at risk of transportation the movements of private vessels like these no longer had any real bearing on his investigation. But Bruno was a good man, and Jacquot didn't want to let him down.

'How did you manage to get all this?' he asked. 'And so quickly?'

Bruno beamed, revealing a perfect set of white teeth bar a single gold incisor that gave him a piratical look. 'I got it from my son-in-law down L'Estaque.'

'And what does your son-in-law do to have access to information like this?' asked Jacquot, flicking through the pages, nodding as though it was invaluable.

'The boy's a marine architect. Been brought in to rationalise – now there's a word – to rationalise berthing facilities in small ports for larger craft. Part of his brief is to track movements between ports. Days in port, days out. One vessel taking up two berths kind of thing. Needs close attention.'

But Jacquot wasn't listening any more, hadn't got any further than that first 'rationalise' before a smile spread over his face. He shook his head in a kind of stunned disbelief, chuckled at the sheer incredibility of it, and passed the last sheet to Marie-Ange.

'*Voilà*,' he said. 'The tenth name down. Now you know why we do our business over lunch.'

Marie-Ange took the page and counted down the list.

The tenth name.

It took her a moment to realise what she was looking at.

MY *Léonie*.

89

BENEATH THE DRIPPING COVER OF a tilting Aleppo pine, Gastal sat in his car five metres back from the corner of rue Cornille and Chemin de Roucas. Just a hundred metres to his left, on the far side of de Roucas, was the main gate of Maison Cabrille, and at the end of a short and tree-shrouded *impasse* almost directly ahead of him were a set of double garage doors, sunk into the side of the slope on which the property stood. It was as good a stake-out spot as he'd been able to find. Close enough to keep effective watch, far enough away to remain inconspicuous.

Before settling on this spot, Gastal had made a couple of circuits around the Cabrille estate and along roads that might overlook it. But the three-metre stone wall that surrounded the property and the line of lime and pine that branched above it made any kind of surveillance a tricky proposition. Rue Cornille was the only real vantage point he'd been able to find. For the first hour he'd been forced to double-park but now he was more discreetly slotted into a line of cars, just two between him and Chemin de Roucas.

From where he sat he may not have been able to see anything over the wall or through the trees or beyond the rising slope, but Gastal was not unfamiliar with the Cabrille estate. According to *DGSE* files in Lyons, Arsène Cabrille had bought the property in the late-sixties and paid in excess of five million francs for it.

Big money then. Big money still. Gastal knew the price because he had the agent's sale brochure from that time, a fold-out prospectus with faded colour pictures of a grand nineteenth-century villa with sea-view terraces and sloping lawns. According to the brochure some renovation had been recommended to bring the property into suitable order – the inference being that the previous owners had done nothing for some years and the place was in a deplorable state – but it wouldn't have taken the new owner long to turn it around. As well as the brochure illustrations, Gastal also had a number of hazy long-distance shots of the house taken by a *DGSE* operative from a boat offshore, and from a Department helicopter flying overhead.

After bringing the villa itself into suitable order, Cabrille had also, over the years, implemented a number of changes in the grounds – seeking planning permits for a two-bedroomed stone lodge, a double garage complex with accommodation above, a swimming pool and tennis court. For a man like Cabrille, a rising figure in Marseilles' underworld, such *permis* would have been easy to acquire, almost as easy as it had been for the *DGSE* to get their hands on copies of those same plans and architect's drawings.

Whatever now lay behind those walls, Gastal was in no doubt that the original purchase price would be but a very small fraction of the property's current value. He also knew it wasn't the family's only residence. In addition to the house in Roucas Blanc there was a winter home in Courmayeur, a holiday home in Martinique and several properties in French Polynesia where Cabrille's trading fleet enjoyed tax-efficient registry in the Futuna and Willis Islands. There was also the cottage in Endoume that Cabrille had bought for Mademoiselle Cousteaux, a small private jet hangared at Marignane, and a fifty-metre yacht berthed in L'Estaque. And now it all belonged to his daughter, Virginie. The sheer scale of her inheritance made Gastal hiss with envy. And squirm with an impossible lust. Just seeing her standing at the graveside had done it for Gastal. He'd seen her pictures, too, in *Point de Vue* and *Sud* – the openings, the exhibitions, the parties. Rich and tasty. Just a scratch over thirty. And still single.

And Gastal was going to bring her down. For the smuggling, for the Lafour girl, for the money-laundering Druot Clinics, for whatever piece of Cabrille chicanery he could get her for – however he could manage it.

If Gastal had had to put money on it – now that Carinthe Cousteaux was unable to supply the name of the freighter with its illegal cargo – he'd say the Lafour girl was his best bet. But it wasn't by any means a sure thing. What he couldn't figure out was why the family should bother with a kidnap and ransom. It wasn't their usual fare and it wasn't like they needed the money, or the risk of possible exposure. Certainly the girl was here, in Marseilles, if only because Madame Bonnefoy had brought in Jacquot to track her down. But did the Cabrilles actually have her?

Watching the house, occasionally checking behind him in the wing and rear-view mirrors, Gastal wondered just how far Jacquot might have got, but felt a rising confidence that the man was nowhere near as close to springing the Lafour girl as he was. Because Gastal knew, he just *knew*, that he was in the right place. And the time was right. And something was going to happen. In the next couple of days that ponytailed chancer would be discredited, Madame Bonnefoy would be forced to admit his own superior policing, and he, Gastal, would be calling Bocuse to book the first of many tables – his future assured.

He had been sitting there for two hours, listening to the rain on the roof of his Renault, watching the main gate and the *impasse* garage, when his patience was finally rewarded at a little after four o'clock. With thunder crackling overhead, a black VW came down Chemin de Roucas, passed Gastal on the corner of rue Cornille and turned up into the dead-end street with no name. Staying low behind the wheel, Gastal saw the garage doors slide open as the car approached. Thirty seconds later it had disappeared inside and the garage doors had closed. Despite the distance, the VW's speed, and his own rain-smeared windscreen, Gastal had managed to make out two men inside the VW, big fellows both of them, real *vrais durs*, as likely as not the pair that Haggar had told him about who had gone to Valentine's workshop and done for the *garagiste*.

He was trying to place them, work them into the picture, when the garage doors slid open again and the VW reappeared. There was just the driver this time, no passenger, and he reversed out of the garage at speed, swinging the car round in a tight turn and then swooping down to Chemin de Roucas. Sidelights on, right indicator flashing, off he went, the car jerking as he changed untidily into second. Wherever he was going, he was in a hurry to get there.

Gastal counted twenty, then started up his Renault and set out after him. By the time he'd turned into the road, the VW was passing out of sight beyond the bend. Gastal increased his speed so as not to fall too far behind, and prayed he wouldn't lose it. Coming round the bend, he was in time to see it swing right through a set of lights and head off down rue Fabres. As soon as it was out of sight, Gastal put his foot down and made the lights as they changed to red.

Rue Fabres was another long bend to the right, a tight squeeze for two passing cars, with no kerbs and a gentle slope that would have led them down to the Corniche if the VW hadn't taken an abrupt, unsignalled left into rue Seneca. If Gastal had been in a squad car, he'd have lit the lamp and hit the horns. Instead, he braked hard to make the same turn and hoped the VW's driver wouldn't notice he was being followed. Dropping his speed, he watched the VW race on ahead until it swooped around another bend and out of sight. This time he kept his speed steady, wondering where the VW was headed. He found out when he came round the bend and saw it pulled up outside a *tabac*. Keeping his eyes on the road, as though the parked VW and its driver, now going into the *tabac*, were of no interest, Gastal dropped down to the next intersection and realised where he was, back on Chemin de Roucas.

A cigarette run.

That's all it had been.

He could have sat tight on Cornille and not missed anything.

In the meantime Maison Cabrille had been left unattended. Anyone could have come in or gone out, and he was none the wiser. Cursing lightly, Gastal swung back down into Cornille, went to the bottom of the street, turned in someone's driveway and came back up to his original parking space just as the VW's brake lights glared again and dropped down out of sight into the Cabrille garage.

Switching off the engine, Gastal settled down to continue his surveillance. It didn't take long for him to start thinking that maybe it hadn't been a cigarette run. Did they know he was there? Had they made him? Lured him away while something more interesting went down?

He soon found out. Minutes later the garage door opened and the VW's driver appeared, holding an umbrella over his head. Gastal watched him walk down to the main road, cross over, and head straight for him. Without breaking stride he came down rue Cornille, stopped by the Renault, and bent down to look through the passenger window. There was a nasty little smile on the man's face as he tapped the glass.

Gastal knew immediately it hadn't been a cigarette run.

But he still tried to brazen it out. Buzzing down the window, he leaned across the passenger seat and asked, 'Can I help?'

'Please get out of the car, monsieur,' the man said. The accent was unmistakable. Just as Alam Haggar had described it – a rough, clipped sound. An islander, certainly not local.

'You what?' tried Gastal.

'I said, please get out of the car. Mademoiselle Cabrille would like a word.'

Before he had a chance to compute that particular piece of information, Gastal heard another tap on the driver's window behind him. He turned to see the muzzle of a 9-mm automatic resting against the glass. The second man from the VW had appeared from nowhere. Just come up behind him like a shadow. He motioned with the gun that Gastal should do as he was told.

'You'd better lock it,' said the first man, as Gastal stepped out into the rain.

'Even round here,' said his companion.

Despite the gun, now slipped away in the man's pocket, Gastal felt a swoop of relief. You weren't told to lock your car if you weren't coming back to it. One of the men even put an umbrella over his head so he wouldn't get wet.

90

WITH TWO RETIRED HARBOUR MASTERS to help, it didn't take long to establish that the motor yacht *Léonie* was a fifty-metre vessel built in 1968 in Portuguese yards. She weighed a little over three hundred tons, had five guest suites, a crew of ten, and had undergone a major refit in Toulon some four years earlier. What they couldn't find out was the owner's name.

'Not surprising when she's registered in Mata-Utu,' said Salette. 'Futuna and Willis Islands. Tighter than a Swiss bank, they are.'

'She'll be a nice-looking boat,' said Bruno. 'The people who built her are good. Arsenal do Alfeite. Real naval architects. She'll have some style, that's for sure.'

'Still a pleasure-boat,' grunted Salette who didn't rate a vessel unless it had sails.

Thanks to Bruno's son-in-law they had also established that MY *Léonie* had left the port of L'Estaque at a little after seven o'clock on Sunday morning after a two-week stay. The time-frame fitted with Elodie being taken from Vassin's home the night before, and a ship the size of *Léonie* seemed a reasonable place to keep someone safely and quietly hidden away – no snooping neighbours at sea. As far as Jacquot was concerned, he'd bet a *pichet* of *rouge* to a case of Bellet that Solange Bonnefoy's niece was on board.

But where was the boat now? Where had she gone after leaving L'Estaque?

Monopolising Tant'Anne's hallway telephone, they found out that MY *Léonie* had not berthed at any port along the coast and that no boat of that name had been reported anchored off-shore.

'She could be anywhere,' said Bruno. 'She'll do twelve to fifteen knots easy, and with full tanks, say forty thousand litres, she's got a cruising range of . . . what? Maybe three thousand kilometres?'

Marie-Ange looked appalled.

But Jacquot wasn't convinced she was that far from port. 'She'll be hiding somewhere, out at sea, out of sight, but not too far,' he told them. 'Any ideas?'

'There's Maritime Control in Toulon,' suggested Bruno. 'They've got the best surveillance in terms of radar. They might be able to help.'

'Or there's the Gendarmerie Maritime out at Corbière,' said Salette. 'They share the same feed, have the same information. And they're a lot closer than Toulon.'

It was Bruno's turn to grunt. 'That means dealing with that know-it-all, Monsieur Gérard "*Je-sais-tout*" Torne. We'll be there all night.'

'Maybe he's not on duty,' said Salette.

But Gérard Torne was on duty. When they arrived at the coast-guard facility on the quay at Corbière, they were shown through to the control room – a dark, windowless space crowded with chart tables, consoles and radar screens – and there he was, a tall man in a sleeveless pullover, Sta-prest slacks and squeaking trainers. He had a long, mournful face, heavy-framed spectacles and a thin black moustache that he pulled at as he talked.

'I wish I could help, monsieur,' said Torne with a weary smile when Jacquot explained that they needed help finding a boat. 'But this is not air-traffic control,' he continued. 'Ships do not have transponders. They are not like aircraft, you know, coming in to land or taking off. Air France this, Air France that. I can't just look at the screen and say "oh, there is your ship". It simply doesn't work like that, I'm afraid.'

He then frowned, began to nod, and the four of them looked at him expectantly, as though he had suddenly remembered something. He hadn't. 'Of course, it's all set to change,' he began again. 'There is a new system being developed to track and monitor vessel movements a great deal more efficiently. Things like vessel identification, position, course and speed. Apparently it works by integrating a standardised VHF transceiver system with an electronic navigation system, such as a LORAN-C or Global Positioning receiver, and other navigational sensors on board ship, which tie in with . . .'

'But you don't have this system at the moment,' interrupted Jacquot. Now he knew what Bruno had meant back at Tant'Anne's. Once the man got going it was almost impossible to break in.

'I regret, monsieur, not quite yet. All we have is what you see in front of you, real-time radar surveillance data supplied by Toulon. Here, let me show you.'

Torne was clearly used to the limited space in the control room and wove his way expertly between the chart tables and desks to one of the radar consoles. Jacquot, Marie-Ange, Salette and Bruno followed more carefully, gathering around him, all eyes drawn to a green line sweeping clockwise round the screen. 'From the maritime monitoring station at Toulon, five hundred metres above sea level, our effective radar range is about eighty kilometres,' said Torne. 'Line of sight, if you like. But the further you go, the weaker the signal. There, for instance, pretty much at the edge of our range are three tankers,' he said, pointing a long bony finger at three tiny green blips within an inch of each other at the top of the screen. 'Approximately south-south-east of us, on a north-easterly heading. MS *Konstantin,* MS *Crude Lavery* and the *Osten* out of Hamburg.'

'I thought you said you didn't have names?' said Jacquot.

Torne smiled patiently, his thin moustache curling slightly. 'I have these names, monsieur, because their departure details are logged with Toulon Control. This one, in the lead, is probably the *Osten*, coming up from Gibraltar, and these two further back from the refineries at Puerto Castellón near Valencia, all bound for Genoa as their destination port. Even if I didn't have their names and

357

details, I would know them just by their heading – where they are coming from, where they are going. It's the third time this year that they have made the same journey. At sea, as in life, messieurs, mademoiselle, there is always a pattern. Day and night. The same routes, the same ships. Ferries to and from Corsica, oil tankers leaving and arriving at Fos-Martigues, trawler fleets working traditional fishing grounds, even naval patrols on manoeuvre.'

Torne looked happily from face to face, tweaking his moustache, pleased to have such an attentive audience. 'But then, there are those who sail and cruise for pleasure, these other smaller indices you see, closer to the coast. All I can say with any certainty is that there is a vessel of some description here,' he said, pointing to a blip. 'Or there,' pointing to another. 'But I can give you no details. Name, tonnage, registration, destination. Nothing.'

'Unless they contact you . . . a distress call,' said Salette.

'Ah, with radio communication established between the vessel and our control facilities, *mais bien sûr*, everything changes.'

'Do you get many distress calls?' asked Marie-Ange.

'At this time of year, plenty,' replied Torne. 'Yachtsmen who think they can handle the kinds of seas we've been having recently, people lost in the fog, and just the other day a couple of crazy divers off Cap Canaille. Swept out, they were. At least they had transponders, or we'd never have found them. Which is what is so good about the new technology, you see, because . . .'

'What about those patterns you mentioned?' pressed Jacquot. 'If you saw something that didn't look right, but there was no distress call.'

'If something looked suspicious, of course we would check it out. And it happens more often than you might imagine.'

'Any examples?' asked Jacquot.

Torne pushed out his bottom lip. It looked like a long shiny slug, the red of it tinged green from the radar screens. He gave the question a moment's thought, then started to nod. 'Last summer we had a ship about forty kilometres out, on the edge of a deep trough called the Maures Escarpment. One of our controllers noticed that it hadn't moved between his shifts. It was outside recognised anchorage spots and close to shipping lanes, so we had the Gendarmerie Maritime chopper go and take a look. Turned out it was on a treasure hunt, exploring a wreck. Not in trouble at all.'

He smiled at them, each in turn, as though he had done all he could and now he really must be getting back to work.

'Anything more recently?' asked Marie-Ange with a smile.

'Pretty much the same thing this morning,' Torne replied. 'Some vessel keeping to station about eighty kilometres south-west of here. We call it "patrolling".'

'Patrolling?' asked Jacquot, his interest piqued.

'Holding a circular course. Not going anywhere. Something like that could have been a drugs pick-up – which was our first thought – or possibly something wrong with their steering, maybe some kind of mechanical failure. If their radio was down too, they'd have been unable to call for help. And that stretch of water, monsieur, can get pretty busy with traffic in and out of Fos-Martigues, not to mention westerly bound traffic out of Marseilles, and on occasions . . .'

'So what did you do?' Jacquot broke in.

'The chopper again. Came in overhead, established radio contact. And there was no problem at all. They were fine. Just testing a new rudder assembly, some big refit, the skipper said. Beautiful boat too, according to our pilot. Real style.'

A beautiful boat, thought Jacquot. Real style.

Nice-looking, Bruno had said at Chez Huit. *She'll have some style, that's for sure*.

'Do you happen to remember her name?' asked Jacquot, an unexpected fluttering in his stomach.

'Not off the top of my head, but I could check.'

Jacquot smiled. That would be very kind of him.

Torne went over to a computer terminal and started work on the keyboard, making his way through a number of links until he found what he was searching for. He looked up from the screen. 'Here it is. Contacted oh-eight-seventeen hours today. Local motor yacht. Out of L'Estaque but registered in Mata-Utu. MY *Léonie*.'

91

BY THE TIME HE REACHED the garage doors leading into the Cabrille estate, Gastal was feeling more confident, a little more in control of the situation. On the walk from his car, the two men accompanying him had been oddly deferential, as though a gun had never been drawn to ensure his compliance, and every effort had been made to keep the umbrella over his head as the three of them walked together up rue Cornille, waited for passing traffic on de Roucas and then made their way up the *impasse*.

'Terrible weather,' said the shorter of the two men, the one with the gun in his pocket, as the garage doors slid open.

'Like all things, you can be certain it will pass,' his companion replied. As they stepped into the shelter of the garage, he released the catch on his umbrella, shook off the rain and placed it against the wall.

The first thing that Gastal saw was a line of cars: a green 356 Porsche roadster, the VW still wet from its outing, a large 4X4 Cherokee Chief and, furthest away, parked beside a well-equipped workbench, the long, low, unmistakable lines of a Daimler limousine. He felt a beat of satisfaction. There, for certain, was the car that Alam Haggar had seen near Valentine's workshop. But no tinted windows. In that regard, Haggar had been lying.

'Would you mind waiting a moment?' asked the taller of the

two men. He gave the same cold smile he'd put on when he'd tapped on Gastal's car window. 'I will phone to let Mademoiselle Cabrille know that you have arrived.'

Gastal spread his hands. 'Of course, not a problem,' he said, and wandered down the slope of the garage to take a closer look at the soft-top Porsche. It was this incline that had concealed the far wall of the garage, a long panel of glass running from floor to ceiling and giving on to a landscaped garden spreading out beyond it. A hundred metres to the right he could see the terraces of Maison Cabrille and to his left, beyond the azure glow of a swimming pool, what must have been the lodge. He was putting his hands up against the glass to cut out the interior reflection when he saw the man who'd gone to call Virginie Cabrille coming back in his direction. He turned and gestured to the view and the cars. 'Beautiful. Just beautiful,' he said.

'"A man should so live that his happiness shall depend as little as possible on external things",' the umbrella man replied.

Gastal frowned. 'Say again?'

'Epictetus, first century AD,' said a voice beside him.

Gastal turned. Once again the smaller of the two men had appeared from nowhere. He gave a smile, and shook his head as though, really, Gastal should have known about Epictetus. 'He was a Greek philosopher,' the man continued. 'Born a slave, became a Stoic. He taught us, among other things, that suffering arises from trying to control what cannot be controlled. Taddeus is a great fan. Reads him all the time. Really a very clever gentleman, Epictetus . . . and my brother too.'

That was when Gastal glimpsed the brother's open hand slicing down towards his neck.

He didn't feel the blow, saw only blackness as he crumpled between their feet.

Tuesday
17 November

92

IT WAS SHORTLY AFTER MIDNIGHT when the Gendarmerie Maritime's coastguard cutter *P.60* slid out of Port de Corbière, passed the Lave beacon and took up a heading of two-three-five degrees, bearing south-west into the Golfe du Lion.

Just a few hours earlier Jacquot, standing at Gérard Torne's desk, had contacted Solange Bonnefoy and told her what he had found out and what he wanted. She in turn had contacted the Préfet Maritime in Toulon, finally tracking him down to a sixtieth-birthday dinner party along the coast at Le Lavandou. Whatever she had said to him over the phone had clearly worked. Permission to proceed with action had been granted. The Gendarmerie Maritime was at Madame's disposal.

There were four of them up in the *P.60*'s wheelhouse – Jacquot and Marie-Ange in standard-issue life-jackets, and the cutter's helmsman, Willi, feet planted apart, hands on the wheel, eyes flicking between compass bearing, radar and the windscreen, its glass panels swept clear of rain and spattering sea-spray by four elbowed wipers. Behind Willi, the *P.60*'s commander, Léo Chabran, rode out the incoming swells from the comfort of his skipper's chair. He was tall and well-built, with broad shoulders and a strong hard face. His skin was tanned from sea and sun and his eyes glittered like chips of grey flint. He wore regulation blue serge trousers tucked into polished lace-up black boots and a thick grey polo-neck sweater that made him look, Jacquot thought, like a U-boat commander. The sleeves had been pushed back to just below his elbows. There was a large black-faced chronometer on his left wrist, and on the top of his right forearm a small tattoo put there so long ago and so softened by a pelt of black hair that its shape was difficult to make out, no more than a pale blue bruise. Sitting in his skipper's chair, he looked at home in the wheelhouse, comfortable and confident with command, the kind of man, Jacquot suspected, who was easy to like.

Certainly Salette had liked him, enough not to argue when Chabran had told them that he could only take two passengers. He had been briefed before Jacquot and Marie-Ange boarded – a seek and search, a motor yacht called *Léonie*, possible kidnapping – but Jacquot had filled him in on the details. He'd listened intently then nodded his head. He understood; he would do what he could.

Up at the wheel, Willi leant sideways for the throttles, easing them forward a notch or two. As the cutter increased its speed, ploughing through a westerly chop past the twinkling coastal lights of La Vesse and Niolon, Jacquot reached for a handhold.

'It will take some time to reach her,' explained Chabran. 'If the weather were behind us, we would make better headway, but it's not.'

'How long?' asked Jacquot.

Chabran spread his hands – big strong hands Marie-Ange noted.

'Two hours certainly,' he replied, checking his watch. 'Maybe a little longer.'

'What's the procedure when we reach her?'

Chabran gave a small shrug. 'Let us wait and see what happens. Right now she is close to shipping lanes in and out of Fos-Martigues. I will keep to the coast then turn towards her. If they see us on radar, which they might, we will be following a path taken by other vessels. There will be no suspicion, I hope. Then we close on them, fast. If they stay within territorial waters – which is where they are right now – we make a simple approach, ask permission to board. A drugs search maybe?'

'What if she makes a run for it?' asked Marie-Ange.

'We are faster, mademoiselle. And we also have the advantage of a small 50-mm canon on our bow, *pour encourager*. And out at sea, who can say what happens?'

He smiled at her.

She smiled back.

Standing so close to Marie-Ange, elbows touching as the cutter rose and fell, Jacquot noticed a small flush rise up into her neck. He looked at Chabran's hands. His left hand. No ring.

'It will get a little bumpier when we pass Méjean, and the wheelhouse is not a comfortable place,' Chabran continued. 'You are welcome to stay, of course. But maybe for now you should get below. There's coffee, something to eat if you're hungry. Just ask one of the boys. And if you want to get some rest, there are crew cabins aft. Dry and clean but very noisy. If anything happens, I'll let you know. But for now . . .' He nodded at Jacquot, gave Marie-Ange another smile.

93

'MY, MY, BUT YOU'RE A fat little fellow.'

Gastal opened his eyes, blinked, and felt a dull ache on the side
of his neck. The next thing he registered was a prickling, sweaty
heat. All over his body. All over his skin. It was then that he realised
he was naked. And restrained. His arms had been secured by leather
bracelets to a beam of wood above his head, and his legs similarly
spread and secured by the ankles to another beam beneath his feet.
It was, he realised, a crucifixion of the most exposed and obscene
kind.

'Such a tubby little man . . .' the voice continued. Soft and teasing
and gentle. A woman's voice. Coming from behind him.

Gastal looked around as far as he could, but he could see no
one, just varnished brick walls, a polished concrete floor, a fabric-
covered door and a double line of tiny spotlights set into what
appeared to be a padded ceiling. The padding looked like foam-
rubber insulation of some sort. He raised his eyes and tried to focus
on it, beyond the lights. Or soundproofing, maybe. One or the other.
And then he saw, with a sudden chill of understanding, why it
might be soundproofing. Against the wall to his left stood two wide
cabinets, doors open, the first fitted with a range of shackles and
restraints, chains and collars, the other with whips and canes and
straps and switches displayed like cues racked in a snooker hall.

But that wasn't all. On his right was a wheeled hospital trolley with two metal shelves, covered in a selection of shiny chrome instruments, and beside it what looked like a large leather trunk, lid open, shadowy interior filled with wired clips, callipers, and what looked suspiciously like the defibrillator paddles he had seen paramedics use. More ominous still was a small drain in the middle of the floor, and a reel of coiled hose by the door.

He was, he realised, in a torture chamber. Despite the heat he felt his balls contract.

'And, oh, what a tiny little *bite* you have,' came the voice again, and this time the folded leather tip of a riding crop flicked out from behind him and smacked against the head of his penis.

Wincing Gastal looked over his right shoulder and saw her, Virginie Cabrille, her jet-black hair gelled back from her forehead, furrowed with the thin tracks of a comb, her face bare of make-up, angled, severe. She was wearing penny loafers, a pair of blue silk slacks, a jumper with a matching cardigan slung over her shoulders, and a single strand of pearls at her throat. She had the look of a schoolteacher – a headmistress he decided, and a headmistress in a not very happy frame of mind. She came round the side of the beams and walked past him, flexing the crop between her hands, turning to give him a stern look before disappearing behind him once more.

'I don't know what you think you're doing . . .' began Gastal, but he was cut short by a vicious swipe of the riding crop across his dimpled buttocks. He let out a bellow of shock and pain and felt himself sway between the beams.

She came round to face him again, stood in front of him, put her hands on her hips and smiled. The riding crop swung from her wrist. But she wasn't looking at his face.

'Ah, there we are, *petit*,' she cooed. 'Come out to play, have we? You liked that didn't you?'

Despite the shivering pulse of fear that Gastal felt, there was now another pulse, altogether warmer, and more visible, that had started to flood through his body.

And there was nothing he could do about it.

Absolutely nothing.

Naked. Spread like that . . .

Despite himself, his body, if not his mind, was starting to respond.

'So tell me,' said Virginie, now tapping the riding crop against her leg, 'wasn't it enough to gate-crash my father's funeral? Did you have to come snooping round here as well? And alone? My, my, but you are a brave little soldier, aren't you?'

'I'm here for the girl,' he replied, making his voice as strong and authoritative as he could, despite the state he found himself in.

'And what girl would that be?' she asked, with a slim teasing smile.

'You know very well. Elodie Lafour.'

'Ah yes, such a pretty little thing. And such a loss.'

'Loss?'

'Of course. Because I'm going to kill her. I have what I need – something to prove that I have her – but now . . . now she really is of no further use. In fact, why don't I do it right this minute? So you can listen in.'

Virginie put down the crop on the trolley and went behind him again. He heard her pick up a phone and punch in just two numbers – internal, he thought.

'Tomas, call Milić. Tell him we don't need the cargo any more. Just weight it and drop it overboard . . . That's right. Good.'

She put down the phone, and came back to stand in front of him. 'There, you see? Easy.' Then she picked up her crop again and pushed its hooped tip against the top of his penis.

He could feel a springiness. Crop and cock alike.

But she didn't seem impressed. 'Not much to play with, is there?' she observed. '*Mais alors*, I think we can come up with something, don't you?'

'This is madness,' spluttered Gastal. 'I'm a policeman. A Chief Inspector. You can't do this.'

'Oh, but I can, Monsieur *Flic*,' she said, and, with a lashing back-hand, laid the riding crop across his chest, sharply enough to leave a long red welt between his breasts. 'And I most certainly will.'

94

JACQUOT WOKE WITH A START, surprised he'd even slept. Down in what passed for a galley – a narrow wooden table, equally narrow banquettes and a ribbed bulkhead devoid of any decoration save lengths of thickly lagged pipes – he and Marie-Ange had been served coffee, eaten some warm baguette sandwiches and, lulled by the close warmth of the room and the lateness of the hour, had promptly dozed off like commuters on a home-bound train. Marie-Ange still had her eyes closed, a wedge of spare cushion pushed between her and the bulkhead. It was astonishing that either of them had got any sleep at all. The hum and whine of the *P.60*'s engine and the distant thump-thump . . . thump as the cutter's prow beat through the sea sent a pulse of power shivering through the ship. Their plates rattled on the wooden table, the surface of their coffee rippled. Everything throbbed. But still they'd slept.

Not that Jacquot had woken by himself. It had been Willi, from the wheelhouse, even now leaning across to tap Marie-Ange's shoulder.

'Skipper says we're about four nautical miles off, and thought you should come topside. I'll get some coffee brought up,' he said and stepped through the companionway.

Up on the bridge everything was in darkness save for a pale blue glow from the instrument panel. Chabran was at the wheel, riding the chop, wipers jerking across the windscreen, the sea-spray shifted from head-on to hit them from the side now. Despite his size and the cramped quarters of the wheelhouse, he had a swift, easy grace, reaching out to Marie-Ange as she came up from below and a swell caught her off-balance.

As he guided her to the skipper's chair and let go of her wrist, the most extraordinary thought entered her head: *If I lick him, he'll taste of the sea.* The very idea of it unbalanced her as much as the swell.

'You've killed the deck lights,' said Jacquot, looking through the windscreen. The last time he'd been in the wheelhouse he'd been able to see the prows cutting through the water, and the tarpaulin-covered shape of the 50-mm canon.

Chabran checked his watch. 'Thirty minutes ago. I didn't want to alert our friends.'

'Won't they have radar?' asked Marie-Ange, still trying to recover herself.

'If they're watching it they'll have a searchlight on us any time now,' replied Chabran coolly. 'But I don't think they are. It's past three in the morning. Even at sea people get tired, and lazy.'

'Where are they?' asked Jacquot, peering through the windscreen.

'You'll need glasses,' Chabran replied, pointing to a pair of binoculars hanging by the door. 'The swell's high and they're running stern on to us. Not much of a target, but you should be able to see them.'

Wedging himself against the bulkhead to counter the jarring and screwing the binoculars tight into his eyes, Jacquot tried to make out something in the blackness ahead. There was no moon, no stars, just a spray of white, like snow, streaking past his line of vision. But gradually a certain form came to the darkness. The *P.60*'s bows breaking through the swell, cresting wave-tops coming in from their right, and there, a blurring flash of orange lights like the lit tip of a cigarette. Clamping his elbows to his sides to steady the binoculars, he finally located the lights, lost them, found them again, adjusted the focus and settled on a half-dozen dancing gold points the size of nail-heads.

Jacquot felt someone nudge his arm. It was Willi with a thermos and a cup. Chabran and Marie-Ange already had theirs. 'Coffee, monsieur?'

'Thank you, that'd be great,' said Jacquot. Putting down the binoculars he took the mug and held it out as Willi poured. The smell was unmistakable. Not just coffee. He caught Marie-Ange's smile.

'It's a cold night,' said Chabran, sipping his brew. 'And late, and we'll need our wits about us, so I've . . . adapted our coffee, *P.60*-style. Had Willi add some Calva. The British may have their rum but we have something altogether better, wouldn't you agree? *Le vrai esprit de l'océan, n'est-ce pas?*'

Jacquot grinned. He'd been right. Easy to like. Exactly his kind of man.

Chabran raised his mug and they toasted one another.

'So,' he continued, surrendering the helm to Willi with a few brief instructions before getting down to business, 'some ground rules, *s'il vous plaît.*' The playful expression turned hard now and serious. 'I must remind you that I am skipper of this ship, and I am in command. You will both do exactly what I say, at all times, immediately and without argument. There must be no misunderstandings about this. We are at sea, the weather is up, and it is dangerous out there. I hope you agree?'

He looked at Jacquot and then Marie-Ange, to make sure that they did. Both of them nodded.

'Good. Now let me tell you what will happen. At the moment we are approximately twelve nautical miles off the L'Espiguette coast. The *Léonie* is still holding her pattern, sailing approximately three nautical miles inside and three nautical miles outside territorial waters. In a moment, if she keeps to pattern, she will turn and come back into home waters. When she does that, I will come in behind her, to block off any escape if she tries to make a run for it.'

'Can't we follow her if she's in international waters?' asked Marie-Ange.

'International Maritime Law is a minefield, Marie-Ange. Let's just say I would prefer to make any approach in French territory.' Chabran turned to Jacquot. 'I am assuming that you are armed?'

Jacquot nodded, opened his life-jacket and showed the grip of the 9-mm in the pocket of his pea-jacket.

'As will be our boarding party. Sidearms only. They will remain holstered until I say otherwise, or our lives are in danger. Understood?'

Jacquot said that he did.

'She's beginning her turn, Skip,' said Willi. 'About three thousand metres, a few degrees off due south.'

Chabran checked the radar screen. 'Take us up to fourteen knots, then bring her round to follow at a thousand metres.'

He turned back to Jacquot and Marie-Ange.

'So, *mes amis*, the game begins.'

95

VIRGINIE CABRILLE WALKED OVER TO the display case
and fitted the riding crop back into its place, black braided leather
against the cabinet's lining of scarlet felt. She ran her fingers over
the various coiled whips and bamboo canes set around it, but
shook her head, as though what she saw there didn't quite seem
to fit what she had in mind. Instead, she turned to the trolley and
picked up one or two of the instruments laid out on its top shelf
– pincers, pliers, and an extravagantly curved tool in shiny steel
that looked as though it might be used to open something up, and
open it very wide indeed. She tested the action. Hanging from
the beams, Gastal heard a ratcheting sound as the tong-like jaws
opened and held. But these, too, seemed not to interest her. In
the end, she settled for a long metal rod with a thick rubber handle
which she waved about like a sabre. Gastal knew exactly what it
was the moment she pressed it against his left nipple. There was
a crackling blue buzzing sound, stars exploded in his eyes, and
Gastal jerked as a burst of high-voltage, low-current electricity
shot through his body.

A taser. A bloody taser, he thought, as she drew the rod away
from the nipple and placed it in his open armpit. Another flash.
Another jolting, buckling burst of power. And another, and another,
as she worked her way along his arm until she buried the tip of

the rod into the palm of his hand, held the burst and lit him up like a firecracker.

He was only able to scream when the power came off, and when it did, with a final, burning crackle, he screamed with all his might, loud and clear and anguished.

'At last, at last, a proper scream,' she cried out, tilting her head like a piano tuner, as though to hear the sound more clearly, to savour it more fully. 'Beautiful, beautiful, beautiful . . . Oh, you did that so well, *mon brave*,' she said, walking back to the trolley and dropping the prod on to it. 'And please don't worry,' she continued, waving to the ceiling, the quilted door, the varnished brick walls. 'As you can see, the room is soundproofed. So feel free. Make as much noise as you wish. Even louder, it doesn't matter. No one will hear you down here.'

Virginie went to the door, reached for a switch and lowered the lights. 'They say that screaming helps,' she said, coming back to Gastal. 'Did you know that? Apparently it lessens the pain, or rather . . . makes it more manageable. Whether it does or doesn't, I cannot say. What I do know is that it greatly increases my pleasure. Because, Monsieur *Flic*, if you do not scream, and scream loudly, and enthusiastically, well, I really won't enjoy myself. And you wouldn't want that, now would you?'

'You're mad, you're raving . . .'

She was quick, so quick Gastal never saw it coming. Not that he could have done anything about it, strung up as he was between the beams. In an instant, the blink of an eye, she seemed to pirou-ette away from the trolley and spin towards him, and the next thing he knew her right foot had shot up between his legs and the toe of a penny loafer had connected with that small, hard stretch of skin and bone just behind his scrotum. The pain speared up through his anus, spine, belly and chest and exploded behind his eyes, howled into his brain.

It was worse, far worse than any direct kick to the genitals. He tried to double up, to somehow absorb the pain, to soften and accommodate it, but there was not enough movement in his bonds

376

to afford him such comfort, the leather bracelets and ankle straps biting into him as he tried to squirm away from the appalling, numbing glory of the hurt. All he could do was suck in air through gritted teeth as though it was the last air in the room. When he could take in no more, he flung it out in a prolonged wail of agony.

'*Oh, mais oui, mais oui, chéri,*' shouted Virginie again. 'Bravo, bravo, bravo! You *are* learning, you *are* learning.' And she spun around delightedly. 'But from now on, *mon petit, un peu de respect, s'il vous plaît.*'

'Jesus Christ, woman,' he gasped. 'This is . . . this is fucking . . .'

'*Attention*, monsieur.' She wagged her finger in his face, 'Tsk, tsk, tsk. I beg you to be careful what you say from now on. And how you say it. I will not warn you again.' She walked back to the trolley, shrugged off her cardigan and draped it across the topmost shelf.

'Now, I know I just told you that screaming gives me pleasure, that it's good to hear,' she began again, turning to look at him. 'But shall I tell you another little secret? Would you like to hear it?'

Gastal knew better than to let the question go unanswered. So he nodded his head. Right now, he knew, he needed to play for time. Time for someone to reach him, to save him. If only he'd brought back-up . . . If only he'd told Peluze where he was going, instead of stomping out of the Sofitel the way he had . . . But he hadn't done either of those things, and given the way he'd been treating Peluze he couldn't see his second-in-command losing any sleep over his absence. For the moment, he knew that he was on his own.

'Well, it's this,' she continued, running the necklace of pearls through her fingers. 'I've recently discovered that sometimes the best pain to inflict, the most satisfying, the pain that gives me the greatest pleasure, is the . . . the quiet kind. Or rather, the kind you don't actually hear. Just the sense that someone is suffering, suffering terribly because of something that you have done. Do you follow me?'

Gastal nodded again.

377

Virginie seemed satisfied with the response, and Gastal was relieved he'd made the effort. Just stay in there, he thought to himself. Don't make her angry. Spin it out as long as you can, as long as you can bear it.

'Shall I give you an example?' she continued, going over to the twin cabinets, closing one of the doors and leaning against it.

'Yes,' he managed. 'Tell me.'

'Yesterday, at Saint Pierre cemetery, there was a funeral. You were there. Why don't you tell me who was buried?'

'Your father.'

'*En effet,* not just my father,' she said with a little chuckle. 'Because, you see, there were two bodies in the coffin. One dead, my father, may he rest in peace. The other, not dead. Alive. Just . . . sleeping. A cheating, double-dealing little shit called Guillermo Ribero who thought he could fool the family, take us for a ride, profit from our generosity. So I put him in the coffin with my dear, departed papa, and I screwed down the lid.

'Now, I wasn't there when he woke up, when he realised where he was and started screaming. I never heard a whisper. Not a thing. But you know what, Monsieur *Flic*? I lived it with him. Thinking about him. Wondering how long he'd live. Wondering what it would be like, in that silky, satin darkness, when the air started to turn bad. I felt it here. In my heart. In my head. Even here,' she said, placing a hand between her legs. 'For many hours, longer than I would have thought possible, I felt the most intense, the most . . . elevating sense of pleasure. That's how good it was. *En effet*, better than good.

'Of course, one of the things you miss is the smell. The smell of pain,' she continued, pushing herself off the closed cabinet door and coming over to him. 'But that's not going to happen with you, Monsieur *Flic. Mais non, mais non* . . .' She sniffed the air. 'Indeed, I can smell yours already.'

Gastal couldn't help a small whimper of fear. If she could do that to this Ribero character, what could she do to him? he wondered with a shiver of terror. Strung up like he was, naked, defenceless?

She was mad, certifiable, and unless someone came busting through that padded door very soon, he knew he was dead meat.

'You are sick. You are fucking sick . . .' was all he said. Only a whisper, no more than that, the words just popping out of his mouth before he could stop himself, knowing in the instant he spoke them that wishing them back would do him no good.

He was right.

Without any warning, without any hesitation, Virginie's fist lashed out at him, straight arm, the ball of her hand connecting with the space between his nose and top lip.

Blood shot up his nostrils, splashed into the back of his throat, its force and quantity making him gag and choke. A tooth – or rather the very expensive crown that he had recently had fitted – was snapped out of his top jaw and spun around in his pulped mouth. He didn't know whether to spit it out or swallow it, but his tongue was suddenly so swollen, so useless, that he was unable to do either. Finally, coughing out a mouthful of blood, he heard it hit the polished floor and skitter away.

Slowly, still reeling from the blow, Gastal squeezed open his eyes.

Virginie was standing in front of him, hands on hips, a penny loafer tapping.

'Now, what did I just say? What did I tell you? Respect, respect, respect,' she said. 'I told you. I warned you, didn't I? But you didn't listen, did you? So there you are. That's what happens down here to naughty little boys who don't do as they're told.'

96

AS THE *P.60* BEGAN ITS turn to take up position behind MY *Léonie* Jacquot didn't need binoculars to see her lights as she danced across the swell just a thousand metres off their starboard side. But without those lights, the yacht would have been invisible. Like the *P.60*, now turning into the chop and taking up position behind her.

Reaching forward, Chabran pulled a cream-coloured microphone from its slot on the instrument panel and pressed the transmit button. 'All hands to station. All hands to station,' he said, then racked the mic back in its holder.

For a moment nothing happened, and then Jacquot was aware of sound and movement – the clang of a bulkhead hatch somewhere below, running feet, and a shadow up on the prow taking position at the canon, removing the tarpaulin cover and swinging the barrel down to take a bead on the *Léonie*, now just a warm golden glow rising and dropping below the swell.

'Someone's sleeping on watch,' said Chabran. 'If they were keeping an eye on their radar screen they'd have spotted us by now. If I was her skipper, I'd have his guts, whoever's up there . . . Still, it's a motor yacht. Navy's different, I guess.'

He reached for the mic again and spoke into it: 'Searchlight on in ten, bosun, and counting . . .' Then he leaned forward and switched to a new channel. 'Time for their wakey-wakey call,' he said to Jacquot and Marie-Ange, and pushed the transmit button again.

'MY *Léonie*. MY *Léonie*. This is Gendarmerie Maritime vessel *P.60*. I repeat, this is Gendarmerie Maritime vessel *P.60*.' The moment he finished speaking the searchlight came on from somewhere above them, a brilliant cone of light shooting ahead through the darkness, silvering the rain and lancing across the *Léonie*'s stern and superstructure. As far as Jacquot could judge, they were now no more than a few hundred metres behind and clearly gaining on her. He wondered whether they'd make a run for it, now that Chabran had introduced himself.

For a moment nothing happened. No movement aboard, no sudden change in *Léonie*'s rolling forward course. It was like following a ghost-ship. But then, as Jacquot watched, the *Léonie* pulled round to starboard and he was hard-pressed not to gasp. As she came beam on to them, caught in the glare of the searchlight, the full sweep and glory of her lines was revealed, from a high prancing bow to a long low transom, the space between taken up by rows of lit windows at deck level and portholes beneath, a second-storey bridge and wheelhouse, and a curving white hull that shone in the searchlight.

Suddenly a voice crackled over the intercom. 'MY *Léonie* to Gendarmerie Maritime. MY *Léonie* to Gendarmerie Maritime. This is Captain Milić of the *Léonie*. How can we be of assistance? Over.'

'We have a permit to board, *Léonie*. I repeat, we have a permit to board. Please hold to and prepare for boarding party.'

Fifteen minutes later, the *P.60*'s boarding party cast off in two Navy Zephyrs and crossed the fifty-metre stretch of choppy water between the two vessels, keeping within the searchlight's silvery beam. As the first Zephyr closed in, the *Léonie*'s crew opened the transom gate and made ready to receive the boarding party, ropes cast and secured. Chabran went first, clambering up on to *Léonie*'s deck, followed by three of his crew. Once they were aboard, the Zephyr's helmsman moved away to make room for the second craft carrying Jacquot, Marie-Ange and four more *P.60* crew, their gunbelts and holstered weapons cinched below their life-jackets.

By the time Jacquot and Marie-Ange had climbed up on deck, the *Léonie*'s skipper had come out from the salon and was shaking hands with Chabran. He was still in pyjamas, his dressing gown flapping in the breeze and pressing against his legs. Keen to be out of the weather, he waved them inside.

After the roll and chill of the open deck, the salon was warm and quiet, plumply furnished and filled with the scent of hothouse flowers and beeswax polish. Introductions made they sat down and made themselves comfortable. The *Léonie*'s skipper, Perto Milić, was all smiles, his face lined and craggy, a small beard tipping the point of his chin.

'So, messieurs, mademoiselle, how can I be of assistance?' His voice was soft and treacly, not a single sign of tension, no tremor in his expression. As though this was something that happened regularly, some guests dropping by, a social call, even if it was nearly four in the morning.

Chabran pulled some documents out of an inside pocket and handed them over – a thin sheaf of papers, curled at the ends where they'd been torn from a fax machine.

'A warrant to search your ship, *Capitaine*.'

'So I see, so I see,' replied Milić, leafing through the papers. '*Mais bien sûr. Pas de problème*. But might I ask why?'

'Not at this time,' replied Chabran, taking the papers back from him and getting to his feet. 'May we begin?'

97

'MY FATHER ALWAYS TOLD ME I was too impulsive, too impetuous,' said Virginie Cabrille, wiping a splash of Gastal's blood from her wrist. 'Always telling me to hold back, take my time. Well, he would have been proud of me now. Twelve years I have waited and suddenly the prize is mine. Offered to me on a plate. An exquisite, irresistible opportunity to cause the most terrible, the most devastating pain. From a distance, of course. Like our friend Guillermo. But far, far worse.'

While she spoke, Gastal tried to make himself as comfortable as possible. By twisting his hands upwards he had discovered that he was able to get a grip on the cords that ran from bracelets to beam, supporting himself for minutes at a time. Then, letting go of the cords and narrowing his hands, he was able to drop a precious few centimetres, far enough for his pointed toes to reach the lower beam and take the weight from his arms. By working between the two, he had found some means of support, some small comfort. But he was tiring quickly. His wrists, upper arms, and shoulders ached, and he was aware of a cramp dancing dangerously around his insteps.

If Virginie was aware of these movements, these accommodations, she gave no sign of it. Instead, she walked behind him and he heard a dragging sound, something being pulled across the floor.

His pulse quickened, and a shiver passed through his body. He wondered what it might be, what new horror she had in mind. He closed his eyes, and waited. The dragging sound passed him and stopped in front of him, and slowly, fearfully, he opened his eyes.

A chair. Nothing but a chair, an old leather club chair placed beside the trolley. Kicking off her shoes Virginie settled into it, drawing up her legs and curling her feet under her. When she was comfortable, she reached over to the trolley and picked up a shiny steel container about the size of a cigar box, laid it in her lap.

'And you know something, Monsieur *Flic*? My father was right. Patience really is a wonderful thing.' She shook her head, as though astonished that it could be so. 'You put a million francs in the bank, you don't touch it, and *voilà*, fifteen years later you check your account and the money has doubled. Just like that. And I have discovered that it is exactly the same with revenge. You make a deposit, and the longer you leave it, the greater the gain.'

She flipped open the lid of the box and trailed her fingers over its contents.

Gastal wondered what was inside it. It didn't take long to find out.

'Of course,' she continued, 'it is not easy, this patience thing. This holding back. But in the end, well, it is so gloriously rewarding. Because while you wait, while you bide your time, it is quite extraordinary how many unforeseen events come into play.'

As she was speaking, Virginie took what looked like an aerosol can from the box. 'You start an action, you commit, and things suddenly start happening.'

She reached into the box again and lifted out a small metal spout and trigger assembly which she screwed on to the top of the can. Gastal saw what it was and shuddered. A blowtorch. A miniature version; the kind a chef might use to put a glaze on a *crème brûlée*. She shook the can, pulled the trigger and a jet of blue flame shot out. She trimmed the spout and the flame narrowed to a hissing blue spear-tip, two different shades, light and dark.

'Not that I planned it that way, I admit. It just . . . happened.

384

Things I could never have dreamt of.' When she had the flame as she wanted it, she dipped back into the box and came out with what looked like a finned dart the length of her little finger. 'Which is what has happened with Georges Lafour. My old teacher, Georges Lafour.'

Carefully she rolled the tip of the dart in the jet of blue flame, took it out, inspected it, put it back in again.

'Thirty years ago *cher* Georges was working in a family business that negotiated beet prices in northern France. Did you know that? There wasn't a ton of beet sold on the market that did not have a Lafour family ticket on it. Percentages. Very small, but enough to keep the family comfortable, to secure a good upbringing and education for young Georges and provide good holidays. And then Monsieur Lafour senior died in a car crash and Gorgeous Georges took over . . .'

Virginie drew the tip of the dart from the flame and Gastal saw the red glow. In an instant, she drew back her arm and flung the dart at him. It hit him in the top of the thigh, and stuck there, drooping. At first there was no pain, just the tiniest impression of a prick, nothing more than the flick of a fingernail against his skin, the tip of the dart no more than a couple of centimetres in length. He looked down at it, and as he did so the red-hot tip buried in his thigh started to make itself felt. A sharp burning sensation, like a wasp sting. He struggled against it, shaking his leg, trying to work it loose. But he couldn't budge it. He looked back at Virginie. She had another dart in her hand and, as she talked, she heated its tip with the blowtorch.

'In a very short time,' she was saying, 'our man, Georges, had moved from beet sales to crop futures . . .'

The second dart hit Gastal in the hip, its red-hot tip striking bone, the burning pain starting up much quicker than the first.

'. . . playing the markets, trading everything from beet to barley, from maize to wheat. And as the business grew, he set up a financial services group to support his dealing and widen his interests . . .'

A third dart pierced Gastal's chest, close to his right nipple.

'. . . and in time that small financial services group became a bank, no less. And he was the boss . . .'

Another dart glanced off his collar bone and punctured his neck.

'. . . and getting richer and richer.'

The next dart was thrown with fury and Gastal flinched as it pierced the skin just a few centimetres below his navel.

'The next thing you know, there are stories about him in the press. This acquisition, that acquisition. Art and culture. Prominence. A society wedding. All the trimmings. And another fortune to add to his own . . .'

Another dart hit home, close to the one in his belly.

'And now, all these years later, the loathsome little *connard* is at the pinnacle of his profession . . . favoured, fêted. About to be elevated to the highest ranks, whispering in the ear of Monsieur le Président no less . . .'

Another dart pierced the inside of Gastal's thigh, high enough for the fins to brush against his scrotum as he squirmed with the pain from the burning puncture wounds.

'A ripe, luscious plum ready for the picking . . .' Virginie shook her head; words, it seemed, had failed her. But she took a quick little breath, and smiled. 'And you know what? You know what's even better? They're not even related, Georges and Elodie. Did you know that? She's not even his daughter.' Another dart hit him above the knee. 'He's just the stepdaddy. He's going to have to do what he's told, to save someone else's child. How noble is that? How perfectly, perfectly delicious. And she's dead, anyway.'

Virginie let out a harsh cackle of delight, and flung another dart. It flew wide, thudding into the beam above Gastal's head. 'That lovely little Elodie's going to cost him dear, mark my words. Ooooh yes. Not money, of course, not some cash-packed briefcase, used notes in low denominations. Nothing so trite, nothing so vulgar. Something infinitely more rewarding, more refined. Something even more satisfying than that cheating dago shit fighting for breath in my father's coffin. And do you know what that is?'

Gastal shook his head, grunted, weeping now with pain and fear, the darts and their gaily coloured fins wobbling as he wept.

'Justice, Monsieur *Flic*. Justice done, and justice seen to be done. *Le double*.'

Virginie let out a long, low sigh, and switched off the blowtorch, put it back in the box, snapped the lid closed.

'But right now, my fat little friend, it's you in the firing line. Call it payback for snooping, for getting in the way, for daring to think I might be bothered by your interest. I am not. You are nothing. No threat. Just a little something to pass the time, down here in my little playroom. You will never provide as great a pleasure for me as the death of *cher* Guillermo, or the imminent downfall of the house of Lafour, but I will try to make it worth my while. And yours, of course.'

Getting out of her chair, Virginie dropped the dart box on to the trolley and went over to the leather chest. Squatting down beside it, she rummaged around inside, and brought out a shiny chrome dildo attached to a spooling length of insulated cable. At the end of this cable was a jackplug which she pushed into a small chrome socket set in the floor. Then she reached in the chest again and brought out what looked like a tube of toothpaste.

'And now,' she said, straightening up, 'I'm going to show you something rather unusual. Made for me by a master craftsman who specialises in this sort of equipment. Tailor-made to my specifications. And very expensive, I can tell you. Oh, and very, very entertaining.'

Clamping the dildo under her arm, she twisted the cap off the tube and squeezed a worm of clear jelly on to her fingers. Dropping the tube on to the trolley, she retrieved the dildo and smeared the jelly over its tip, and up and down its sides, until the silvery mirror shine of the chrome was dulled.

'It's a little messy, this stuff,' she conceded, wiping her fingers on her slacks and leaving a dark, greasy stain. 'But it works brilliantly. Not just as a lubricant, you understand, but as the most amazing conductor. Just you wait and see.'

Virginie stepped right up close to Gastal – close enough for him to smell her perfume through his snot-and-blood-filled nostrils – and moved the tip of the dildo around his nipples. He felt a tiny vibration followed by a very gentle pulse of electricity, just a soft tingling that danced across his skin, nowhere near as searing as the taser, strangely arousing as a matter of fact.

'Electricity,' Virginie murmured. 'Such a clean, pure power, *n'est-ce pas*? But don't worry,' she continued. 'It gets stronger. You see that socket there? In the floor?' She nodded back towards the chest. 'It's a combination timer and rheostat. Over the next hour or so, as I show you a few more tricks, the vibrations will increase, and so will that tiny pulse of electricity. Gets to be some fun, I can tell you. And all these little darts, all those sharp little tips . . .? Well, they're also part of the kit. They may have cooled but they are there for a reason. Tiny little . . . receptors. To create a circuit, do you see? As the power increases, you'll feel them start to react, pick up each little shock, amplify it.' She reached up, pulled the last dart from the wooden beam and, without a thought, plunged it into his cheek.

'Oh, I should just mention, there is one small . . . downside. When my little silver friend here is properly inserted, there's really no way to get it out again. Look here, you see?' She pointed to a tiny row of backward facing spines half-way up its jellied length, and then made a circle with her thumb and forefinger. 'I push it up, *comme ça*, then I bring it down, like so.' As she slid it down between her fingers Gastal saw the row of spines rise like a spikey collar, and catch. '*Et voilà, c'est en place*.' She shrugged, smiled. 'So it doesn't drop out, you understand.'

She gave him a pat on his dart-free cheek and walked behind him, trailing the cable after her.

'So, let us see. Ah, yes. Here we are. Now, just relax, relax. And whatever you do, Monsieur *Flic*, don't forget to scream.'

98

THE MY *LÉONIE* WAS CLEAN. No sign of Elodie anywhere on board. From stern to prow, from bridge to engine room, from the anchor chain compartment to the aft inspection hatches above the twin screws, Chabran's boarding party had opened every door, every cupboard, turned every mattress and checked every possible hiding place. And found nothing. A clean sweep.

When they'd finished their search, the *Léonie*'s skipper, Petro Milić, was waiting for them in the panelled dining room off the main salon. He had shaved, brushed his hair and changed into khaki drills, a sharp crease on his trousers, epaulettes on his pocketed shirt. He smiled at Jacquot, Chabran and Marie-Ange as they took their seats at the dining-room table, its wooden surface polished to an impossible shine. He was drinking coffee, but he didn't offer them any. Beside his cup and saucer was a stack of passports and work permits belonging to his crew, still gathered in a corner of the main salon, where they'd been brought before the search began, so that nothing could be concealed, nothing spirited away. Apart from Milić and his second officer, Rohan Kostić, both of them Croatian, the *Léonie*'s crew were either Vietnamese of Filipino.

'As you requested,' said Milić, with a tight smile, sliding the paperwork across the table. 'I think you will find that everything is in order.'

While Jacquot and Chabran started through the pile, Marie-Ange pushed away from the table and wandered around the dining room, slipping through a mirror-panelled door into the small galley that serviced it. As she did so, she saw in the mirror Milić's eyes follow her. Something in the way he looked at her gave her a strange, unsettling sensation. She recalled a game she had played with her father when she was a little girl. Hot or Cold. When they'd played it, her father hadn't needed to say 'Hot' when she was about to find whatever he had hidden for her, or 'Cold' if she strayed too far away. She just had to look at him to know. The way his eyes held her.

And that was the feeling she got from Milić, watching her, just as her father had done.

Something had been hidden, she was suddenly sure of it.

Or maybe someone.

And she was close.

Hot.

And getting hotter.

Carefully she examined the narrow galley. It reminded her of the same working spaces on commercial airliners. But where an airliner's galley was stacked with scuffed metal containers and tea and coffee and water dispensers, the *Léonie*'s galley was sleek and stylish, oak panels concealing a half-dozen cupboards. The first ones she opened contained glassware, crockery, table linen. Another was a chiller, packed with condiments – everything from ketchup to cornichons. There was also a small fridge stacked with white wine and beers and mixers and bottled water, a freezer with an ice dispenser, a microwave and two warming ovens set above a wood counter, wide enough to carry whatever was sent up from the kitchens below.

Marie-Ange paused, frowned, reached out a hand.

Two ovens? Why would there be two ovens? she wondered.

And then she realised that one of the ovens wasn't an oven at all, even though its black glass door was the same as the black glass doors on the real oven and microwave, even though the controls were identical.

390

Or almost identical.

Off and On, for the microwave and oven.

But Up and Down for the second 'oven'.

Not an oven at all.

A dumb waiter.

To bring up the food from the kitchens below.

No one searching this small space would have thought to check a pair of ovens, open their doors, look inside.

Behind her, Marie-Ange could hear Milić answering questions from Chabran about the tests they were carrying out on *Léonie*'s steering system, but as she turned away from the dumb waiter she could see his eyes flicking nervously over Chabran's head . . . watching her . . . watching her . . . Just like her father had done.

'Jacquot,' she said. 'I think there's something . . . '

That was when the lights went out and shots rang through the darkened dining room.

99

IT WAS THE SECOND OFFICER, Rohan Kostić, standing in the arch between dining room and salon, who killed the lights, drew a gun and fired. In the darkness there were strobing yellow flashes from the gun's muzzle, the shattering of glass, the whine of a ricochet and a groan from the dining table.

Jacquot had just picked up another passport when he heard Marie-Ange call his name. As he turned in his seat, he saw Kostić slide one hand into his jacket and reach out for the light switch with the other. He sensed immediately what was going to happen next. As the room was plunged into shadowy darkness and the first shots rang out, he pushed back his chair, slammed the galley door shut on Marie-Ange, and was out of his seat, coming round the side of the table, reaching for his own gun.

As he chased after the fleeing Kostić, a looming black shape racing across the salon towards the aft deck, he tried to remember the layout of the darkened cabin but forgot the two steps that led up to it. He went flying at exactly the moment that Kostić blasted out another couple of rounds towards the dining room. He heard the bullets whine like angry bees over the top of his head and knew that, but for the steps, they would have caught him full in the chest. Looking up, he saw Kostić turn and head for the aft deck doors.

When he reached them, he snatched them open and a gust of chill air swept into the salon.

Jacquot leapt to his feet just as the spotlight from *P.60* blasted through the cabin windows. When the boarding party had clambered up on to *Léonie*'s deck, Chabran had ordered it to be turned off. But someone aboard the cutter had heard the gunfire and its glaring white light now shafted through the darkness and spilled over the rear deck. Crouching as he ran, Kostić let off another couple of rounds at the spotlight but without hitting the target.

Flicking the safety off his gun, Jacquot dodged from cover to cover – an armchair here, a sofa, a pillar there – until he reached the sliding doors in time to see the gunman leap over the transom. There was another shot, a scream of pain and a heavy splash. Jacquot raced through the door, across the deck and reached the yacht's transom in time to see the *P.60*'s helmsman, Willi, floating in the swell, and Kostić in one of the Zephyrs. As he backed away from the *Léonie*, he let off a couple more rounds at the second Zephyr's outboard engine and her black inflatable sides. Throttling up a roar from his own engine, he swung the Zephyr round and raced for the shelter of *Léonie*'s starboard side, away from the searchlight, powering off into the darkness, putting distance between himself and the cutter.

Hard to port, with a matching roar, the engines of the *P.60* growled into life and Jacquot saw the cutter swing wide and start to give chase, its spotlight snatched away from the *Léonie* and lancing through the darkness.

But Jacquot didn't have time to watch. Willi, the helmsman, was still in the water, unconscious, face down and spinning away, caught in the pull of the passing Zephyr, his body only kept above the swell by the bouyancy jacket he was wearing.

Without thinking, Jacquot threw down his gun, leapt over the side and into the water. He remembered it was November and how cold the sea would be in the millisecond before he hit the surface, plunged under, and came up spluttering and breathless from the numbing shock. Flailing his arms, he struck out for the floating man, there one minute, gone the next, in the chop. Pushing away the freezing water with heavy sleeves, spending more time below the surface than above it, Jacquot finally reached Willi and flung out a hand for the collar of his bouyancy jacket. Turning back to the boat, gasping for breath, spitting out mouthfuls of seawater, he heard a stutter of gunfire to his right, and the answering rat-a-tat boom of the *P.60*'s canon. Then, gloriously, a lifebelt sailed over his head, a line of rope sliced past his cheek, and five seconds later the lifebelt reached him. Tucking one arm through it, still clinging to Willi with the other, Jacquot felt himself hauled through the water in jerking tugs, banging up against the sports deck, arms reaching down for him, the two of them hauled up out of the icy water.

Teeth chattering, shaking from head to foot, Jacquot sprawled on the aft deck.

'*M-m-m-merde*, but that was fucking cold . . .' he managed.

100

TWO AÉROSPATIALE PUMA HELICOPTERS, bearing the red,
white and blue chevron livery of the Gendarmerie Maritime,
came in low over the *P.60* and took up station, the first over
Léonie's upper deck, the second holding a hundred metres out,
just off the cutter's bows. Rotors thundering, spotlights shivering down from its belly, the aircrew of the first Puma threw
out ropes to each side of its cabin, and a dozen armed combat
troopers abseiled down to take control of the *Léonie* and rein-
force the *P.60*'s crew. After it peeled away, the second Puma
took its place and a metal basket was lowered for the first of
the passengers brought up topside to be airlifted out. Ten minutes
later, the last of them brought aboard, the Puma's side door was
secured and the pilot tipped away from the *Léonie* and headed
back to the coast.

There were five of them in the main cabin: Jacquot, Marie-Ange
and Elodie belted into their seats, Léo Chabran and his helmsman,
Willi, strapped on to stretchers. Both men had gunshot wounds,
the helmsman with a bullet in the thigh, Chabran with bullets in
his upper arm and shoulder, the first shots that Kostić had fired
blind into the dining room. Both men had been sedated, their heads
swaying to the beat and rhythm of the Puma's mighty rotors clat-
tering above them. As for Kostić, the *P.60*'s crew had retrieved his

bullet-shredded inflatable but were still searching for his body when the Puma took off.

The choppers had been called in after Jacquot was hauled from the freezing water, his icy soaking clothes stripped off him out on the aft deck, his numbed, cramping body towelled dry and an insulating blanket flung round him. Dry clothes had been brought out to him, and with help from a member of the *P.60*'s crew he'd struggled into them, but it had taken half an hour for the trembling and the shaking and the teeth-chattering to subside. Back in the salon he was settled on a sofa where Marie-Ange brought him a tumbler of Cognac and set to rubbing warmth and feeling back into his arms and his back and his hands.

'You are mad,' she'd told him, in a proud, scolding sort of way. 'Mad, mad, mad.'

But Jacquot wasn't really listening. On the sofa opposite, curled up in a corner, was a young girl. She had blonde hair, tear-reddened eyes, and an angry red mark across her mouth from the duct tape her captors had slapped on her. The *P.60*'s medic was working on her.

'Elodie?' Jacquot asked. 'Are you Elodie?'

The girl nodded and gave him a tight little smile that made her eyes well with more tears.

'Is it really over?' she asked in a tiny voice.

'It's over,' he replied.

'Are you taking me home?'

Jacquot nodded. 'Yes, we are.'

The girl nodded again, then looked away, as though she had no more words.

'She's fine,' whispered Marie-Ange. 'Fine, but badly shocked. She was in that lift, the dumb waiter. When we opened the door, there she was, half-way down, packed away like a contortionist in a box. Her hands were bound, and there were chains on her too,' continued Marie-Ange softly. 'Around her ankles. It looked like they were going to dump her overboard. Another few minutes and she really wouldn't have been here. We made it just in time.'

And now Elodie Lafour was sitting with them in the helicopter, a blanket wrapped around her shoulders, her eyes wide with a kind of stunned disbelief, as though she still couldn't quite credit what was happening. That she was going home, her ordeal at an end.

Jacquot looked at his watch. Nearly three hours' sailing to reach *Léonie*, but a little less than twenty minutes to make it back to the coast, coming in to settle with a bump on L'Estaque's floodlit football pitch. Looking through the window, he could see a police car and an ambulance waiting for them, lights flashing, and beside them a single black saloon. As the whine of the engine subsided, two figures emerged from the car. He recognised them both, the two sisters, Solange and Estelle.

On the seat opposite, looking out of the window, Elodie saw them too. In that single moment her young face crumpled and her body was wrenched by a hiccuping burst of tears, spilling down her cheeks. Marie-Ange put out a hand, squeezed her arm. The girl turned away from the window and looked at them both, tried to smile through the tears but couldn't hold it.

'I think I'm in trouble,' she managed. 'I am going to get so told off . . .'

'I don't think so,' said Marie-Ange.

'Maybe just a little,' nodded Jacquot with a gentle smile.

With the smile came a sudden draft of cold wet air as the Puma's door was pulled open, whipping into the cabin. One by one the stretchers were lifted out. When there was room to move, Elodie unbuckled her seat belt and rose to her feet, turning to Jacquot and Marie-Ange.

'Thank you,' she said. 'Thank you for finding me.'

And then she went to the door and one of the aircrew held out a hand and helped her down the steps. Jacquot and Marie-Ange followed, in time to see Elodie break into a run across the pitch, arms wide, and her mother start forward. A moment later they reached each other, clung to each other, swaying together in the rain.

'Don't go crying or you'll start me off,' said Marie-Ange.

'All in a day's work,' replied Jacquot.

She gave him a look. 'If you say so.'

101

SOLANGE BONNEFOY JOINED MOTHER and daughter, briefly clasped them tight, then set out towards Jacquot and Marie-Ange. A metre away, with a soft rain shawling in across the stadium lights, she stopped in front of them.

For a moment, it seemed to Jacquot she didn't quite know what to say, what to do. So he decided to do it for her and made to step forward. She beat him to it. Before he could react, her arms were around him, trapping his own in a tight hug. Two swift squeezes were followed by three darting kisses to his cheeks.

'You will never know . . . you will never know how much . . .'

Each word came out as a kind of strangled sob. As though to keep herself in check, to provide some distraction, she turned to Marie-Ange and repeated the hug, the kisses.

'I'm so sorry if I was rude to you, my dear, or unfriendly. I had no right to be.' She sniffed loudly, wiped her eyes, glanced over her shoulder. Her sister and niece were getting into the car.

'You'll miss your ride,' said Jacquot.

'They're going back to my apartment by themselves. It's been arranged.' She shook herself, squared her shoulders. 'And anyway, there's still some business we need to attend to.' The examining magistrate was quickly gathering herself. 'We have been busy during your pleasure cruise.'

'Why don't I leave you to it?' said Marie-Ange, reaching for both their arms, a double goodbye. 'I'll go in the ambulance with Captain Chabran and Willi. See them settled. If you need me, I'll be at the hospital. Or home.' She looked at her watch. 'Or maybe I should go to work.'

At the edge of the pitch, the second stretcher was lifted into the ambulance and secured. A paramedic started to close the doors, the lights began to revolve and flash.

'I'd better hurry,' she said, and started off, calling out to the paramedic as he jumped up into the cab. He waited for her, and Jacquot watched Marie-Ange clamber aboard, the door close, and an arm reach out of the window and wave to him.

It was the wave that did it. He felt a sudden twist of regret that it was all over, at an end – the time they'd spent together – and that they would soon be going their separate ways again, had already started to do so. He also remembered the flush on her neck when Chabran had smiled at her, and felt another unexpected twist. When Léo Chabran woke up, he'd find Marie-Ange at his bedside. Lucky, lucky man, he thought.

'She's a beautiful young girl,' said Solange Bonnefoy.

'You're not the first who's remarked upon it,' replied Jacquot, aware of the word 'young', and, deliberate or not, the attendant 'too young for you' subtext.

'But let's be going,' she continued, taking his arm and leading him to the squad car. 'I'm getting soaked.'

Settled in the back seat, with the ambulance leading the way out on to Boulevard de Rove and turning right for the city, Solange Bonnefoy brought Jacquot up to date.

'While you were gone, we found out about MY *Léonie*,' she said. 'It took my new best friend, the Préfet Maritime, to provide the information, with no need to go through official channels. She might be registered in some South Pacific atoll, but the Préfet knew her. Apparently she had once been owned by his uncle, would you believe? And he had actually sailed on her as a young man. She was called *Calypso* back then, he told me. He also knew the man his uncle had sold her to, the man who changed her name.'

'And that would be?'

'Monsieur Arsène Cabrille.'

The name instantly rang a bell. 'The one who died? He was buried yesterday. Or Sunday.'

'Correct. Wreathed in noble causes, but still smelling of the sewer. Everything above board, but a great deal unseen below – though we never managed to pin anything on him. A very clever man by all accounts. A wily old fox. And now it's his daughter in charge. Virginie Cabrille.'

'And it was this daughter, Virginie . . .?'

'It would seem so. A warrant has been issued for her arrest and there's a squad getting ready to serve it. Should be fun.'

'Gastal will love it. Headlines. Just what he always wanted.'

'Not Gastal. It's one of your boys, Peluze, in charge. He couldn't locate Gastal. Gone missing. The last time Peluze saw him was yesterday afternoon, at the Sofitel.'

It was then, as they left the tree-lined avenues of L'Estaque, that something struck Jacquot. It hadn't been more than two hours since they'd found Elodie. Yet there was her mother, Estelle Lafour, waiting for them. There was no way she could have made it to Marseilles so quickly.

'Madame Lafour got down here very fast?'

'She arrived last night. In quite a state. Apparently there was a ransom demand.'

'From Virginie Cabrille?'

'She wouldn't say. Wouldn't tell me. But I assume so. Apparently Georges was dealing with it. She just said that it was over. That he had done what they wanted.'

'He paid? How much?'

Madame Bonnefoy shook her head. 'I don't know. But I'm sure we'll find out soon enough.'

Up ahead the domed bulk of the Cathédrale de la Major loomed out of the darkness.

'You want me to drop you at headquarters?' she asked, as they approached the turning for rue de l'Evêché. 'You up to it?'

'I wouldn't miss it. So long as Peluze doesn't mind.'

102

CLAUDE PELUZE HAD ALREADY LEFT for Roucas Blanc by the time Solange Bonnefoy dropped Jacquot at police headquarters. Being Jacquot, it didn't take long for him to persuade the desk sergeant to provide a squad car and one of the night-duty uniform boys to drive him out there.

Peluze was a good cop and hadn't taken any chances. He'd known this was likely going to be more than a cuff and custody job, and as Jacquot and his driver turned into Chemin de Roucas they came up against a pair of squad cars drawn across the road, lights flashing. A hundred metres further on another couple of squad cars had been similarly deployed, effectively blocking off the road outside the gates of Maison Cabrille. Police tape had also been strung across the road and across rue Cornille. Some early risers stood behind it, looking up the slope.

Jacquot didn't have a badge, but his arriving in a squad car convinced the two gendarmes manning the tape that he was who he said he was, Chief Inspector Daniel Jacquot of the Cavaillon force, formerly with the homicide squad in Marseilles. They let him through.

'There's been shooting,' said one of the gendarmes, as he passed. 'We got the all-clear a few minutes ago. But you'd better watch yourself all the same.'

Jacquot nodded his thanks and set off down the road, turning into the *impasse* where a group of caped gendarmes stood beneath the trees, smoking and talking amongst themselves. As he passed, there was the sound of a screw cap being removed from a flask and a couple of tipped heads. Up ahead, two ambulances had been reversed into the entrance of a double garage. Slipping between them, Jacquot smelled the sharp, antiseptic warmth of their brightly lit interiors, and as he stepped past and headed into the garage, the equally familiar scents of gunfire and spilled blood and emptied bowels drifted up to him. Someone had been shot in the guts, thought Jacquot. That's what often happened with a stomach wound. You just . . . popped it.

There were four cars in the garage, their sides punctured with bullet holes, not a single intact windscreen or window between them. With shattered glass fragments crunching underfoot, Jacquot made his way down the gentle slope, taking in a vivid, still-dripping splash of blood on one of the garage's white breeze-block walls – a head-shot, had to be; a puddle of blackening blood backing up against the wide front wheel of a Jeep Cherokee and leaking around it; and a broad smudge of it slanted across the humped bonnet of a vintage Porsche. Its matt green paintwork made the bloody smear look more blue than red. Over by a workbench, beside a pockmarked limousine, paramedics were working on one of the uniform boys, the last of four body-bags being zipped up.

As Jacquot stepped away from the cars and through what had clearly once been a set of sliding glass doors, he heard a familiar voice.

'I heard you were back in town.' The gravelly voice belonged to Peluze, sheltering from the rain under a striped awning. His collar was up, his tie undone and a cigarette smouldered between his fingers. 'You just missed the fun.'

The two men embraced. It had been a long time.

'You're looking good,' said Jacquot, taking in the stubble and the military buzz-cut. 'Just as I remember you.'

'Sorry I can't say the same for you. You look like shit. I should

403

have you in a line-up. And what the fuck happened to the pony-tail?'

'Line of duty,' replied Jacquot. 'So what's been happening here? One of the guys outside said there'd been shooting, but I wasn't expecting this.'

'Who was? We didn't bother to ring the doorbell, but we weren't expecting World War Three.' Peluze nodded as the first of the black body-bags was wheeled past on a gurney. 'Two *gorilles*. Just two of 'em, but they took out three of ours. One of them was working at the bench back inside, the other was upstairs doing crosswords, would you believe? Crossword puzzle books all round. He couldn't have been much good. Not a single clue filled in. Down here, the guy at the bench didn't wait to ask who we were. Just took one look and started firing. His buddy joins him and it's fireworks, Bastille Day, but we got them in the end.'

'And the woman, Virginie Cabrille?'

Peluze nodded over Jacquot's shoulder.

'*Quand on parle du loup*,' he said. Speak of the devil.

Jacquot turned to see a young woman coming down the garden pathway, escorted by two gendarmes, hands cuffed behind her back. She looked like a librarian, he thought: well-tailored slacks, twin-set and pearls, penny loafers.

Except for the gelled hair. It gave her a punky, rebellious look.

And the blood. It was everywhere. All over her clothes. Her throat. Her cheeks. It clearly wasn't hers.

As she drew closer, she caught Jacquot's eye and held it, a searching, quizzical look, then turned her attention to Peluze. With a disdainful shrug, she pulled free from her escorts, and headed in his direction. It was clear she wanted to say something. The gendarmes tried to hold her back, but Peluze raised his hand. He could deal with this.

For a moment she didn't speak, just looked at Jacquot's companion. The only sound was the distant moan of an ambulance or squad car down on the Corniche and probably heading in their direction, and the soft breezy whisper of rain on the awning above their heads.

'*Je suis vainqueuse encore*,' she said, at last. I still win.

Just that.

Then, with a smile at the two men, she turned back to the gendarmes and they led her away, into the garage and out of sight.

'Win what?' asked Jacquot.

Peluze shrugged, took a drag on his cigarette.

'She's mad as a fox, if you ask me.'

'How's that?' asked Jacquot.

'She lives in the lodge over there,' replied Peluze, pointing towards a cluster of lights in the trees to their left. 'That's where we found her. Watching TV, smoking dope and drinking scotch.'

'And that makes her mad? Far as I remember it's what most of the squad do on their nights off.'

Peluze grunted, then nodded to the lodge path. 'Well, here's one who won't be doing it ever again,' he said.

Coming down from the lodge, Jacquot made out the reflective jackets of three paramedics pushing a stretcher trolley, its wheels skittering along the path.

'An old friend of yours,' said Peluze, indicating the body-bag as the trolley passed them. 'I can't say I'm sorry, but no one deserves what he got from La Mam'selle.'

The name just sprang into Jacquot's head. 'Gastal?'

'*Le même*. According to the medics it was a heart attack. But what he went through, there were a dozen things he could have died of first.'

'She did it?'

'Crazy. Mad. Like I told you. She had a basement . . . sound-proofed, the lot. You wouldn't believe what we found down there.' Peluze gave another grunt, shook his head as though he couldn't find the words. 'And I'm supposed to have given up,' he said, looking at the cigarette between his fingers, taking a last drag, then flicking it away. 'Some hope.'

405

103

Paris

AS VIRGINIE CABRILLE HAD INSTRUCTED, the message she had sent to Georges and Estelle Lafour appeared in *Le Monde* that Tuesday morning, first edition only, a boxed announcement in the centre of page three, printed in a bold eighteen-point typeface and bordered in black like a funeral notice. Which, to all intents and purposes, it was.

The message ran:

My name is Georges Lafour, President and Chief Executive Officer of Banque Lafour et Finance Mondiale, in Paris.

In 1986 I raped a young woman. Her name was Nathalie, she was twenty-three, and at that time she was a scholarship student at the Institut d'Etudes Politiques.

Afterwards I told her that if she reported the incident I would deny it, and that I would ruin her career. Like many others, she did as she was told.

When she fell pregnant, I forced her to have a termination. During the procedure, one of many I have paid for, her heart stopped. She did not recover.

I declare myself personally responsible for her death, and the death of her unborn child. And I declare myself guilty of the crime of rape.

Georges Lafour
Banque Lafour et Finance Mondiale
Rue Baranot
Paris 75004

But Georges Lafour never saw that page in *Le Monde*, did not wait to see what would happen when Virginie's message was published – the strict condition for the release of his stepdaughter. Nor did he wait to see how many other women would step forward, how quickly his world would come tumbling down, how swiftly and certainly he, in his turn, would be ruined.

Instead, as Virginie Cabrille was led from her home, and as bound bundles of the first morning edition thumped on to pavements around Paris, around France, Georges Lafour felt a cold winter rain spatter on to his trembling shoulders and soak through his shirt as he opened his office window and climbed out on to the fifth-floor parapet above rue Baranot.

He looked at the sky, closed his eyes, took a final breath.

And then he jumped.

An office cleaner, heading home after finishing her night shift in the offices of a large insurance broker, heard a muffled cry, loud enough to draw her eye across the street, in time to see something blur past the lower windows of a Marais townhouse and smack hard into the pavement.

She found a public phone and called the police, stayed until they arrived.

'I knew at once what it was,' she told the officer. 'But I didn't go to look.'

104

Marseilles

AT A LITTLE AFTER MIDDAY, Jacquot came down the stairs at Auberge des Vagues.

It had been a long morning, a long night too. After a guided tour of Maison Cabrille with Peluze, he'd called in at Solange Bonnefoy's apartment where Estelle Lafour gathered her resolve to thank him, without breaking down, for finding her daughter. He then crossed town to the Témoin hospital where Léo Chabran was now conscious, watched over by a solicitous Marie-Ange.

After his brief few minutes at Chabran's bedside – all that Marie-Ange would allow – she'd come down in the lift with him, walked him to the hospital entrance.

'Till we meet again, Chief Inspector,' she'd said.

'*A la prochaine*,' replied Jacquot, not altogether sure how to respond, how to end it. He'd held out his hand which she ignored, leaning forward to kiss him, on each cheek, close to the mouth. She smelled of roses. Sweet and rich. There was a gentle, knowing look in her eyes as she drew back, a look he hadn't quite been able to fathom, and a few minutes later he found himself outside the hospital, thinking to himself that Chabran was indeed a very fortunate man, and that he, Jacquot, was just a little bit . . . disconcerted.

Which made him think of Claudine.

Back in the hospital reception area, he'd ducked into a phone booth and dialled her number, his eyes settling on Marie-Ange as she waited for the lift back to Chabran's floor.

'*Oui? Allo?*'

The lift doors opened, Marie-Ange stepped inside and turned. She didn't see him. The doors closed.

'It's me, Daniel.'

He'd heard the catch of her breath and then the sudden muffled sound of crying, tears spilling out.

'You bastard, you bastard, how could you?' she sniffed, when she managed to catch her breath. 'I've been so worried . . . I thought . . .'

And he'd calmed her, and told her how sorry he was, that it would never happen again.

There'd been a long silence after he said that.

Her voice, when it came, was tiny. 'You promise?'

'I promise.'

'You promised before.'

'This time I mean it.'

'Are you coming home?'

'I'm coming home.'

Back at the hostel, he'd stripped his dormitory bed, stuffed his few belongings into his duffel bag and lugged it down the three flights of stairs to reception. He was coming round the last landing when he heard the phone on the reception desk start ringing. It didn't take long for Madame Boileau to pounce on it.

'Auberge des Vagues,' he heard her say. '*Oui, oui, il est ici. Ne quittez pas, monsieur, il arrive maintenant.*'

As he came down the last stairs, Madame Boileau beckoned him over.

'*Téléphone*, Monsieur Muller,' she said, holding out the phone to him. He came to the desk and took it from her with a nod of thanks and a smile.

'*Oui*? Muller here.'

'It's Yionnedes, at Poseidon.'

The voice and the names were unfamiliar. Jacquot frowned, trying to place them.

409

'The shipping agent, on Chamant. You remember?'

'*Ah, mais oui.*' Jacquot smiled again.

'It's just we have a place for you. Second-Mate. Marseilles to Salvador. Bahia. MS *Carabella*, carrying motor parts. She leaves tomorrow from the Mirabe Basin. If you are still interested?'

Jacquot looked at the rain hammering down in the street outside and thought of Bahia. South America. Palm trees and blue skies and warm golden sand between his toes, rum cocktails and grilled fish on the beach . . . He had always wanted to go there. And now so close.

'Monsieur Muller? Are you still there?'

Jacquot shook away the blue skies and looked back at the rain, remembered what was waiting for him in the Luberon.

'A day too late, monsieur,' he said with a sigh. 'A day too late.'

Now read an extract from Martin O'Brien's new Jacquot novel

BLOOD COUNTS

Published by Preface

Prologue

THERE WERE ELEVEN BULLET WOUNDS in the two bodies – six in one, five in the other – but only two of these wounds had been fatal.

The first of the killing shots was effected by a 9x19mm parabellum cartridge fired from a police Beretta 92G at a range of no more than ten metres. Milliseconds after leaving the muzzle of the Beretta it entered the skull of Taddeus Manichella two centimetres above the right eyebrow, mashing a path through the soft tissue of the frontal lobe and exiting four centimetres behind and below the left ear.

The second killing shot was another 9x19mm parabellum cartridge fired at a similar range, entering Tomas Manichella's chest four centimetres to the left of the mid-sternal line, shredding the muscly anterior wall of the heart, cutting down through the lungs and lodging in the lower spine.

During the police pathologist's autopsy which followed the shoot-out in the Roucas Blanc district of Marseilles only four cartridges were retrieved from the bodies, leaving eighteen entry and exit wounds. None of these wounds was treated except for the massive cranial damage to the back of Taddeus Manichella's head where a wedge of gauze dressing was applied and bandaged into place to contain the splintered remains of the skull and to prevent any further leakage.

After three weeks in police custody, the refrigerated bodies of the twin brothers were shipped on an overnight SNCM ferry from Marseilles to their home in Corsica. For ease of transport the thick black plastic bags that contained their bodies had been put into two deal coffins. On arrival in Ajaccio, after the passengers had disembarked from the vehicle ramp and companionways, the cargo hold was opened and the coffins discretely transported to a dock-side warehouse. It was there that two women took possession of the caskets, driving them back to the family home in the village of Tassafaduca high in the hills above Corte.

As is the custom in such remote and isolated settlements the first thing the women did was open the caskets, unzip the bags and lay out the bodies on trestle tables in the kitchen. They did this alone, at night, after the children had been settled in the roof space of the old family farmhouse and their elderly parents seen off to bed. By the light of a low-wattage ceiling light and a scattering of home-made candles, the two sisters washed their brothers' bodies and plugged their wounds with a thick poultice of honey, chestnut flour, macerated myrtle leaves and crushed arbutus berries.

Wounds washed with love, plugged with hatred.

They worked in silence, one sister to one brother, their fingers soon red and aching with cold, the putrefying stink of the bodies barely disguised by the smokey tallow scent of the candles and the sweet perfume of the honey and herbs. When the two bodies had been properly prepared and dressed in clean clothes they were returned to their caskets with red coral charms clasped in their hands, and the night-time shadows of the old farmhouse were filled with a light tap-tap-tapping as the lids were secured for the final time.

At eleven o'clock the following morning the caskets were taken from the family home and carried in black-shawled procession through the steep tilting streets of Tassafaduca to the church of Sant' Anselmo. There, with family and villagers crowding into the icy nave, prayers were said and blessings given, before the brothers were delivered to the village's small hillside cemetery. Here, the

414

caskets were lowered into a single shallow pit that had taken two days to dig with spade and pick-axe, jerking and tipping on their ropes, their rough wooden edges scraping against the stony sides of the grave until they lay five feet down, one beside the other, heads pointing north.

Another month and the two coffins would have been left in a barn, or a fire would have been lit and kept alight long enough to soften the ground for digging. But the snow had not yet come, just a dusting on the peaks of distant Monte Cinto in the west and Pica Tassa to the north. In its place, that bleak winter morning, came a chill, shawling drizzle that silvered the mourners' best black homburgs, stiff black suits and woollen headscarves, all hands gloved or pocketed against a sharp little breeze that whipped through the chestnut trees and snatched at the brown tufted grass.

On these hillsides Taddeus and Tomas had played as boys, and as young men they had learned to hunt here – boar and partridge – before the summons came to leave the island and serve their master. At twenty they had gone, and more than twenty years later they had come home for good, attended now by a handful of mourners. There, carried in his favourite chair by four nephews and set beside the single grave, sat the twins' nodding father, and beside him their shawled whiskered stub of a mother shuffling rosary beads through crooked fingers, their two sisters, assorted cousins and uncles, and the elders of the village of Tassafaduca, its slate walls and steeply pitched roofs crowding together on the slope below the cemetery.

No tear was spilled. No flower was laid. Just pale faces framed in black, and dark, dulled eyes cast down to the hard ground. They had done this before, all of them gathered there. In these distant hills they knew death, just as they knew life. And neither held any surprise for them. It was the way things were. Life and death. Just that. And as the single, hollow bell of Sant' Anselmo tolled through the valley of Tassafaduca, taken up by the nearby campanile of Cabrillio and Borredonico and Scarpetta, the first shovel of earth and stone drummed over the wooden lids of the twins' coffins, and the mourners turned their backs on the grave and made their way home.

But it wasn't over. In these dark and haunted highlands, nothing is ever over.

And the brothers Taddeus and Tomas Manichella were not forgotten.

Towards the end of a long, bitter winter, in the second week of March, on the first clear night of a new moon, an old man and two women set out from a house in Scarpetta and in single file, accompanied by a bleating goat, they climbed through the forest to the place of the stones.

It was after midnight when they reached their destination, a slope of open ground pillared with seven stone columns set in a leaning oval around a worn slab of granite. In short order their torches were switched off and a small bundle of dried rock-rose stems and rosemary was set alight upon the slab. In the brief, flickering, smokey light, a litany of muttered chants was followed by the swift, gargling splatter of blood from the goat's sliced throat. Salt was scattered with a crackle over the burning twigs, a splash of olive oil and water added to the warm pooling blood and the fingers of the *Mazzeru* drawn through the brew. Turning to the two sisters, the spell-caster drew the old signs in ash and blood and oil on their brows and cheeks and wrists, and blessed their endeavour.

Three weeks later, four months after burying their brothers, with a stiff ocean breeze licking at their scarved heads, the two sisters stood on the deck of the ferry Mistral and watched as the coast of France drew closer and the gold skirts of the Madonna atop Marseilles' Notre Dame de la Garde winked at them in the dawn sunshine.

There was work for them to do here, and as they stepped ashore at the Joliette ferry terminal the passenger door of a black limousine opened.

As promised she was there, waiting for them.

416

1

IT WAS A SPRING WEDDING. A country wedding. A twenty-minute drive from Cavaillon, on the northern slopes of the Grand Luberon, under a sky the colour of milky topaz, in a meadow as green as parsley. And most of the guests, Jacquot could tell at a glance, were country people. The suits the men wore gave the game away, either too tight – not yet old or worn enough to justify a fresh purchase – or a size too large as though room had been left for growth, or its owner had shrunk with age. Collar tips were turned up, ties were loud and wide, faces nut brown, stiff hair brushed flat. Their smiles and gusts of laughter were as broad and as big as the land, and their voices rang out in a jolly *patois*.

As for the women, Jacquot decided, their outfits were gay and colourful and festive but had about them a sense of 'best'. They looked like the kinds of dresses that had served as long and as well as their men's suits, bought from a catalogue, or a market somewhere, or years earlier from fashionable boutiques in Cavaillon or Apt, or cut from patterns on kitchen tables. Taken from creaking *armoires*, hung up in the shade to air out any mustiness, maybe dry-cleaned for the occasion, they were worn with an easy, comfortable familiarity.

The only items of dress that appeared to cause any real discomfort, however, were shoes, men and women's both, Jacquot noticed.

417

Brightly polished, sensibly heeled, but he could sense their pinching grip, their stiff ungiving edges, the way their owners swayed between the tables set beneath the trees, the way they stood chatting in groups, lifting a foot like a horse lifts a hoof, just to ease the weight off biting leather. And when they started to dance on the large squares of ply pegged out on a stretch of level ground, not a few of the women kicked off the offending items. Harder for the men – stooping for all those laces.

It was late afternoon now and the rain that had threatened had failed to show, the sun still bright and warm as it slipped down through the branches, dappling the cloth on Jacquot's table – thick white damask crumpled now, ringed and stained with spilled wine, spotted with grease from the hog-roast sandwiches they'd all fetched themselves from the firepit. It was, Jacquot decided, tipping back the last of his coffee and glancing at his watch, just about time to call it quits and head home. It had been a long day.

They had arrived at the church in St Florent at eleven that morning – Jacquot in linen suit and loafers, Claudine in a matching light blue jacket and sleeveless dress that he hadn't seen before. She looked long and lean in it, the jacket high off the waist, the satin sheen sharpening slim hips, firm breasts and flat stomach, tanned legs in blue court shoes, long neck sliced with a single string of pearls, dark hair caught up and combed into a tight little chignon. They'd sat at the back of the church, by the stone font, because they weren't really family enough to claim anything closer to the altar. The invitation from *famille* Blanchard had been sent to Claudine for the help she'd given the bride's younger sister preparing her art-work portfolio for admission to Aix's École des Beaux Arts. When their daughter was subsequently awarded a place, Blanchard *Père et Mère* were convinced that Claudine, who sometimes lectured at the school, must have pulled some strings with the admissions board, rather than believe in their daughter's talent. And so, the invitation.

As for Jacquot, he recognised some of the faces from town, men and women both, knew one or two of the names, had once sorted out a quarrel between two of them over a boundary wall, for which

418

both parties – now reconciled – gave him bone-crushing handshakes and mighty slaps on the back. And though he didn't know it when bride and groom came down the aisle arm in arm at the end of the service, he knew the groom too. Or rather, it turned out, the groom knew him, or knew of him.

Standing in line at the firepit, the young man had come over to Jacquot and introduced himself.

'Noel Gilbert, Chief Inspector. Police Nationale, Marseilles. I saw you at Roucas Blanc last year. The Cabrille place.'

'Daniel. The name's Daniel,' he replied, taking in the sharply-cut black hair, spikey on the neck and above the ears, the red cheeks, the tiny shaver's nick on the point of the chin. He didn't recognise the lad, but he remembered the Cabrille place in Roucas Blanc, the shoot-out he'd missed by a matter of minutes, the blood on the garage walls, on the floor, the sharp scent of cordite and the tell-tale faecal stink of a stomach wound.

'You were there? With Peluze?'

The younger man nodded, let go shaking Jacquot's hand. 'If it wasn't for Chief Inspector Peluze I wouldn't be here now. Pulled me down behind an old Porsche when the bullets started flying. What a noise in that garage. First time under fire and, well, I suppose I was frightened. I didn't know what to do.' He shrugged, spread his hands in a there-you-are gesture.

'You'd be lying if you'd said any different. We all would. And it doesn't change. Don't let anyone tell you otherwise. A gun's always a gun. And a bullet may be small . . .'

'She's clear, you know? Off the hook.'

Jacquot frowned, took another step closer to the firepit, the smell of roasting pork thick and succulent, carried on a smoky breeze.

'The Cabrille woman . . .?'

'Mademoiselle Virginie Cabrille. All charges dropped.'

'*C'est des blagues.* You're kidding?'

Gilbert shook his head. 'Nothing. Free to walk.'

Jacquot was stunned by the news. Kidnap, attempted murder, murder . . . It couldn't be.

'But the Lafour girl on her boat? And Chief Inspector Gastal in her basement? And the two *gorilles* . . .?'

'She had a lawyer down from Paris. Slippery as a peeled grape, he was. He wouldn't let us pin a thing on her. No charges filed.'

Jacquot noted the 'us' – the police as family, the team. He had a feeling this young man might go far.

'So you're not in Marseilles these days?'

'Cavaillon,' replied Jacquot. 'They put me out to graze.'

Gilbert took this in, nodded, cast around for his new wife. They both spotted her at the same time, a dozen tables away, surrounded by a gaggle of great-aunts and grandmothers, a tall, big-boned country girl in an off-the-shoulder gown that showed a generous swell and plunge of cleavage. In church the shoulders, and cleavage, had been concealed, her hair piled high beneath the veil; now the veil was gone and the hair was loose, a bundle of black curls tumbling over bare white shoulders. She had a lovely smile, thought Jacquot, and twinkling mischievous eyes. Gilbert had chosen well.

'You better go rescue your wife,' said Jacquot, stepping up to the hog-pit now, first in line at last, and holding out his two plates. Fat wedges of pork were carved off the haunch and dropped onto them, along with blistered belts of crackling, thick slices of buttered bread and a healthy sprinkle of rock salt on the side. 'Never a good idea to let the old ones give the young ones too much advice.'

'I think you might be right. So . . . if you'll excuse me, Chief Insp . . .'

'Daniel. At weddings I'm Daniel, remember?'

'Okay, okay. Thanks . . . Daniel.' He held out a hand to shake, but had forgotten Jacquot's loaded plates. For a moment Gilbert wasn't sure what to do, a pat on the arm or back just a little too familiar with a senior officer, even at a wedding, even if said senior officer had told him twice now to use his christian name. Instead, he'd lifted his hand – somewhere between a wave and salute – and had hurried off.

'You're dreaming.' It was Claudine, her shadow falling across the table, her hand sliding over his shoulder. 'Whoosh,' she continued, pulling out a chair. 'That old farmer sure knows how to rock and roll. Had me in quite a spin.' She guided a stray wisp of hair into the loosening chignon with long, delicate fingers, slipped off her shoes and laid her legs over Jacquot's knees. 'And you sitting here, a million miles away.'

'I was thinking . . .'

'Don't tell me if it's work . . . It's been too nice a day,' she replied, reaching across for the plastic camera left on each table. She wound on the film, pointed it at Jacquot and pressed the button.

'*En effet*, I was thinking,' said Jacquot, 'that maybe it's time I took you home . . .' He dropped a hand to her leg and let his fingers trail up her bare brown shin, rubbing her knee with his thumb when he reached that far, knuckles idling at the hem of her dress.

She gave him a long, cool look. 'I can tell when you're lying, Daniel Jacquot. And it won't work, you hear?'

'What? It's the truth.'

'And you want to leave? Just as things are hotting up?' She glanced back at the dance square. The DJ's amplified but strangely muffled voice spread between the tables and out across the pasture. The sun had slipped behind the hills now but already there were lit candles on tables and lanterns in the branches. They darkened the sky, brought the night closer.

'You were the one who said she was tired.'

And it was true. At breakfast Claudine had complained of a poor night's sleep, the second or third in a row, and had sighed deeply at the thought of a long country wedding.

'That was earlier. Now I'm not.'

Jacquot shook his head and chuckled.

'So? I've changed my mind. I'm a woman, I'm allowed. That's what we do, didn't you know? Just to keep you men on your toes. Talking of which . . .'

'Three dances – two fast, one slow,' he told her. 'The slow one to get you in the mood.'

'Three fast, two slow. I need priming.' She leaned foward and ran her fingertips across his cheek.

'It's not fair. You're younger than me.'

'You want it the other way round, you should have settled on someone else, someone older, someone closer to your own age, *hein*? In their sixties, or maybe even their seventies; with one of those frames to help them get around.'

'You drive a hard bargain, Madame.'

His fingers flicked at the hem of Claudine's dress.

She brushed them away as she might a settling fly and raised her chin in that way she had – as though trying to see over his head. Haughty as hell. God, how he loved her when she did that.

Through the trees the first bluesy, bursting rhythms of a Jackie Wilson number blasted from the speakers. Both of them knew the song. A favourite. *Higher and Higher*.

'Okay,' he said, shifting her legs off his knees and pulling her to her feet. 'You win.'

'That's right,' she replied, gripping his arm as she bent to pull on her shoes. 'And don't you ever forget it, Daniel Jacquot. *Allons-y*. We dance.'

2

IT WAS A DARK NIGHT, a widow's velvet, no moon, no stars, just coal black clouds blotting out all light save a distant sulphurous glow over Cavaillon. At a little past three o'clock in the morning it was cold, too, with a taste in the air that the promised rain might soon start to patter down.

The two women reached their car, a battered black VW, after crossing two fields, the same fields they had used to make their approach, two black shadows taking a path between straggling, catching vines. One was tall, thin and stoop-shouldered, the other short and buxom. Both were breathless as they steadied each other down the bank and stepped onto the stony lane where they had parked. When they'd viewed this route a week earlier, it had been in bright sunshine and the advantages were clear to them – flat ground, packed earth, hard to track or search, and out of sight of any residents. Also there were no ditches, no hedges of any account and the route a straight diagonal from their car to the grounds of Le Mas Bleu.

But the total darkness that early Sunday morning had thrown them. They had brought no torches for obvious reasons, and had banked on the light from stars and a high quarter moon to show them the way. This had not happened. Maybe, too, it was the very flatness of the land that had surprised them, both more used to clambering up and down slopes and sliding inclines. It was as if, in the darkness, on this level ground, the earth between the vines cut into narrow gutters, they didn't altogether trust their luck or instincts.

But this had been their first outing, and despite all the problems they hadn't anticipated – the cloaking darkness, the stumbling route, the creaking stairs on the top landing – they had acquitted themselves well. Everything had gone as planned, even if the couple were still making love when the pair of them slipped into the room, forcing them to wait in the shadows until the action had come to a breathless, panting end. Younger sister had enjoyed this unexpected treat and lay coiled and tight, listening to the sounds from the bed, while elder sister gritted her teeth and prayed the whole thing over.

From the moment they'd set out, not a word had passed between them. Now, in the safety of their car, they spoke.

'It was good,' said elder sister, starting the engine.

'Taddeus and Tomas would be pleased,' said younger sister, buckling up her belt.

'As it should be,' replied elder sister, reaching an elbow over the driving seat to reverse the VW back onto the road.